MW01137384

Deo Vindice

BY

Robert W.P. Patterson

ISBN: 1-58500-297-6

About the Book

For students of the War Between the States there are often moments of reflection when facts and events are placed aside and the question is pondered, *"What if...?"* One such a question often considered is, *"Could the South have won the war?"* Recorded history gives glimpses to us that the South did indeed come close to achieving some of its goals which in turn might have led to, if not outright victory, at least a negotiated peace.

In such a momentous conflict, it seems unlikely that relatively small-scale events could have had the far reaching effects to have changed the War's direction. But for a moment consider... *What if the Battle of Gettysburg had never been fought? What if England had recognized the South as an independent nation? What if....?*

DEO VINDICE is a work of historical fiction based upon real people, real places and actual plans. Many of these events, although real, are unknown to the average reader. One must wonder if a few of these events had been different, would history as we know it have changed?

You be the judge.

To my Arlene
The grandest Southern Lady of them all...

FORWARD

Many scholars of the War Between the States have said the South could never have won the war for its independence that was waged from 1861 to 1865. Since the outcome of this war is now so much a part of our history, indeed the very pivotal point in our national history, it is difficult to imagine it otherwise. However, the events of this period often changed and in doing so, what might have become history, became lost in the pages of quiet archives.

DEO VINDICE tells a story that requires very little imagination on the part of the reader, and very little poetic license on the part of the author. The events could very easily have happened and in fact, a great many of them *did* happen or were *planned* to happen. Proposals, movements, war plans and political actions in this story are woven together from actual material of the day to make a fascinating story. The people, places, times and decisions all made up the ingredients that became, *or changed*, what we call history.

You will recognize most of the players. The other players are known well by me. Their comments reflect what I feel they would have said in the situations in which I have placed them.

To the serious student of history and to the Civil War buff, I hope you enjoy the hidden nuggets of personality, actual history, quotes, and historical connections that only you will glean from the story.

To the reader desiring to perhaps see the issues of the war in a different light, I hope you will listen to what is said by all the players.

To the casual reader wanting to curl up with a cup of coffee and a good book, I say enjoy!!

To each of you, I say *remember...*

R.W.P. Patterson

I

II

In April of 1861, the 7th Mississippi Infantry went off to war with 811 men.

In April of 1865, there were 75 of them left.

Today, few remember, fewer care.

I do

DEO VINDICE *…God Vindicate Us…*
From the Great Seal of the Confederate States of America

PROLOGUE

The two officers sat together looking across the river at the distant smoke from hundreds of campfires. Their faded uniforms showed the wear of long campaigns and hard times. Their faces reflected years of war as recorded by eyes which had seen too much, too quickly. A brilliant orange glow from the fading evening sky seemed to confirm that this was more than just the end to another day.

Slowly the younger officer said, "I just can't believe it's over..."

"Me either," quietly answered the colonel, feeling old far beyond his 24 years. "I thought it would never end. So many hard fights...so many good men...and now, it's finally over. I never thought I'd live to see it end. Now that I have, I don't feel much like cheering. I just want to...." His words trailed off as he put his good hand to his eyes.

"I know...me too," said the other young colonel, feeling embarrassment for his friend. He scratched hard in the dirt with the small stick that young men always seem to pick up.

Looking up he said, "Rob, you know, it will be really hard to try to forget all that has happened and to be friends again...with them". He stared at the distant smoke.

Robert leaned back against the tree He, too, stared at the smoke hanging low over the trees. "I know, but we must. Besides, Chris, most of them are just like us when you get right down to it. They did what they thought was right... just like we did."

Christopher flared back, noticeably agitated, "Like us? No! They weren't like us at all! We fought for our country, but they...!"

Robert raised his hand and closed his eyes as if to calm his friend's rising voice and to the settle the waving stick now pointing menacingly toward the river in front of Richmond. "Easy…easy.. It's over.. Thanks be to a merciful Lord, it's over."

Calmness returned to Christopher as he went back to his scratching in the dirt. The light was dimming rapidly. He looked up again.

"Rob...you know, we almost lost this war?" He paused. "Did you ever think about what would have happened if we had lost?"

The older colonel paused for a long time, looking at the smoke now fading from sight and slowly shook his head, "I don't want to ever think about that...."

VI

THE NORTH ATLANTIC

Even in late June, the dawn in the Atlantic was cold and damp when the weather was overcast and unsettled. "We will be in for a little blow," Lieutenant Thomas Addison thought as he shuddered trying to shake away the chilly Atlantic wind. Still, being here on the *USS Octorara* headed south for blockade duty off the coast of South Carolina was far better than a long patrol far up in the North Atlantic. Now that's where the cold really....

"Ship ahoy!" Addison spotted the newly appearing ship in the increasing light and was putting his glass on it even as the lookout was calling out the sighting and direction. As Addison turned to call below for Captain Collins, he found he was looking at the captain.

"Good morning, Mr. Addison, what do we have?" Leave it to the skipper to sense another ship.

"Morning, Captain. Just off there to port, looks like it might be a Brit. She is holding a southerly course. She could be headed south for a turn in to the Carolina coast." He steadied the glass, "She's not a big one. We should be able to better tell in a minute or two."

Commander Napoleon Collins had been in the U.S. Navy most of his life, having left the farm in Iowa in 1831 to become a midshipman. He was now more at home on the oceans of the world than he ever had been on the sea of corn and grain of the Midwest. But Captain Collins was more than just a sailor, he was a fighter. He had a reputation of caring little for formality and discussion when fighting was an available option. In a world where oceans were international roadways and diplomacy was constantly needed to prevent conflicts, Collins could be the proverbial bull in the china shop.

"Looks like she is going to stay on course and hold her sail," Addison said.

Collins smiled, "Port two points, let's stay with her, Mr. Addison."

"Aye, Captain," Addison replied as he turned to the helmsman. "Looks like it was not going to be quite so cold this morning after all," he thought.

"Cap'n, she is turning to stay with us. I don't think we can outrun her," said the *Mount Blanc's* first mate, as he watched the *Octorara* through his telescope. "She appears to have the speed and she's moving to intercept us." He looked at his captain half hoping he would turn away. The mate had no desire to even get close to an American warship.

"We are in international waters," said the English captain. "I'll not run at the sight of a bloody Yankee tub," he snarled.

Captain Peters had no love for the American Navy, or Americans in general for that matter. His family had been sailors for generations. They had met the Americans first during the Rebellion, then during the naval actions in 1812. He had heard all the sea stories. Now it was his turn, only he was not aboard a man of war. The *Mount Blanc* was a sloop and unarmed. The British flag was his only armament, but it was all he needed. The American Navy would not be foolish enough to challenge the British flag at sea.

It was well known that the northern states had imposed a naval blockade on southern ports due to the southern *insurrection*. It was also well known that there was a lot of argument over the legality of placing a naval blockade against one's own countrymen. England had somewhat reluctantly agreed to abide by the imposed blockade as long as it was truly enforced as required by naval law. In doing so, England instructed all English shipping to observe the blockade, or be subject to the American Navy's enforcement of it. As in any conflict, there were latitudes and abuses by both sides over this issue.

To many Englishmen, the Northern Americans were far too arrogant and free with their interpretation of their rights at sea. It seemed that the U.S. thought a large part of the Atlantic was an American lake, subject to patrol, search and seizure as decided by U.S. naval forces. When England had taken this same approach to an excess, the War of 1812 had been the result. In 1861, this blockade was a bitter pill for English merchantmen who considered it an obvious fact that England

2

was the undisputed master of the seas.

Added to the English aggravation was the fact known to all sides that there was a great deal of money to be made in southern ports ripe with cotton and eager to trade for almost everything offered. Obviously, war materials in particular were high dollar cargoes. The threat of capture or sinking was not as great as the northern navy made it sound. To some English maritime merchants, the profits were well worth the risks. Besides, real danger only came when a ship actually approached the southern coast or its ports.

Little of this had any effect on the *Mount Blanc*. She was well off the American coast on a southerly course out of Newfoundland, bound for Jamaica with no intention of approaching the Confederate coast. She was carrying a cargo of salt and, she was flying the Union Jack. That would protect the *Mount Blanc*.

"She is flying the Union Jack, Sir" said Lieutenant Addison steadying his telescope. "She's an English sloop." Addison looked at his captain to see his reaction. They had captured twelve blockade runners so far, several of which were English. Most had been headed from the Bahamas for Charleston or Savannah. They had missed a few, but not many got past Captain Collins. Here now was something a little new, a British merchantmen still in northern latitudes, international waters, headed south, but not seemingly toward the coast.

"Sir, she could be headed to the Caribbean. We are pretty far north yet. Shall we just track her south and make sure she keeps well clear?"

"This Englishman is as close as he is going to get to Charleston. We will turn him and send him back to Queen Victoria with a clear message," said Collins. Addison looked at his captain and then at the English ship. Surely Collins was not going to stop the Englishman this far north. They weren't even off the Rebel coast yet. The British sloop cut a white wake at its bow as it bore on its course.

"Set your course to intercept her, Mr. Addison." Addison

hesitated, but only for a brief second. Years of naval discipline saw to it that he responded as commanded first, then he considered the order.

He gave the necessary commands to bring the Octorara into range of the Englishman. "Captain, we are still several hours from being abeam the Rebel coast. Do you want to pace her and stop her off Virginia?" Lieutenant Addison had both said what was on his mind and asked for clarification at the same time.

"Beat to quarters, Mr. Addison. All ahead full." The Lieutenant again responded immediately, and just as quickly a young Marine was beating the drum signaling the crew to action stations. The steam boilers began to throb heavily. Addison turned to look at the distance now closing between the *Mount Blanc* and the *Octorara*. Was the call to quarters the answer to his question?

Captain Collins now answered, "This Englishman is likely coming down from Canada. He probably plans to parallel the coast looking innocent enough, and then run for a Rebel port after he has given us the slip." Collins looked up at the eastern sky. "We will have some weather this morning and it will come up very soon, well before we get off the Virginia coast. I don't want to lose this one in poor visibility." Collins smiled slightly and turned to his first officer, "If his papers and cargo show he is not headed to Jeff Davis, then old John Bull has nothing to worry about."

"The wind is picking up, Cap'n," observed the *Mount Blanc's* first mate. "Looks like the weather...."

Captain Jarvis cut him short, "Add canvas to her, Mr. Wilkes. Full sail." He continued to observe the American ship through his telescope, "The Yankee has turned and is coming for us. I'll not be stopped by him or any other American in international waters!"

Like his counterpart on the *Octorara* , Mr. Wilkes responded at once. The English crew did likewise. The idea that England's merchant fleet and the Royal Navy were as good as they came, was no myth. They were good, they had proved it time and again. It seemed they would need to prove it once

4

more to the American warship now determined to stop them.

Both captains were watching the approaching squall that had been developing in their path. *Mount Blanc* was closing on the darkening area of the squall, even as Octorara closed on *Mount Blanc.*

"Sir, the American is closing," reported Wilkes. We won't outrun his steam."

Captain Jarvis never stopped watching the U.S. warship. "Helm, a little port - a little more - now, steady up!" "Mr. Wilkes, have a dozen of the new empty carpenter chests pulled from our cargo and brought top side. Double quick!" Wilkes leaned over the rail and gave the order that sent half a dozen seamen running. The chests appeared on deck in moments.

"She runs well," Collins said as he smiled to himself. "Sir, see how she bears port a little to keep the angle to slow our closing," noted Addison. "Yes, she can run but she can't escape," said Collins who was now really into the chase. "Captain, they are throwing something overboard! Look to the starboard side. Now port…more to starboard." "Can't make it out, but whatever they are, they are floating high in the water. What the….?"

Collins was looking hard with everyone else at the floating objects now dead ahead. "Starboard your helm a little. We will steer to pass them on our port side. Keep those objects well clear of our paddle wheel." The Confederates had made use of floating torpedoes with some degree of success, and perhaps the Englishman was doing the same. In any event, whatever these boxes were, they were easy enough to miss with a slight course correction.

"He is steering to starboard. He is trying to dodge the boxes!," Wilkes called out.

"Port a point, helm! That's it! That's it! Now steady up!," commanded the *Mount Blanc's* captain.

The closing distance between the two ships now began to slow slightly as the two course corrections once again opened an angle between the two ships. The sky was becoming darker now as the ships pressed toward the squall.

Captain Collins turned sharply to the helmsman, "Put your bow on that sloop's stern and hold it there!" He looked back at the sloop. "Very smart, John Bull," whispered Collins. "I turn starboard, you turn port, the angle increases, the chase slows. Nice move, but you won't get off the hook that easy. I'm too close! It will just add a few seconds to the time I need to get you in range, then a shot across the bow and you'll heave to!" The sky darkened still more. "Mr. Addison, ready on guns one and three! At my command, I'll turn starboard. I want a shot close across her bow and one across the stern!" The gun crews now angled the big guns as much as possible to fire forward early in the turn.

Addison thought..."Two shots instead of one...both from a rear quarter position in a turn...there would be little room for error!" He told the gun crew to make the bow shot wide to starboard to clear the sloop well forward. The shot across the stern could be closer since the Englishman would be moving away from it.

Captain Jarvis looked first at the storm front and then at the American ship as he planned his escape. "Three minutes more and we will be in the squall, Mr. Wilkes. Be ready to take off canvas quickly and when we are obscured, we will swing to port and then circle north before turning eastward. I want to get well clear of this infernal Yankee!"

"Two more minutes," he thought! It was now raining hard. *Octorara* was coming on fast. It would be very close. Not yet.. Not yet. NOW! "Hard to port, helmsman, turn us into the squall! Look to your topside, Mr. Wilkes!"

"Sir, she is starting to enter the squall. She is fading and will be out of sight in a minute!," Addison was now sure they would lose sight of the Englishman.

Collins barked the commands in rapid succession... "Right full rudder! Fire when the guns bear!" He leaned forward and shouted at the gunners, "Make it close, lads!"

The rain was starting to pour in earnest now on the *Mount Blanc* and she was starting to fade from view. Seconds passed. Then the number one gun thundered followed two seconds later by number three gun who was aiming close through the rain and smoke at an almost faded target.

The two 24-pound projectiles followed the *Mount Blanc* into the rain. Hardly was the report from the guns gone, when Collins called out, "Hard to port! Steady up on where the Englishman went in and follow her!" Captain Collins was determined to be right on the sloop when it came out of the squall line. The *Octorara* was now moving very fast and the Englishman was out of sight.

Now unseen by the Americans, the *Mount Blanc* was leaning over hard in its turn to port when the round from number one gun passed the starboard side and hit the water well ahead. Everyone heard it pass and hit the water, but in the rain, it was hard to see.

"My God, he's is firing on us!," screamed Wilkes above the increasing storm. It was the last words he would ever speak.

The second shot that was supposed to be close and across the stern of the ship, slammed into the ship's wheel station as *Mount Blanc* continued its hard turn to the left. The cannon ball could not have more deadly if it had been planned that way. The *Mount Blanc's* helmsman was killed instantly as the heavy ball tore away the ship's wheel and him with it. Captain Jarvis was knocked half way through the hatch and knocked unconscious by the debris. First mate Wilkes died almost immediately from the metal and wood shards that cut him down.

Now without steering, the loose rudder of the *Mount Blanc* began to center itself swinging back from its hard left turn. The driving squall winds pushed the full sails over to the left forcing the ship into an ever harder turn to the right. The ship rolled heavily. Crewmen were now grasping at anything trying to just stay aboard. The English ship was in serious danger of rolling over. Then out of the driving rain, Octorara appeared. The *Mount Blanc's* crazy "S" turn first left then right had placed the sloop right in the path of the on rushing warship.

"Hard to Port! NOW!!" Captain Collins yelled at the top of his lungs.

He had seen the sloop appear out of the pouring rain and it

took only a second to see that it was healed over and crossing his bow. A hard turn to port was all the choice he had to avoid driving amidships into the Englishman. Everything seemed to slow down as the big man of war began to turn to the left. They weren't going to make it.

"Hold On!!," Collins again yelled as he grasped the overhead handrail with both hands.

The *Octorara* was now rolling over to the right as she turned ever harder to the left. Collins clinched his teeth waiting for the collision, but somehow the bow of the warship missed the sloop. He watched in surprise and shock as the floundering sloop passed off to his right only feet away. He could see the rolling ship, under full sail, with its shattered wheel station. "What had happened? No! It couldn't be our fire that did that! We fired well clear! We only fired warning shots!" his mind yelled at him.

About 45 minutes later the squall line had passed by and the crew of the *Octorara* could see the *Mount Blanc* drifting, seemingly helpless, its sails now down in disarray. Captain Collins brought the his vessel abeam the disabled ship, but stayed well clear of it. He dispatched Lieutenant Addison with a small party to board the sloop. Shortly, Addison was on his way back to report. As Addison climbed back aboard, Collins noted he seemed almost ashen.

"Sir, the ship is the *Mount Blanc*, an Englishman last out of Newfoundland bound for Jamaica with a cargo of salt, tools and wooden ware. Sir...it appears that one of our warning shots hit the Englishman right
in the helm. The Captain is down and seriously hurt, the First Mate is dead, as is one of the crew. The helm is shattered and she cannot steer with out repairs".

"You say it we hit her with one of our shots?," Collins asked, as if looking for a mistake.

"Yes Sir. One shot apparently went across the bow well forward, but the other hit the wheel station dead center. There is no doubt...the shot smashed the helm and took out about everybody on duty there. It was hard to think solid shot could do that. If it had been an explosive round I could see how...." Addison decided not to finish the comment.

"Why did he run?," Captain Collins wondered aloud.

Addison responded, "The second mate said he heard the Captain say since they were well clear of the southern coast and not approaching land by course or distance, he would not stop for a search." Collins was glaring at Addison as he continued. "Their Captain is badly hurt and unconscious, so no one really has the details to piece this together right now."

The lieutenant hesitated..."Sir...the mate asked why we fired on them. I tried to explain it was a warning shot. He obviously did not accept my explanation. He did ask for medical help and repair assistance. Shall I see to it?"

Captain Collins was leaning forward on the railing looking at the sloop now dead in the choppy waters. "Give him what ever help he needs. We will assist in temporary repairs and escort him to Gosport."

Collins mind was racing. "Why did he run? How did they hit the sloop with a warning shot? I shouldn't have fired two shots. Well, one thing was certain, the Englishman was not bound for Jamaica. He was headed south for a southern port sure as sin! He would stake his reputation on that!" He considered that thought. His reputation might be the least of what he had at stake here. In any event, there would be a lot of explaining to do. Blockade duty would have to wait for awhile.

9

RICHMOND

President Jefferson Davis read the telegram again hoping to see more than was there. Things were not going well for the Confederacy and he desperately wanted to receive some good news. Secretary of War James Seddon stood quietly, feeling the weight of the news for both himself and his President. Davis read it again, "I arrived this evening, finding the enemy in force between this place and General Pemberton, cutting off all communication. I am too late...GEN J.E. Johnston. " The words struck like a blow. "I am too late..." Davis thought of the men trapped in Vicksburg. He thought of his Mississippi home, Briarwood. He thought of his family members and his friends and the importance of Vicksburg to the South. He thought of a Union controlled Mississippi River.

Looking up and speaking in a military like command he said, "We must send additional help, Vicksburg must not fall!"

Seddon replied, "Yes Mr. President, I am confident that General Pemberton will do his best to hold out until help can arrive. We could send additional forces from General Bragg to help General Johnston, if you concur."

"Yes, Mr. Seddon, see to it immediately, but we must not forget General Bragg's necessities. He must not be unduly weakened in Tennessee. General Johnston must be strengthened, but regardless of resources or reinforcements, he must hazard an attack to relieve Vicksburg." Seddon left the room to start the effort. Davis wondered if Lincoln, only some 100 miles away from Richmond, was thinking about Vicksburg too. He thought, "If only I were in command of Johnston's army the field, I would attack! Vicksburg might still be saved by a bold stoke!"

General John Pemberton looked through his field glasses at the Federal army that surrounded him and had Vicksburg under siege. The trenches, artillery and troops seemed endless. General Johnston's last message had told him to try break out and escape to the northeast, but he could see no way to breakout. "My army is trapped in the city, and Vicksburg will fall," he thought. "Without Johnston's help, my army will fall with it." His thoughts became barely audible words, "Johnston... come now...let me hear your cannon thunder into the Federals before me!"

Behind him, he heard the muffled thump of one of Admiral Porter's ever present naval mortars as the round fell short, landing among the civilian houses just over the ridge from his entrenchment's. The reality of it was, it was the Federals that controlled the thunder.

Pemberton remembered that President Davis had told him that he must defend Vicksburg and never let it fall into Union hands, but there seemed little he could do to stop it. General Johnston had told him that whatever he did, he must not lose both the city and his troops. Now he was close to doing both. The city and his army had been under siege for over a month now, and no help was coming from his General or his President. Pemberton pondered his options. They were not good.

Turning to his Adjutant, Pemberton instructed the colonel to call for all division commanders to join him within the hour. More heavy mortar rounds fell. These were closer.

Soon his generals were assembled. General Martin Smith, like Pemberton, a northerner by birth; Carter Stephenson, a West Point educated Virginian; John Forney, a North Carolinian that called Alabama home and John Bowen, a Georgian stood quietly facing Pemberton as he spoke. "General Johnston is not coming." No one moved. "The General has instructed me to consider leaving Vicksburg and to withdraw our forces to the northeast. I need your council and your estimate as to the practicality of this option." He waited.

Finally General Smith spoke, "Sir," he took a deep breath, "I do not feel that such a withdrawal is any longer an option available to us. Our supplies are exhausted and our troops are too physically weak for such an operation."

"I agree," said Stephenson, "The enemy is just too strong. We would have to force a break in his lines to get out. When we start to concentrate our troops, Grant will see the concentration.

He would likely break our defense that is now weakened elsewhere in our line before we were ready."

General Forney spoke, "What if we prepared at night to break out at dawn, pushing toward Yazoo City and then on toward Canton to link up with Johnston"?

"Mass at night and attack Sherman at dawn followed by a fighting withdrawal?," Stevenson questioned. "Few of us would probably make it. I agree with General Smith, the troops are just too weak. We would surely suffer grievous losses."

"It might be that if we could break out, the Yankees would move on Vicksburg rather than follow us and likely the Army could escape." General Forney immediately regretted that he had used the word *Yankee* in front of Pemberton, a native Pennsylvanian and Smith, a native New Yorker.

"The Federals are strong enough to take the city and pursue us at the same time," said Smith. "If we could break through, we would be out in the open without any defensive works to help us. We would be in a dead run with tired troops."

The discussion ebbed back and forth for some time.

"I will stay and hold them." John Bowen's measured words silenced the exchange. "Sir, my boys and I can hold the enemy while the rest of the command evacuates. I think if I concentrate and strengthen the line at selected points, we should be able to gain you the time that you need to break out to the south. I don't think Grant would pursue you into south Mississippi."

His fellow officers were clearly moved by General Bowen's offer to sacrifice himself and his command so they could escape. Bowen was very ill and they all knew it, but no one knew how ill he really was. He would be dead in two weeks from dysentery. All eyes were now on Pemberton.

"General Bowen, the sacrifice and contribution of your brave soldiers from Missouri and Arkansas have been, and continue to be, a source of strength and pride to this command and to our cause." The other officers softly voiced their agreement. Pemberton paused and thought for a few moments.

"Gentlemen, I feel I have your counsel on this matter. I believe we will gain little if Vicksburg is lost and in doing so, the lives of much of the command are sacrificed trying to join General Johnston in a desperate escape. The few troops that got through would likely be so demoralized, so ill equipped and so spent from such a fight that they would be of little value to the Confederacy as a fighting force. I do not wish to give up another life just to put off the inevitable a little longer. Much to my dismay, I see no alternative but to seek the best terms for our surrender...." Pemberton's words fell like a heavy weight on the gathered officers. Terms? Surrender? Did it have to be?

Pemberton looked at his generals, his friends, his fellow soldiers." I will look to secure terms on July 4th, I think on this day, they will be generous. I know my people."

General Stevenson wondered to himself, why that day? What was the significance of July 4th over any other day? Then he remembered. How quickly the 4th of July had become just another day in the Confederacy. However, to the people of Vicksburg, Mississippi, the 4th of July would never be just another day.

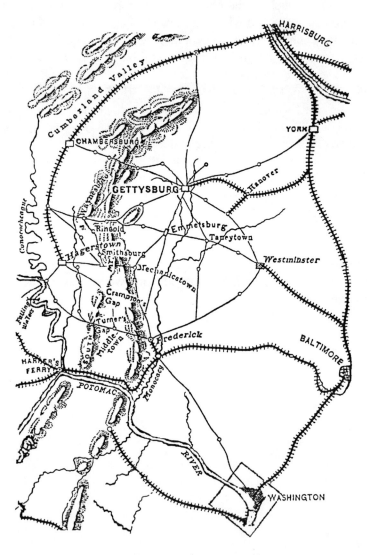

GETTYSBURG – FEDERICK

14

PENNSYLVANIA

It was still very early-just after dawn. The Army of Northern Virginia was again moving south through Pennsylvania.

Reining up hard, Lieutenant Hart called to the mounted officers watching the marching troops, "Beg pardon, Sirs, where might General Lee's Headquarters be?" A dust-covered Captain pointed toward a hill-side and several small dirty white tents almost obscured under a small cluster of trees. "Thank you kindly, Sir" he called, as he threw a salute, wheeled and spurred his horse all in one motion. The lieutenant truly was an expert horseman. Moments later he arrived at the headquarters' pickets.

Keeping his rifle ready and his eye on the young rider, the sergeant called over his shoulder, "Courier comin' in, Major!" Major Walter Taylor, General Lee's adjutant, was already moving toward the dismounting rider.

The young officer saluted, then began, "Sir, I have a message for General Lee, " he said, hoping to get a chance to see General Lee up close.

"Very well, I'm Major Taylor, his adjutant, I'll give it to him."

The young Lieutenant hesitated, but as General Lee stepped from his tent, Lieutenant Hart caught his breath, and snapped to attention, "Yes Sir, message from General Hill." Hart removed a message from his leather pouch and handed it to Major Taylor.

"Water your horse and relax for a minute, the General may want to send a reply. Sergeant James!, see to this officer." The sergeant nodded and gave a soft salute as he motioned for the lieutenant to come toward him.

"Message from General Hill, Sir." Major Taylor handed the paper to his commander. "He still looks tired and worn out," Taylor thought to himself.

"Thank you, Major," said Lee unfolding the paper. After a few moments of reading the message and without looking up he said, "Please ask the courier to come here. I want to reply to this." Taylor turned toward the lieutenant, now some distance away getting a drink of water. The lieutenant was still watching General Lee. Raising his hand, Taylor beckoned for the young officer to come. The lieutenant was there in seconds.

"The General wants to send a reply," said Taylor, motioning for the lieutenant to report to the General.

Lee nodded in reply to the young officer's salute, and said, "What's your name, Lieutenant"?

"Sir? I mean Hart, Sir. I'm Lieutenant J.J. Hart from Mississippi." The General smiled slightly, "Lieutenant Hart, this is very important, so you listen carefully now. My compliments to General Hill. Inform him that I concur with General Heth's move into the town, but I do not wish for him to become engaged there. I do not want his command to begin any major action until we have assembled our full force. Ask General Hill to please keep me informed. Do you understand?"

The young officer stretched another half inch at attention, "Yes Sir, General Lee's compliments...," he proceeded to accurately restate the full message back to Lee.

"Fine, that will be all," said Lee nodding to Major Taylor who then walked the young officer toward the pickets.

Just when Lieutenant Hart was mounting his horse, a general accompanied by two colonels rode up to the dismount point. As they returned his salute, Hart recognized the tall general with the long dark beard, wide brimmed hat and cigar. Longstreet! It had really been some morning. He had just talked personally with General Lee and now here was General Longstreet right up close as well! Being a General's courier really had advantages. Lee and Longstreet in one morning! He must not forget this day and the place where this happened. June 31st and the place...what was that small town nearby? Gettysburg...Gettysburg, Pennsylvania. He would have to try and remember that name.

James Longstreet was a serious man who seemed to have little on his mind except his duty as General of I Corps, Army of Northern Virginia. He had always been a professional soldier, but he had not always been so single minded. Today, he was more serious than usual as he knew a battle was close at hand. It would surely be a major confrontation. They were in Pennsylvania, and Longstreet knew there could be no mistakes. He must confer with General Lee.

"Good morning, Sir," Longstreet said after removing the unlighted cigar from his mouth and saluting formally.

Lee saluted and smiled, "Good morning, General." He was truly glad to see Longstreet on whom he depended so much.

Longstreet spoke carefully, "Sir, I have just received information that the main body of Union troops are coming from the south toward us. Lead elements of their cavalry will be in contact with us shortly. There is at least one, maybe two brigades of cavalry now entering that town down the road there." Lee showed great interest, but little surprise.

"How did you come by this information, General?," Lee asked.

"I have a man that came in last night with the details," Longstreet replied.

"A man?," Lee inquired.

"Yes Sir, he is a civilian, a Mississippi man who often scouts for me."

"General, I have little confidence in a civilian scout..," he paused. " I can not understand why General Stuart has not reported...."

Longstreet continued, "Well, Sir, I have found this man to be most reliable, and without any other information..." Having made his point about Lee's Cavalry chief, Longstreet continued. "My man says the lead infantry element is marching hard and it is Reynolds's Corps. The whole army is headed this way, coming fast and converging on this town to our front where the roads come together here. Gettysburg, it's called."

Lee was about to speak when Longstreet added, "There is something else too, my man says George Meade has been made commander of the army, replacing Hooker." Lee looked away as if pulling up the service record on this new commander from some mental file cabinet. This last bit of information seemed to preempt the news of the Union Army's movement.

"Meade.. are you sure? Lee puzzled.

Longstreet replied, "Yankee newspapers say Joe Hooker was relieved. My man said some of the papers told of Hooker asking to be relieved."

"I thought this might be coming as before," said Lee, "but I expected Reynolds to get the command."

"So did I. Do you know Meade?," Longstreet asked.

"Yes, and I can tell you that General Meade will commit no blunder to my front, but if I make one he will take full advantage of it. How long has Meade been in command, do you know?"

"Not long. A week...two at the most ," Longstreet answered.

Lee was already planning as he moved toward the map on his table. "We must act now to take advantage of this new change, Pete." General Lee did not call many men by their nickname, but James Longstreet, was among the few he did. "Meade will take some time to organize his command to fight. He is new and will be cautious, but only for a short time. While he hesitates, we will strike."

Longstreet had seen this concentration and glint in his commander's eyes before. Lee will make his army appear vulnerable, and when Meade attacks, Lee will again defeat the Army of the Potomac, just as he had done before. It was truly an opportunity in the making.

Longstreet spoke, "If the roads will just not get washed out in the rain. We can move rapidly to a defensive position, we could then...," Lee interrupted Longstreet's developing plan.

"Here," Lee said pointing to the map, "Here, south of the town. We will take this high ground and pull him into an attack. When he does, we will defeat him." Longstreet saw that Lee planned to force Meade into an attack by just being in place before he arrived. Lee reasoned that the Federal troops would be tired from the march up the Tanneytown Road and Baltimore Pike, but Meade was surely under pressure to attack and destroy the Army of Northern Virginia. It would be a battle Meade could not refuse, and one he would not win.

Lee turned to dictate the order to move all troops toward the town of Gettysburg. Longstreet, ever the defensive soldier, was still looking at the map and the high ground. He tapped his finger the map as he spoke. "That hill, Culp's Hill, and this ridge, the one starting at that cemetery just south of the town and running down to these two hills. Good terrain. Hold this high ground and the Federals will be chewed up trying to take them. It could be Fredericksburg all over again! There was just one problem. We are north of the town and not in position. Union cavalry will be coming up fast from the south. We have to get there first. We must sweep them away and move quickly through that little town."

A rumble caused both men to look toward the south and then at each other. No mistaking that sound, it was artillery, but whose and why? The two generals had the plan, now it was time to act.

Lee soon mounted to ride forward, as the headquarters of the Army of Northern Virginia already began to move to follow him. Longstreet departed to rejoin his headquarters at Cashtown. Firing toward Gettysburg seemed to be growing.

Lee found A.P Hill moving toward the sound of the battle. "General Hill, who is firing ahead?"

"I'm not sure, Sir, but General Heth is supposed to be there and I think it is likely his fire. By your leave, Sir, I am riding that way to see for myself. I'll send word to you as soon as I can!" With a nod from Lee, Hill departed at a full gallop.

Longstreet arrived at his headquarters having made his way back through the sea of troops now making their way toward Gettysburg down the Chambersburg Turnpike. The troops were moving slowly but steadily. He needed to bring his troops up fast, but the approaches were clogged. Longstreet thought, "We will be late and the Federals will beat us there for sure. If they get control of the high ground south of the town, we will be in serious trouble."

Lee received the reports with inward agitation. It was apparent that the Union cavalry was holding up the Confederate advance until Reynolds's infantry could arrive to join in the battle. Confederate forces were also arriving now, but still not fast enough to suit Lee. Rodes, Early, and Pender arrived one after the other and moved into position to engage.

Lee had not wanted to fight this way, but a good commander made the most of what was presented. The Federals must be moved from the town and pushed before they could assemble and organize in numbers. Lee ordered a general attack.

One Confederate division after another pushed toward the Federals. All General Heth had wanted was to enter Gettysburg to raid a shoe factory that he heard was there, and now a major battle had developed over shoes in a warehouse! So be it! The weight of the reinforced Confederates began to crack the blue line. At last they were breaking! Maybe it wasn't too late.

Lee observed the Union forces falling back and Confederate troops entering the town. It had been a hard fight following a hard march. His troops were just unable to muster up the strength to pursue retreating enemy. The day had been won, but Federal troops were now moving south, up the ridge past the cemetery just outside the town. They too were exhausted, but they began to dig in.

Lee thought, "We won the day, but they are going to hold the high ground we had wanted... the high ground we had planned to use against them."

Union cavalry and the lead infantry units had paid a high price to buy time for the Army of the Potomac, but they now had the better of the terrain. Lee knew this will make it harder, but no matter, in an all out fight he also knew his boys could take those people.

Amid all the developments, Longstreet arrived. "Sorry I couldn't get my boys up any faster, General, but it looks like you whipped them good without us, he said smiling around his cigar."

"God was again kind to us," Lee said with reverence. "I trust he will be so again tomorrow." He was looking toward high ground past the town.

Longstreet's smile was now gone as he looked at Lee. He removed his cigar slowly and in measured words he said, "I wish we could have taken that high ground. We could have had them." It was a statement and a question all at the same time.

Lee never stopped looking at Gettysburg as he said, "We will take them tomorrow."

Longstreet knew his commander all to well, and he knew this was his answer. He is not going to stop, high ground or no high ground. Lord in heaven! He is going to continue to press the attack to the Federals and them on the high ground!

"General Lee," Longstreet tried to be calm and deliberate, "We have won a victory today even though we did not plan to fight here. The enemy is hurt, but he is far from spent. He has superior numbers and with it, he now has the high ground which gives him a great advantage. But he will have the advantage only if we choose to give it to him by attacking. We can disengage and move on toward Washington or Virginia and choose the next ground to fight him. Meade will follow and when he does we...."

Lee turned toward Longstreet and interrupted, "Retreat? We can not retreat after this victory today." He again looked south of the town, "The enemy is there and we must strike him. I want us to destroy those people before they grow any stronger and we can do this, right there. We will hit their flanks; they will break there."

"Sir, there are worse things than moving away." Lee turned and stared at Longstreet. He had never been taken to task by one of his generals like this before. Longstreet continued, but in a softer tone, "Sir, we want to finish this battle, but we have fewer troops, poorer equipment...."

Lee again interjected, "General, we have fought this entire war under such conditions. Had we waited for the ideal time and place to fight, you know we would have already lost this war."

Longstreet continued, "I know, Sir, but you have always placed us in the best possible position to use what we had. This looks like Fredericksburg all over, only *they* are on Maryes Heights!" These words seem to touch Lee, but he said nothing. With his lips drawn tight, he just turned and looked toward the hills to the south. Longstreet knew the decision had been made.

After a minute or two, he slowly came to attention, saluted and said, "I better return to my command, Sir." Lee turned and saluted.

Longstreet was heart sick. He had not handled that well. He had appeared to question his commander's judgment rather than strongly presenting the facts of the situation as a matter of counsel. Longstreet respected no man more than Robert Edward Lee, and somehow he had to tell him so.

As he walked away, he slowed, then stopped and turned to look back at Lee who surprisingly was watching him depart. Lee smiled slightly and nodded as if to say all was forgiven. With that, Longstreet slapped his leg with his gloves, took a deep breath and walked back to Lee. He was calm and composed now as he removed his hat, "General, you know I will draw my sword and personally lead the attack up that ridge if you but wish it so. My Corps will give you everything we have to give, as you direct." James Longstreet had apologized as only a soldier could. He had offered to die or to sacrifice his command without question.

Lee was moved by this honest gesture. He reached out and took Longstreet's arm. "Walk with me, Pete."

After a minute, Lee began, "Pete, we must soon end this war. The South can not continue to fight on for an indefinite time. We have the superior army, but it is being consumed in battle after battle. We have no limitless supply of men and equipment as do the enemy. England does not appear to be prepared to help us, and without help…" he left the rest unsaid. "I am very tired and in all honesty, I am not in good health." "You are my most experienced commander," he smiled, "my old warhorse." "I depend on you more than you know," he said softly. Then he stopped and the smile faded. "You feel very strongly about this attack tomorrow. Do you honestly feel it is not possible to carry it, even with massed troops and massed artillery?"

Longstreet was unbelievably being given another chance to discuss the attack with General Lee. He spoke carefully, "General, the enemy is digging in as we speak. He has the ground, the men, and the artillery to stop us. If I were in Reynolds place, I would pray to God that we would attack." Lee was listening intently, but he was still not convinced.

Longstreet continued, "We *might* just carry this off. I don't honestly think we can, but we might. It took a considerable effort to clear the town today, and the enemy has been converging out there ever since. Our losses tomorrow on these hills, win or lose, will be heavy, and as you said, we just can not afford the losses. If we should have particularly heavy losses...it could cost us the war." Lee was now listening to his trusted lieutenant carefully.

Longstreet was again becoming intense, although very respectful. "Sir, I urge you to reconsider. Let us take the victory today and move to new ground. We know it is not a retreat, but if the enemy thinks it is, so much the better. They will follow us to a battlefield of our choosing, and no one chooses ground better than you. The enemy has taken losses, but we both know he must follow us, and when he does, we might just be able to destroy him once and for all." Longstreet was now done. He had said it all, he had made his case, but Lee said nothing. Longstreet knew it had not been enough. The commander of the Army of Northern Virginia made no response, he just stood with his arms folded just looking at those hills.

Finally without turning, Lee said, "General Longstreet, thank you for your honesty, I do greatly value your counsel. I will give this matter some thought."

Longstreet replied with a simple, "Yes Sir". He saluted once again and departed for his headquarters at I Corps. Tomorrow would be a very long and painful day for his troops.

Longstreet tossed and turned, but slept little through the night. Now he was up and studying the map again. He always hated to lose sleep before a battle since he worried about its keeping him from being as fresh and sharp as he needed to be. In truth, he also knew the battle and its needs would take from him what was required and leave his body to suffer later. Like a baby in its mother's womb, the battle took what it needed first. War used soldiers up well before their time.

Major Sorrel pulled back the tent flap and seeing his commander was up, ducked slightly to enter while carefully balancing a cup of steaming coffee in his hand. "Good morning, Sir," he said in a quiet tone. "I wasn't sure you would be up yet. General Lee has called a staff meeting for an hour from now, so I brought you some coffee."

Longstreet rubbed his face and nodded.. "Thank you, Moxley. Coffee sounds good. Go ahead and get our mounts ready to go."

"They are being brought up now, Sir," replied Sorrel. Longstreet nodded again, his mind was again on the upcoming battle and the part I Corps would play in it.

If Lee would agree, Longstreet would send a force around to the right and try to flank the Federal line. This might just work out if he went wide and hit the flank hard. He must talk with General Lee about this. One last swallow of coffee. Quarter of five. It's still dark. Time to go and see what the day holds for the boys.

General Lee was looking over his map for the hundredth time. Dawn would be here shortly and his generals were on their way to get their instructions. He had studied the situation again and again, and did not like what he saw. No matter, he must defeat the Army of the Potomac soon. He must make the best of the situation and bring the weight of his army against the Federals, and he must do it quickly.

He went over it again, and once more he was drawn to the Federal flanks. "If we can break either the right or left flank, they will collapse and we can very likely end it all right here, right now. They have the high ground, but we have the momentum. I have Longstreet and Hill and the magnificent Army of Northern Virginia. There are none better and they are ready for a fight. This must be the battle that breaks the Federal army, yet we *must* avoid the heavy losses. There just are no replacements." He did not like the decision he was going to make, but there was no escaping the course of action. He could not afford a mistake. He had to decide. "We must...."

Major Taylor kept Lee from arriving at the same distasteful

answer he had repeatedly come to. "Sir, General Hill is arriving and the other commanders are now here."

Lee began to button his coat as he moved toward the entrance of the tent, "Very well, Major." Light was beginning to just show in the east.

The Corps commanders of the Army of Northern Virginia and their selected division commanders came to attention and saluted as General Lee entered the briefing tent. "Good morning, Sir," they collectively said to their general. No one was particularly cheerful, but all seemed alert and ready for their orders and the battle they knew would come this day.

"Good morning, gentlemen," Lee looked over the assembled officers as he returned their salute. "Everyone here?" he asked.

Generals Ewell and Hill nodded that they were as Lee looked around to confirm that the key officers were indeed present.

Then he began, "Gentlemen, as you all know, destruction of the enemy force in the field remains our primary purpose. We must defeat the enemy once and for all."

Lee paused for some time. "However, after careful review and consideration, I am convinced that this is NOT the place to accomplish this task." Ewell looked noticeably puzzled, if not somewhat disappointed. A.P. Hill was likewise surprised, since his conversation with Lee earlier had convinced him that there would be an attack and a major battle here today. Longstreet slowly put his cigar in his mouth holding back a smile. He had convinced Lee after all it seemed.

General Lee began to explain his plan, now pointing at the map before them. "I propose to disengage the bulk of the army and move in this direction." He ran his finger southwest through South Mountain, then south, then east through the Catoctin Mountains toward Frederick on the road to Washington. Several officers openly smiled and looked at each other. Washington! At last! Now they would let the Federals experience what Richmond had experienced these past two years!

Lee quickly brought them back to focus, "I do not expect that we will actually attack the Federal capitol. I plan to destroy the enemy reserve corps here at Frederick. The enemy will move quickly to stop us and when he does, we will use his haste, our good plan, and our superb army to destroy him once and for all!" He waited for a response.

"Sir?," General Ewell spoke. Lee nodded. "We won a substantial victory here yesterday. Will it not be counter productive for morale and spirit of the troops to move away from the Federals when we have such an opportunity here?"

The commander of the Army of Northern Virginia seemed to have been waiting for this question. It was one he had pondered over and over. He responded, "It is true that we won an impressive victory here yesterday and I have considered that. However, General, this victory is out of proportion to the battle that is surely to come. I must say honestly to you all, I feel we could very likely defeat the Federals today. Right here. But we must be certain of this victory. A near victory will not do, nor will just any victory do."

"Consider the facts. The enemy grows stronger each day. If we fight now, and win, but in doing so we take heavy losses, we can not look for help. We are in enemy territory and it is no secret that the South has little left to send us. If we win a victory without completely destroying his army, the enemy will again move away to replenish and refit. We will be unable to pursue and continue the fight. No Sir, we must plan carefully to assure total victory as much possible. This next battle must be decisive. We must completely defeat these people."

The generals now understood. They would indeed fight, but their commander wanted as much in his favor as he could get. He would not trade his army away for a victory, he wanted to end the war! How exactly did he plan to defeat the Federals? The Army of the Potomac was just over the tree line and they had no intention of letting Lee's army just walk away to fight another day!

"The plan to defeat the enemy in the next few days will require the greatest effort of all of our forces. *Timely movement without hesitation* or delay is a primary factor here." Lee was looking at his Corps commanders, particularly at Longstreet.

"For this plan to succeed, coordination and control will be paramount. " He placed his spectacles on and looked at the map, "We shall proceed in this manner."

"General Longstreet, you will demonstrate this afternoon before the Federal left here, near these two hills. Give the enemy great reason to believe you will attack momentarily. Your demonstration should start after lunch toward early afternoon today. The days are long this time of year, so early afternoon will do well for us."

Lee continued, "You should give the appearance of preparing for an attack, but I want you to look disorganized. Get some of your troops into position late in the afternoon, but appear that owing to the now late hour, you decide to wait for an attack early tomorrow morning. You should make use of cavalry, artillery, and wagon movements to appear that you are strengthening here-in the wood line west of-Emmittsburg Road. Then, well after dark, as the enemy settles in and continues to prepare for your attack in the morning, you will disengage the bulk of your Corps. You will move southwest through Fairfield and then *rapidly* towards Boonsboro, turning to go through Turner's Gap…here. Proceed toward Frederick looking for a suitable location west of the Catoctin Mountains where you can hold until the rest of the army can assemble with you. I stress that you must give the appearance that your main body is still in place at Gettysburg even as you move south." Lee looked at Longstreet, "Is this clear so far, general?"

General Longstreet paused, then responded, "Yes Sir, you mentioned cavalry."

Lee replied, "Correct, General Stuart will provide cavalry elements from his command for this work. I would suggest General Imboden, who is already detached, join General Jenkins' brigade for this duty." Lee looked at Stuart who was still smarting from his *little talk* with his commander about being gone too long and being out of touch.

Stuart quietly voiced a simple, "Yes Sir". Longstreet indicated understanding by nodding as the generals all looked again to the map.

"General Hill, when General Longstreet's main body moves south, you will immediately fall in behind him and follow in close order with most of your Corps. This will place you second in the movement. The cavalry elements from General Stuart that I mentioned will remain behind when you depart. They will keep up campfires and the appearance that there is a strong force before the enemy lines. They must appear to be infantry and not just cavalry." Lee was looking over his spectacles waiting for confirmation of understanding from General Hill and General Stuart.

A.P. Hill responded, "Yes Sir, I follow immediately behind General Longstreet." He was thinking that this was a lot of people to be moving at night, but if it could be done, the Army of Northern Virginia would do it. Moving south would certainly help the men to move smartly, as everyone was ready to get out of Pennsylvania and get on home soil.

Lee nodded and now looked to Richard Ewell, "General Ewell, you will follow General Hill immediately as he moves to follow General Longstreet. In like manner, detached cavalry elements will stay behind as you depart. As you move through the mountains past Fairfield, you must watch to your rear and be prepared to hold up any enemy elements that might try to follow us. I do not foresee this happening, but if it should, you must provide us time to get the army south and in place to fight."

"Very well, Sir, " Ewell answered. "But should the enemy follow us through the mountains, rather than move south from Gettysburg, or if he does both, how will we address such a move?"

General Lee responded, "I do not think the enemy will follow you in any real strength. If your rear guard is alert and strong enough, it will be able to handle any cavalry units he should send against you. I fully expect that General Meade will be late in moving, and by the time he realizes we are disengaged, we will make sure he knows we are now *south* of his main force. General Meade will be forced to move due south directly toward us to cut us off from attacking Baltimore or Washington."

Dick Ewell replied with a nod of his head and a "Very well,

Sir."

"General Stuart, the main body of your cavalry will be out in front of the army as we move south. You *must* maintain contact with the main body and keep me informed as we proceed. I want to be very clear about this. I *must* know what is to our front. The Army will be advancing in column and we can not engage piecemeal." JEB Stuart was looking almost embarrassed at the specific guidance he was being given. Lee continued pointing at the map, "Just southeast of Hagerstown, we will turn east and move through the mountains here." He pointed toward the small dot on the map called Middletown. The enemy may well be on his way to close on us by the time we reach this point, but if not, we will continue south toward Frederick. You must also have elements of your cavalry take and secure the bridges across the Potomac at Williamsport, as well as the fords there and here at Falling Waters for our possible use."

"The bridge here across the Monocacy southeast of Frederick may need to be destroyed, so be ready for this order should it come. *Do not*, I repeat D*o Not*, destroy this bridge until you receive orders from my headquarters to this effect."

Lee continued, "General, after you have cleared the way to Frederick, be prepared to turn north to contact the enemy and determine just where he is and how he is approaching us. At this point, you must delay him and gain us as much time as possible without becoming decisively engaged."

"General Stuart," Lee smiled warmly as he removed his spectacles, "as a cavalry officer you are unsurpassed. You must find the way for us and then provide us some time as prepare for the enemy." Stuart was deeply moved at the compliment given to him before his fellow officers. In an instant he knew that all was truly forgiven. He returned the smile, "Yes Sir, I will get you some time."

Lee again continued to Stuart, "Once you have accomplished this, return directly to the main body by way of Frederick City. The enemy will surely be following you, and I want you lead him right to us. Once you rejoin us, you must quickly move to protect our rear and flank from any approach from Washington or Baltimore. By this time, Washington will be in a panic and the Meade's forces will be moving as quickly as possible to try and stop us."

General Hill raised a question, "Sir, reference to Washington, do you think the Yankees troops there will be sent against us?"

"No," Lee said as he leaned on the table looking at the map. "The troops in Washington are not prepared to meet us in the field, and the government would never leave the city undefended. I expect they will man defensive positions in or near the city and wait for us to attack."

"*And* pray to the good Lord all the while that we do not do so!," loudly interjected George Pickett. Everyone laughed as Robert E. Lee smiled. Spirits were high.

Lee hesitated as the seriousness of the moment returned, "I expect the enemy to move south out of Gettysburg by forced march. Meade will want to fight us immediately, hoping to catch us strung out as we move toward Washington. The enemy will probably want to catch up to us at Frederick, only we won't be moving, we will be waiting. He will be trying to stop an attack that we never intended to make. They will be the ones that are caught. Gentlemen, we *have* the army and we *will have* position. *Here*!" Lee was pointing at the hills of Monocacy just south of Frederick. "*Here* we shall defeat the Federal army once and for all."

The assembled commanders realized this plan was bold, just as were always the plans of Robert E. Lee. They also realized the Army of Northern Virginia had a reputation for accomplishing such bold plans. This one would be no different. They were going to make a long and dangerous night move. Then place themselves between the Federal army and Washington. The enemy will surely come at them like a charging bull!

For the next half hour or so, details were discussed and the commanders looked at the maps, asking questions, making plans and coordinating their efforts. They discussed the need for being seen to prepare for an attack at Gettysburg , but at the same time, not being too obvious. The need to avoid observation as they prepared to move, the need for quiet but fast movement, the need for route reconnaissance before dark, the need for troops to rest while looking as if they were preparing to attack, these were but a few of the topics of discussion. The coordination would continue through the day as preparations were made, but they

had to start now before the Federals might decide to attack. But no, the Federals would not attack. They had the good positions and were not about to give them up.

Shortly, General Lee dismissed his officers from the formal briefing. He talked individually with his Corps commanders alone before they left, stressing the need for rapid and steady movement. He encouraged them, pointed out specific details and wished each of them well as they left. Longstreet was the last to take leave of his commander. Lee walked with him to his horse.

"Pete, your counsel yesterday was important in helping me reach this decision."

Longstreet was uncomfortable and immediately replied. "General, I hope I did not step out of line with my comments, I would never...."

"No," said Lee, "I asked you to speak up and you did. I need officers who will give me their honest opinion. Now, our plan is in place. As I mentioned to you, I have not been well physically. Should anything happen to me, you must see this plan through. One thing I do want to mention to you. I have noted that of all my Corps commanders, you in particular tend to get too far forward and place yourself in greater danger than necessary."

"Sir, nothing will happen to you. You will outlast us all!" Longstreet was trying to speak and not seem dramatic.

"Well, you take care of yourself and stay well clear of the front line. That's an order," said Lee as he smiled and walked a few more steps. Then he stopped and faced Longstreet, "General, for this plan to succeed , you must move quickly, you must be bold, strike hard, and you must win decisively. I am convinced that this battle could well determine the war. That's why I have *your* Corps leading in this march. I want you to help me end this terrible conflict."

Longstreet realized just how much Lee really had come to depend on him since he had lost Tom "Stonewall" Jackson. He was deeply moved, "My Corps will give you everything we have, General."

As he mounted up and rode back toward his headquarters, James Longstreet had much on his mind. It was shaping up to be a very long day just as he had thought it would be, but it was certainly different than he had expected. When he looked toward the Union lines, he felt relieved that there would be no fight here today.

For a moment, he wondered what would have happened if the two armies had indeed fought at Gettysburg, Pennsylvania.

WASHINGTON

Secretary of War Edward Stanton walked briskly toward the President's office to tell him of the latest war news. His face had an appearance of grimness, which, in truth, was his normal outlook on most affairs. Stanton was an unlikely ally of Lincoln. He had been an early critic of Lincoln's administration. The president had silenced him by asking him to join the administration and help change that which he disliked so much. Stanton surprised many people by doing just that. His stern administrative hand quickly brought order to the massive expansion of the military. He demanded accountability from suppliers of war materials, as well as those for whom it was intended. He worked well for Lincoln, but he was never a close friend of the president. It was thought by some that the only people he disliked more than rival politicians were Southerners. He hated Southerners.

Learning that the president was alone, Stanton entered following a slight knock on the door. "Mr. President, I have just received some news and I wanted to update you immediately."

Lincoln leaned back from the papers on his desk and smiling softly, he said, "Good news, I trust Mr. Secretary." Abraham Lincoln needed good news. Robert E. Lee was still running loose in the north somewhere unchecked and had captured York, Pennsylvania only last week. At the same time, Lincoln had been forced to replace Joe Hooker with George Meade. This made the fifth commander for the Army of the Potomac since the first battle of Bull Run. On top of that, the Peace Democrats and more and more people were becoming vocal in their opposition of the war which was dragging on and with more and more casualties after every battle. Good news would do nicely. If only there were some.

"Well, I think you will find this very encouraging, Mr. President", Stanton replied. "General Meade has sent news that he has run down Lee and will look to engage him today or tomorrow, if Lee does not disengage and run." Lincoln raised his eyebrows, but said nothing. Stanton continued, "And the very best possible news from Vicksburg. As we expected, General Grant says the Rebels there have asked for terms. Vicksburg is ours!"

Lincoln smiled and nodded his approval. "Mr. Stanton, that is indeed good news. Very good news! This will insure return of Federal control over the Mississippi River soon. As I recall, there are only one or two areas on the river that are now still in Rebel hands. Is that not correct?"

Secretary Stanton answered without hesitation, "Yes, Sir, Port Hudson, is still holding out, but should fall quickly now."

"Good! It has been a long time in coming. General Grant has done a great service for the nation with this victory. The people will be very pleased to hear of this! Now, about General Meade." Lincoln was again serious, "You said Meade has 'run down' Lee?"

"Yes, Sir, near a small town in southern Pennsylvania. Gettysburg, I believe its called."

Lincoln again leaned back as he started into one of his famous frontier illustrations, "Running down Lee and wondering if he will fight reminds me a little of a coon-on-a-log fight. You know, that old coon will run from a pack of dogs all day if he can. Once cornered, such as when placed on a log in the middle of a lake, he will turn on the dog, tear his nose off and drown him if you don't have a good dog. Many times as not, the coon comes out on top." Lincoln smiled, "I trust we have a good dog in General Meade, Mr. Secretary?"

"General Meade is a very able commander, Mr. President. He has an excellent chance to completely defeat the Rebels," Secretary Stanton replied. Stanton really hated it when Lincoln started into his old 'buckskin and coon hat' stories from the backwoods of Illinois. Lincoln really could be such a country bumpkin! A knock at the door drew their attention from the conversation of Meade.

Secretary of the Navy, Gideon Welles, and Secretary of State, William Seward, entered the room and stopped just inside the door. Welles spoke first. "Excuse me, Mr. President, I was hesitant to interrupt, but I think you gentlemen might need to hear this information together. I caught Secretary Seward in his office and thought you might want him to join us as well."

"Certainly, Mr. Welles, you all please come in." The President motioned as he said, "We have just received very good news from General Grant in Vicksburg."

It was obvious to Lincoln that Mr. Welles was not sure how to proceed. "Mr. Stanton has just provided us with some good news, but I perceive that you do not have such good news to offer," observed Lincoln.

"No, Sir, Mr. President. I had just heard about Vicksburg from Admiral Porter, when I received this dispatch from Virginia requiring urgent attention. News has come to me indicating a new potential problem concerning the British. We have had another situation occur at sea between a British merchant ship and one of our warships," Welles paused.

They all well remembered the *Trent* affair, when a U.S. man-of-war had taken two Confederate commissioners enroute to England off an English mail ship by force. This act almost gained the Confederacy the recognition it wanted and brought England into the war on the side of the South.

Welles continued, "A dispatch from Gosport reports that one of our sidewheel steamers, the *USS Octorara*, tried to stop an English merchant ship at sea, when the Englishman decided to make a run for it. Our warship fired a warning shot and - well somehow - this part isn't clear yet. It hit the English vessel killing the first officer, a crewman and seriously injuring the captain."

Edward Stanton's face flushed at what he was hearing and in a voice of unbelief he asked, "How in blazes can you hit a ship with a warning shot? Who...," he stopped as President Lincoln stood up.

"Two killed you say? Where is the English ship now?" asked Lincoln.

"Yes Sir, the dispatch says there were two killed and the captain badly injured," continued Secretary Welles. "The English ship just arrived at Gosport and was escorted in by the Octorara. I'm told our personnel did render such assistance as they could," said Welles, as if trying to put a little good news into what was an otherwise dismal situation.

"The report said the Englishman tried to run?," asked Seward.

"That is what I understand from the report I received," answered Welles, "The English vessel was ordered to stop, but instead it tried to make a run for it. The initial report is very sketchy. I have asked for a full report immediately."

"Well, if the Englishman failed to stop as ordered, that is their problem, not ours!" exclaimed Seward. "The maritime laws pertaining to running a blockade are very clear. If you fail to halt when ordered to do so, you suffer the consequences!" Seward seemed satisfied with his own interpretation of the incident.

"I rather think the British government will take a somewhat different view of this matter, Mr. Secretary," Lincoln said. "They will take as dim a view of such an incident at sea as we would. What else can you add Mr. Welles?"

"Not much, Sir," replied Secretary Welles as he looked at the message in his hand, "The ship was damaged and was helped into port. We are trying to assist by making repairs as necessary. The wounded officer is in our hospital at Gosport...wounds are serious.. additional information to follow in a formal report. That's all, Sir, there are no other details provided."

Lincoln paused and then spoke, "Mr. Seward, we must immediately let the British embassy know that there has been an incident at sea and that we are investigating the matter with the greatest dispatch possible. I imagine that the crew members of the English ship are probably telling their story to the British embassy personnel even as we speak. Please express my personal regrets to Lord Lyons at the loss of life that has been reported. Don't say too much until we know more details, but let them know that we are taking the incident *very* seriously, *very* seriously indeed. Tell Lord Lyons we will provide information to him just as soon as we can confirm what has occurred and why."

Lincoln leaned forward on his desk and spoke very deliberately, "Mr. Secretary, there must be no finger pointing or verbal accusations until we know more details. British subjects have been killed by American military personnel and whatever the reason behind this incident, there will likely be a major crisis come of this."

"Yes, Mr. President, we will handle this very carefully," replied Secretary Seward. Seward had no love for the British and Lincoln knew it. The President had made his point, although it was unnecessary. Seward also understood full well the seriousness of the matter before them and whatever his opinion of the British, he would be very diplomatic in this matter.

Lincoln now looked at Secretary of the Navy Welles. "Mr. Welles, we must have the captain of our warship.... What was the ship's name?"

Welles answered, "*Octorara*, Sir. She is a new paddle steamer." Welles looked at his papers. "A ... Captain Collins is in command."

Lincoln nodded, "Yes, *Octorara*. Captain Collins. Have Collins immediately report to you personally to render a full and detailed report. We must know all the details, with nothing left out or overlooked. Make sure ALL the details are provided to you by Captain Collins. In fact, have *Octorara 's* first officer also accompany Captain Collins so as to provide additional details as necessary."

"Yes, Mr. President," said Welles. "I will see to it at once. May I add, a naval court of inquiry is normal procedure in such matters. I suggest that we consider such action as well."

"Very well, I leave this to you and Mr. Seward, replied Lincoln. "Mr. Welles, I want you to again inform our naval commanders to exercise extreme caution when it comes to dealing with ships at sea in the vicinity of our blockade. When word of this gets out their will be tensions with other ships at sea, theirs and ours. There must be no more incidents, or we may well lose control of the situation with disastrous results."

"Of course, Sir, I understand," answered Welles.

"Render all aid possible to the English ship and the wounded," Lincoln continued. "Gentlemen, I expect us to hold our ground if we are in the right on this matter. If we are in error, we must not allow such an error lead us into a conflict with the British. This will likely be a most difficult situation."

Lincoln was looking out the window and watching the work crews going and coming from the new capitol dome project. "Please inform me just as soon as you have more information. Thank you, gentlemen, I will let you get to these matters without delay."

The three cabinet officers excused themselves and left Lincoln alone. He now felt very tired. Tired, alone, and with bad news...this seemed the natural state of affairs ever since he had become President. Once again, it was happening. The good news of Vicksburg had scarcely been delivered when it was over shadowed by bad news from the Atlantic. Was there no end to it?

At least the Mississippi River was clear to the Gulf now. This would help in the Mid-Western states where support for the war was lagging badly. His mind went back to the incident at sea. How will our people react to this incident? What will the British say? They had threatened war over the TRENT situation when it happened and no one was even killed there. Lincoln hoped the English sea captain did not die, but he did hope that somehow it was this Englishman that had precipitated this incident.

THE BRITISH EMBASSY

"No! By heaven, not this time! England will not be blamed for this mess!" Lord Lyons slammed both hands flat on the desk. "How could they be so stupid!" Normally the picture of a calm and collected diplomat, he realized that this was more than a difficult situation. It was a very *bad* situation. Lyons called for his private secretary in order to begin the dispatch that would quickly be on its way to London.

He wanted so much to keep his country out of this war. His beloved England had already experienced more than its share of young men lost on battlefields and seas around the world. Lyons knew it only took an incident such as this to put a nation on the course to conflict that would be almost irreversible. Based on the stories he had heard from the Mount Blanc's crew, the U.S. Navy had perhaps this time given the enemies of the United States more than enough ammunition to start a new war with England. He could just imagine the anger and passion on the Parliament floor. Queen Victoria would publicly call for calm, but privately she would be seething with anger at the apparent master-of-the-sea attitude the U.S. was again demonstrating. The Queen was a very hard lady indeed when pushed too far.

Lyons was remembering how he had tried to talk to Seward after the *Trent* affair. At that time an over zealous American naval officer had forcibly taken two Confederate Commissioners off the English mail packet even though they were under the protection of the English flag. Lord Lyons had told Seward that both nations had to be very careful not to precipitate any more incidents. Seward had expressed an attitude of more or less, "YOU be careful...WE are at war."

There had been serious saber rattling over the *Trent* affair, but this time there would surely be demands for action, for punishment ...for WAR! He would do his best, but this time it would be up to the Americans to do most of the work. This situation was of their making.

"Secretary Seward," he thought, "you will have to be at your best, for you have pulled the tail of the English Lion once too often." He motioned for his secretary to be seated and then he began. "To Prime Minister Palmerston. Sir: I have the unhappy duty to report...."

GETTYSBURG

The lamp flickered, making its light dance around the map as General Longstreet talked to his Division Commanders. "By now, General Stuart is moving the bulk of his command south behind the mountains. We must be start within the next two hours to follow him. General Hood, you will lead out. You must, I repeat, must stay on the move behind the Cavalry with all the expediency you can muster. You will not only be the first elements leading the army, you will be the first to arrive at the new position."

"Sir, where exactly do you want these new positions?," General Hood asked motioning toward the map.

"Somewhere near here - just east of Middletown or just this side of this pass leading to Frederick. Stuart will find us the general area and I will be with you, or in front of you, to tell you the exact area we will occupy when you arrive." He looked at the other commanders as he spoke deliberately, "Once there, the boys will be bone tired, but you must not let them rest until you know they are ready to move to attack the Federals in Frederick. Your presence and visibility before the troops is vital. The men will work as long as they see you moving among them, so stay visible. Make your officers do the same. Lastly, keep me posted on where you are."

His commanders all nodded understanding and agreement. He continued, "Gentlemen, the Federals have a huge army and when they find we are moving toward Washington, they will come after us with a vengeance. If they rush head first, and we are prepared with our second wind, we can catch them coming off the march piecemeal, trying to stop us. It could be Fredericksburg all over again, only more so."

He paused, looking at the map, and spoke carefully, "I know you have heard this before, but I think you can really see it here. We have the best opportunity we have ever had to whip the Army of the Potomac once and for all."

Longstreet looked up, tapping his finger for emphasis as he spoke, "But understand this...we can not make mistakes, we *can not* be slow in our movements, we can not be sloppy in our security, and we must be ready for the fight of our lives." He looked in their faces, "Are you up to it?"

General Pickett smiled as he twirled his mustache, "I, for one, shall look forward to admiring Mr. Lincoln's new capitol building as I tour it, just before General Lee arrives!" Everyone laughed and agreed they too hoped this would lead to the army marching on Washington. They were eager to go.

RICHMOND

"Gentlemen, it appears God has indeed intervened on behalf of the Confederacy!" President Davis seemed to almost be gleeful as he prepared to tell the assembled Secretaries of the Confederate Executive Departments the news he had just learned. He began, "Secretary Seddon has just informed me that a Federal Navy warship has fired upon a British merchantman, and in doing so, has killed several English seamen, including the Captain of the vessel. The British ship was, we understand, unarmed, carrying a cargo bound for Central or South America, and it was in international waters well away from any of our ports."

The looks on the faces of Davis' Cabinet members ranged from great surprise to outright delight. Davis continued, "Upon learning of this news, my first thoughts ranged from unbelief that such a thing could happen, to the idea of giving the Union Naval officer a medal with the thanks of *our* Congress!" Everyone laughed heartily and made various comments of agreement with this ludicrous proposal.

Stephen Mallory, the very capable Secretary of the Navy, spoke above the fading laughter, "Mr. President, do we know why a Union vessel would fire directly upon a merchantman flying a British flag?"

"No, we have only synopsis of what took place for now," answered President Davis. Then in reference to his previous position as U.S. Secretary of War, Davis said, "I know from my time as U.S. Secretary of War that the standing orders against firing on a merchant ship are very specific and very restrictive. I can not imagine that even during a illegal *blockade* such as they have put in place against us, would they become so brazen as to fire upon the ships of other countries."

President Davis now assumed a serious attitude. "I will tell you this. It can be reasonably assumed that England will not pass this act of war off as they did when Commissioners Slidell and Mason were high-jacked by the Yankee Navy. Knowing how close they came to breaking relations with the U.S. because of this previous incident, it is reasonable to assume that they may well take action of some sort this time. What we must do is to immediately find a way to make this situation work to our advantage."

The Secretaries were by now all with, or ahead of, where Davis was directing the meeting. Judiah Benjamin was the first to speak. "Mr. President, we will surely hear of the repercussions from this event shortly through our State Department contacts in London. It is obvious that we should make every effort to push for recognition for our government. For some time now, I have considered several options that could have very positive effects to help us, given the right conditions…conditions just such as these."

Davis leaned back from the table and motioned for Benjamin to continue, "Excellent, Secretary Benjamin, are you proposing to discuss these options now? " asked Davis.

"Actually, Sir, I would prefer to assemble my notes and discuss these ideas with you before I present them as firm proposals. This would allow me time to prepare details so as not waste the valuable time of you and the other Secretaries," replied Benjamin.   With this, the other Secretaries now wondered what Benjamin was planning. They knew he was not worried in the least about their "valuable time," and he was seldom unprepared for any idea he wished to discuss.

"Perhaps your right. It is close to lunch. Let us adjourn for now and meet again at 2 o'clock this afternoon. This will give each of you time to consider the news and how it could effect your area of responsibility." President Davis moved his chair back and the Secretaries all stood. Davis was almost smiling, "Please return promptly prepared to discuss any proposals you think appropriate."

As the President left the room for his office, the assembled secretaries began somewhat excited conversations about the unfolding events. Judiah Benjamin did not linger long before he left the room heading directly for the President's office. Entering, he found Jefferson Davis talking to his personal secretary. As they both turned to him, Benjamin said, "Excuse me, Mr. President, I was wondering if I might meet with you at one o'clock or one-thirty before we all assemble again? I have several specifics of which I would like to brief you before I do so in the meeting."

"Of course, Judiah," replied Davis. Come by at say...one o'clock and we can chat before the meeting at two. Davis' private secretary was making the note on his calendar. This would make it official. After a few pleasantries, Benjamin headed for his office. As he entered, he told his waiting secretary that they would be working through the regular noon hour. He had much to do.

Time rushed by and soon Benjamin was seated before the President presenting his idea. "Mr. President this proposal I am going to present to you will seem radical, but I ask you to please hear me out before you make up your mind as to its worth."

Davis seemed a little surprised. "It must be truly radical for you to ask that, but by all means please proceed, Judiah."

Calmly, Benjamin began, "Sir, it is no secret that the war is not going well for us. We have had some great victories, but many of the setbacks and even many of the victories have sapped our manpower and resources. We have been trying to buy time to at least get recognition from the English, if not outright intervention on our behalf. This attack on a British ship by the Union Navy presents us with a great opportunity, as you earlier pointed out." Davis nodded agreement as Benjamin continued.

"We may not have a second chance to seize the moment as we do now, and therefore I propose we do all we can to give the English government *every* reason to recognize our government. Actually, Sir, what I propose is that we *remove* every major stumbling block that stands in the way of recognition. We should provide such strong incentives, that it will be difficult for the English government to refuse recognition."

"Mr. Secretary, we all have wanted to arrive at such a formula, I hope that you have really developed such plan," said Davis.

"I think I have, Mr. President. Lets consider what we all

know as facts now. The *main drawback* to the Confederacy being recognized by the English parliament is our attachment to the institution of slavery. On the other side of the coin, the greatest *asset* we have to offer the English, and in fact, France and Spain as well, is our cotton," Benjamin paused.

"Surely, you don't suggest that we *abolish slavery* and *give our cotton away*, do you?" Davis said in a somewhat humorous tone.

"Basically, that is *exactly* what I propose, Mr. President!," replied Secretary Benjamin as he moved forward in his seat to continue. Davis looked absolutely shocked at this statement.

"We know that international slavery is dead, our own Constitution prohibits such trade even though the U.S. Constitution does not. Some of us who sit at this very table don't personally care much for the institution of slavery, but all of us support the institution as being undeniably legal! We are, in fact, fighting for our independence to preserve the rights of States to decide when, where, or even if this issue and other such issues should be addressed. It also is an undeniable fact that, for now, our entire economic system is primarily based on the production of cotton, which, in turn, is supported by this most peculiar of institutions."

"All this means that slavery in the present South is a basic necessity for our nation's survival. Unfortunately, England, the one country that could do the most to help us gain our independence, abhors the institution she helped bring to our shores. Now she even leads the world in the fight to outlaw slavery."

"The last piece of this complex situation rests in the fact that we have sought to achieve a great victory over the Union armies in the field. We hope that a substantial victory will swing English sympathy to our side when they see we have accomplished our independence on our own. Once Southern independence appears to be *fait compleat,* it would be easier for the British to maintain relations with the U.S. while recognizing a nation that it had no part in helping establish."

"So there we have it - Cotton is king. Slavery makes cotton

king. England wants and desperately needs our cotton. Many Englishmen wish us well against their twice fought adversary, but England cannot tolerate slavery, therefore she can not lose face in the international community and risk yet another war with the United States by giving even tacit support to the Confederacy, which is so deeply tied to slavery. So we must ask ourselves, how do we break this cycle and make it work to our advantage?" Secretary Benjamin could see he had Jefferson Davis' attention.

"I would propose that our government strike an agreement with England to *abolish slavery* in the South at some date in the future, say...ten years in the future. We can establish some mutually agreed date that would be acceptable to both our government and the English government. The condition for this agreement would be immediate and uncompromising recognition of the Confederacy as a free nation among other nations. Mr. President, this would do several things. It would place England in the position of leadership in the effort to make the world free from slavery, which is one of the goals of the British government. Conversely, if England turns down this opportunity, it would be refute this expressed goal as well as to make England appear fearful of the United States. British recognition would identify us as a free nation with all rights and privileges due us. This would give us access to British ports for trade to purchase openly the items we need to defend ourselves and continue the fight for our independence. This agreement to eventually abolish slavery would also identify the Confederate States of America as a nation making every effort to join with other nations of the world in establishing and maintaining high standards of conduct and excellence. By setting it years into the future, we would have plenty of time to work out how to accomplish this without destroying our economy. "

Benjamin did not give the President a chance to interject as he continued. "As for the cotton, you know we have taken the approach of holding *all* cotton back from the market. We hoped it would drive English merchants into feeling they must run the U.S. blockade to get what this product from us. So far, this has not had the desired effect, and I don't think it ever will. Mr. President, I propose now that we consider doing just the opposite! Instead of holding cotton back in hopes they will fight to *buy* it, lets make it available for *free* and see if they won't fight to come and get it! We might charge some relatively small "tax" that we could use to purchase military arms, but in essence, the cotton would cost nothing to those willing to come and get it!"

Jefferson Davis, could hold back no longer on this idea. "Judiah, of course you know the cotton of which you are offering to give away is the property of the cotton merchants and the states. It is not ours to give away! On top of this, we can not afford to just give all our cotton away!"

"But of course, Sir. I would not propose that we give it *all* away, or even most of it. Let's say we told the English we would make some 50,000 or perhaps even 100,000 bales available! This would raise such a demand from the merchants in England, I think they would surely feel the risk of running the blockade was more than justified. If in the process, English vessels were fired upon and perhaps another incident were precipitated, who knows how the Royal Navy would respond? They might be forced to offer protection to vessels flying the English flag to the point of fighting with the Union Navy. Think of what might come of that!

It was just such a situation I was thinking about when this latest naval incident took place. While I truly regret the incident for the English, I must say that I see great opportunity in it for us. In light of the critical tension now arising between the English and the Yankees, the proposal I have just described appears absolutely made to order!"

President Davis was more than impressed, he was enthralled. Benjamin could see that the President's mind was racing to consider the options and alternatives. "President Davis, I have known you for a long time, and I will not insult your intellect by telling you this is a simple plan. We both know it is not. It is most difficult and it carries with it great political risk. This will not be popular in some individual states, nor do I think it will it be easy to get Congress to back it. However, Sir, I am sure it *is* the opportunity we have been praying for, and one that must be seized at once, if it is to have the desired effect."

Jefferson Davis was a politician, but he was also President. He saw the risks to himself, but he also saw the great opportunity for his country. His country would always win out over his personal ambitions and his personal security. He saw the far reaching implications in what Judiah Benjamin was proposing. He felt he was at last seeing a ray of sunlight through the very dark clouds of war. For the rest of the hour, more questions and possibilities were explored as the two men discussed the idea. What if the government bought the cotton from plantation owners on credit, and paid for it after the war? If the government helped offset the loss of slaves to slave owners, would enough states consider elimination of slavery at some future date? Such federal meddling is just what had led to the conflict in the first place! How quickly could contact be made with England? Who should be the emissary to approach the English? Should Congress be addressed openly or in secrecy?

Lunch had come and gone when finally Jefferson Davis closed the discussion. "Mr. Secretary, I am not sure all that you propose is in the realm of possibility, nor am I sure we would even want to do all that you propose. However, I must say that I think that your ideas could have a major impact on the outcome of this conflict. We must discuss this at once with the other Executive Secretaries. When we join the others, please be prepared to present your concept and answer questions as necessary." In saying this, Davis had agreed to have the proposal discussed at the highest levels, but would let Secretary Benjamin test the waters to see how it was received. At the proper time, he could throw the power of his office behind the plan, assuming it had a chance to be really considered. If it met with total opposition, he could allow it to die on its own without damaging the office of the President. The two men left to return to the meeting room where the other secretaries were now waiting. As they entered, the assembled men stood for their

49

President.

"Gentlemen, please be seated! I trust that you all had a good lunch. May I say that Secretary Benjamin has some very profound ideas to present to us as we start off our discussion of ways to maximize the developing events of the day. I would encourage you to be open minded. Consider what he will present in the light of how it would affect your area of responsibility and our nation as a whole. When he is done, we will discuss the matter and consider other ideas and proposals as you may wish to do."

Judiah Benjamin began slowly setting the stage for the points he wanted to make. He addressed the issues somewhat differently for this presentation than he did for President Davis. He knew that the idea of agreeing to eliminate slavery would be *more* than just unpopular with some of his peers, and the idea of *giving* cotton away would probably bring several of the secretaries to their feet! Benjamin began by explaining that after two and one half years of war, victory was still not in sight. The drain on the limited man power of the South was being felt more and more. The financial strain was apparent to everyone and really needed no explanation.

As he continued into the general points of the plan he could see several of the other secretaries were grasping the idea that if this worked, victory for the Confederacy might be at hand. Once he had finished presenting the plan, he waited for response. It came quickly. Secretary of the Navy Stephen Mallory was enthusiastic in his support of the plan, and stated that he could already envision the British Navy entering the war! Secretary of War Seddon likewise favored pursuing the idea. He was in favor of most any plan that would bring some relief to the Confederate Army. They both questioned the authority of the Confederate government to make any agreement on the issue of freeing the slaves without the states first agreeing to it.

Opposition to the idea was also quick in coming, and Vice President Andrew Stephens led the charge. This was most predictable, since the Vice President was unfortunately often found being in opposition to things that Jefferson Davis supported. In this case, his points had great validity.

He began, "Gentlemen! Gentlemen! The very idea that the Confederate states would agree to eliminate slavery, which is as noted the basis for our labor system, is totally unrealistic! What would replace it? How would the owners of this property be compensated? England certainly won't pay the bill, and surely none of us would propose that the Confederate government compensate them! As for *giving* cotton away to the English merchants instead of *selling* it to them - well, I would not like to be the one to present this plan to Congress! They will laugh you out of the chamber, assuming they don't cane you out of it first!" Several secretaries muttered in basic agreement, but did so in less than an audible volume.

Just as Secretary Benjamin was about to begin his defense of his proposal, President Davis spoke, "May I say Vice President Stephens has presented very clearly the exact arguments that this proposal would face before the open forum of Congress." Davis was now very stern in his delivery, "I will say to you, my closest co-workers and fellow Southern patriots assembled in this room, the conduct of the war is going in such a manner that we can not afford to dismiss any serious plan that might have a positive effect on the war effort. We must go over such ideas in great detail and view them from every possible standpoint! You gentlemen above all others know the seriousness of the situation for our new nation. We have thus far been unable to bring this conflict to a satisfactory conclusion. We are being bled white by the losses, while our enemy appears quite willing to accept such slaughter of their forces. Our economy is slipping under severe pressure and unless we can relieve it...." Davis never finished the statement.

The President was now looking around the table at the secretaries, but he was avoiding looking directly at the Vice President. " I, too, see difficulties and limitations in this proposal and I see great difficulties, but I also see great possibilities in it. With what little we have discussed so far, I would favor a serious discussion toward an attempt to develop the idea into a full, detailed plan." Davis had surprised Judiah

Benjamin by how quickly he had come right out and given presidential support to the concept.

President Davis continued, "I know there are many questions unasked and as I said, there are many other questions that must be addressed and resolved to make such a plan plausible. However, we are the senior officers of the government and it is up to us to hammer this out." Davis was now back in control of the direction of the meeting and the issues to be addressed.

"This is the way I would like for us to proceed. We should now take the remainder of this meeting to raise and list questions pertaining to this proposal for attention and discussion. We will also raise and discuss other items that relate to the current naval incident as we know it. As additional information arrives about what happened and how the English are reacting to this incident, it will be immediately presented to the group for discussion. Lastly, before we adjourn for the afternoon, we will break into several committees for continuation this evening and tomorrow. I would suggest that one committee form with the task of considering the proposal to negotiate an elimination of slavery.

A second committee will be formed to address the proposal of providing a limited quantity of cotton to England and for that matter, possibly France. Finally, a committee will form to discuss and develop other questions and resolutions to other situations that might arise from our actions. In this latter regard, such questions might be concerned with France's and Spain's attitudes and possible responses to our actions, in what ways might we use our Naval forces and shipping facilities to aid English merchants or others approaching Confederate ports. We should also consider what other actions we might take to place U.S. Naval forces in a compromising situation whenever and wherever possible."

"We will form these committees before we adjourn for dinner. We can meet after dinner tonight to begin our discussions, and continue tomorrow. We will work day and night until we have come to some resolution and decision about a course of action. Whatever the course of action you recommend, it must be quickly determined and we must act upon it. I assure you the Northern government is at this very moment trying to salvage the situation to keep it from becoming more of a disaster than it already is."

The President urged, "Gentlemen, I would also remind each of you in the strongest of terms. What we are discussing here *must absolutely* remain in this room! We can not discuss it over dinner, with our staffs, or even with our wives!" Some of the group inwardly smiled at this comment and wondered if Varina Davis would be privy to what was going on. "If this proposal gets to any congressman or senator before we have the details worked out, or God forbid, if the information were to get to a Northern spy, the results would likely be more devastating than we could imagine! I *ask* you, I *implore* you, with all the power of my office, I *instruct* you. *Do not* discuss any part of this subject beyond this gathering. Understood?"

Most everyone said yes, nodded and made affirmative comments in agreement to those around them. Vice President Stephens said nothing. He looked at President Davis and then at the men around the large table. He felt offended that he had been addressed in such a manner. Bad enough that he thought the whole idea to be idiotic, but to be talked to like a school boy! No wonder the war was not going well with such persons making decisions!

Judiah Benjamin had noted the Vice President's demeanor during President Davis' comments. In truth, Benjamin was perhaps the most capable officer at the table. He could see that Stephens was not impressed by the ideas presented, and that he certainly was not happy with the approach and instructions just provided by Jefferson Davis. It was no secret that the President and Vice President had less than a good working relationship.

"What a weakness in our government," Benjamin thought. "Just when we need every senior officer working and contributing with more energy than they normally had to offer, the Vice President was folding his arms!"

Benjamin then reflected that there were always two sides to every coin, and perhaps it was not fair to think that Stephens was letting personal feelings enter the discussion. After all, the Vice President's comments had been very realistic. Everyone knew that President Davis could, indeed, be very stubborn when he made up his mind on an issue. Perhaps this was just an honest difference of opinion about an issue that would force people to fully take sides. Certainly, there would be no middle of the road on these issues! So be it! The good and the bad points of the plan would surely come to light as the Executive Secretaries labored during the coming hours and days. Time now to grab a bite of dinner. He had not eaten since early this morning and suddenly he was very hungry.

GETTYSBURG

Sporadic actions in the afternoon and the seemingly confused massing of Confederate troops had indeed led troops of the Union left flank to think there was a major attack forming. They expected the attack to come across the fields of Gettysburg at any time. In response, Federal forces had shifted up and down the lines in an attempt to meet the expected attack.

As the hot afternoon bore on and afternoon shadows lengthened, senior Union commanders began to realize that the Confederates would not, or could not, organize sufficiently to attack in force as first expected. The realization was met with disappointment for some Union soldiers who knew they had excellent positions for a fight and just wanted to get on with it. Others were glad to have another day to rest and another day to just be alive.

General George Meade had just finished being briefed by one of his staff officers who explained that the Rebels had formed twice in apparent preparation for an attack, but in doing so, they appeared "...confused and indecisive." They now seemed resigned to the fact that owing to the late time of day, it was too late to launch and carry through a major attack before darkness. Considering these factors, it was the opinion of the staff that any Rebel attack would not come before dawn.

General Meade was a careful man, but he was not a man who was slow or hesitant to act. He was well known to be an officer who could evaluate a situation and act if the opportunity presented itself. He was in command of the most powerful Army the United States had ever fielded, and he was looking for an opportunity to use it to destroy the Rebel invasion of the North. Yet, something did not appear quite right about all this. Robert E. Lee and his Army of Northern Virginia had been threatened and mocked by more than one Commander of the Army of the Potomac. Lee had defeated each of them in turn, or at least fought them to a standstill. Lee was many things, Meade reflected, but "confused and indecisive" were not among them.

Meade thought, "While we sit here and think him confused,

Lee will set about to whip us where we sit! He is probably up to something, but what?"

General Meade pondered the map on the table before him, Lee would never go deeper into Northern territory with the Army of the Potomac on his heels, since he could wind up cut off and unable to get back to Virginia. He has no reason to go West, or does he? He thought for a time about this, and returned to the questions when he determined there was indeed no reason for Lee move West. Lee could possibly flee South towards Virginia. It could be difficult for us to stop him and bring him to battle once he got started. This might be possible, but why would he do this? He came here to fight, not to run away. Meade stared at the map, if he comes East, he runs right into us and a major fight! He nodded his acceptance of this idea. This must be Lee's plan. This is what the Army of Northern Virginia does best - fight! But how? Likely, he would not just come at us directly, head on. Perhaps on the right flank - here at Culp's Hill. Why the apparent confusion and indecisiveness? Was there a change of command among the major units? This might be a possibility. He must check on reports of this. Perhaps... then his eyes moved across symbols of his own lines and the terrain of Gettysburg.

Union forces were arrayed in the form of a fish hook, with the eye of the hook at the southern end. It was the left flank of his forces. Meade now was looking at two hills, one large and one small. He thought, "Our forces are not overly strong here. If Lee could take these hills and break our lines at this point, he could very likely roll our lines up and our entire defensive position would collapse into...." He pondered. The Confederates could turn and move south easier from this flank than from the northern end of the fish hook. If Lee attacked these hills in force and failed, he would be on the southern flank in a better position to move south. If he indeed did break our lines, he could defeat the Army of the Potomac and have a clear route to move South toward Virginia with little to stop him. Or, God forbid, the Rebels could move on Baltimore or even Washington.

For some time, General Meade worked these options back and forth as he studied the map. At last he came to the conclusion that the two hills at the 'eye of the fish hook' and the one at the tip of the 'barb' would likely be keys to the coming battle. He reasoned that the attack would come at first light, and it would come in force. He could foresee a savage fight. Longstreet, Lee's most seasoned commander, is who Lee would probably choose to come at him. It would be an action that would be pivotal for the success or loss in the coming Battle of Gettysburg. General Meade began to write out orders to move reinforcements into these positions. Troops would have to move in the dark. By first light, these positions would be strong enough to stop the most determined of attacks.

"The Confederates will run into a 'hornets nest' when they come up these hills," he thought.

At the same moment, General James Longstreet was closing his traveling desk in preparation to pack up his headquarters for the forced march south. Longstreet quietly reflected how pleased he was that there would be no assault on the Federal lines tomorrow at Gettysburg.

As he buckled on his sword and pistol, Longstreet called for his aide, Major Sorrel, who appeared in seconds.

Longstreet gathered his gloves and several other personal items as he spoke to his aide. "Moxley, everything is ready here. When the light begins to fade, tell the boys to strike the tent and be ready to move on short notice. They are to fall in and move with General Pickett's division. You and I will leave in a few minutes and move toward General Hood's headquarters. When we move out on the march, I will position toward the front of the column."

"Yes Sir," answered Major Sorrel. "I have prepared a bed roll and some rations for you. I knew we would be moving rapidly. I also knew you would want to be forward. It appears that tomorrow will likely be a very busy day."

Longstreet smiled and replied, "You're right about tomorrow, Moxley." He hesitated putting his cigar in his mouth, "*Very* busy."

Minutes later, General Longstreet, Major Sorrel, the command's colors and two courier/guards were riding toward General Hood's headquarters. Troops that had been pulled back were sitting in the trees along the road. Officers and NCO's were briefing troops in various sites. Wagons were being loaded, and everywhere men and animals were moving in what seemed to be a slow, sleepy pace. Longstreet knew this was just an appearance and was done only to conserve energy for the night march, and to avoid making a great din of noise that armies made when they moved in a hurry. When the troops recognized their Corps Commander, some saluted, others raised their hats, some even waved and smiled. All did so with the intent of showing deep respect and affection.

After meeting a young Major sent to meet them, General Longstreet's party was soon riding to General Hood's headquarters. Longstreet dismounted and turned to General Hood who saluted, smiled and extended a cup of coffee to his commander.

"Guess we have time for a cup," said Longstreet. He looked around at the wagon, tents and flags still flying.

Hood noted his commander's observation as he poured a second cup of coffee for himself. "The wagon's are packed and the tents are empty," said Hood. "I thought it best to give the appearance of business as usual, just in case some Yank is watching. We can be packed and moving in five minutes."

Longstreet nodded, "Yeah, J.B., I was just surprised to see you sleep in a tent. Guess that's a habit you picked up after you left Texas and came back east to civilization."

Hood's eye twinkled, "Tent's not for me. Its for my aide. He's from South Carolina…can't rough it."

Longstreet, a South Carolinian, chuckled and raised his cup in salute, and took a long drink of the coffee.

After a few seconds, Hood spoke again, "Pete, you did real good talking General Lee into not pushing this battle here. I think we were about to get in over our heads on this one."

"What makes you think I talked him out fighting here?, Longstreet said softly as he swirled his coffee around in the cup.

58

"Bob Lee is not a man easily convinced to change his plans."

"Let's just say that word gets around, General," Hood smiled. "Besides, Dick Ewell said General Lee mentioned that you were really against this set up. One of his staff said something to one of my staff… and well…. Anyway, I think you were surely right. I had a bad feeling about this one. I am glad we are moving south, even if it is *south Pennsylvania*."

Longstreet replied, "There is no guarantee it won't be worse where we are going. You know, if Meade figures out what we are up to, he could get troops south to meet us before we can concentrate and get in position. He could make it real interesting."

"Yeah, he could, but he won't," replied Hood. "By the time he figures out what has happened, it will all unfold just like General Lee said. They will come at us fast and strung out, trying to stop our taking Washington or Baltimore. If we have good positions, we can hammer them into ground just like Fredericksburg."

Longstreet remembered Fredericksburg. He really did not like to remember it, but it was often very real in his memory.

Lord, how the Federals had wasted good men there!

"You're right about one thing, J.B. Having a good position to hold is the key, and I mean to have the *good* position! That's what made this fight such a bad risk. The Yankees have the good ground here and they know it. That why they won't move quickly. We have to reverse the positions and let them come at us just like they did at Fredericksburg. I always said Fredericksburg wasn't war, it was murder." He threw the last sip of coffee into the fire, "We need to get in that business again so we can end this thing!"

General Hood took Longstreet's cup to put it away, and as he turned he said, "And that's exactly what we will do in the next couple of days, General - end it! I need to ride up ahead and make sure the boys are ready to start when it's time. Would you care to join me?"

"Sure would, I need to move around rather than just wait for the *parade* to start," said Longstreet. Soon the two men were mounted and moving toward the left flank of Hood's Division. Hood's Texas and Alabama troops were now stirring. In less than an hour, they would be the lead division, and the move south would start in earnest.

General J.E.B. Stuart was already moving. Having met with his commanders and detached those elements with instructions to keep up the facade of staying in place, he had the remainder of his command slowly moving in elements westward. They would cut through the mountains toward Fairfield begin the ride south. Stuart had detached his artillery to come up later with following elements and he was riding well forward with General Wade Hampton's command. General Fitzhugh Lee's troops followed close behind. What Robert E. Lee had said about "JEB" Stuart was true, there was none better at operating alone to scout , probe and provide intelligence. This time, however, he would not detach himself from his commander to operate alone. Stuart's cavalry command was truly the eyes and ears of Lee's army - an arm extended. This mission could well be the most important of the war thus far. Stuart knew he had to do it just right and with all the stealth, speed and thoroughness for which he and his troops were famous.

"General, we have ridden circles around the Yankees before, but I swear this is the first time we ever started riding south to do it," said Wade Hampton in a joking tone.

"Yes, and I am more concerned about this ride than the others we have done. If we can get far enough south and turn east, we should be able to find a good position for the infantry." He turned in his saddle and looked to the rear as he continued, " I have in my mind to find a position quickly, get the infantry coming up and in place. I want us to get free to ride out to hit the enemy as they try to hurry to come south when they find we are gone from here. I figure they will be coming like hounds after a buck! I think we can get some good licks in and slow them up before they ever get to Longstreet's lines. If we can keep moving hard and get in place, we could really buy some time for our boys."

Hampton also looked to the rear as he remarked, "I just hope

General Longstreet doesn't make a Sunday walk out of it. I was a little surprised that General Lee put him to lead out on this one. I have to tell you, I don't think that speed is something he is exactly famous for."

Leaning over toward Hampton, JEB Stuart smiled and said, "Well, I'll tell you this much, his boys may not be as fast as Tom Jackson's, but they move pretty good and can flat kick your teeth in when they get into it. We just need to buy them a little time, and that's something *we* are good at!"

Both men smiled and began to pick up the pace a little to close the gap between the horsemen in front of them. The light was almost gone.

Well behind Generals Stuart and Hampton, the road was becoming full of troops moving from what had been their camps. Almost without a word the men moved from the trees and on to the road. Each unit struggled to keep its distance from the unit to its front. First hundreds filtered on the road, then it seemed that thousands were moving. Still there was little noise to say that Lee's Army was moving.

Most wagons were off to the side of the road, letting the infantry pass. Only a few interspersed wagons moved between the units of troops. Artillery and caissons were now moving at a regular pace. Ammunition wagons followed the artillery, doing the best they could to keep up. Troops moved aside to let a battery pass here and there, but no one stopped. At first the columns seemed to crawl, but in reality they were moving steadily…moving away from Gettysburg. They gained speed as they moved through the mountains and started to turn south.

Some thirty five miles to the south, Captain Jerimiah Ivy was riding up and down the same road encouraging his cavalrymen to close up and keep a sharp eye out. He told his men that the Rebs were still pretty far away, but there was a chance they might bump into some of them running for home. His men were cavalry troopers of the 26th Pennsylvania Emergency Volunteer Militia Regiment, a militia unit of Pennsylvanians formed to help throw the Rebels out of their home state. Their unit had been called to ride out to help the

Army of the Potomac. Some were too old to fight, some were too young to fight, and most of them were ill-prepared to fight. All of them were in the wrong place this night.

Seventeen year old Privates Jeremy McTavish and Hans Stocker were tired, but they were excited with the advent of fighting "the Rebs." Hans was the bugler for the unit. It was a special job and one of which he was most proud.

"Hans, you think them Rebs will still be at Gettysburg when we get there?" asked Jeremy.

Hans replied, " Yeah, I reckon they will still be there. I hear that they is good fighters and don't run from nobody, lessen they be whipped."

"And we are just the boys to help whip 'em and send 'em a runnin!" added a grinning Jeremy.

"I never been this far from home, Hans, have you?"

"Oh Yeah," said Hans, " I went most all they way to Baltimore one time with my Pa. He was...."

"You will be going to Richmond at the point of a Reb bayonet if you don't hold down the gab and move up!," said Sergeant Thad Peoples as he rode by leaning over toward them and pointing them to close the gap.

The two young boys looked startled, but didn't answer. They spurred their horses and moved up.

Mr. Thad Peoples, or *First Sergeant* Thad Peoples as he was now known, was the town blacksmith. He seemed a bit old and round to be doing such a young man's work the boys had thought. Every time they had a parade, he always looked out of place among the other young gallant looking troopers. They had to admit, he sure was good with horses and men. He was so big and strong, that you did what he said as much out of fear of being jerked off the horse by him, as you did just because he was the First Sergeant.

"Cap'n, I think we might want to be resting the horses shortly. We've been pushing them pretty hard," said Sergeant Peoples as he came along side Captain Ivy.

"I agree, the men are making good time," answered Captain Ivy. " It's too dark to see enough of the mountains ahead, but I am pretty sure we are getting close to Hagerstown. We will give it a little more time to check out location, then we will stop to give the men and the horses a rest."

"Right, Sir," said Sergeant Peoples. "I was over this way in '58, and I think we are probably about 8 or 9 miles from Hagerstown, best I can recall. With your permission, I'll send a couple of men ahead to see how long before we cross a stream or river where we can water the horses."

"Good idea, Thad," said Captain Ivy as he turned in his saddle to try and see if the men were closed up.

It did no good. It was too dark to see more than a dozen riders back. In the length of time he looked, the First Sergeant was on his way to get two men to move ahead.

Campfires were now sparkling along the Confederate tree line at Gettysburg. Soldiers from General Imboden's and General Jenkin's cavalry tended fires and kept up the look of an army bedding down for the night. The occasional clanking of pots and pans, the playing of guitars and banjos as well as other such noises drifted across the lines toward Union lines giving more credence to the facade being shown. To Federal pickets, it was just another night before a big battle.

"Captain, it's about eight miles to Hagerstown according to the two riders I sent out. Do you want to stop now before we get into the town?" Sergeant Peoples asked.

"No, let's get to the edge of the town before we stop. We can rest there a bit, then walk our mounts through the town. The men need the stretch and we still have a ways to go tonight. I want to try to get to Frederick before we hold up. That should put us at Gettysburg sometime tomorrow afternoon or so. Think the boys have a few more hours in them, First Sergeant?" asked Captain Ivy.

"Yes Sir, the men are ready to go," replied Peoples, "the horses will be worn out pretty good after today, but a good night's sleep and some feed should get them going tomorrow."

The first of JEB Stuart's cavalry was now coming out of the pass at South Mountain after passing Fairfield, and was turning south. They were some fourteen miles from Hagerstown and moving steadily. Scouts from the lead elements were fanning out to the front to keep the column from being surprised. The roads were in good shape and the weather was clear. Stuart decided to send a company due south to see if there was a short-cut that the cavalry could take. He wanted the following cavalry to find the Hagerstown to Frederick road without going into Hagerstown. If the advance company found a way, they were to send riders back and direct the cavalry units to take the short-cut. The wagons and infantry would continue via the road to Hagerstown. Quickly, a company of the 1st North Carolina Cavalry moved ahead and veered off the road to disappear south into the darkness.

At Frederick, some twenty miles from Hagerstown, the 7,000 men of the Army of the Potomac's Reserves under General French were bedded down for the night. General Meade had these men ready to move up to Gettysburg if needed, or to move on Lee's army once it was defeated. For now they were well clear of the coming action. Plans were to rise early and be ready to move out toward Gettysburg, if needed.

Several hours passed. Captain Ivy's troops and horses that had rested for a time were moving again. They had walked their horses through the streets of Hagerstown before again mounting up. Shutters had opened but only a few lights were noted as the town folk peered out into the darkness to see if it was Union or Rebel horsemen moving through the town in quietness. The rest and walk had done them all good, as men and horses were tired after the long journey. Still, they had a ways to go to get to Frederick where they could finally bed down and get some real rest.

As Privates Jeremy McTavish and Hans Stocker moved past the last building of Hagerstown, they both were tired to the point of almost not caring if they saw the Rebs or not. The idea of just getting out of the saddle and getting some sleep was becoming paramount. It seemed to the boys that Mr. Peoples wasn't tired at all! He acted as if he were just getting mounted for another afternoon ride! In truth, Sergeant Peoples was also feeling the long hours, but he made sure no one noticed. They were now clear of Hagerstown and headed southeast toward Middletown and Frederick.

One hour later the company from the 1st North Carolina Cavalry found the Hagerstown to Frederick road about 7 miles east of Hagerstown. After dispatching riders to proceed back they way they had just come, Captain William Stokes took the remainder of the company and started toward Frederick. He wanted to see how far it was to the mountain pass. Within 30 minutes his unit crossed a small stream. From there, he saw the shadow of the mountains directly ahead. He knew he was only a few miles from the pass.

"Few more hours it would be light," Stokes thought. Turning to his sergeant, he quietly said, "Pass the word. Move well clear of the road on the north side and rest up a bit. I want no fires, no smoking, and *no noise*." He added to Lieutenant Harry Leche who was right beside him, "Ole JEB coming up behind us, and only Yanks ahead. This seems like a good place to take breather." Soon they were clearing the road, and his men slowly rolled out of the saddle. After watering their horses and loosening saddle cinches, most of the troopers lay down right where they were standing.

Some twenty minutes later, the North Carolina soldiers again mounted and were on the road moving back toward Hagerstown. They had been on the road for Hagerstown about an hour when Captain Stokes was surprised to see riders approaching him out of the dark. He put his hand up to stop his troops just as Captain Ivy was doing the same. The Federal troops were half asleep in the saddle having been on the move half the day and most of the night. They did not see or hear the signal to stop. Quickly the column piled up like a train that had its engine derailed. While no one was hurt, about 15 horses and riders were now all pressed together. Then the Confederate commander saw the Union Cavalry pennant.

"Yankees!" he yelled, as he drew his Navy Colt and aimed at the first figure to his front. Before he could shoot, gunfire went off all around him as him. His troopers had begun to fire into the now spinning and churning group of Union soldiers. A shotgun, two handguns, then a half dozen handguns all began to fire. Shooting was coming from everywhere it seemed. Two Pennsylvania soldiers went down, their terrified horses bolting into the darkness. These horses were not used to the noise of gunfire and when startled, they became a handful to control. A horse, shot through the head collapsed into a ditch, trapping his young rider.

Now the Federals began to try to fight back, but their firing was wild. The Confederate officer raised in his stirrups and called to his men,

"Lets take 'em boys! Charge!" As the battle-hardened Southern cavalrymen charged into the shattered Union column firing and screaming, the boys and shop keepers from the quiet Pennsylvania countryside wheeled about and spurred their horses towards Hagerstown. Weary from the hard march, and half asleep in their saddles, the Volunteer Militia had thought themselves safe in their own country side. The Confederates were far to the north, and the Militia never expected to run into an enemy cavalry unit bearing down on them out of the dark. As had been demonstrated time and again, the difference in seasoned veterans and new replacements again become apparent.

As the volunteers were off toward Hagerstown, Lieutenant Leche was having some of his men gather the wounded and count the dead.

"Looks like the Yanks have about five or six dead and 10 or 11 wounded, Lieutenant," said a lean and grizzled Corporal. "Not sure if we found 'em all, a couple went off into the country side pounding leather. We got a couple of them that are hurt pretty bad."

"How many of our boys hurt?," asked Leche.

"Looks like none back here... don't know about the bunch that took off with Cap'n Stokes," said the Corporal. " We're gittin' the Yankee-wounded together, and I got the Deacon watching 'em."

Leche looked turned in the saddle and was looking down the road toward Frederick. "Right, get the boys formed up and get ready to move out. If there are more Federals in the area, this ought to bring them. In any case, Captain Stokes will be back in a bit and we need to be ready to move."

The Corporal laughed as he turned to assemble the men, "Right, Lieutenant, I speck Cap'n Stokes has chased them Yankees half way back to Hagerstown by now! And guess who they gonna to run into? Wonder who will be the most surprised, them or old JEB?" He turned to the men moving all across the road, "All right! All right!.. Let's go.. Let's go... Form up!"

Young Private Jeremy McTavish had come to his senses, only to find that his horse, which was shot in the head, was lying across a fallen tree with him half way pinned underneath. He had fallen next to the tree and the tree had stopped the dying horse from falling on him, or at least most of him. His left arm was pinned, but with painful effort, he got free. The Confederates were less than fifty yards away gathering on the road. They couldn't see him if he stayed low.

Jeremy's mind was racing. "What do I do? Which way do I go? Do I give up? No! Rebs might shoot prisoners. I have to run, get back to Hagerstown! No! That's where the Rebs were headed. Frederick! I have to get to Frederick! I have to warn our Army that the Rebs are here!" He was shaking from shock as he tried to look at his arm. It had numerous small holes in it that hurt like fire, but the bone wasn't broken. "Shotgun! Lord Almighty, I was hit by a shotgun! Worry about that later! I have to move... now! McTavish crawled a few yards and decided to get up to a crouch and try to make it into the woods by running low. Just as he was getting started, he tripped over something and went face down into the ground with a thud. He froze.

A Confederate trooper heard the thud and wheeled his horse around, drawing one of his .44 pistols from his belt. He rode slowly toward the sound. The he saw it. A dying horse. The animal kicked a time or two and moaned. The young North Carolina soldier thought he should shoot the horse and end its misery, but no more shooting. Sadly, the horse would just have to die on its own. No sense in leaving that Yankee saddle. He started to dismount, when the Corporal called for him to get in ranks. The young trooper hesitated.

"Now!," said his Corporal, "unless you want to stay here and to tell the Yankees which way we went?" At that point the trooper wheeled about and moved off down the road. McTavish breathed a mouth full of dirt and grass.

As he turned to see where the Reb had gone, he saw what he had tripped over.

"Mr. Peoples!" He recoiled back by the sight and lost his breath for a moment. First Sergeant Peoples had a bullet hole just under his left eye right through his cheek. The Sergeant was wide eyed and his mouth was open as if in disbelief. Blood was everywhere. Jeremy began to sob. He covered his face and his mouth with his good arm so he could not he heard.

He thought, "Not Mr. Peoples, Not Mr. Peoples! He is the blacksmith, he shouldn't even be here! He was too old! He..." He sobbed. "Hans! Where is Hans? Did he get away? Was he captured? He was right next to me when we all ran into each other and the Rebs. " McTavish wiped his face that was smeared with blood, dirt, and tears. He tried to compose himself. "No! No! I can't think about that. I have to go! I have to get to our troops in Frederick. I have to tell them about the Rebs." He crawled a few more yards and then stood up behind a tree in the wood line to get his breath. The Rebs were moving away. "I have to stay in the woods along side the road for a bit, then I can get on the road and run!" He started stumbling through the trees, trying to keep the road in sight.

By now, the still fleeing Union troopers were slowing down. Their mounts were exhausted and the riders were getting strung out down the road. Captain Stokes had sent a rider back to tell Lt. Leche and the men left behind to hold their ground there. As he rode, he formed his company to prepare to meet the Federals if they turned back on him. Stokes knew what lay ahead. He knew that it wouldn't be long before Union troops would run headlong into the lead elements of General Hampton's Division. Stokes knew he only had to be in a place to block them from running. Soon he heard a short spasm of gunfire, then silence again. He slowed to a trot and sent two scouts out to make contact. The column had not gone far when the scouts came back telling him they had made contact with the lead troops of Hampton's Legion.

Most of the Federals had been taken prisoner. Some scattered and one was wounded in the brief exchange. But the Federal Captain had surrendered after coming to the conclusion that the country side was over run with Confederates. Hampton's troops were soon on their way again with hardly a lapse in the movement.

When word of the militia cavalry encounter got back to Generals Stuart and Hampton, they began to figure the word was probably out that the Confederates were on the move. Some confusion and a period of questions to and from Federal headquarters would give the Confederates some time. The two generals dismounted with the other troops to walk their mounts as a "rest period on the march." A courier came riding up from the forward elements with news that several of the just captured Federals said they had been enroute to Frederick where General French was encamped. It was confirmed that French was the Reserve for Meade and the Army of the Potomac.

"By George, we might bag the lot this time, Wade!," exclaimed Stuart. His courier hurried off toward the rear to take this news to Stuart's other commanders and ultimately to General Lee and Longstreet following somewhere behind.

General Hampton, always one to ride to a fight, smiled as he said, "Those reserves will have a lot of cavalry as well as considerable infantry, you know. For an Army Reserve, it could be 5,000 or 6,000 men. They won't fold up just because a few cavalry brigades come at them."

"We won't hit them alone. Longstreet will be up with his boys and we will pile into them together. I don't figure these Reserves will stand up to our boys and Longstreet's Corps when we crash through them!" Stuart was smiling as he sensed another of the surprises he loved to spring on his enemy.

"I just hope Longstreet gets here quickly. He doesn't move like Jackson used to…! JEB Stuart interrupted, "General Lee is with General Longstreet. Longstreet will move all right! We just need to look to concentrating our command before we cross the mountains. Any word from Fitz and Rooney? "

" Fitz Lee is close on our heels and is moving right with us. No word on Rooney yet, but if I know him, he will be close in too, " answered General Hampton. "Sir, looks like another courier coming in."

The courier was a Lieutenant from General Hampton's 1st North Carolina company that had just captured the Federal militia. "Captain Stokes compliments, Sir! The Captain said to please inform the General that General Rooney Lee's brigade is presently coming south, cross country off the road between Hagerstown and Waynesboro. We found a direct route and General Lee, I mean General *Rooney* Lee, will not go through Hagerstown. He should be arriving somewhere along this road in an hour or two. Captain Stokes said to please watch for him. Also, he said to tell you he is closing on the mountain pass and will hold there."

"General Hampton spoke first, "Tell Captain Stokes that I have his message. Tell him that he is to scout ahead to locate where the Federals are, but he is not to be observed and *must not become engaged*. If he finds the enemy, he is to send word back to me on the double. Is that clear?"

"Yes Sir!," the young Lieutenant replied about to wheel about to leave.

Then JEB Stuart spoke, " Also tell Captain Stokes that General Stuart said 'Well Done!'   What's your name, Lieutenant?," asked Stuart.

"Leche, Sir... Lieutenant Harry Leche."

"Well, Lieutenant Harry Leche, you take that message back to your Captain and tell him he has done the 1st North Carolina proud this night!" Leche grinned, saluted and wheeled to bolt off toward his unit.

Stuart continued, "I'm telling you, Wade, its falling into place. I think we may just well catch the Yanks looking the other way on this one!"

Private McTavish was now on the road stumbling as he half ran and half walked toward Frederick. He was in the mountain pass now, and the hills, loss of blood and sheer exhaustion were

70

rapidly taking their toll. He fell, but got up. He went on another few hundred yards, and again fell. He lay there crying and talking to himself with his face in the dirt, when he heard something right in front of him. He looked up to see a horse only feet away looking at him. Then he saw the rider, .44 pistol out and pointed at him. McTavish thought the Confederates had come back. Then he saw the shoulder epaulets. It was a Union officer. "Help…me, " he muttered. His face fell into the dirt. Quickly he felt the water pouring down his throat and across his face. He reached for the officers arm.

"You're all right soldier, " said the Captain. "What happened to you? What unit are you with?"

The boy was getting his breath back now. "Rebels! Rebels!, " he stuttered out. "Back there… hundreds of them..! They hit us out of the dark.. killed Sergeant Peoples!… The Captain, Hans.. they…"

"Whoa! Easy!," said the Captain trying to calm him so he could make sense of the bits and pieces. "You say Rebs are behind you? McTavish was nodding yes and pointing. "They attacked you?" asked the Captain. The boy again nodded yes over and over.

"What's your unit?.. Speak slowly now…It's all right," comforted the Captain.

"26… 26th Pennsylvania Militia…E-Company…Cavalry. We were going to Frederick on the way to Gettysburg to fight… Rebs! They rode right into us. It was awful!"

"Easy, son. Can you stand?" asked the Captain. Another nod yes. "Any of your boys coming behind you?,"

"I don't think so... just Rebs... hundreds of 'em!"

"Come on. Lets get you mounted and get out of here. You can double with me. I'll get you to Frederick. What happened to Captain Ivy, do you know?," asked the Captain.

"No... No Sir. There was so much shooting, my horse went down and…." Then Jeremy realized he had not told this officer who his commander was. "How do you know about Captain Ivy?," he asked puzzled as he was helped on the horse and followed by the officer.

"He is my brother-in-law. I came out here tonight to meet your company and show you the way into Frederick. I suppose he isn't coming now." The Captain swung up on the saddle behind the young soldier to hold him. "Lets ride, you've got a report to make!" He turned and holding the young trooper with his arms he spurred his horse through the mountain pass.

Captain Stokes was slowly letting his horse walk down the center of the road as he approached the mountain pass known as Turner's Gap. He turned in his saddle, and pointed at the Corporal behind him, circled his finger in the air, and the pointed down the road. "Keep about a hundred yards ahead. Heads up!"

"Yo!," responded the lean Corporal as he darted out ahead of the column.

"It will be light in an hour or so," said General Lee.

"Yes Sir," replied Longstreet. "Looks like the men are getting a bit strung out, we might need to slow the lead columns to let them close up."

Lee was quick to respond, "A fast pace by lead elements always strings the rear columns out, but we must maintain this pace. Let the lead elements continue, and please speak to your commanders to close up the rear gaps as expeditiously as possible."

Longstreet dutifully passed Lee's orders to his subordinates to carry out. Upon returning to Lee's side, he leaned over and said, "General, I only thought it best that we stay concentrated. If we meet the enemy on the march, it would take time to assemble."

"I agree, General, but if we take too long to get to get to Frederick, piecemeal or concentrated won't matter. *Time* is our enemy here. We must make it our ally. Indeed we must concentrate forward...that is why I instructed your men to close swiftly from the rear." Lee waited and then with a twinkle in his eye he continued, "Besides, General, how would you slow Texans down? It is in their very nature to move rapidly toward the enemy! You are indeed wise to lead with them!" Once again Lee had answered a question to his actions with firm instruction, with courtesy, and yet complimented the person who asked.

FREDERICK

As the first hint of day stirred in the east, the Federal Captain passed through the sleepy guards heading for Corps Headquarters, still holding the young wounded Private McTavish on the saddle. As he reigned up before the Headquarters tent, he called for the startled sentries to get a doctor and help his rider down. He turned to yet another arriving sentry and told him to tend to his exhausted horse. Within minutes he was talking with the General W.F. Smith's Chief of Staff who was trying to get fully awake to understand what was being said. The captain related the full story as he had seen it and as had been told by the wounded private.

"Colonel, that's the story I got from this private," the Captain continued. "He said there were *hundreds* of Rebs. It is obvious that there was at least a fair number of Rebels out there, since they shot his unit up. I know for a fact that his unit was coming, as I went out to meet them. He was all that showed up. I thought it best to bring him straight here."

"You did well, Captain. Can the boy talk? The Captain answered in the affirmative. "Good, then lets see what he can add to this."

The tent fly opened and the Captain came out leading the now wide awake Colonel who was clad in his trousers, boots and undershirt. They walked to where the young soldier was lying propped up next to a tree, while the doctor worked on his buck shot riddled arm and side. His blood and dirt-caked face had been wiped off. The young face was much calmer now that he was among his own.

The Colonel knelt down, "Sounds like you had a night of it, son. How about your telling me exactly what happened to you and your unit?"

Jeremy tried to straighten up a little, but grimaced in pain as he moved. The Colonel bid him to relax and just talk. The young man told him of the long ride, going through Hagerstown and seeing no one, then the face to face encounter, the fight, his horse going down, the Rebels on the road, Mr. (Sergeant)

Peoples terrible wound, and his escape and meeting with the Captain.

The Colonel listened intently and asked several questions. "Did you see any men on foot?   Did the soldiers have any flag or colors? How many troops did you actually *see*? "

To all of the questions Private McTavish tried to answer as best he could. After ten or fifteen minutes the Colonel patted him on the leg, and told him to take it easy that the medical personnel would care for him now. Soon General Smith was up and dressed and the Colonel was explaining the young Private's story. The Colonel motioned for the Captain to join them. After saluting and a brief explanation of the preliminaries, the General said, "Lets look at the facts here. It is obvious that there were Rebs on the road toward Hagerstown and an action did take place. This soldier said there were hundreds - or at least dozens of Rebs on the road. But he was under his horse and out for a time, so who knows how many there were. We have to remember, that these boys are home town militiamen. These Rebs are Lee's Army of Northern Virginia, and a few of them go along way against untried militia!"

The Colonel was looking at the Captain, who spoke, "Yes sir, but to think that a patrol of Southern Cavalry could put an entire company on the run? Seems pretty odd. I know the commander. That's why I was out there. He is my wife's brother. He is no veteran, but unless he was heavily outnumbered, I'm sure he would not run."

The Colonel interjected, "Its not a case of your brother-in-law running. You have to face it, Captain. He may have not survived the action on the road. Without their commander, the unit could have scattered and gotten lost. Under fire, in the dark, officers and NCOs down…it has happened to more seasoned troops."

General Smith continued, "Still, we can't assume a few Reb cavalrymen are hunting chickens in the rear either! We have to check this out at once and send word to General Meade, telling him of this development. Colonel, write up a dispatch immediately to General Meade for me to sign. Explain the situation, and tell him we are investigating the report. Tell him I will keep him advised. " He turned to the Captain. "Captain, you have had a long night. Are you up to resting a bit and going out with a detachment to help them investigate this?"

"Yes Sir, I would very much appreciate that opportunity. I will need a fresh horse, and I will need to let my commander know where I am. Outside of that, a good cup of coffee and a biscuit would do nicely," said the Captain.

General Smith put his hand on the Captain's shoulder, "Don't worry, son, you will find your brother-in-law. This is just probably some of JEB Stuart's wild bunch out creating their usual pain the britches for us! Your brother-in-law is likely in Hagerstown having breakfast!" He smiled, "After all, I don't think Bobby Lee's Army is on that road coming after us! General Meade has seen to that!" The men smiled at the General's joke, as they saluted and then set about their tasks. General Smith looked at the dawn sky and thought to himself, "July 3rd... looks like rain."

Captain Stokes was looking toward Frederick through his English binoculars. He thought, "My Lord, there are several thousand troops there! I wonder if General Longstreet knows this? These troops are pretty relaxed, but then why not? They have no reason to fear us, we all are in Gettysburg!," he chuckled.

"Cavalry, infantry, trains, hospital, not much artillery. No, there shouldn't be much artillery. Guess they are all deployed at Gettysburg. Enough! Better get out of here and get this to Headquarters." He returned to his horse who was obviously tired. "Come on, Cindy, old girl. We still have a lot of work to do. You can rest later today. Stay with me a little longer." He worked his way back down the trail where his nine man detachment was waiting. "Lets ride, boys. We've seen enough." As they took off down the road, he began to tell his Sergeant what he had seen just in case they got split up and only one of them made it back.

As the Confederates rode off toward JEB Stuart, a Union Reserve Cavalry troop in Frederick was saddling their horses and making preparations to leave on an all day patrol toward Hagerstown.

Within an hour, Captain Stokes was back at the head of the pass where his company was waiting.

"Rest of the Brigade is about an hour back of us, Captain. The 1st South Carolina and Cobb's boys are leading now and will be here shortly," reported Lieutenant Leche.

"Fine! Harry, here's what I want you to do…," said Stokes, as he was writing about what he had seen and making a penciled map. After a few more verbal instructions, he ended by telling the Lieutenant, "When you find General Hampton, tell him that I will stay here until the command arrives. Tell him that I will *let any Federal unit come through* that is going *towards Hagerstown*, but I *will attack and try to hold any unit trying to go back toward Frederick*, if I think they know we are here." He added, "Tell him to be alert, for I won't be able to warn the column if a Yankee unit rides through headed that way. Got it?," Stokes asked.

"Yes Sir, got it!" "Then ride, Harry, and hurry back!,"

Captain Stokes slapped Leche's horse and Leche was off.

B troop of the 6th Ohio Cavalry was slowly moving from its bivouac area to the Hagerstown road. Their mission was to check the road and the area all the way to Hagerstown and back. It would be a long dusty ride, and most of the men were thinking about Gettysburg. They wanted to see what was going on there, not ride around in Maryland on a hot and muggy July day. Then again, perhaps they could find some of JEB Stuart's boys. That might be interesting at that!

Leche had been on the road for about thirty minutes when he saw troopers of the 1st South Carolina Cavalry. He passed them waving his hat. He was surprised to find General Hampton and General Stuart just behind this regiment. He reported to them and was on his way back in only a few minutes. In another half hour he had arrived at his company. As he was telling Captain Stokes the details, they saw the scout posted up the road coming at a dead gallop, waving his hat. Reigning in hard, he pointed back up toward the pass and yelled, "Yankee cavalry…looks like a full company! They are headed this was about three or four miles back!"

"All right boys, clear the road! Lieutenant Leche! Send a rider back to warn the column, now! Maybe they can bag 'em and we will get any strays that try to get back home! Move lads, get clear and into the tree line! The Confederate cavalry cleared the road and Stokes rode up and down to make sure no one was showing and that the road was clear. It looked good. He spurred his horse over a ditch and disappeared into the trees right next to Sergeant Purvis. They waited. About thirty minutes later, the first of the blue coated troops passed in front of them. They were looking and riding with a purpose.

"These were not militia," Stokes thought to himself. "They likely won't panic in a fight." In minutes, they were gone. He waited another ten minutes and then moved to the road with Sergeant Purvis.

"Tell all the boys to move to only one side of the road. If we charge out of the woods on any of these Yanks coming back, I don't want the boys firing at each other in a cross fire. You take two sections up the road toward the pass. Don't let anyone through! Shoot the horses if need be!"

"Right Cap'n," the Sergeant turned and was moving troops in a minute.

The 6th Ohio was moving steadily and was well clear of the approach to the mountain pass now. The trees were heavy, but the terrain was easier to traverse. All at once the commander of the Union forces saw two riders in the road up ahead. One had a flag and the other had his hand up. As the troop halted, the commander saw the flag was a white flag! They were Confederates and it appeared they wanted to surrender! The Union commander and the Captain with him rode forward with their troop following.

"Good morning, Sir!," said the Confederate officer as he saluted. He was smiling and dressed in faded gray and had a large turkey feather in his hat.

The Federal commander halfway returned the salute as he asked "And just who might you be, me Bucko?"

"Sir, I am Captain Isaac Thomas, of General JEB Stuart's command, Confederate States Army! I ask you to hear me out and think very carefully before you react."

The Union commander paused and looked around before replying. "Speak, Captain Thomas, You have one minute."

"Very well, Sir. I am instructed to ask that you and your men lay down your arms and surrender at once!" The Union commander looked positively surprised at the audacity of the Confederate. Captain Thomas continued, "You are completely surrounded by more than a full brigade of troops who are at this moment looking at you and your men down their rifle sights. For the last five minutes, you have been riding into our unit's position. I am instructed to ask you to weigh your options carefully, so as to avoid useless bloodshed."

"What in blazes do you mean surrounded! I see only you and I certainly don't see any brigade!," said the Union Captain.

"Look behind me, Sir...far down the road to where I point," replied the Confederate officer who stood in his Stirrups and removed his hat. In a slightly sweeping motion, as if to introduce his troops, he used his hat to direct their attention down the road. About 200 yards in the direction he was pointing, dozens of men were slowly riding out to the roadway from the trees. "And behind you," he pointed his hat back toward the mountain pass as another group of Confederate cavalry took to the road.

Obviously surprised, the Union officer recovered quickly and then said, "Looks like just enough for a good fight to me." The Union officer began to move his hand toward his holster.

The Confederate officer leaned forward, his smile now gone and he spoke in a very serious tone. "Captain, when this white flag drops, most of your men will go down with it. There are riflemen in the woods all around you and more in every direction." He motioned with his hat and over a hundred troopers stepped slowly just clear of the trees enough to let the Union troops see the rifles aimed at them. "Your brave act won't mean a thing to you or most of your men who will be dead in seconds. Why sacrifice your men for nothing? You have nothing to gain here!" The Union officer was looking for a way out.

The Confederate spoke again, " Sir, I will give you our terms once more. Surrender your arms and avoid a useless disaster. If you refuse, we will not wait for you to fire the first shot!" The Confederate officer raised slightly raised his arm in the direction of the white flag, "Sir, your decision?"

The other Union Captain spoke to his fellow officer, "You better do as he says, most of your troops won't even make if off the road. These boys do mean business!" Now the Federal cavalrymen were beginning to move around in ranks as their mounts sensed the tension.

The Confederate again loudly spoke. "Your answer, Sir!"

"Very well!...Hold your fire!" "We surrender."

The Confederate sat back and moved waved his hat in a circular motion, at which time the men in the wood line began to move forward as did the mounted soldiers. He saluted the two Federal Captains and said "I salute you, gentlemen, for your wise decision and for saving the lives your brave men. Tell your men to dismount, lay down their weapons and raise their hands." The Union commander complied. Confederate soldiers were now moving though the stunned and shaken blue ranks taking weapons, belts, hats and moving the soldiers off the road into groups. It had been a bloodless victory. It was the only such victory to come.

HAGERSTOWN

Back at Hagerstown, the first of Longstreet's columns were coming out of the town starting toward Frederick. Generals Lee and Longstreet were off the road under a tree looking at map spread on the ground.

"General Longstreet, let us continue toward Middletown here. Our cavalry is on the road and going through Turner's Gap to the south. I am told both routes are clear and the two roads will allow us to converge more quickly. Do you agree?"

Longstreet looked at the map for a few minutes and then said, "Yes Sir, I agree. I would also send the artillery and wagons by the southern road to keep the northern route clear for infantry."

"Very well. Please give the orders to your men, and let us be swift in these movements. It is full daylight now and we must move before the heat is upon us." Lee set about writing a message to General Ewell. He noted at the end of his text, " I request you provide me… with reports of your progress… at every few hours. Have you heard from A.P. Hill?"

Major Taylor summoned a courier and the party mounted to again proceed in the march. No sooner had the courier departed than another courier arrived from JEB Stuart. Message delivered, he galloped off toward the front of the seemingly endless column.

"General Stuart is keeping us well informed!," Lee said with satisfaction. He says our cavalry is now at Turner's Gap in force and appear to be undetected as of yet. I have asked General Stuart and General Ewell to meet us at Middletown at 10 o'clock this morning for a council. I want to try and coordinate a swift strike against the Federals in Frederick before dark if possible."

Longstreet was surprised. "General, do you think the men can come off a 30 mile road march and fight a major battle like this? Lee looked at him somewhat disappointed if not puzzled. Longstreet continued, "I mean perhaps we should move into place tonight and strike them at first light. We would be rested enough to drive them to Baltimore if need be!"

James Longstreet realized he was again questioning his commanders decisions and plans. He thought it necessary to at least discuss the options.

Lee replied, "Time! Time, Sir! You must understand if we have successfully moved this Army away from the enemies' main force, it is because we have done so with great expediency and without being discovered. However, if we hold up to rest, we may forfeit all we have gained. If the enemy can concentrate his main force with his reserves and do so before we are fully prepared, our task will surely be more difficult, if not impossible. Our men will be tired, but if we fall on the enemy as he prepares to retire, our infantry and cavalry together will break him and send him running. Our troops can rest and late tomorrow or the next day we can then face General Meade when he comes after us, as he will." Lee was experiencing chest pains. The pain was coming more and more often, but he smiled a tired smile, "I expect Mr. Lincoln will see to that part for us!"

Longstreet simply stated, "Yes sir," and decided not to press the issue anymore. General Lee's mind was made up. Longstreet thought, at least we are not charging the Federals at Gettysburg as we might have been!

Lee was looking at his watch, calculating time, planning his actions. He spoke to Longstreet, " General, I am going to move forward now. Rendezvous with the other commanders at Middletown at noon sharp!"

"Yes Sir, I will be there! And sir…" Longstreet said smiling, "Don't get to far out front! We don't want to have to come get you!" Lee smiled as he saluted and moved ahead with his party.

It was about half past noon when General Ewell finally arrived at Middletown to join the other assembled general officers. He apologized for the delay and reported that the roads were almost clogged with troops and artillery moving forward. He added that the artillery was being slowed from moving rapidly by this congestion.

General Lee explained that was in part why he had called for this council. He said the main force of the infantry was now some two hours or less from Frederick. Most of the cavalry could attack the town in an hour if need be.

"The enemy reserve force has been located and found to be in Frederick. There are at least two divisions with additional cavalry totaling some 6000 men. General Stuart's scouts report that they have no emplacements or positions prepared and they do not seem to be alert for an attack. They appear to still believe the fight will be to the north, at Gettysburg. If we hit them hard this afternoon, they will not be ready and they *will* break. We will destroy them as a unit and by morning they will be scattered all over the country side. That will effectively eliminate the enemy's reserves for the coming battle." The officers were listening and looking with a great deal of doubt, but an equally great understanding of what was possible here.

"I did not plan to fight a battle before the main body comes to us, but we have a great opportunity here. We can reduce the numerical advantage of the enemy by eliminating his reserves first." Lee continued pointing to the map lying on a barrel top. "We will use our infantry to strike them directly from our present location... two divisions abreast coming out of the woods here. Our cavalry will strike them from the south by circling around the mountain. They will approach northward along the rail road to make a coordinated attack on Frederick." Lee paused and continued. "We must destroy these units to the point they can not reform and become effective. Enemy stragglers to the south should be permitted to cross the Monocacy River south of Frederick, particularly infantry. If they panic and flee to Baltimore or Washington, the effect will be very detrimental on the enemy capital and its population."

"Not to mention the effect on ole Abe," said Longstreet. Everyone laughed.

Lee again continued, "General Stuart, you will see to it that your strike on Frederick is well coordinated with our infantry attack for maximum effect. Take some of your artillery with you to support the infantry as they attack. I want you to also oversee the bridge across the Monocacy. Again, stragglers should be allowed to flee south, but no enemy can be permitted to come toward Frederick. Be prepared to destroy the bridge

83

immediately, if ordered to do so. Is that clear, General?"

Stuart replied in the affirmative. General Lee nodded at James Longstreet. "General Longstreet, you have led the way here, and your men will have the opportunity to make the first strike against the enemy. I recommend two divisions, one deploying left and one right as we come through the pass into the wood line. Your divisions should attack from the woods across the open area here west of the town. They can roll across the bivouac area and right through the town. As you force the enemy from the town and into the surrounding country side, General Stuart's men will strike from the south. The cavalry should attack shortly after they hear the main action begin. I expect this action to be over quickly. Coordination is the key here, but the terrain, the approaches, and the ability of our cavalry to observe and hear the action as it commences should make this straight forward."

General Lee looked at his officers as he continued, "Once we have captured the town and have destroyed and dispersed the enemy, we must *immediately* set about to prepare our positions. The enemy headquarters will know of our actions and dispositions almost as soon as the fight is over. I expect he will be moving toward us no later than tomorrow before dawn. General Stuart, please send couriers immediately to Generals Imboden and Jenkins with instructions for them to withdraw tonight to cover the approaches to our rear. In particular, insure the fords at Falling Waters and Williamsport are secured for our possible use. As soon as this action is over and the area is secure, you must rest and then be prepared to move northward. You will have to tell us where the enemy is, and what he is doing. I will talk with you tonight after we are in Frederick."

As General Stuart acknowledged his instructions, everyone was thinking about the men and the attack to come. The men would be very tired after such a difficult forced march. To make a spirited attack would be asking a lot, but these officers also knew that Lee was correct in his assumptions. To wait till morning could mean the Army of Northern Virginia could well be facing a coordinated artillery, cavalry and infantry defense in a hastily, but substantially fortified town. There was little doubt that the Confederate Army could take the town tomorrow morning, but it would surely be much more costly, and the delay could buy precious time for the Army of the Potomac only 34 miles away. It had to be as General Lee had said. It had to be now!

As always, Lee asked for questions, and several were raised, then answered. The Generals asked and discussed necessary details...the artillery was being delayed...go with what was available. No problem with daylight... it was light until 8 p.m. in July. Some ambulances and medical staff must be passed forward. Perhaps they could follow the cavalry moving south. No, they must stay on roads. Soon the discussions faded.

Lee spoke. "Gentlemen, I will ask a lot of you and of our Army in these next few days, but it must be asked. Today we find ourselves in the enemies' homeland, in an effort to keep him from ours. We did not ask for this war, but let us prosecute it quickly and resolutely so that it may end quickly. Virginia and the South are to our backs. Let us purpose not to allow these people to again violate our homeland! May God vindicate us. **Deo Vindice!**"

The officers straightened up and saluted as Robert E. Lee moved to where Traveler was resting. "Major Taylor, tonight we will rest in Frederick!"

Walter Taylor grinned and said, "Yes Sir, I shall look forward to perhaps providing you with a nice room for the evening!"

"Perhaps," answered Lee.

Soon after the general departed, troops were pouring into the area near the mountain pass. Cavalry troops and a few artillery pieces were moving slowly off to the south. This created more room for the arriving infantry. The area was filling with the troops of Longstreet's I Corps. Several Union riders and couriers were taken prisoner as they came westward through the pass, but no large units had come down the road. A battle was about to start, yet the Confederate troops were sleeping and resting as best they could. There were no complaints, no murmuring, and no noise to quiet. The men trusted *Marse Robert* and knew he would do what was needed, as it was needed. They also were too tired to complain. A little sleep and rest was more important than talk. They would be ready when the time came.

FREDERICK

In Frederick, General Smith's Chief of Staff was trying to find out if there had been any word from the company of 6th Ohio that had departed that morning. "I specifically told their commander to keep us informed during the day!," he growled.

The Major behind the small field desk looked over a disarray of papers and commented, "Yes Sir, I know. I checked with both the regimental headquarters and the Provost Marshal and no reports have come in. In fact…," he did not finish the statement.

"In fact, what?," said the Colonel.

"Well… the Provost Marshal said *no one* has come in from Hagerstown all day, " replied the Major.

"What do you mean *no one*? You mean no couriers, no patrols…nothing?" The Colonel was now looking out of the tent toward the mountains.

The Major said. "No Sir, no one."

The Colonel stood silent for a few seconds and then spun around, "Where is General Smith?," he barked.

He said he was going to General Jenkin's Headquarters to see the general, Sir."

"I am going there now. Contact the commander of the 6th Ohio Cavalry and ask him to meet me at General French's Headquarters immediately!"

The major hesitated. "Yes Sir." He began to look for his hat.

"NOW!," bellowed the Colonel. The Major was gone in a flash without his hat.

Although it was only few minutes, it seemed like an hour had passed when the Chief of Staff reigned up hard at General French's dismount point. He threw the reigns at the soldier on duty and saluted neither him nor the guard. They could see that the Colonel was not going to stop to be recognized. The General's Headquarters area was on the western side of the bivouac area, so as to allow the officers access to the roadway. It also kept them away from the bulk of the troops with all the smells, noise and traffic caused by masses of men huddled together. The officer walked hurriedly toward the generals who were now standing outside a large tent. He looked past them about a half mile across the tents and across the fields toward the mountains to the west. Suddenly he stopped. Deer, rabbits and small game began to bolt from the woods. The tree line seemed to be moving! "NO!," his mind screamed.   He had seen this before... at Chancellorsville!! It was massed infantry driving animals before them as they moved through the woods! A shot rang out, then several shots followed by a steady popping as Union sentries and soldiers began to react to the ranks of gray and butternut clad troops emerging from the wood line.

The generals were stunned for a moment. The Colonel, in a fit of frustration and anger, pointed toward the wood line and sarcastically yelled, *"General Lee has arrived!"*

Bugles began to sound as troops ran everywhere. Many soldiers half clothed, barefooted, without weapons and caught ill prepared were running toward the center of the camp and toward the town beyond. Men with rifles were trying to form up. More bugles. An artillery battery was desperately trying to form and get into position to engage the advancing Confederates. Their officer tried to clear a path of running men so the guns could fire. Other troops in blue were double timing in a semblance of order toward the edge of the camp to face the massing gray and brown lines now quickly moving toward them. So far there was little noise and firing coming from the advancing Rebel line, but they were closing steadily.   Solid ranks of infantry.   Their bayonets glistened in the afternoon sun.

A company of Pennsylvania Volunteer Militia Infantry had been drilling when the attack began. As if it were part of the drill, the company commander halted the men,. He held them in ranks and turned them about to face the Confederates. After a command to load, they stood waiting for the range to close. It was obvious most of these volunteers wanted desperately to run. Like the regulars they were meant to replace, they stood their ground. Not one broke. Not one ran. Fifty-four men stood in two lines facing the massed attack. The Confederate line to their front slowed and then stopped. The Confederates were aiming -

aiming at them!

The young commander quickly ordered the militia to the *"Ready, Aim*," and as he dropped his sword, and yelled "*Fire!*," both Blue and Gray ranks fired. Over 200 guns fired against 54. When the smoke cleared, only eleven Federals were still standing. Everyone else was on the ground, some turning over in pain others crumpled in a pile. Still others collapsed together, unmoving. Cries were coming from up and down the line.

The Union officer stood stunned with his pistol in one hand and his sword in the other. He looked to see the gaps in the Confederate infantry close. The lines now start to run toward him in dead earnest. Then he heard that terrible scream - the Rebel yell! Like banshees in great anger, it was a terrifying sound rising above the noise of the guns and the carnage taking place. He raised his pistol and fired toward the advancing line. Events seemed to slow down to something unreal. He did not hear the pistol go off and he thought it misfired. He cocked the hammer and fired again, and again. It jumped each time, but the sound was covered up by the roar of rifles going off all around him. Now only three of the Pennsylvanians were standing where seconds ago there had 54 men in two lines. One of the three was grabbing his rifle by the barrel to use as a club. Another was trying desperately to reload. The last one was cocking and firing his rifle over and over, but it was no longer loaded. In an instant, they were all gone as the Confederate line charged over them. As the young militia officer again aimed to fire, a rifle butt slammed into the side of his head. Everything collapsed into darkness.

Federal troops on the east side of Frederick were having only a slightly better time of it. When the first sounds of gunfire increased, bugles sounded and men rushed to form up. As a company assembled, it was double-timed off toward the sound of the developing battle. By now, the Headquarters of the Reserve of the Army of the Potomac had been overrun. Most of General French's staff were taken prisoner or killed as they tried to make a stand. General Smith's Chief of Staff had been captured as he tried to organize resistance on the west side of the bivouac area. The General had grabbed a horse and galloped off to the east side to try to get men formed to fight. His wounded horse fell dead as he arrived on the east side of Frederick.

Union officers tried desperately to assemble men where they could. Here and there, small groups organized and returned fire into the now screaming Confederate onslaught, but there were too many gray and butternut soldiers for small groups of men to stand against. In places, the Confederate attack slowed as Federal sustained fire became effective. Some Federal units were standing to meet the attack. They could only slow the advance for a time, they could not stop it. Union troops flowed back through the streets and between the buildings of Frederick, firing as they went. Small units collected and merged with other small units. Here and there an officer, sergeant, or corporal tried to rally the men. A corporal from Pennsylvania took command of a unit made up of men from New York, Michigan and Minnesota. One Private was yelling at twenty men to line up and fix bayonets. The men were responding. For a time, it looked like the Union soldiers were recovering from the initial force of the attack. Then, the Confederate artillery began. It was no more than two batteries, but it slammed directly into the Union soldiers who were trying to form. First infantry, then artillery and now they saw Confederate cavalry. The dreaded gray troops on horseback were sweeping past the edge of the town, cutting down Union troops trying to form in the field for a counter attack. The mounted soldiers of JEB Stuart were armed with several handguns each. Some had sawed off shotguns. They used all of these as they galloped across the field, crashing into troops, firing as the rode. Again and again the blue ranks dissolved, unable to find a place to organize and form. Many Union troops were now running for their lives or surrendering. They had no where go and no weapons.

Confederate losses were light, considering the action. Several hundred were killed or wounded. Most of these had come from the leading ranks that absorbed the point blank fire of the Union troops who had massed their fire before they were overrun. The 18th and 21st Mississippi of Barksdale's Brigade were badly hurt, as they tried to take an artillery battery that was able to turn and fire before it was taken. At least three of the guns had fired double grape shot into the ranks of Mississippians at a range of only 25 yards. The effect was terrible. Some forty Confederates were cut down in seconds by the three guns. But still they came. Once reformed, the remaining infantry returned the fire with their rifles sweeping the batteries of the Federals standing at their guns. The artillery pieces that were taken became known as the *Mississippi Battery*, a tribute to the terrible price paid by that state's soldiers to take them.

General Hampton's Brigade had cut through the Federal infantry and headed north before reversing to again face south. They were blocking and intercepting fleeing troops on foot, riders trying to head north toward Gettysburg, and elements of Union cavalry units that were trying to get to the Army of the Potomac. Scouts were also deploying northward to see what Union forces might try to come to General French's assistance. It appeared there were none.

General Fitz Lee's Brigade was moving eastward to provide a screen for the Frederick operation. As expected, numerous troops on foot, wagon and horseback were streaming down the Baltimore road across the Monocacy Creek bridge. Lee's troops captured a few of the slower ones. This helped urge the others along. A strong Confederate force was observing the bridge from a distance, but did not try to interfere. When it looked like at last, the Federals were going to try to burn the bridge behind them, Fitz Lee's men swept down and captured it. This forced the men in the wagons to flee toward Baltimore and Washington.

Back at Middletown, Robert E. Lee was receiving reports from the battle. "Resistance collapsing. Enemy pockets still fighting in the town. Enemy casualties heavy. Many prisoners taken. Our casualties light to moderate." He looked up from the message toward Dick Ewell.

"Report from General Longstreet. The attack is progressing as planned."

Lee did not seem particularly pleased with the news. He

looked toward the battle some three miles ahead. "We must hurry and take the town and disperse these people," he said, almost to himself.

He was about to express a wish to hear from JEB Stuart, when another message arrived. It was from Wade Hampton. Lee read it and nodded affirmatively.

"Good. Very good. General Hampton has blocked the major escape route toward Gettysburg and says there has been no activity observed coming from there! He has many prisoners." General Ewell was almost smiling as Lee said, "I don't think General Meade will know about this battle until it is too late!"

General Stuart was with the two batteries of his Horse Artillery that been able to get forward to join him in the attack. He was yelling instructions to the commander.

"Our troops have part of a Yankee Battalion holed up in the center of town! I have ordered our boys to back away from there for a few minutes. Place all your battery's fire on and around the town hall, and see if a few rounds will loosen them up! Aim well and fire when ready!"

Captain R.P. Chew and Captain W.M. McGregor saluted and set about to get their guns working on the new target. Soon the seven guns of the two batteries were firing. After three rounds per gun, General Stuart ordered them to cease firing.

Waving his plumed hat as he rode by the guns, he called out to the two Captains, "The infantry is signaling to stop! I think your guns have shown the Yankees the error of their ways!"

The artillerymen cheered him wildly and waved their hats in response, as Stuart rode toward the mountain pass to find General Longstreet.

"Good afternoon, General!" said JEB Stuart. He saluted and then dismounted. Removing his gloves and his hat, he wiped the sweat from his brow. "It looks as if the town is about ours. Have you received any reports from your people?"

"Just heard a few minutes ago from McLaws," said Longstreet . "He said it's about done. Some resistance, but he expects it to be over within the hour. JEB, you did a nice job sweeping those Yankees on the east side, and that was a pretty tune your Horse Artillery played on the town square! You saved a bunch of my boys today!"

"Why thank you, James! Southern cavalry is always happy to assist our infantry brethren!" Stuart grinned and bowed with a slight flowing motion of his famous feathered hat.

Stuart then added, "And may I say, sir, your Corps looked magnificent today! They hardly slowed up while taking the town! Truly well done!" Stuart grew a little more serious, "I did notice that one brigade took some heavy losses when taking that Yankee artillery position on the northeast side of the town. Who was that?"

"Part of Barksdale's Brigade. The Mississippi boys paid a price today. Lost several officers in that," replied General Longstreet. "Did you know Colonel Griffin or Colonel Luse of the 18th Mississippi? We lost them both today. Griffin dead and Luse badly wounded."

General Stuart remarked, "No, I didn't know them, but when I saw this develop, I was about to lead a charge across the town and try to flank those guns. I could see it coming, but couldn't get to there in time to stop it. I was going to make sure there was only one volley, when the rest of those boys took the guns. Brave lads! That will be one to remember!"

"Yes, and it *will* be remembered too!, said Longstreet who paused then asked, "JEB, do you agree that it is safe for General Lee to bring his Headquarters forward now?"

"Yes, but perhaps it would be well for General Lee to hold here with you. Let me insure the town is secure and fully under control before he comes in. I'll send word to move up from here. Agreed?", Stuart asked.

Longstreet concurred. The two men discussed a few details and then Stuart, his colors, and his guards galloped off toward the south side of town.

GETTYSBURG

In Gettysburg, word had not yet reached General Meade's Headquarters of the disaster to his south. He was meeting with other general officers trying to determine why Lee had not attacked today. He spoke to the half dozen commanders standing around him.

"Lee should have attacked this morning at first light, " Meade said. "He has lost the better part of the day now, but he could still come at us any time. Comments? Observations?"

General Slocum spoke first, " The enemy looked to be organizing for an attack, but it never materialized. My front appears fairly quiet for now. I used the time to prepare our positions. The other officers grumbled in general agreement.

General Winfield Hancock then expressed his concerns, "General Meade, we have noted only cavalry and small units on foot moving to our front as well. I tell you this, the Rebs are up to something!"

"I agree," said Meade.

General Sykes spoke up. "Sir, we have the good ground here. Perhaps the Rebels are looking to draw us out of these positions and get us to attack him?"

"That's a possibility, but I don't think it's likely. Lee knows we won't blindly go after him and he can't sit there while we grow stronger." Meade paused, arms folded, then added, "We have good positions, but I do not propose to sit here and leave the advantage of maneuver to Lee. Let's see what he is up to. General

Pleasonton, I want your cavalry to perform a reconnaissance of the enemy where possible. Probe in several places. See if he is moving or dug in…how organized…Al, you know what we are looking for," he smiled. "But tell your boys not to get tangled up to where they can't get loose. Clear?"

General Pleasonton, nodded and responded, "Right sir, we will see what we can find out and do it as quickly as possible."

General Meade addressed the group. "Gentlemen, the rest of you use your assets to see what you can find out. If nothing has come up by dark, we will send some scouts out on foot to the other side to see what is going on. Meanwhile, let us be on the alert on our flanks and even to our rear. The Rebels did not come into Pennsylvania to bivouac. They knew they would fight us, and Lee will try to gain every advantage he can get. We must give him none! Keep me informed. We will meet again tonight if the show does not begin by then! I won't keep you any longer. Thank you, gentlemen."

As everyone filed out, George Sykes, who had taken command of V Corps from his friend George Meade, paused to speak privately with the new Army commander. "Sir, how is it going up here? Anything I can do to help?," asked Sykes.

Meade smiled, "Yes, tell me what Lee is up to!"

Sykes said, "Well, I can tell you what he is *not* doing. He is not running away! That much I have learned about Bobby Lee!

Meade asked, "Do you think he might be planning a *night* attack? That would help off set the terrain advantage against him. I started to mention that, but the coordination is so difficult, I keep thinking that the Rebs just couldn't pull it off.

Sykes responded, "The Rebs have a habit of doing what's difficult, but I agree with you in this case. Jackson was our running around the front lines after dark at Chancellorsville, and got shot by his own men for the effort! Imagine Divisions or even Corps of men moving around like that in unknown territory. No, I don't think they would try that.

Meade nodded in agreement and said, "Well, Al Pleasonton should be able to get us a better idea of what's going on." He smiled at Sykes and patted him on the shoulder. "You take care, George. The next few days will likely be some hard ones."

Sykes returned the smile and said, "You too, George."

As General Pleasonton was calling for General Gregg of the 2d Division to start his reconnaissance , Confederate General Dick Ewell's troops were coming out of Turner's Gap and into the Frederick area. Some sporadic fighting was still going on, but the main battle was over. Frederick was in Confederate hands. Federal troops were scattered north, east and south. Union soldiers were riding their horses into the ground trying to get word to Gettysburg. Others were trying to get to Baltimore and Washington to warn authorities that the Rebels were surely right behind them. One rider met a company of cavalry on the road coming from Washington and told the commander about the battle in Frederick. After hearing the story, the commander started to continue, then considered it best to return to Washington. He decided there was little one company could do if the whole Reb Army was coming this way. Moving anywhere was the last thing General Lee and Longstreet had on their minds. In fact, they were having problems keeping the troops of First Corps even on their feet. Troops lay down next to dead bodies and the wounded only to fall asleep in seconds. They were exhausted from 24 hours of hard marching and the battle just finished.

Longstreet rode slowly through his worn out soldiers. He was almost in tears as he looked at them. "No army in the world could match these men!, " he thought. "They are truly magnificent. I am privileged to be their commander! But I must move them as General Lee has instructed. Only then, they can rest."

He called for his division commanders and instructed them to get their troops on their feet once more and move them south of the town, south through Monocacy Junction. It was the same in every army. One more mile, one more move, only then can they rest. Once there, some would begin the task of resupplying and rearming, but most could just sleep. First Corps would now become the Army's Reserve. They could regain their strength as the other troops prepared the positions for the Federal Army that would surely come.

It was late afternoon now. A disheveled major from General French's Headquarters was trying to maintain his composure to make his report to General Meade who was ashen faced.

"Calm down now, Major, just tell me what happened," said Meade.

"Oh! It was bloody awful, General! the Major replied. The Rebs came out of the wood line. Our boys tried to stop them, but they just kept coming! They came through the mountains somehow and hit us on the western side of the bivouac." He gulped some more water.

"General French - what happened to General French?," asked Meade.

The Major continued, "I saw him ride toward the town. If he had stayed at the Headquarters, the Rebs would have got him sure. They didn't even stop when they went through the Headquarters area. The Rebs just killed or captured them all! Our boys tried to rally on the eastern side of town and join up with some of our cavalry. Just as it looked like we were going to be able to form, Rebel artillery and cavalry hit them from the south."

"From the *south* you say?," asked one of the generals..

"Meade put his hand up to quiet the officer.. "Wait! Let him continue. Casualties, man, how many casualties?"

The Major was shaking his head. "I don't know. There seemed to be hundreds down on the west side. There was a terrible fight going on in the town, and on the east side… I just don't know.... There were men down and men running everywhere. This way toward Gettysburg, there were hundreds on foot, running and walking - all spread out. Most were on foot. I saw a lot of men head south too, but…. I don't know… I don't think many escaped. Oh Lord, General, it was awful!"

"How many Rebels did you actually see?," asked Meade.

The Major rubbed his forehead "There were 2000…maybe 3000 that came from the wood-line right at the Headquarters' area. I couldn't see much more from where I was. As I rode out, it looked like several *thousands* of them coming into and around the town."

"Think carefully now, were they infantry or cavalry?" asked Meade.

"I don't have to think about that one, General!" the Major answered. The ones coming from the woods were infantry! Gray and Butternut infantry!" The other general officers were stunned at what they were hearing.

"Did you see any other of our officers that escaped?, Meade asked.

"Yes Sir, there were some, but no one I knew. Some were on foot, but I didn't stop. I rode as hard as I could to get here to bring the word to you. I knew you had to know! I...."

"Its all right. You did the right thing. Colonel, get this man some food and drink. Put someone with him. Major, if you remember anything else, anything at all, get it to me. You understand?" said Meade. The exhausted officer nodded in compliance as he was shown away.

"Infantry!" General Hancock was looking at Meade. "Do you think its Lee?"

"Who else could it be, ?" said Meade. "Still, I want to know who is to our front. If we pull out and head south we could get caught in the open, or we might wind up with Lee on *these* positions! Win, we must send out a force to see what's to our front. Get some of your boys together and see to it. I *have to know* specifically what is out there. I'll send more cavalry out, but I need an infantry report on our front and I need it *now!*" General Winfield Hancock departed immediately.

By now, more senior officers were arriving at General Meade's Headquarters. The word was spreading like wildfire as survivors were straggling in on horses and wagons. Rumors flew... *The Rebs were only a few miles back and coming this way.! Thousands of them! The were marching on Baltimore!...No, they were advancing on Washington!...No, both Baltimore and Washington! It had been a massacre! Thousands were dead and it happened in minutes!* Units began to reposition themselves to meet the Confederate Army that *had been seen* coming up the Emmitsburg Road. Bugles blew and troops were moving all over. Cavalry mounted up in force to move south to intercept the horde that was reportedly charging north. Infantry prepared to move. They didn't know to where or when or why they were to move, but they were ready.

Meanwhile, Longstreet's Corps was resting recovering from the battle, while Ewell Corps was preparing positions in and around Frederick. A.P. Hill's Corps was also preparing positions as well as marching the mass of prisoners off to the south west. He wanted to get them clear of the coming fight.

Almost 2200 men had been captured, including General French their commander, who was wounded, but not mortally. It was estimated that 1400 Federals had been killed or wounded. The rest were scattered across the country side and now headed for Baltimore, Washington, or Gettysburg. Not knowing if Lee's Army had defeated the Army of the Potomac or not, most men headed for the relative safety of the cities and their populations.

As the light dimmed in the late afternoon, the Army of the Potomac worked to prepare to attack, or to be attacked. In Baltimore and Washington, there was a growing panic as soldiers arrived with stories of disaster. President Lincoln called an emergency meeting of his cabinet. While at Frederick, the men of the Army of Northern Virginia prepared their positions, rested and waited.

It was July 3d. Day one of the Battle of Frederick had ended.

By 3 a.m. Stuart's Cavalry was again on the move. Captured Federal cavalry horses had provided many fresh mounts for Stuart's men. The few hours rest had done its magic for his hardened troops. The supplies taken at Frederick replenished and restocked the Confederate cavalry for their next task, which was to intercept and delay the enemy.

Shortly after dawn, with lamps still burning from an all night session, a worried Abraham Lincoln was writing yet more messages to General Meade. Enough stragglers and survivors from Frederick came into Washington and by way of Baltimore to paint the Cabinet a picture of the disaster that had unfolded. The Cabinet had discussed dozens of options from the government fleeing the city for New York, to making a fight of it with what ever was available. Emergency telegraph messages to the Governors of Pennsylvania, New York, New Jersey, Maryland and Delaware went out calling for all available militia and volunteers be sent to Washington and Baltimore immediately. *The enemy is at the gate*!

Lincoln tried repeatedly to get information as to where the Confederates were actually located. His best information indicated that the Rebels were still at Frederick. He thought this was logical due to time and effort spent to move and fight. He expected Lee would move on Washington sometime today, and would likely attack the city early in the afternoon. He figured if Lee attacked Baltimore first, this would give Meade time to get to Washington first. Lincoln did not think Lee would risk being cut off from crossing the Potomac into Virginia. Military scouts had been sent out in every direction to watch and look for the Rebel Army. As of yet none had reported. Had they not found the Rebels? Were scouts captured too? Had Lee gone south into Virginia from his victory?

One thing was certain. The capital must be protected! Lincoln sent a message to General Meade via telegraph from Washington to Baltimore to Hanover. Because the lines were still down, it had gone by courier from there. The instructions were very clear. *Move to protect Washington and the government at all costs*! The President further instructed Meade that, … *if the opportunity to attack and destroy Lee's Army presented itself*, he was to *seize it without hesitation.* Lincoln reasoned that Lee was outnumbered and had no home state assets of supplies and population to draw upon, therefore Lee was as weak as he would likely be to fight a major battle. He urged Meade in the *strongest of terms* to find Lee and fight him before he escaped and had to be dealt with again at a future date. As the first rays of the day glowed in the east, President Lincoln's message was being given to General Meade.

Meade read the message carefully. *"Protect Washington…attack and destroy Lee…"* The message agitated him. "What does he think we are doing out here?" Then the professional soldier in Meade took hold. "The Commander-in-Chief is only trying to help by making the orders clear. He is doing what he must for the nation; I must do the same," he thought. Meade now knew from his reconnaissance in force that Lee had indeed withdrawn from Gettysburg and moved south to attack the Army's Reserve force. It seemed almost impossible, but Lee had done it. Cavalry units were now racing south to see if Lee was still in the Frederick City area. To the west, some Rebel cavalry units had been engaged and others were observed holding the pass from Fairfield through South Mountain. He would let Pleasonton handle that later, but for now the task at hand was to move to protect Washington and intercept Lee if he tried to attack the city. He called for his commanders so the Army could be readied to move.

Some fifteen miles south of Gettysburg, units of General Fitz Lee's Virginia Cavalry ran headlong into the 2d Brigade of General Judson Kilpatrick's Cavalry. The fight was sudden and violent. Lee's men were getting the best of it, when the 1st Brigade of Kilpatrick's Cavalry arrived on the scene. Seeing the immediate danger, JEB Stuart led the remaining troops of Lee's command into the fray to attempt to allow Lee to disengage.

It was during this action that General George Custer personally charged to seize the colors of Stuart's command. Custer shot the color bearer and wrested the colors from him, but just as Custer pulled the colors down and was about to carry them away, he was hit in head by a pistol shot fired at point blank range from Private Richard Norton. Custer died instantly and collapsed from his horse. Union soldiers fought to get to him, while Southern soldiers fought to get their colors. Quickly an intense hand-to-hand action developed at this site. Horses fell, sabers flashed from every quarter while gunshots hit men and animals alike. A Confederate soldier finally galloped free of the melee carrying Stuart's colors wadded up in his hand, the staff having shot away. With some difficulty, the Confederates disengaged and rode hard southward to get space between them and the Federals who were following.

The soldier with Stuart's colors rode near to Stuart and held them up. He yelled for the General not to worry as the colors were safe! Then the soldier noticed the General was hurt. Stuart's right arm was not only hanging limp it, but his sleeve was completely red with blood and he was having increased difficulty at the pace they were riding. The soldier called for help. Without ever breaking stride, men rode up to help steady their commander. Stuart could not continue with out medical help, so the column halted just long enough to put a tourniquet and a hasty wrapped bandage on his arm. It took only a minute.

That was enough to stop the bleeding and they were off again. Riders stretched out ahead to look for help as they headed south. Help was not needed however, as the Federal cavalry had no intention of charging into the country side where they might be ambushed or overpowered. They were content to follow from a distance. They wanted to know where Robert E. Lee was, and they figured that the Reb cavalry would lead them right to him.

Both sides had taken losses, but in this action. The more numerous Federals had clearly gotten the best of the fight. The wounding of General JEB Stuart made it a serious blow indeed to the Confederates. Fitz Lee slowed up and then changed directions slightly to allow General Stuart and a strong escort to continue in front of them toward Frederick. They still had a hard ten miles to go to get the General home. He was hurt badly, but he would live.

Kilpatrick sent a messenger riding back to Meade tell him that he had engaged and bloodied a brigade of Confederate Cavalry who was proceeding northward up the Emmitsburg Road. He was now following the Rebels southward, but he would not engage unless he had a strong advantage. By the time Meade got this message, the II Corps followed by the I Corps of the Army of the Potomac were already starting to move down the Emmitsburg Road. Meade read the report and took it to mean that Robert E. Lee was still south of Gettysburg. He considered after the forced march and then the fight at Frederick, Lee would have to catch his breath and rest a bit before he moved on Washington. Meade thought, "We must catch him before he gets to the capital!"

MONOCACY

Confederate Commanders inspected the positions their men had been working hard to prepare.

"More logs, deeper pits, pile rocks higher, clear brush. Put stronger abitis in the road ways leading into that line!," they ordered. The men were clearly tired from the last 48 hours and had not prepared as well as they would have normally done. The officers and Sergeants pushed harder.

"Sweat now lads, so you don't bleed later!," one was heard to yell out.

One Colonel pointed toward Frederick City and said, "The whole Yankee Army will be coming right through that town, down that road and right into your position. Dig boys, dig! They are coming, they *are* coming!"

A badly hurt JEB Stuart finally arrived. His wound was serious, but he was alive. In the field hospital the doctors worked quickly.

They tried to save first his life, then his arm. Lee came to see him, but Stuart was unconscious having been exhausted by the ride and the loss of blood. As Lee left the hospital tent, he noticed it was about to rain. By the time he got to his Headquarters, the rain had started. It quickly turned into a torrential downpour. Lee knew the heavy rain would slow Meade down. As more and more troops and wagons came down the Taneytown Road from Emmitsburg, the road would turn finally into a mire and the fields would flood. The greater part of Kilpatrick's cavalry was now riding hard back up the Emmitsburg Road to return to General Meade. They followed the Confederate Cavalry and watched them enter Frederick City.

Lee thought, "Meade will press no action today while his men are strung out and tired from a 32 mile march on bad roads. Every hour the enemy marches, we rest." Lee wanted Meade to attack, attack while the Federal Corps and divisions were strung out and tired so they could be defeated piecemeal. Lee also knew that Meade would make no mistake unless he was led into one. Lee called for his Corps Commanders.

Soon the Corps Commanders were in Lee's tent trying to keep the pouring rain from soaking the maps on the table. General Wade Hampton was now the acting commander of Stuart's Cavalry.

Lee spoke to Hampton, "God was kind to spare General Stuart in spite of his serious wound. I am ever grateful for this."

Hampton answered, "That He did, Sir. I am told the doctors may well be able to save his arm as well. A day should tell us for sure."

"I pray it will be so, General, but in any event. I would prefer General Stuart with one arm to most officers with two." Ever the gentleman, Lee smiled, "But, General Hampton, we are indeed fortunate to have you to stand so ably in General Stuart's place."

After pausing, Lee continued. "As we stand here, the enemy is moving toward us. Their lead units will arrive before long , but his following columns will be slowed as road conditions deteriorate. If Meade would attack us without concentrating his forces, we could surely inflict grievous losses upon him and could further reduce his numerical advantage. Therefore, I propose to give him a target he will be tempted to attack. We will leave it to Mr. Lincoln to provide the additional impetus to help General Meade commit to battle before he is ready."

"General Longstreet, your Corps has been refitting and resting from the last action, while the other Corps have been preparing positions. With your Corps off line, our defenses are spread too thinly to hold under a concentrated attack. If the enemy sees a weak front, the temptation will be there to attack before we can reinforce these lines. Also, if two or more divisions were formed on the roads to our front as if preparing to move south toward Virginia or toward Washington, his immediate response would be to try and stop this movement. If these two situations are presented at the same time, they might just cause General Meade to attack almost from the march as his troops arrive."

Lee continued, "I would expect the enemy to attack in such a situation as soon as he could bring at least two Corps to bear…three at the most. The other units will be still be coming from Gettysburg, and they will be slowed by the difficult road conditions. Perhaps with the judicious use of our cavalry, we could slow them even more so."

Longstreet spoke, " Sir, I think this plan has much merit, but you know only too well that George Meade is not Ambrose Burnside. He may not fooled so easily."

Lee removed his spectacles, "You are correct General Longstreet, Meade is not Burnside. He is however, commanded by the same President, and *that* man is surely calling for Meade to save Washington by attacking as soon as possible, the invaders who now move freely through their country. In short, I plan for Lincoln to pressure Meade to attack us, and I think Meade the soldier, will do so."

General A.P. Hill had been listening and now asked, " Sir, if the enemy attacks us, do you expect to be able to cause serious damage to his units before he sees the danger and withdraws to regroup? He only has to be patient and consolidate before he comes at us."

"I do not expect the enemy to be patient and wait for his Army to arrive. But if he does, then we shall deal with him as we did at Fredericksburg. Yet, I say again, if he thinks we are moving on Washington and we are not ready to engage him when he arrives, he *will* attack. If the Meade comes at us with two or three Corps without waiting for his other units to arrive, I am sure we can inflict a great damage upon at least one Corps and possibly more. We have already eliminated his reserves, and that, in conjunction with this next action, will further reduce his capabilities. If the enemy continues to attack our positions after a failure, and I feel he will be compelled to do so, we can so weaken and demoralize him, that our opportunity to finally defeat him on the field will be at hand."

"Gentlemen, before we left Gettysburg, I told you that we must bring this campaign to a decisive conclusion. I said then that we have the Army to win this coming action, and I tell you now that we have the ground as well! If the enemy gets bogged down on our front with great casualties, we will attack and destroy him when that opportunity presents itself. The effect of such a victory could reach far beyond the battlefield here today. I ask you to give this your all."

The assembled officers then got down to the serious planning for the defense of the ground they now held. Artillery, egress roads, interior lines for movement, ways to mask movements of troops and hide concentrations, reserves, cavalry…each subject was covered and coordinated. Movements and times of action were planned in detail. It would be a somewhat complex operation, but if understood properly it could be executed keyed to events, almost without orders for the most part. Lee knew this coordination and understanding was important. Poor coordination had cost him a total victory before. They continued their discussions as reports of the advancing Federals began to come in. Then they dispersed. It was time to lay the trap.

GETTYSBURG

Two hours passed. Off to the side of a muddy road under a stand of trees , General Meade sat in the back of a wagon under a top covered with oil skins. He was listening to a soaked cavalry officer telling him that the Confederates had been seen just south of Frederick City . He was told the Rebels appeared to be in force and were not moving at this time. Meade ordered his reconnaissance to keep watch and let him know when and if the Confederates moved. Within the hour, Meade was consulting with General John Newton of I Corps and General Winfield Hancock of II Corps. He told them what he knew so far and asked for their evaluation.

Hancock replied first, "General, my scouts also confirm that the Rebels are south of Frederick in the Monocacy Junction area. Looks like at least one Corps, perhaps more, is there preparing to move with some units lining the roads. I would say they appear to be getting ready to move toward Washington."

General Newton agreed, "I think Washington will be their target if we don't stop them. If they strike the capital and get into the city, it could be difficult to have a pitched battle without destroying Washington!" The men were silent for a moment.

"What could Lee gain by taking the city?," asked Hancock, "That is, assuming he could take it. He certainly could not hold it, and I don't think he would destroy it."

Meade replied, "No, Lee would not destroy it, but General Newton is correct about the fact that it would suffer greatly if we had *force* him out. If the Rebels could capture the city and any part of the government, we might be forced to treat with him on their terms to save the city from ruin and destruction. The factions that are calling for peace now would have an even stronger voice. England might even recognize the Rebels! It could be a political disaster."

General Hancock again spoke firmly, "Lee won't reach Washington. My Corps is first in the march and if Lee has not moved out yet, or not moved too far, I will hold him up long enough to let the Army catch up and get at him. We can stop him here in Maryland." He was looking at George Meade to see what he would say.

"I had thought this too, Win, but if Lee is already moving, I don't think you can get in front of him before he could get to Washington. You might hit him in the middle or toward the rear of his force and slow him up. On the other hand, if we can strike him *before* he moves, he won't ever get started for Washington. That's what we need to do. We need to attack him *before* he can start moving. But I am concerned... you say you see one Corps or more is south of Frederick?"

Hancock again confirmed the report. "Then that leaves the major part of his force unaccounted for," said Meade.

Hancock said, "It could be that *all* of Lee's army is there, General, and we can't see it." He paused, "You don't think he would have split his force and sent part of it toward Washington do you?"

"No, I don't think he would do that. We have at least an equal, if not stronger army. He would not risk getting caught with his forces separated in our territory. He *must* be concentrated near Frederick. That is where we must attack him."

George Meade turned to the II Corps commander, "General Newton?

Newton rubbed his hand through his soaked hair and slung the water off on the wagon floor. "I don't know, Sir. I don't like it. We are talking about a hasty attack off the march with the Army strung out in column on a slow road in a heavy rain. If Lee is not caught out of position, and he usually isn't, at least not very often .... Our two Corps could pay a heavy price. Perhaps it would be best to wait until the rest of the Army arrived."

George Meade pondered these thoughts before he replied. "If I could afford that option I would choose it. If we wait and he gets a jump on us again, we may not be able to stop him should he move on Washington.

"What if we turned east before we got to Frederick and moved to take up a position between the Rebels and

Washington?, Newton asked.

Hancock interjected, "That would be a good option, John, but we are looking at a forty to fifty mile march to get in place, and we have to go through Frederick, because there are few, if any other roads." He nodded out the back of the wagon, "This is holding as a hard rain. If it continues, the roads will break down and the rivers will shortly rise to impassable levels. I just don't see how we could make it in time if Lee moves first. I think he would if he saw what we were doing."

General Meade said, "I think these are good ideas, and I have an idea to try to do both. I will send the major part of the cavalry to block off any Rebel forces from Washington. If the Rebels are moving toward the city, the cavalry can delay them up till we catch up. On the other hand, if we press hard and can catch Lee in the Frederick area before he is about to move, we could engage him with at least two, maybe three Corps. That would hold him until the rest of our units arrive to then bring the full Army to bear. Once we see we have caught him, I can recall the cavalry."

Both Corps commanders agreed it sounded like a viable option from what was available.

Meade added. "Gentlemen, President Lincoln has sent me specific orders and they are very clear … *Protect Washington! Attack and destroy Lee, if the opportunity presents itself.* It would appear that the opportunity may just be here. You both will have to press equally hard. You can not get strung out. Win, you must get into position to attack, but you must wait for John to come up before you attack. Facilitate his movement into position with yours. If the Rebs are off guard, we will attack with First and Second Corps only. If he is in place, we will hold him and not attack until the rest of the Army comes up. Understood?"

The two Corps commanders said they understood. Meade continued, "There must be no misunderstanding here Gentlemen. A two Corps attack will be made *only* if we have to do so, or if the enemy is vulnerable to it. Otherwise, we wait for the full Army to assemble." Again, the two generals nodded agreement and said they understood.

"Very well, I will let you return to your commands. I will brief the other Corps commanders and see about getting the cavalry on its way for their part in this plan. Win, John, both of you be alert. Be flexible and use your assets to keep you informed to your front and flanks. With our cavalry dispatched, we lose a vital asset here." The two Generals stood somewhat stooped as they put on their rain gear. A few details and general comments were exchanged, and then the officers saluted as they departed.

A short time later General Alfred Pleasonton arrived to be briefed on what had been discussed. Then he was quickly on his way to begin the movements General Meade had ordered. One by one, most of the other Corps commanders made their way to Meade's wagon headquarters in the rain. The roads were becoming more and more difficult to traverse because of the mud from the still falling rain. It was past noon and the lead elements of First Corps were now ten miles north of Frederick. It would take some two to three hours to reach the city. The rains were getting worse.

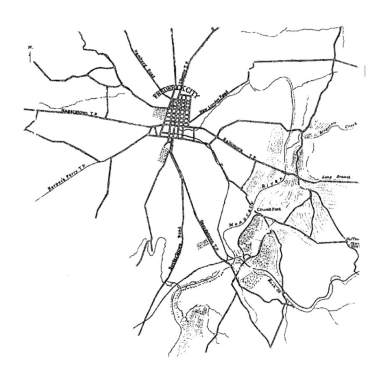

FREDERICK - MONOCACY

MONOCACY

General Lee had just received word that the Federals were about 3 to 4 hours away. He called for the Corps commanders to meet with him at once. Within the hour they had joined him in his tent. He asked how their positions looked. Each commander commented on the strengths and weaknesses of their positions as he saw them. Lee planned to put one division from First and Second Corps in front of the defenses on the Georgetown Turnpike and the road crossing at Crum's Ford. They would form up as if to move and therefore, be the bait to help bring the enemy forward. At first indication that the Federals were coming at them, these forces would pull back within the prepared positions.

Elements of Stuart's cavalry, now commanded by Wade Hampton, were sent toward Washington to provide warning of any force that might come from the capitol, as well as to give increased alarm to the enemy government. A large portion of the cavalry force moved south down Buckeytown Road. It would serve as a rear guard and if needed, they would be able to come up the road to reinforce either flank as a reserve force. Artillery was placed for maximum effectiveness where their field of fire would be enhanced from the high ground.

Just before he dismissed his commanders, Lee gave them one last order. "Be prepared to attack from your positions if the opportunity develops. I will send you this order if necessary, but do not move from positions without orders. Make no mistake, the enemy has a very strong army coming at us. We have defeated his reserves, but his main force is most formidable. We will let him spend his energy attacking our positions. But if a situation develops where we can catch the enemy in the open or unable to deploy, we need to be prepared to attack. Consider this possibility as this action begins." With this, Lee bid his Corps commanders farewell and sent them on their way to see to last minute preparations.

It was now just after two p.m. and General Hancock was riding into Frederick following elements of the 6th New York

Cavalry who led him into the town. From a position near the Georgetown Turn Pike, he looked through field glasses at the hills south of the city. After a minute he said, "Lord! Its just as the scouts said, there are at least two, maybe three divisions of troops on the road ahead! It looks like they are preparing to march. We must get into position! Captain Johnson, send an courier to tell all division commanders to move as quickly as possible through Frederick. Tell them the city is clear and that the Rebels are south of the town."

Now pointing at the map, Hancock continued, "General Caldwell is to move through the town and place his right flank on the Harper's Ferry Pike at a point - here - near Prospect Hill. His left flank will anchor on the Georgetown Pike right about where it comes out the town. Where we are now is good. He will be on the Corps' right flank. Understood? Then General Gibbon will take center position, and General Hays will assume the left flank. Divisions on line facing the enemy. Place artillery to support a general attack. Read that back to me."

Captain Johnson was just finishing writing the last of the instructions and he read them back. They were correct. Then Hancock continued. "Now, send messengers to General Newton and General Meade. My compliments…Tell them both that Second Corps is entering Frederick City. Ask General Newton to join me. Tell him where I am. Tell General Meade that we have the enemy in sight, at least three divisions on the road making preparations to move. Second Corps is preparing to attack on his order." In a moment the Captain was gone to make copies and send couriers on the way.

General Hancock looked through his glasses at the hills beyond the Confederates on the road. There were soldiers on the hills and he could see some fresh emplacements. He wondered was this in place to protect the Confederates from attack before they could move, or if the Rebels planned to stand and fight. It looked like it might be a good defensive position. He was too far to see for sure, but no matter. If he could get in position and attack these Rebels in the open before they moved, the Second Corps could defeat them easily. He looked at the skies. The rain had subsided, and although the fields and roads were soaked, the visibility was improving. There were about six hours of daylight left. That was plenty of time to fight.

In less than an hour, Hancock's division commanders were with him. He showed each of them what he wanted and they departed to complete their division's placements as they came through the city. First Division was trotting into line to get formed. Second Division was starting to deploy when First Corps commander, General John Newton rode up.

"Afternoon Win, what do you have?," asked Newton.

"Well, the Rebs are still here, John. They were forming to march when we arrived. Since I sent you the message to come up, they have spotted the first of our troops arriving. Looks like they are going to swing around and deploy to fight."

Newton was looking through his field glasses at the hill sides, "Where are the rest of them, Win? There are a lot more on the loose than just these boys."

"I don't know, John", Win gestured. "There are some troops on those hills and what appears to be considerable entrenchments. I have not seen a lot of troops there. They are either behind the hills or perhaps they have moved further south and these are the troops to follow up."

As they discussed the matter, they saw a large party riding up. It was General Meade and General Daniel Sickles. They exchanged salutes and General Meade immediately asked for an update as he too looked toward the troops forming some two miles away. Winfield Hancock filled him in on the dispositions, plans and situation as he had found it.

"They look like they mean to fight where they are. I don't like it," said Meade. "They must know they are outnumbered three to one."

Hancock said, "Sir, it looks like they came down from the hill sides to move and we caught them. They stopped when they saw us arriving. Once we deploy two Corps for an attack, I would expect to see them try to get back into the emplacements they prepared. "

Meade turned to his officers, "I agree with General

Hancock. Comments?"

Newton again raised the question of waiting. "General, it will soon be late afternoon. I feel that I must again ask if it would it not be prudent to wait until more of the Army arrives so we could bring it to bear on the Rebs at first light?"

Meade continued to look across the fields with his field glasses and spoke. "Well, I think we have stopped them before they moved on Washington. We waited at Gettysburg and Lee moved before us. If we wait now, the Rebs will have all night to prepare for us to attack, or God knows, maybe even to move south once more and again threaten the capitol. If we attack now, we can surely take those divisions to our front before dark."

Then Meade made the decision. "The enemy may have moved south, or they may already be on the road to Washington. In any event we can deal with this Corps to our front now, and not have to do so later. They appear to be the last troops to move, and I propose hitting them now rather than waiting. We can reduce Lee's force while this opportunity is at hand. Do we agree?,"

General Meade paused for comments from his commanders. Of the assembled Corps commanders, Hancock and Sickles favored the attack, Newton said he still thought it best to wait till morning. Meade decided to take the majority decision and attack immediately. After a short discussion about coordination of times and Corps boundaries for the attack, the general officers departed to take up stations.

As Hancock arrived, his artillery was setting up forward of his lines to engage the Confederates on the road. The guns were almost in place. Hancock was looking at the Rebel formations to decide where and when the artillery would concentrate its fire, when he saw the Rebels begin to move. Just has he suspected they would do, the formations were moving rapidly back through the roads leading into the hills. The opportunity to attack them in the open was slipping away! Hancock called for a courier and turned his glasses toward I Corps.

"Come on Newton...Get in place!," Hancock muttered to

himself.

His courier arrived. "Take this message to General Newton. I will start artillery fire in fifteen minutes and commence a Corps attack in thirty minutes. We will go down the Georgetown and Buckytown roads to attack the hill sites to our front across the railroad." The young officer was gone in an instant riding hard toward II Corps.

General Hancock took off riding as well. He was sitting erect in his saddle at a light gallop across the front of his leading divisions. As he rode by he raised his hat to his troops and their colors. For this, he was met with a tremendous cheer from each unit he passed. Before he could finish his ride, the cannon of I Corps roared to life. The men cheered at first, then they settled into watching the fire impact in and around the Confederate troops who were still trying to move through the passes on the roads leading south. Many of the troops were clear of the road, but others were crowding into the pass as the rounds accurately hit among them. They jogged and ran just as fast as they could, but casualties were being taken by those still in the line of fire.

James Longstreet watched this through his glasses and waited. "We must let them commit to the attack," he thought. "Hood's troops are paying a price for this...I must make it count!"

Several of Longstreet's staff officers looked at him waiting for the order to return fire. He waited. When at last it seemed everyone would burst with the tension, Longstreet turned to COL Walton and said, "Colonel, you may silence those guns to our front."

"Yes Sir!" the colonel quickly replied. With that he took off his hat, held it high and then quickly dropped his arm. Almost at once the trees and brush that had been covering the artillery on the hilltop near the pass was cleared and the guns responded.

As planned, only some sixteen cannon fired, but the effect was immediate. The Federal artillery slowed as rounds from the twelve pounders hit around them. One round was on target and killed or wounded most of a gun crew. The other first impacts were close, but not accurate enough to damage or destroy the

116

Federal guns or crews. It only made them hit the ground and stop firing as they looked for the source. The Union artillery officers quickly spotted the smoke from the now exposed Rebel guns, and they set about to bring their guns to bear on these new targets. As they did so, the Federal advance began with hundreds of men starting down the roads and spreading across the fields coming south from Frederick. More Union artillery began to try to reposition forward to support the infantry against these new targets.

Confederate artillery fire was now falling more accurately among the forward placed Union artillery pieces. The Union gun crews were being killed and wounded with each volley from the Confederate guns. The Federal guns began to return the fire with a vengeance. According to plan, Colonel Walton signaled to slow the fire from his guns. He wanted to conserve ammunition for the approaching sea of blue making its way across the muddy fields and roads toward them.

General Newton watched as his troops moved forward toward the hills and down the Baltimore Turn Pike. As he strained to view the distance hilltops, he saw Confederate troops stirring and other artillery now becoming exposed. As these troops moved into their positions or came up into sight, Newton could see these were the troops they had all wondered about. Newton could now see what was developing.

He said to his staff officers around him, "I should have seen this! The Rebels are massed in those hills. They are waiting for us!"

George Meade could also see the situation developing. His troops were half way to the hills now. He stood with arms folded as he watched the advance and said to Dan Sickles, "Lee is not moving. He is there - in force - and we are attacking him with two Corps and no reserves." He thought to himself, "I should have waited. Well done, General Lee. I won't underestimate you again." Meade turned to Sickles, "General, I need your Corps up here *now*! How long will you take to get them on the field?"

"Sir, the lead division of my Corps is at least an hour from

Frederick," Sickles replied.

Meade said, "We don't have an hour! See to it that they move as quickly as possible. I want your Corps to come straight through the town and to form on the right. Be prepared to follow I Corps on my order. We are committed to this attack. If Hancock can break the enemy on his front, I want you prepared to follow him up. If he falters, I will need to use elements of your command to reinforce him. Do you understand what I saying here?"

Dan Sickles answered, "Yes Sir, I will move as quickly as possible and get word to you when we are into position. We will advance on your order."

After a few other comments, Sickles and members of his staff turned and galloped off to the north toward his command. He did not know that his Corps was not an hour away, but rather it was almost two hours away. They had been slowed by the heavily traveled muddy roads and flooded fields.

General Dick Ewell gave his men instructions to take their positions and to let the enemy get well within range before they commenced firing. Some half mile out from Ewell's front, there was a steep hill, across which the Baltimore Pike ran. The hill helped shield the Union troops from some artillery fire, while it forced them to move either down the Pike, or go around the sides of the hill to avoid a steep climb over it. Dick Ewell knew there would be a hard fight on the road and bridge where it crossed the Monocacy river. The rains had started to flood the river, so the troops would have to take and hold the bridge as a major crossing.

This would be a key point. True to this, he could see the blue clad troops now double timing en-mass as they approached the first hill to their front. They had grit, noted Ewell, but it will take more than grit this day. They were covering the ground in pretty good order Ewell thought. They must be tired from the long march and the wet ground should have slowed them, but they were coming hard. These are regulars, but then again, a great deal of the Army of the Potomac fought like regulars as this war dragged on.

As the troops of the 147th New York pressed toward the bridge, they began to narrow into a wedge converging on the entrance to the stone bridge. Confederate artillery was now firing steadily into the approaching ranks as well as toward the Union artillery who was shelling the Confederate positions. Some fifty yards before the Federals got to the bridge itself, the Confederate line rose up from the trenches and rocks, aimed at the mass of troops and in one instant fired a massive volley that engulfed the hill side in smoke. Before it fully cleared, a second line of troops fired, then a third, then the first line now reloaded fired again, and again, until fully a half dozen thunderous volleys of rifle fire had poured across the river at the bridge. The first charging ranks of Union troops had gotten about ten yards on to the bridge, when the first wall of lead hit them. Those not dropped in the first or second blasts were caught in the third. Men dropped like wheat cut down before a scythe. They lay piled face down on top of each other, falling dead on the soldiers in front of them. Some fell side by side as if struck at the same time. Others lay twisting and rolling in pain from wounds that had brought them down, unable to continue and unable to escape.

The charge had been shattered as it merged into the narrow width of the bridge crossing. Soldiers now fell back toward their lines, some firing, some helping wounded comrades, some just running to get out of rifle range. One tall soldier from New York calmly walked toward his lines as men around him ran. He was reloading his rifle as he walked, then he stopped, turned, took careful aim and fired before resuming his pace to the rear, stopping only after reloading to again turn and fire. Bullets splattered in the mud and against rocks all around him. Another soldier running past him was hit, but the tall soldier was not scratched. In all, the main charge had taken just fifteen minutes from start to end.

On the Confederate left flank, Union infantry and cavalry tried desperately to force a crossing of the Monocacy River. Adding to the increased river current and the rising water level, Southern artillery and infantry located on the high ground across the river poured a steady fire into the troops who were trying to cross in the open. Men and animals were swept away in the current which was much stronger than it looked. The attack here deteriorated quickly and the troops began to withdraw behind the nearby tree line in an effort to seek safety.

On the right flank, Union forces faired little better. Again, the key was the bridge that crossed the river and lead to the pass through the hills. The Federal troops had made a valiant effort, but the concentrated fire from the artillery and infantry was just too intense to overcome no matter how great the courage. Union soldiers littered the bridge having almost gotten across before they were cut down.

To the rear, Union officers tried to reform their units for another charge. Artillery was deployed further forward to better support the infantry. It was difficult at best. The troops were bone-tired from the long forced march from Gettysburg over wet roads. Now they were spent from a costly attack and the wet ground that was made even worse from the troops moving across and back over it. Riding back and forth waving hats and swords, the mounted officers began to form up regiments for a second attack. Here and there, some officers dismounted to take up positions to lead the attack that was to come. It was mid-afternoon. Soon darkness would be falling. They needed to make the most of the available light.

Northern artillery limbers and caissons sat in disarray as field guns were hastily repositioned forward and began firing. The shorter range was deadly to the Confederates. The Union infantry could see the effect. Cheers went up as their guns pummeled the hillsides near the bridges. The troops began to form and move toward the river and those bridges. Then Confederate artillery answered with one cannon after another, thundering a reply. Explosions tore holes in the advancing ranks. Rounds aimed at the Union artillery exploded in the air showering the area with shards of metal. Large chunks of mud and dirt-cart wheeled into the air as rounds impacted near the gun crews. Still the Union artillery maintained its fire and took its losses. Here and there an artilleryman spun around or reeled backwards as he was hit by Confederate sharpshooters who now had the range. The Union infantry was moving ahead steadily. They went from a route step to a double quick and the troops began surging forward going around, over, and on top of the dead and wounded from the previous attack. They felt this attack carrying forward!

A major yelled and waved his empty pistol in the air, "We'll take the Rebs this time…We'll roll them up and push them off the high ground this time!" They could now see the bridge ahead. It was littered with dead and wounded.

Colonel Nathan Tines raised his sword and with his other hand pointed at the bridge, " Forward boys, drive them off of our soil!"

The lines now surged forward with everyone trotting and running for the stone bridge. They were going to make it! Then the Confederate artillery and infantry unleashed another massive volley of fire into the charging ranks. Men in blue fell by the dozens, seemingly all at once. The 1st Minnesota took four artillery blasts in rapid succession across its line. More than two dozen men fell in the first two ranks. Rifle balls whizzed by like a thousand angry hornets, while the crack and thud of a lead ball finding home sounded steadily throughout the men still running. The fire grew more intense, and still they charged. More men stumbled and fell. The sounds grew to a roar, broken only by the crash of artillery explosions. They were on the bridge! As the Union soldiers surged forward, they saw a log barricade across the far side of the bridge. Then they saw the two cannons behind it! Several men stopped to aim and fire at the cannon, while others fired on the run. It was all in vain. At virtually point blank range, the two 12 pound Napoleons fired seconds apart into the packed ranks of the Union soldiers and literally swept away everyone standing on the bridge. Lines three ranks deep that were just reaching the bridge were cut down by the canister shot that came across the bridge. This was followed by a volley of infantry rifle fire, then another, then another…. The attack was again decimated and reeled back. As fresh troops ran into the dead, wounded and those falling back, the field around the bridge became a killing ground. The carnage was incredible. It was Fredericksburg all over again, only worse. Hundreds were down with many units virtually shot to pieces.

General Hancock was watching through his field glasses and could see the second attack crumble. "My God, they are being torn apart!" the words seemed to explode from him. He began to ride forward as his staff officers tried to convince him to stay back out of range of the artillery and rifle fire. "I must get them back!," Hancock was saying to himself. The exhausted, bleeding and wounded men falling back from the last attack were obviously spent. They had just come too far, too fast and hit an entrenched foe who was waiting for them. It was another disaster.

Hancock soon rode up to General John Gibbon who was calling to his men to form up in an effort to again advance or retreat as the orders came. "General Gibbon, get your men formed and pull them back toward the town. We will...." Hancock never finished the order. An artillery round hit just next to his horse. The explosion blew the horse completely off his feet and rolled him over on his rider. The horse, now crazed with pain, tried to get to his feet but his front legs were both broken. Each time the helpless animal tried to get up he fell yet again on his now unconscious rider. Finally a staff officer with General Gibbon shot the mount and dragged General Hancock free. It appeared that both of Hancock's legs were badly broken and a metal shard had pierced his arm. General Hancock's war was over.

As the divisions tried to regroup, reports were coming to General Meade. A staff officer read a message just brought in by courier, "Sir, II Corps has been unsuccessful in trying to cross the river. Casualties heavy. They are forming to try again."

Meade nodded and said, "Any word from General Newton or General Sickles?"

"No Sir, not yet"

Meade peered intently through his field glasses, "Very well."

Moments later another courier arrived. " Sir, General Hancock is down! He was wounded by artillery fire! General Gibbon has assumed command."

"How badly is he wounded?," asked Meade.

The courier continued, "It seems he is broken up badly, Sir. His horse was hit and it fell on him. Looks like his legs, maybe his hip, and his arm could all be broken."

Meade shook his head in disappointment and said, "Keep me posted."

Now he wondered about John Gibbon. Meade knew Gibbon was a good man, but he wondered if he was up to commanding a Corps in such a fight. Well, men rise to the occasion or quickly fall away he reflected. He wondered about Newton and how he was fairing. From his observation, it appeared Newton's I Corps was doing little better than II Corps. If only Sickles could get III Corps here before dark. They still might carry the day.

Lee watched the battle raging before him. He knew there was little chance of the Federals breaking the Confederate line that was well entrenched and that poured a withering fire upon their attackers. He looked past the Federal troops and scanned the rear area wondering how far back the next Corps was now.

"A third Corps of their army must surely be coming up, but it appears they have slowed even more than I expected," Lee commented

"Yes Sir. I don't care if they all stopped for coffee and a smoke, I am just glad they are late," replied Longstreet. "We can hold this ground till winter if need be."

"The enemy is paying a hard price to get at us. Another hour or so at this rate and his two Corps to our front will be relatively ineffective." Lee lowered his field glass and looked at Longstreet, " If the enemy throws yet another Corps into this fight today, we may have an opportunity to cut him down to where he will have to withdraw or face destruction on his own soil."

Longstreet replied, "If the other Corps doesn't arrive soon, there won't be an option for them to attack. The daylight will be gone. That means that tomorrow the Federals should have at least another three Corps or so available. It will be a tough fight, but I think we can still take them no matter what they assemble and send at us. That river is not going down for a few days. Those bridges are nothing but killing grounds."

"Well, it's up to General Meade now." Lee again had his glasses trained on Frederick. "It appears his next Corps is arriving from Gettysburg." Lee and James Longstreet could see mounted officers and the first of a large infantry column coming out of the city. The infantry was moving toward the Confederate left.

"They probably will form up behind Hancock's Corps to reinforce him." said Longstreet. Lee looked at the sun. Longstreet could see his commander's mind racing ahead to figure his battle plan. Lee looked at the stone bridge. Fighting was going on there, but most of the Federal troops were pinned across the river and could not force a crossing here or at the railway bridge just up the river to Dick Ewell's front.

"General Longstreet," said Lee, "I want you to move your Corps reserves to a position behind General Hood's troops along the Georgetown Turnpike with all haste. Then, at my command, begin to withdraw first your artillery. Then pull the majority of your troops back from the Monocacy bridge site. Pull back no more than 25 yards from the bridge and dig in to hold at all costs. When this is done, pull the remainder of your troops at the bridge back to join them."

Longstreet said nothing for a moment and then he said, "You are going to give them the bridge, General?"

"Precisely, Pete, " answered General Lee. "We will give them the bridge, or least just enough of it to think they are across. Then let them have nothing more. They will cross the bridge. We will stop them just on this side. The forward commanders will call for more support. As soon as the enemy commits the newly arrived Corps forward, we will attack with a powerful force to push the troops at the bridge back across the river. With the new Corps now engaged, they will commit to a full attack. We will have them under our guns piled up at the bridge site. We can cut them down to size before dark."

124

"Yes Sir. I just was thinking, the Yankee army has lost a lot of good men on that bridge. I'd hate to take those kinds of losses to get it back." Before Lee could speak, Longstreet added, "but I see your plan. We don't have to take the bridge, only push them back across it and keep them from crossing it."

"Correct," said General Lee. "You must only give them a few yards on this side of the river. As soon as that new Corps of the enemy commits forward, you must attack! Don't wait for his troops to become engaged. Your reserves will be in place to charge forward in support of, or through, Hood's troops at the bridge. For extra impact, your artillery can concentrate there for five minutes before your attack. It should help break them. I will have General Ewell bring his reserves up behind the railway bridge just up river in case the enemy tries to take both bridges at the same time. This will put Ewell's troops adjacent to your reserves. It comes to it, we can shift troops either way. Time is of the essence, General. Order your reserves to move now."

General Longstreet set about ordering a division from McLaws and one from Pickett to move to the location specified along the Georgetown Pike. General Lee had a courier on the way to General Ewell in short order.

"Thank God you have arrived," said General Gibbon as John Newton surveyed the situation. "Hancock is wounded and I have assumed command of the Corps."

"Yes, I heard Win was down. How is he?" asked Newton.

"Not good," said Gibbon, "and we have had the devil to pay here today as well."

It was as I feared," replied Newton. "The Rebs are dug in and we can't get at them across that infernal river!."

General Gibbon responded and pointed. "There are two bridges we must take to cross that river. A stone bridge on the right - there - and a railway bridge about a quarter mile up stream - there - just to the left of those trees. Take either or these, and I think we can get across the river…"

General Newton finished the statement, "…and be directly under the guns of the Rebs…a delightful prospect!"

"General Gibbon looked directly at Newton and continued, "

A lot of men have fallen here today trying to cross that river, General. If we take either of these bridges and force a crossing, we can crack the Confederate line and split his force. We could roll up the whole Reb army here!"

"What does Meade say," asked Newton?

Gibbon replied, "Well, he has had us make three attacks so far. Now that you are here, if you will follow us up with your artillery and infantry, we might be able to take it. What do you say?" As the two men looked at each other, a courier was approaching at a full gallop. He was almost yelling as he began his report to General Gibbon.

"General Caldwell's compliments, Sir! He reports that the Rebs are giving way on the stone bridge! He will be attacking with the 1st Division shortly! He asks for any support you might give, and asks that the Corps be prepared to follow the Division up as soon as we take the bridge site. He said he doesn't know how long he can hold without support. Our losses have been heavy. That's all, Sir! What shall I tell him, Sir?"

General Gibbon looked at Newton and paused as he responded to the courier's question, "Tell General Caldwell that II Corps is moving to follow the 1st Division's lead."

With his eyes fixed on John Gibbon, Newton added, "Tell General Caldwell that *III Corps will be joining II Corps* following the 1st Divisions lead." The courier's eyes flashed as he saluted and replied "Yes Sir!" With a quick spin and hard spurs, the courier was on his way back toward the fighting.

Newton turned in his saddle and looked back toward Frederick City to see his troops coming steadily forward. "John, I will have III Corps elements come on line and follow as soon as they arrive. I'll pass the word to Meade to tell him what we are doing. I'll also deploy the artillery forward as fast as I can. Don't hold up to wait for us. We are pretty strung out. Just know *we will* be coming."

"That's good enough for me. By the way, thanks, General," said Gibbon.

Newton replied with a smile, "Right, good luck to you. I better go get the boys to shake it up. See you across the river."

With that he turned and headed off toward his troops.

Robert E. Lee was watching intently to see if the Federal troops were moving forward. General Hood's Texans were almost finished pulling back from the bridge. So far there was no surge forward by the Federals. It seemed like ten minutes passed. Then Union troops began to inch forward. A U.S. flag came up near the bridge. An officer stood up and waved his sword, and the ground literally rose up. The enemy was charging! He watched for a moment, then shifted his field glasses to the rear. Troops were forming far back, but not moving forward. They were not ready. Again he looked at the charging Union troops. These were brave men indeed, but he knew they would not succeed. They were at the bridge now. The charge picked up momentum. The Union soldiers were getting across the river! They sensed a break through! Once across the bridge, some soldiers started to the right and left to seek cover. Others charged ahead. Men were falling, but the attack was advancing quickly. Then like a huge explosion, the Confederates fired into the charging mass of troops. The charge collapsed. NO! It was rising up and coming on again! A second explosion of rifles and a cannon, then rapid firing by the men only yards from the bridge. The charge was gallant, but again it failed. No troops could advance against such concentrated fire. The troops now running across the bridge were getting over the bridge only to seek shelter behind the rocks and shattered trees near the bridge. Those who took shelter behind the bodies of fallen comrades were soon dead or dying themselves as the Confederate infantry on the high ground picked them off in rapid order. The Federals were across the river, but they held the bridge with only a handful of troops. They could not hold out for long.

Colonel Patrick Kelly of General Caldwell's 1st Division, was about 200 yards from the bridge behind a shattered stump and two fallen tree trunks. It was about as safe as one could get under the circumstances. Kelly had a Lieutenant by the collar of his uniform pulling him close. He was shouting over the rifle fire and explosions. "Get to General Caldwell! Tell him that the 2nd Brigade has crossed the bridge! *We hold the bridge*! The Lieutenant nodded rapidly as Kelly continued. "Tell him our casualties are heavy! We can not hold this position for long...We must have support! Do you understand?" Kelly pulled the young man's collar hard, "We must have support now! "

"Yes Sir, I have it!" "All right son, now go!" In a second the young officer was half running half scrambling off to find General Caldwell. Kelly watched the Lieutenant run about twenty feet and then pitch forward face down.

Kelly grimaced and started to turn to find another man to send. Then he saw that the Lieutenant was on his hands and knees now wiping mud and blood from his face. He looked around, regained his composure and was up and off again on a zigzagging run toward the rear where the horses were being held. He had only tripped over a dead soldier and knocked the wind from himself for a moment. In minute or two he was out of sight. Kelly peered around the tree stump where he was sheltered from the lead and iron rain.

"The boys are holding that bridge," he thought, "but we must hold it a while longer!"

Longstreet was watching the action at the bridge. General Hood's Alabama troops had the enemy contained at the bridge. It appeared that they could hold this position for some time. He looked toward the rear of the Union attack. Other units were forming. Behind them, more Federal troops were coming from the city and trying to form up. It appeared that the troops were about to charge again with those coming off the march to follow as they arrived! General Lee had been right again in his predictions of how the battle would develop. Longstreet sent orders to Colonel Walton to have Alexander's Artillery Battalion to strike the massing infantry as soon as they came into range. He instructed the Washington Artillery from Louisiana to conserve its fire until the massing infantry approached the bridge, then to concentrate its fire at that point. He wanted continuous artillery falling on the infantry as they crowded together to cross the bridge.

"Maximum casualties before they cross the bridge," he thought. "If we cut them up, Hood will have an easier time of it on this side of the bridge." The blue force was now beginning to surge forward.

Artillery rounds hit all over the Southern positions. The Federals were also massing and coordinating their artillery fire. Confederate artillery slowed as the batteries came under intense fire, forcing gun crews to seek shelter. Here and there a field piece was hit by fire and collapsed or turned over. Instead of intensified artillery fire on the advancing Federal troops, Confederate firing was reduced. The Confederate divisions and the Corps artillery were being punished. Only the Washington artillery was not being pummeled. This was because it was not firing like the other batteries. Union artillery began hitting in the area near the bridge where Hood's Division was holding. Longstreet could see this was having a terrible effect on the troops there. About all the troops could do was claw into the ground and keep low as the rounds hit in an almost constant barrage. Union troops were less than 300 yards from the bridge. Confederate artillery was taking a toll but it was not enough. Some of the Confederate guns were now firing at Federal artillery! General Longstreet gritted his teeth. "Didn't they get my instructions! The infantry! The infantry! That's where the fire should be directed!"

Federal infantry was moving in mass now only some fifty yards from the bridge. Longstreet could see the Federal flag. It was the green flag of the 69th New York, an Irish Brigade. Just then the guns of the Washington Battery opened fire. The impact of the volley from the Louisiana guns was immediate. The concentrated infantry began to fall in great numbers as the rounds hit all among them. Their flag went down and disappeared in the smoke. The Federal line slowed, reeled back, then reformed. The flag was up again and now the line began to surge ahead once more! Artillery rounds continued to fall, as troops reached the bridge and started to charge across it. The Federal artillery had lifted from the Confederates near the bridge and the guns were now firing on the Washington Battery. John

Hood's troops were up and firing at the charging infantry. The Confederate losses from the artillery pounding had its effect, as they tried desperately to put up enough fire to halt the blue onslaught.

James Longstreet watched this battle and saw what was coming. If the charging infantry were stopped, it would take everything Hood could muster to do it. When the next wave, and then the next wave behind that hit Hood, he would be overrun. Longstreet knew he must send the Corps reserve in now! Longstreet called for a courier. He instructed the courier to go to General Barksdale and tell him to advance at-the-double to reinforce the Hood's Division at the stone bridge. Then he turned again to look toward the Union rear. He could see at least three if not four brigades of troops were coming right behind the attacking Corps. "They are coming in force to cross the bridge and cut our defense in half," he thought, "and if they succeed, we could lose it all right here." He looked at the defenders at the bridge.

The Confederates were firing at will now, reloading and firing as fast as they could. The Federal line staggered. Losses were horrendous. But in the midst of this, the blue line reformed and again charged ahead. It finally crashed into the Confederates who were standing to receive the attackers. This was combat at its worse. Hand-to-hand with rifle butts, bayonets, knives, sabers, pistols and shovels. The attackers and defenders were merged and Union troops were streaming across the bridge.

Just as the Confederate line was reeling back and about to break, General William Barksdale's Mississippians charged up the road toward the bridge. They slammed into the exhausted troops of the 69th and 63rd New York. Almost at once the Federal line began faltered. The Union troops had come too far and were just expended. The fresh Mississippi Brigade charged with the Texas and Alabama troops to force the Union troops back across the bridge. The Union forces had the preponderance of troops, but could not bring them to bear across the narrow stone bridge. Just behind the Confederates, two artillery pieces were being manually rolled toward the bridge once more. The Federals also tried get cannon forward, but just could not do so with the Confederate artillery and rifle fire pouring down on them from the high ground. Their horses quickly went down, and they could not move the guns across the bodies and the muddy, churned up roads. As the Union troops in the rear pressed forward once again, they began to crowd into the forward elements who were beginning to fall back. Confederate artillery and infantry in the hills were taking a fearful toll as their fires poured into the bogged down troops. Casualties mounted rapidly.

After what seemed like a half hour of complete carnage, the Federal troops began to try to fall back, taking casualties with each step. Confederate troops at the bridge once again had the bridge site under control, having been reinforced by the 17th and 20th Georgia. First rifle fire, and then artillery fire tapered off. The sun was setting, and the day's fighting was almost over. The Federal commanders surveyed the scene and knew it had been a blood bath. General Meade would have to be content with the thought that Washington had been saved, that is, if it had ever been really been threatened. No one wanted to think about that.

Robert E. Lee was also looking over the battlefield. Results at the Baltimore and Ohio railroad bridge to General Ewell's front, and at the Baltimore Pike bridge to General A.P. Hill's front were similar to what had happened at the Stone Bridge before James Longstreet. The B & O railroad bridge was now burning, having been doused by coal oil and set on fire by Confederate troops in a desperate effort to stop the advancing Federals. Lee could see that the destruction of the enemy had not been all that he wanted it to be. But the enemy had been dealt severe blow and it had happened in one afternoon. Coupled with the destruction of the Federal reserve at Frederick City, two corps and elements of third corps had been heavily mauled. The Union forces were now cut down from seven Corps to something on the order of five and no reserve.

So far it had been a stunning Confederate victory, but

General Lee knew tomorrow was another day. All could still be lost. Five Union Corps were still a powerful force with which to contend, and his Army of Northern Virginia had also taken losses. Hood, Johnson, Early, and Heath's Divisions had each fought hard and paid a price for the day's victory. Confederate losses were way out of proportion to Union losses, but with Confederate forces always outnumbered, any loss had a great impact. Lee knew he could not be pushed off these hills unless he made some grave error. He did not plan to make any such error.

General Lee waited to allow his commanders time to attend to their troops, then he sent for them to join him at his headquarters. It was well after sunset when the last general arrived. Spirits were high and the officers were offered and accepted a cup of coffee as they joined their Commander. Lee talked with each of the generals as they arrived as to the condition of their Corps.

Then Lee addressed the group, "Gentlemen, once again our Lord has granted us victory on the field of battle. Our thanks to Him for this day."

"Amen," the officers agreed almost in unison.

"I trust the Army is bedded down for the night," Lee continued, "but let us be sure we are vigilant." Everyone was nodding in agreement. "Let us look to the 'morrow's actions and needs."

Lee put his glasses on and leaned slightly over the map table illuminated by two lanterns hanging from the top of the tent.

"The enemy has taken a hard pounding. I do not expect that he will come at us again as he did today. I think he will look to overcome us on a flank. Since he can not risk putting us between his force and the enemy capitol, I expect he will choose the northern flank to attack." Lee was now pointing at the map, " He will likely try to cross or ford the Monocacy up river at the New London Road bridge - here and here - near Hughes Ford. More likely, he will try and use both fords. General Hill, this means you will receive the main attack. What is you position like and how well do you think you can hold it?"

132

General A.P. Hill responded. " Sir, I thought this would be coming, so I have had the boys dig in whenever we were not fighting. We have a good ground and are dug in like a bunch of ticks. I feel we can hold against what ever they throw against us. My one concern is that the high terrain will make it difficult to get reserves forward if needed. My reserves are deployed forward. May I suggest that some general reserves be positioned closer to my Corps' area so they could respond if needed?"

Lee agreed and instructed that I and II Corps provide a Brigade each and position these units just behind III Corps. Hill asked for some additional artillery and this was also granted. General Longstreet asked about the availability of the cavalry off to his left flank. He was told that it would be used only if absolutely necessary. Some of these assets were being moved to join Wade Hampton's force now down the Baltimore Turnpike. Other options and ideas were discussed, but it was agreed that this was the most plausible actions of the enemy.

After some time, General Lee gave a final instruction to his generals. "Be prepared to move out in short order if need be tomorrow. We will likely have another hard fight. I want you to plan to move quickly if called upon to do so." Lee did not elaborate. His officers knew he did not want to do so. They needed only to be ready to move as he said. They would see to it.

As the officers departed, General Lee asked General Robertson to remain a moment. When the other officers were gone, Lee told Robertson to get the word to his commander, General Wade Hampton, to avoid becoming engaged tomorrow.

"I think there is a possibility that a large portion of the enemy troops may be in place between Monocacy and Washington, " Lee said. "If troops are coming from Washington or Baltimore, the enemy to our front may swing north and then come down to join them. If this occurs, the area will be thick with enemy cavalry and troops on the move. They can be coming and going from any of several directions. I don't want General Hampton to get caught or get engaged where we cannot help him."

133

General Robertson was listening carefully as Lee continued, "Our Army may pull out and move south if the situation requires it. Then I would need General Hampton to screen and provide rear guard for us. This means he must, I repeat, *must* keep in contact with my headquarters on a regular basis and not get too far removed so that he cannot respond to this plan. You understand me, General?"

"Yes Sir, I understand."

As they walked out into the night, Lee added, "If we do move south, we will have to have cavalry to keep us informed. This will be vital. General Hampton will understand what we need when you tell him to be prepared for the Army to move south on order. The key here is communication. He must keep his elements in contact with me on a regular basis. You must convey that to him."

"Yes Sir, I will, and I will personally see to it that we stay in contact with you," said General Robertson.

"Excellent, General," Lee responded. Please give my regards to General Hampton." With that, Robertson came to attention, saluted and departed.

General Lee looked up at the stars. The skies had partially cleared and it had become a rather cool night. Suddenly he was very, very tired. He wanted to rest, but before he did, he decided to walk over to check on JEB Stuart. He prayed for his young officer and his friend as he walked. God's will would be done.

General Meade was not looking at stars this evening. He was watching the courier ride off toward the telegraph to send the message to Washington telling of the hard day the Army of the Potomac had experienced. He knew the lamps would be burning all night in the War Department and would likely continue to burn in the White House long after his dispatch arrived. The news was not good. Two of the Seven Corps he commanded had been mauled. His reserves had been scattered. The enemy was still entrenched solidly, prepared to continue the fight. Lights from the hospital set up in the town hall and the stable area were shining brightly, as the hundreds of wounded were being treated. Shadows and moans of pain made the night an eerie scene. It was always like this after a big battle. He lighted a cigar to have a smoke before his commanders assembled to discuss the day's battle and plan tomorrow's actions.

General John Newton dismounted in front of the small hotel in Frederick City that was now George Meade's Headquarters. He saw General John Gibbon and General John Caldwell from II Corps approaching the hotel. Generals Sykes, Sedgwick, Howard and Slocum would soon be there as well. The officers each saluted and spoke cordially as they arrived, but each man was subdued in tone and manner. Only General Sedgwick seemed to be past the events of the day. He even acted mildly pleased.

"Gentlemen, join me if you would," said Meade as he turned and headed into the hotel toward the parlor now turned war room. Guards at the door and in the alley outside the windows provided some security from prying eyes and ears. After bidding the officers to be seated, General Meade began, " Today was not exactly a banner day for our Army. Coming off a hard march, we went into a fight almost in column and paid a high price for it. I take full responsibility for this. Your units performed as well as any commander could expect under the circumstances. Some units were remarkable in their gallant efforts today. I will be recommending these units, their officers and their men for decorations." He looked at John Gibbon. "You had several units that were particularly valiant at the fight for the bridge today, General. New York units I believe?"

General Gibbon replied, "Yes Sir, the 69th, 63d and 88th New York were at that bridge."

"Who is the Brigade Commander and how bad were their losses," asked Meade.

"Losses appear to be around 50 to 60 percent, Sir." Most everyone grimaced, shook their head or looked down at the floor. "That was Second Brigade of my old Division, the First Division. Colonel Patrick Kelly was the commander today. He didn't make it back."

"Yes…well…" said Meade.

John Sedgwick then spoke quietly as if to try to cheer everyone up, " One thing we did do today, General. We kept Lee from moving on the capital! That was our primary goal. Today's fight accomplished that."

Meade replied before anyone could add or comment. "Well, I doubt if Washington will look at it that way. In any event, we must look to tomorrow. It is obvious to me after today that this is a bad situation we find ourselves in. The Rebels have an excellent position. If they could hold it today the way they did, tomorrow will likely be no better. General Sedgwick is correct about our primary mission. Our mission is to protect Washington *first*, and then to destroy the enemy if possible. We have taken serious losses and I propose to sit out tomorrow to let our troops rest. Then we will reposition the Army between the Rebels and Washington. If he wants to attack, it will be on our terms and the ground of our choosing. If he moves away to the south, we may get another crack at him. Comments, gentlemen."

The generals all looked surprised. Sedgwick spoke first. "Sir, I respectfully disagree with holding and then withdrawing our Army."

Meade replied, "Its not a withdrawal, General, its a reposition. We are going to reposition the Army."

"Yes Sir,... reposition. I would recommend that we attack again while we have Lee's army before us, only this time we attack his flank. I have looked at the enemy positions and I feel we could likely hit him on his left with a diversionary attack. This would hold their troops in place while the main attack comes down on his right from the north. Our troops could cross the river up north without a fight and would be in a place to hit him where it would be hard for him to reinforce. The diversionary attack would again hold needed troops from moving to reinforce his right. May I add, it would also put the bulk of our force between the Rebels and Washington. Sir, I think this would have a great chance of success,"

Meade hardly moved as he stood with his arms folded. "Comments?"

General Slocum spoke next. "Sir, I think what General Sedgwick says has merit. We have Lee here outside of Virginia. If we can hurt him enough so that he can not fight us, but he cannot run either, then he might be forced to surrender!" Meade noted that some of his officers were seriously considering this. However it was obvious that others did not buy into it either.

General Meade spoke, "What General Sedgwick says does indeed have merit, but we must consider several issues here. First, we have taken heavy losses in the past few days. I Corps and II Corps have reduced effectiveness,. III Corps also has taken serious losses. Our reserves are, for all purposes, lost to us. We are still superior in numbers, but on that ground that Lee has, a two to one advantage is woefully insufficient. We simply cannot bring our numbers to bear at any point to guarantee success. The northern flank does look like the best chance. I also looked at it as an option." He continued, " But, if we attack as proposed, then we, too, are separated without an option to reinforce or support the other attack. While Lee could not easily move troops, we could do little better, as we would now have the river between us. Lastly, consider this, if the northern attack were to fail, the Confederates could sweep down from their positions. *If they did, they could roll us up,*. The road to Washington would be wide open!"

"I might add I, also, considered the enemy's left as an option to attack. Again, the river stands in our way. Plus, this puts us on the southern side of the Rebels, giving them an option to rush Washington while we struggle to cross the river under fire to give pursuit. No, we cannot let him get between us and the capital."

"Of course, the other option open to us, is more of the same as we tried today. But I refuse to ask that of you and your troops. Based on these considerations, gentlemen, unless someone has another proposal to discuss, we will go with my original plan. We hold for a day, then reposition the Army." The assembled officers were strangely quiet.

"The Rebels are likely looking for us to continue the attack tomorrow. We should give an appearance of preparing an attack, but stay close. We will rest the troops, and move day after tomorrow. I will contact Washington and tell them of our plans and see if replacements are available. If so, I will have them move to join us. We will meet tomorrow morning to work out details. Any more questions?" There were none, or at least none that were voiced.

The Battle of Monocacy was over. The Army of the Potomac would take heart in that it had kept the Rebel Army from moving on Washington. They would call it a victory despite its grievous losses. The Confederates would also claim victory. Even though they had not destroyed the Union Army as hoped, there was little doubt that the Confederates had by far gotten the best of the battle. However, in truth, the victory or loss would be determined in the halls of Washington, Richmond and London by men who took no part in it. Such was the way of modern war.

WASHINGTON

President Lincoln read the message from General Meade very carefully. Finally, he spoke, "Its been another disaster! The news is as bad as Fredericksburg." He closed his eyes and slowly shook his head from side to side, "My God...What will the people say?" Members of his cabinet stood silently and listened as Lincoln went over details from the message. "We have taken heavy losses... First and Second Corps have been rendered partially ineffective...The Rebels are just south of Frederick, Maryland in Monocacy. They have strong defensive positions. Although he says they, too, have had serious losses, General Meade feels he cannot dislodge them without further risk to the Army. This could put the capital in jeopardy. He proposes to wait one day and then...," Lincoln was now reading directly from the message, "... reposition the Army back toward Washington on better ground so as to better defend the capital."

"Reposition back? It sounds like a retreat to me," said Secretary Seward. "I don't understand what he means by '...further risk to the Army'.. I thought what the Army did was always a risk! If he would..," President Lincoln cut him off by speaking.

"We must all remember...General Meade has done what he was ordered to do. He was told to protect Washington from Rebel attack and *then*, *if possible*, attack and destroy the enemy. He did what was asked of him in protecting the Capital. He has not been successful in destroying the enemy as of yet. But perhaps he has inflicted heavy losses upon the Rebels and they will more easily be defeated in the next action."

William Seward did not exactly see it that way. "Mr. President, in the last week we have lost the Army's reserves and now most of two Corps. I would suggest that we can hardly accept many more such victories!"

Secretary of the Army Stanton interjected, "Mr. Seward, I think the President is correct in his summation. General Meade was told to protect the capital and he has done so, at least so far. If he can drive the Rebels back into Virginia, I think it would be appropriate to say that the enemy has accomplished little of what he set out to do!"

Seward was clearly agitated, "What he set out to do was to run through our territory at will and defeat our Army in the process. It appears he has done just that! I seriously doubt that the European powers will consider this last battle a great victory for the Union!"

Lincoln spoke up, "Gentlemen! Of course we all are deeply troubled and disappointed in the events that have taken place at Monocacy. No one feels this more than I, but we must look to the positive side of this battle. We must make from it what we can for our people, our European friends, and for the morale of our Army. We must not sink into a morass of despair. We must also give the Army our full support so that the sacrifice that they made was not made in vain. General Meade has asked for additional help in troops and supplies. That is what we must turn our attention to at this time. We will say to the nation that losses were high, the sacrifice was great, but the nation's capital and its government still stand as a light to the oppressed."

Abraham Lincoln had again made a decision to press forward and to make from the situation what he could for the country. Still he wondered what the people would say. Many, many families would be touched by the losses, and he knew that this could not long continue. The price was becoming a burden the nation could not sustain.

"Mr. Stanton, please send for General U.S. Grant. I would like for him to come to see me as soon as practical. I think he may be the man for the task ahead." Sam Grant was about to become the new Commanding General of the U.S. Army.

RICHMOND

It was late in the evening and President Davis was meeting with several of his cabinet members when one of his military aides, Colonel Ayers, came into the room in a great hurry. Obviously in an excited state, he could hardly contain the smiles as he gave the message to President Davis. "Sir, this just arrived for you by courier from General Lee no more than a few minutes ago."

From the excitement of his aide, Davis could tell it was important news, but he was not sure if it was good or bad. As he read it, he quickly felt his sprits raise and then soar! "Excellent news, gentlemen! General Lee tells me that the Army of Northern Virginia has given our country a great victory!" Everyone smiled and commented with thanks and excitement as well as no small amount of relief that the news was not bad. "General Lee says the Army has fought a major battle near Monocacy, Maryland, and has inflicted grievous losses upon the enemy with only moderate losses to our Army. He estimates the better parts of three Union Corps have suffered heavy losses and are now ineffective. In addition to this, the Federal Reserve at Frederick has been almost destroyed and scattered!"

"By God, that's cutting them down to size!" exclaimed Secretary of War Seddon. Everyone was exuberant at the good news being read to them.

Davis continued, "General Lee says the Army's morale is high. The present positions are excellent, and the prospect for a still greater victory are high, should the enemy decide to give battle tomorrow! He says he expects that the enemy may decide to withdraw toward Washington to defend the capital, and if so, our Army will likely return into Virginia."

Davis looked up and was smiling very confidently. "Well, gentlemen, this certainly is good news, good news indeed! It appears our Army has struck a mighty blow for freedom, and the Lord willing, the Army may strike an even greater blow tomorrow!"

Judiah Benjamin was particularly excited. It was obvious he

was thinking of more than just this one item of good news! "Mr. President, this gives us an exceptional opportunity! If we would now act upon the proposals made in our recent meeting concerning a schedule to eliminate slavery and make cotton available to the English merchants, we would...."

Jefferson Davis interrupted, "You mean your proposal to free the slaves and give cotton to the British?"

Benjamin replied, "Yes Sir. This victory is simply made to order to promote these actions! It will have the greatest possible effect when ..."

"It may be that we don't have to make such a concession after such a victory, Mr. Secretary. I think it would be well to wait and see what develops from this. After all, our Army has been victorious thus far, and it may well be even more victorious in the next few days to come. Europe may see that we are winning our independence and the time is right to recognize the Confederacy." Looking at the other members of his cabinet, he posed the question, "Would you gentlemen not agree?"

Vice President Alexander Stephens was not present as usual, so his strong opinion was not voiced. Steven Mallory had agreed strongly with Stephens and now he voiced his opinion, "I very much agree, Mr. President. I had my doubts how we as a government could ever convince the states of this Confederacy to sign into such an agreement. Like the Vice President, I too was not in favor of such a move and I fully agree with your present conclusion.

"Mr. President...Gentlemen. If I may...." Secretary Benjamin rose to address the assembled leaders and received a nod from Jefferson Davis. "You all know that I, too, believe completely in what we are fighting for, and that is the right to make our own decisions and choices in accordance with established law. But, gentlemen, we must understand that this belief in principle of law will not give us the victory in and of itself! From the time our nation was formed, we have had to make a great many decisions based on what Lincoln, Washington, or the Federal Army forced upon us. In short, we responded to circumstances in which we had little control and usually no input. They have been the aggressors in our land. They have been the ones who set forth decrees to the world and presented initiatives that worked against us. Now, we have an opportunity to strike a bold stroke against our enemy *first*! We can do this by taking from them the one cause they are trying to use to rally the world against us! We can negotiate an end to slavery, rather than having it used against us and maybe even eventually *taken* from us. We can have slavery end on our terms, when the change can be absorbed by our people. In doing so, we will say to the world we have fought for our rights. We have paid the price for freedom. We deserve our independence and a place among nations of the world!"

"I am convinced that England would want to stand with us if we were to agree to eliminate, *in time*, the one obstacle to their recognition of the Confederacy. This will, indeed, be viewed as a concession by the Europeans, and so be it! It will work for us far beyond any other action we could take. Washington will be unable to do *anything* to counter it! Add to this, the offer of almost free cotton to a cotton hungry nation like England, top that off with a great military victory in the field, and our position will be the strongest it has been since the Confederacy was formed in Montgomery!

Benjamin continued in a very serious tone, ""Make no mistake, gentlemen, we are far from winning this war! This victory that General Lee and our great Army has wrought was done with *moderate* losses. However *moderate* this might be, these are losses we are having an increasingly difficult time replacing. This victory today can easily be replaced with a reversal tomorrow. This could come not due to any failure on the part of our exceptional officers and our magnificent Army, but simply due to the enemy's overpowering numbers and inexhaustible flow of the supplies of war. I submit, Mr. President, we can win every battle and still lose the war! We should not let this perfect opportunity slip away, for if we do and then we later try to offer these concessions when we are forced to do so, they may be viewed as being too little, too late. Gentlemen, I urge you to at least consider and discuss the

143

options we have discussed. The time is right! We, the elected government, have a great opportunity to follow General Lee's victory with an even greater victory and win this war!"

The room was still. Everyone was looking to President Davis. He finally responded, "Your argument is strong and persuasive, Mr. Benjamin. I must tell you that from my heart, I am firm in my belief as to the rights of the individual states to make these decisions rather than for the central government to do so. I also know that what you say has great truth. We must take action to move toward victory and not solely depend on the military victories of our Army or the weariness of the Northern people to end this war. Still, what you propose is very difficult. You are proposing we yield a right that we felt so strongly about in 1860 that we left the Union rather than give it up! "

Secretary Benjamin responded, "No Sir, not really. I am proposing that our government negotiate a policy change on behalf of *all* its states. What the Northern controlled government did to us for years was work to change policy to suit the Northern and Western states fully at the expense of the Southern states. I think I can say that as Southerners, we will never have an issue dictated to us by *others*. But as Southerners, we are likewise free to negotiate the same issue if it be the will of *our* people. Therein lies the strength of our Independence!

Once more Jefferson Davis responded, "I again say, Mr. Benjamin, you make a strong case of your point. This much I know, this issue is serious enough that it must have immediate resolution. We will indeed discuss this and come to a decision. If we are to act, we must do so quickly. To fail to do so will be an act itself, so let us continue this discussion." The discussion did, indeed, continue. Passions flamed. Then reason prevailed, and then the cycle repeated itself. It would be a long night.

LONDON

The British Foreign Secretary, Lord John Russell, entered the room where Prime Minister Palmerston was seated, deeply engrossed in the papers on his desk. It was a gray, overcast day and the rain was falling slowly, but steadily.

The PM looked up and over the small glasses on the tip of his nose he smiled, "Good Morning, John, and how are you this beautiful English morning?"

"Very well, Sir. I was about to leave for a ceremony at Portsmouth this morning when this dispatch arrived. I thought it best to bring it you immediately. It's from Lyons in Washington."

"You look serious. I trust the United States has not fired on us again?" He motioned for Lord Russell to be seated.

Slightly smiling, Russell replied, "No, but it seems the Northern government does have other problems." He handed the message to the PM who leaned back slowly in his chair to read the long message.

Upon finishing it, the Prime Minister removed his spectacles and asked, "How serious do you think this is?"

"Well, there were numerous dispatches that accompanied this one, but this sums up the situation best. According to Lord Lyons, the Federals have had a serious loss in Maryland just west of Washington. As you will note, Lyons says the Northern government is claiming victory in the defense of its capital, but he says it does not appear that this was the case. Our observer with General Lee's Army, Colonel Fremantle, has gotten word to Lyons that the Confederates destroyed two, perhaps three entire Federal Corps with only light to moderate losses for the effort. The Confederates circled the Northern army and attacked their reserves, destroying these first. Then they pulled the Union forces into a fight and thrashed them rather handily. After the action, the Federal Army withdrew back near Washington in what appeared to be an effort to protect the capital."

"The Confederates did not move to attack?," asked Palmerston.

145

Russell replied, "No, they moved back into Virginia. They either decided against the attack or…"

"Or perhaps they never had in mind to attack the Northern capitol in the first place," finished the Prime Minister.

"In any event, it looks like another strong victory for the Southern government. Very much like the affair at Fredericksburg where the Federals were seriously pummeled," said Russell.

"Well, if the Confederates hoped to continue the fight, they needed a victory after that fight near Sharpsburg, Maryland. It appears they have gained the needed victory and have given Mr. Lincoln another set back." Palmerston paused, "This might be more of a set back than they know." He was now looking at the papers on his desk. Then looking up, he said, "I meet with Her Majesty this afternoon to discuss the situation caused by the American warship firing on our merchant ship. The Queen is, to put it mildly, *livid*. This news from Maryland may well have a bearing on what the government does in response to the situation. Following my meeting with the Queen, I have called for a meeting tomorrow morning with Lord Herbert, the Duke of Sommerset and Admiral Milne. I would like to have you join us. Incidentally, I believe you know Admiral Milne, don't you?"

"Yes, he commanded the ship that took me to Egypt on my first posting to the embassy there. We became good friends down through the years, but I am surprised he is home. I would have thought him at sea. He still commands the Atlantic Squadron does he not?," asked Lord Russell.

"Yes, that's precisely why he is coming to the meeting tomorrow. He was in port getting new armament for the last of his battleships. He came to London to discuss the American situation. When I found out he was in the city, I called for him to join us. It is fortuitous that he is here."

"Meeting with the Secretary for War, First Lord of the Admiralty, and the Commander of the Atlantic Squadron… I would say the situation sounds foreboding," said Russell.

Palmerston replied, "As I said, Her Majesty is … well… upset. She was quite put out when that Northern warship stopped the *TRENT* at sea to remove civilian passengers. We avoided a conflict at that time because everyone on both sides worked hard at resolving the problem. This time, I'm not sure that will be enough. British subjects have been killed and that won't be resolved with a diplomatic note. I must tell you in all honesty, John, I don't have a good feeling about this situation. Have you received anything new from the Americans on this?"

"No, nothing new," said Russell. "Lyons said that Secretary of State Seward has been kind, attentive and friendly to him beyond anything he has seen since arriving in the American capital. It seems obvious that the American government is trying to gain some friendly points to help them in this situation. "

"Yet, they do this without so much as a slap on the wrist to their naval officer who acted so irresponsibility! Well, I think they will find that it will take more than a smile and dinner party to resolve the matter this time!" Lord Palmerston was clearly agitated. "Anything from the American Minister?"

Russell responded, "I met with Mr. Adams two days ago. He continues to express the regret of the U.S. government, but not much beyond that. He is waiting for instructions from Washington. I tend to think the Americans are waiting for us to respond to what has happened, so they can know how to reply. Considering you have a meeting with Her Majesty today, it appears he may not have long to wait."

"Quite so," replied the Prime Minister.

The remainder of the day passed with a noticeable flurry of activity at the Admiralty. Clerks and couriers moved up and down the halls carrying reports, lists, documents and manifests to the offices of the men that were to attend the Prime Minister's meeting. The lamps burned late into the evening.

Wednesday was a much improved day. The sun was shinning and it was looking to be a beautiful day in London as Prime Minister Palmerston called the meeting to order from the head of the table. Lord Russell sat at the Palmerston's right with Lord Herbert next to him. The Duke of Sommerset and Admiral Milne sat on the Prime Minister's left. The secretaries for the

Prime Minister and the First Lord of the Admiralty sat to the side to record meeting notes as necessary. After a brief thanks to all concerned for their attendance and a courtesy introduction of Admiral Milne, Lord Palmerston began to address the substance of the meeting.

"We have a most serious situation before us today. For the past two and one half years, we have tried, with the utmost diplomacy and tact, to avoid becoming entangled in the American Civil War. This conflict has raged beyond anything that most of us expected and now, due to American miscalculations and brashness, the war threatens to involve us as well." He continued, "I have asked the Duke of Sommerset to summarize the recent naval events involving a North American warship firing upon the unarmed English merchant ship MOUNT BLANC. Lord Sommerset?.. Please."

The First Lord of the Admiralty began slowly and clearly explaining the events that led to the firing upon the MOUNT BLANC and the resulting death of the men aboard the ship. While each of the men in the meeting knew of the situation, the agitation created by the realization that an English ship had been "attacked" and Englishmen had been killed, was clearly visible. Even so, these men were all professionals and not a word was voiced until the Duke of Sommerset concluded his comments.

Immediately, Palmerston continued by asking Lord Russell to give a summary of diplomatic exchanges and actions to date as pertained to this event. This, Lord Russell did in a very logical order, explaining the sequence of messages, consultations, and responses. He also included the 'unofficial' expression of regret conveyed to the English government by Confederate Commissioner Mason on behalf of the Southern government. He then added his perception of their unexpressed, but certainly heartfelt delight at the North American's blunder in this whole matter. Russell said that it was his observation that the North Americans, indeed, seemed to be seeking a way out of this situation. He also noted that the interest in a speedy resolution to this situation appeared due more to a need to get back to their war, than it did due to a sincere regret over the affront to England. He ended by saying that diplomatic efforts were ongoing even as they met today.

After Lord Russell concluded his summation, the room was quiet for moment. Prime Minister Palmerston seemed to be weighing his words almost as if he did not want to say more.

Finally, he spoke, "Gentleman, I met with Her Majesty this past afternoon for a considerable period of time. Her Majesty is deeply distressed that this matter before us has developed. She had hoped the war in North America would pass us by with our not having to choose sides to directly support. The Northern government has made it clear that if we decide to openly support the South in its bid for independence, the North would consider this an act of war. Even if they did not respond by going to war, British-American relations would be greatly damaged for the foreseeable future. On the other hand, if we were to openly support the North in this war and the South were able to sustain its claim to independence, England would have deeply alienated a major trading partner and potential ally in North America. As you know, neutrality has been England's course, and we have sailed it well in these dangerous waters until now."

"The recent events upon which you have just been briefed, namely the *second* incident at sea now resulting in the death of English subjects and the seemingly indifferent attitude by the Northern government have forced Her Majesty to reevaluate our strict neutrality in this matter. Add to this the just reported major Southern victory very near the Northern capitol, and we see that an overall Confederate victory is still very possible, if not likely." Lord Palmerston again paused, as he knew the serious impact his words were about to set in motion for England. "Her Majesty has instructed me to ask Parliament to immediately withdraw our proclamation of neutrality and to consider recognizing the Confederate States government as a new, independent nation with all the rights pertaining to such status." The men at the table were looking at each other as eyebrows raised and deep breaths were drawn. They understood well that this meant war with the United States was now very likely.

Palmerston continued, "Her Majesty has specifically instructed me to work diligently to help us avoid a direct conflict with the United States if at all possible. She feels that a strong attitude and resolve will demonstrate to the Northern government that England will protect Her rights and subjects as necessary. In short, if England's neutrality at sea is not respected, then England will choose another course. The Royal Navy will protect Her Majesty's subjects and interests, and will respond appropriately when necessary. "

"It is Her Majesty's wish that every effort be made on the political level to explain to the Americans that we do not wish war with them. If they will respect British rights, we will conduct business and relations with them as with other nations. So far, they have treated the sea's of the world as a merely a place to wage their war as they see fit. They act as if anyone who ventures to cross their path is subject to whatever action they deem appropriate. I need not tell you that England will not be dealt with in this manner!" Palmerston was obviously becoming more passionate as he spoke, "The American's penchant for unruly and rascally behavior has led them to this. We will now deal with the Northern government in a manner befitting their attitude toward us. Likewise we will deal with the Southern government in a manner befitting *their* attitude toward us. When the war between these two peoples ends, then we will deal with the government or *governments* as may exist at that time. However," he now spoke very slowly emphasizing his words, "If war is made on England, then England will go to war without hesitation or reservation."

The room was quiet as the men absorbed the full impact of the unfolding events. They were men of high position and great responsibility, but each was after all, still a man with all the fears and concerns that comes to men who know what war is really about. Lord Palmerston had made the Royal position clear, now it only remained to see if Parliament would follow Queen Victoria's wishes and recognize the Confederate States.

Palmerston again began speaking, "We will work as hard as possible to avoid war. We must hope for the best, but we must prepare for the worse. To this end, we must immediately begin to prepare for conflict at sea and on the North American continent. Lord Herbert, I would like for you to begin to formulate plans for strengthening naval forces in the Atlantic and Gulf of Mexico regions as the Admiralty deems necessary. Plan for the transport and protection of our Armies to Canada. We must arrange for such transport as will be required. Logistics planning, equipment, weapons and munitions factory openings should be set in motion. We will not wait to initiate these efforts, but we will begin *now.* Please formulate a battle plan for naval and land forces. I would suggest that you consider land actions only on a limited basis, at least for now.

Lord Herbert raised the first question, "Minister, are we to assume the Southern forces, particularly their armies, will be an ally to us?"

"That remains to be seen," replied Palmerston. "We are not looking to gain an ally in a fight. We don't want to fight if we can avoid it, but I will answer you this way. What we immediately need is a concept of operations and force structure. Consider a plan concept both with and without Confederate forces. This will give us a view of the situation either way it might develop. In reality, if the North decides to make war on us, the Southern government would surely become our ally since they are already at war with the North." Herbert nodded in agreement as his secretary continued making notes on the points being discussed.

Palmerston now looked to Lord Russell. "I will need to go to Parliament this afternoon, and I want to meet with the leadership prior to my addressing the assembled Houses. Following my address, I will need to see the American minister. I would like you present. If all appears to go well at Parliament, I will then formally receive the Confederate *Commissioner.* Assuming Parliament will follow through on the Queen's wishes, we will confer Minister status to Mr. Mason and provide him with an appointment with Her Majesty so he may present his credentials. We need not rush the appointment with the Queen, as I hope to bring a concession or two to Her Majesty when she receives the new Minister. Lord Russell, you will also need to meet with the French ambassador and brief him on what we are doing. I would expect France to quickly follow our recognition of the Southern government since they have been favorable to the idea for some time, but get a reaction from him. If he hesitates, you must press him. We need immediate French recognition of the Confederate States to strengthen our position in avoiding war. I'm sure Commissioner Mason here in London will quickly be in contact with the Confederate Commissioner in Paris. What is his name? Simmons…? Sable…?"

Russell replied, "Slidell, Sir."

"Ah yes, Slidell! The Frenchman from Louisiana!"

"Gentlemen, it may appear that we are moving quickly in this matter without regard to American opinions or comments. Let me be very clear - this is exactly what we are doing! We will extend recognition to the Confederate government as soon as we can work out the timing and make it as advantageous to us as possible. Meanwhile, we will prepare for war praying that war does not come, and we will inform the Americans about *what* we doing, *as* we do it. We will not ask, nor consult, with the American government in this matter. Their reaction will be limited to just that, a reaction. The Northern government lost their options with Her Majesty through their repeated irresponsible actions."

The Prime Minister leaned forward on the table. "Well! This has been a full day so far, and it is not yet noon. I know you probably have questions, so let us discuss those questions that pertains to all of us and then we can dismiss to allow each of us to look to our tasks.   There is much to be done. If you have specific questions of me, I will remain for a few minutes for your pleasure." He looked around and Lord Herbert of the Admiralty began by asking several questions as to time tables, transfers of naval assets in relation to ports of the Empire and treatment of Confederate vessels.   After some discussion, questions moved on to Napoleon III and expectations of French reactions and possible cooperation. It was generally assumed that France would see this as the perfect opportunity to tighten its hold on Mexico and reestablish a strong French presence in North America. Questions and comments continued for some minutes with Lord Palmerston finally standing to excuse himself.

"Gentleman, I must leave you and get to my office so I may prepare to address Parliament. Please feel free to continue your discussions as you deem necessary." He looked around the table and then said, "We have much to do. We must do it well for England." With that, he turned and left the room, being followed by his secretary and assistant.

Lord Herbert and Admiral Milne were the next to leave as they adjourned to the Admiralty to continue detail discussions and planning. The meeting room was soon empty. Now all the offices began buzzing with actions and a mood of excitement at the events became evident.

THE CONFEDERATE COMMISSIONER

Commissioner Mason was precisely on schedule for his appointment with the Prime Minister. Upon arriving, he was ushered directly into the PM's office. At the best of times, James Mason looked somewhat serious. His high forehead was accented by his somewhat long graying hair on the back of his head. He was dressed in a smart dark suit with the vest, watch chain, cane and high top hat of the day. He carried a small portfolio with his official papers of introduction and authorization from the Confederate government. Although Mason seldom smiled much, this day he looked outright pleased as he entered the Prime Minister's office. There he was announced, then greeted by Foreign Secretary Russell and Prime Minister Palmerston. As the men were seated, there was very little small talk although pleasantries were exchanged.

Palmerston then came right to the point, " Mr. Mason, in an effort to maintain a strict neutral position in the matter of the war between the Northern government and your government..." Mason was thrilled at the reference to the term *"your government"* being used for the first time. It was a tacit recognition that the Confederacy was in fact, a *legitimate government!* He sat listening and trying not to show his pleasure in this meeting as Palmerston continued, "...Her Majesty's government has felt it not in England's best interest to recognize the Confederate States beyond that of a *belligerent* party. You are aware that for us to go beyond this is to practically invite war with the United States. It appeared to be a risk in which England had very much to lose, and very little to gain. We think, perhaps, this situation may now be changing."

Mason was clearly pleased as he smiled in approval of what he was hearing. Still he did not speak.

Palmerston continued, "You no doubt have heard of my meeting with the Queen followed by my visit to Parliament. You have surely surmised that these are the reasons for which I asked you to come here today. Am I correct?"

"Yes sir, I am aware of the general subject of your address

to Parliament. May I say my government deeply appreciates what Her Majesty has proposed through your eloquent presentation."

Palmerston nodded politely in response to Mason's thanks, then continued in a serious vein. "Sir, these are very perilous times for us all. Your people are at war for their existence. My country is trying to avoid a war that can only bring heartache and sadness to our people. May I speak candidly with you without offense being taken?"

Mason was surprised by Lord Palmerston's frankness, but he quickly replied, "By all means Mr. Prime Minister, please..." Mason's demeanor was kind and open as he felt the Prime Minister's concern in addressing these issues.

"Sir, we in England wish the South no ill will. In fact, we wish you only peace and prosperity. We are deeply distressed at the suffering you are experiencing for what you consider the rights of the Southern states. Please understand that we are also saddened by the suffering and pain of your Northern neighbors whom you only short time ago called brother. War is a terrible enterprise with pain and grief its only attributes. For that very reason, we have tried desperately to maintain a position that would not antagonize either peoples. However, our good intentions have repeatedly been dashed to a point that make strict neutrality impossible, and may I add this was not by our hand? You are aware, Sir, of the recent deaths of English subjects at the hands of the American Navy?"

"I am, Sir. A most regrettable and unforgivable incident from what we know of it, and one I know only too well from first hand experience, " replied Commissioner Mason referring to the *Trent Affair* in which *he* was personally involved. Actually, Mason was thankful for this recent incident. It could only aid the Southern cause. In fact, he thought it might just be God's answer to Southern prayer.

"This last incident has caused Her Majesty to decide that *strict* neutrality is a course Great Britain can no longer maintain. To this end, we will be taking steps to curtail American interference with English shipping. Such steps could have great impact on your country, Mr. Mason. It is Her Majesty's intention to treat *both* the North and the South as *separate and equal nations* in our dealings for commerce and trade. At the request of the Queen, diplomatic recognition by England to the world of your nation is now being *considered* by Parliament"

Mason was aware that he had obtained much without having to even ask, but the greatest prize of all, full *diplomatic recognition*, was still not quite in hand. His political savvy now smelled a deal in the works. He was closer than ever. The question was what did Palmerston want? He decided to let the Prime Minster keep the lead. He would not address or offer any comment until he got Palmerston to come out and say what was wanted.

"Mr. Mason, now comes the difficult part... the part for which I asked your indulgence and for you not to take as offensive."

Mason responded quickly, "But of course, Sir."

Palmerston was now firm, but kind. Plain, but not condescending. "You know that human slavery has been opposed world-wide by England. Our nation has taken the lead in trying to have slavery eliminated from the civilized nations of the world. I must tell you that in the case of the Southern states, it has been *the* major issue prohibiting a serious consideration of recognition for the Confederacy. At this very moment, when so many in Parliament are upset with the United States and would gladly give recognition to your county to bring it into the family of nations, the issue of slavery is again creating a stumbling block for you." Palmerston paused for a reply.

Commissioner Mason was somewhat more stern in his appearance at this mention of slavery. He was a staunch supporter of the *particular institution*. He had no hesitation in defending both slavery and the Confederacy's right to maintain the institution until *the states* decided not to do so.

He calmly replied, "Mr. Prime Minister, it is true that our governments disagree on this subject, and while I could do so, there would be little purpose to our debating the issue. I, personally, am one who supports slavery as both a legal and justifiable institution. However, even if I did not feel this way, this is the position of my country and it is something beyond my authority to negotiate."

"You noted that my country is fighting for its life right now, but please understand. The Southern states did *not* engage in this war over the issue of slavery as an institution, because *the then* Constitution of the United States did in fact permit slavery to exist. When it became obvious that a coalition of Northern and Western states planned to subjugate the Southern states by changing the constitution on this subject in particular, thirteen Southern states exercised their right to leave the Union. They did so by legal secession, also permitted by *our then* Constitution. It was at this time, the tyrant Mr. Lincoln decided to make war on us. If he would leave us in peace, the war would end tomorrow! Sir, the *issue* that brought us to war was *not* slavery, but it was the *right* of a state to decide how it will deal with slavery or any other issue not expressly addressed by the U.S. Constitution. In the South, we call this States Rights. While slavery is an unacceptable institution to some, this opinion can not be *forced* on any state to accept. May I also point out, Sir, that while the Confederate States Constitution *bans international slave trading*; the United States Constitution *does not.*"

"One last point, Mr. Prime Minister. The elimination of slavery in the British Empire had very little effect on Britain. Your economy is not built upon it, and does not depend on it. The Southern agricultural economy, however, does. Our economy would quickly collapse without this institution to support it. It would be suicide to eliminate it in one fell stroke." Mason tried to not sound over passionate, while being clear about what he could and could not do as a Confederate representative. " In any event, if you are suggesting that elimination or modification of this institution is a requirement for recognition, I must say my government would surely be forced to remain independent. We would continue to stand alone against the aggression of the United States, an aggression your country is now experiencing first hand." Mason had basically drawn a line in the sand and told the Prime Minister of England this could not be crossed. He hoped he had not gone too far.

"Mr. Commissioner, I am disappointed that there is no room for negotiation" said Palmerston.

Mason replied, "Again, Sir, I must point out that we are in a war over the *right* to decide such an issue. Perhaps if my government was recognized as an equal nation among nations, there would be an opportunity to discuss such issues." Mason now tried to appeal to the strength and honor of Britain as he brought the conversation back to the issue of recognition.

"Lord Palmerston, your government is magnanimous and gracious in discussing and resolving difficult issues with other countries. However, we both know that England could never be forced or coerced to do this. My country only asks the world for the same right. The right of free men to decide. It is something ingrained in us by our heritage - an English heritage." Palmerston and Russell both smiled at this remark.

"I again suggest that if we were recognized as an equal," Mason constinued, "perhaps we could jointly work for some alternative to this institution. Now Sir, as we noted, we should not debate this issue, yet we almost begun to do so. Let me ask, what I can do to encourage Her Majesty's government to give immediate recognition to the Confederate States?" Masons waited to see what Palmerston would place on the table next.

Lord Palmerston was impressed by the short exchange and Mason's argument, yet there was much to gain for much that was about to be given. "Commissioner Mason, I understand your position and that of your government, but I reiterate, you have everything to gain and we have much to lose. Let us get to the heart of the matter. What concessions can your government offer Her Majesty's government for such high risks that would be assumed if recognition was given?"

The question could not have been stated much more straight forward Mason thought. He liked that.

"Sir, my government knows you have wide spread unemployment and serious financial losses in the manufacturing areas where cotton was once used for a host of manufactured goods. Just as *we* are impacted by the loss of trading with you caused by Northern aggression, your country is suffering at the same hands, with little care for the impact on your nation. If recognition is given *immediately*, my government is prepared to make cotton available to English mills at a cost *far* less than has ever been offered. This pricing would be offered to Great Britain *only*. Such an offer would be guaranteed for a considerable period of time. Fully understanding the position Her Majesty would assume in granting recognition, I am authorized to offer 100,000 bales of cotton to Her Majesty's government *at no cost whatsoever strictly as an expression of the good will* of the people of the Confederacy! This cotton can be sold by your government's representative right from Southern docks and ports to any and all merchants as you see fit, with all funds going to the British treasury. There would be no taxes or costs levied on this cotton. It was thought that this might be helpful to Her Majesty, should the North be foolish enough to press the Royal Navy."

Palmerston showed a perfect poker face. "Your government's offer is very kind, Mr. Mason." He and Mason were silent, one considering the offer and the other waiting to see if more would be required.

Palmerston finally spoke, "You mentioned the Royal Navy. What about access to naval ports for the Royal Navy for refit, supplies, crews, etc.?"

Mason replied, "Full access to selected Southern ports. Of course you understand that we currently have limited capability for refitting naval vessels and for resupply, but we would offer such as we have, with a priority second only to our own naval forces. As for crews, you would be free to solicit *volunteers* if needed." He smiled, "I emphasize that this would be strictly *volunteers*. We too have pressing needs for personnel." Mason had just made it clear that the Confederacy was strapped for manpower. At the same time he reminded the Englishman that the South well remembered the War of 1812 when the *impressment* of American seamen into British naval service had

159

been a key factor in causing that war with England.

Palmerston asked, "And your expectations for this?"

Mason answered directly, "Full diplomatic recognition of the Confederate States of America with all the rights and privileges pertaining to such recognition. England's support and influence toward other European governments to grant us recognition."

"Commissioner Mason, I am prepared to say to you that what you request is very possible, but there remains that previous issue we discussed. That may well stop this from happening. I simply must convey to you the very strong feeling of the Queen and Parliament on this matter. I ask you to officially inform your government that if it is willing to make some concession, some pledge, some movement toward an alternative to this latent obstacle that you now embrace, I can assure you the recognition and support of England. I ask you to please convey this to your President with my personal assurance of support for full recognition should he be able to take this course. Mr. Mason, due to the sensitive nature of this matter, I shall not put this in writing. I leave it to you to convey this information to your government as you deem appropriate. Sir, events are proceeding rapidly. I urge you to do this with all haste possible."

Mason's heart was pounding. He had just heard the offer of recognition and support from the Prime Minister of England! The goal for which he had striven so hard was almost within his grasp, but he would not, he could not give such an assurance on his own considering the conditions. After some additional discussion as to time and procedures, Commissioner Mason took his leave of the Prime Minister and Foreign Secretary. He had much to do.

THE UNITED STATES MINSTER

"Shortly after ten in the morning, the American ambassador arrived in the office of the Foreign Secretary. He knew he was about to hear bad news. The word had spread about the Prime Minister's address to Parliament and the subsequent discussions and exchanges that were made by that body.

"Good morning, Minister Adams" said Russell.

"Good morning, Lord Russell." The air was thick with expectation and the tension was evident on the part of the American minister.

"Minister Adams, thank you for coming on such short notice." Russell motioned for Adams to be seated and then he paused, "Sir, you are no doubt aware of the recent visit of the Prime Minister to Parliament in which recognition of the Southern states was discussed."

"Yes Sir, I am. I trust it will remain only discussions without serious consideration," replied Adams.

Lord Russell was very serious in his demeanor as looked directly at Adams. "Well, I am afraid it has gone beyond that point. I have just been notified that Parliament has agreed to extend recognition to the Confederate States government *provided* they meet certain conditions. The announcement will be made public later today. Before this was done I wanted an opportunity to speak with you."

"Lord Russell, *Please...* I urge the British government to reconsider such a step," Adams requested. I have made it explicitly clear that my government has said it will regard such recognition of the insurrectionist Rebel states as a declaration of war against the American people. Sir, I *must stress* the need for reconsideration here. The finality of an announcement and its consequences are unthinkable for both of our nations."

Russell replied without hesitation. "I, like you, am placed in a difficult position. We must follow the orders of our government without question. In my case, I fear the decision of Her Majesty's government is irrevocable. Please understand, however, that this does not *have to mean war* between our countries. We simply must do all we can to try to avoid blindly rushing into a war neither of us wants! I must say to you in all honesty and candor, the events at sea first over the *Trent* situation, and then over the *Mount Blanc* situation, have convinced many people in this country that the United States is little more than a loose cannon on the high seas. However, I personally don't believe that. Mistakes have been made...serious mistakes, but we must both try to work through them."

"Lord Secretary, my country has repeatedly expressed its profound regret at these incidents, even though we feel the latter incident was not all our fault that it occurred. You must know that we, too, want desperately to work through this difficult matter. England is about to take the major step we begged you not to take namely, extending recognition to Rebels who seek to dismantle the U.S. government! Surely, there must be an option other than this!"

Russell responded calmly, but directly. "Mr. Adams, the United States has indeed apologized. It apologized for the *Trent* incident, but now its happened again, only this time was an incident in which English subjects, *unarmed* English subjects, were killed by actions of your navy. To date, no action has been taken against the responsible officers, no plan was proposed or discussed with us as to how you would guarantee such incidents would be avoided in the future, but rather the attitude appears to be that a simple apology from the United States is sufficient. It was almost as if to say, 'sorry, such are the fortunes of war'!"

"Lord Russell, surely you know we do not feel that way toward Britain!" Adams was almost pleading as if to make a point. "We truly regret these situations. I can not believe a nation who supports the abolishment of human slavery just as we do, would seriously consider joining in the cause that would perpetuate it! England's efforts to eliminate slavery have been those of a leader of free nations, determined to eliminate this abominable practice from the face of the earth. Sir, how can England turn its back on this cause?"

This approach somewhat agitated the Foreign Secretary who

thought it rather presumptuous of a country that showed such little *finesse* in its international affairs, as to question the motives of Great Britain. However, Russell was a diplomat and keeping his temper and control was a mainstay of his profession. It was something at which he was very good.

"I must say Mr. Adams, it is the United States that seems to have trouble controlling its naval officers on the high seas. You should not expect the nations of the world to be too understanding when the very basic requirements to operate at sea in peace or war are repeatedly ignored." Adams opened his mouth to speak, but Russell raised his hand ever so slightly as if to ask for an opportunity to finish his statement.

"As for the issue of slavery, you are correct. England *is* the leader of the world in working to eliminate this practice across the world. We were, Sir, the leader in this fight long before the United States ever decided to deal with the issue." "If I may be straightforward in this matter. Your government, in trying to deal with this difficult issue just for your own country, has found itself embroiled in a war that has split your nation asunder. We have managed to achieve considerable results without going to war."

Now, having made several stinging points with the American minister, Russell continued. "President Lincoln has made little secret that he favors releasing the slaves from their bondage. From our vantage point we observe that the Southern states are totally dependent on the institution slavery. Had some plan been devised to allow the Southern states to find a workable option or alternative to slavery, perhaps the terrible war in which your nation now fights could have been avoided?"

Adams shook his head negatively, "Sir, you do not know the Southern mindset. They like slavery, they promote it, they relish in the idea of owning men, women and children as one would livestock. No, we tried talking. The South would have none of it!"

"Perhaps so, Mr. Adams. Perhaps this terrible war has changed their attitude, or perhaps a different approach has found favor. In any event, I am at liberty to tell you that Great Britain

163

has apparently done what your government has been unable to do through the force of arms. Her Majesty's government discussed the matter of slavery with representatives of the Southern government, and they have expressed a willingness to make just such an agreement as we are discussing. They are willing to agree to work toward the elimination of slavery in the Confederate States."

Adams was stunned. He felt his face began to flush as he sought to control his expression, while at the same time he tried to come up with some reply to this staggering news he had just been told. "Lord Russell, you say the Rebels expressed a willingness to make an agreement. You must remember - these men are traitors to the government of their birth, Sir. I submit that a *willingness* to discuss slavery and the *abolition* of slavery are two very different things. I can not believe they would do this no matter what they promised you. It is clear to me that *recognition* for their evil society is what they seek, and they will say or do anything to get it!"

"I understand this issue before us is a very emotional issue, Mr. Adams. I understand your reluctance to outright acceptance of what I have told you. But you call these men traitors. Could it be that perhaps the need for an immediate and uncompromising answer to the issue of slavery is what brought your nation to Civil War? I must tell you that your Southern neighbors see themselves in relation to you as your father and grandfather, whom I knew well, saw themselves in relation to England. Your ancestors are considered by you as patriots in a struggle for independence and the rights of the colonies to govern themselves apart from England. The Confederates see little difference in seeking to leave your Union of states, and say, in fact, that your Constitution does not prohibit them from doing this. Our King George did not listen to the colonies, and England found it self in a war. Perhaps if Mr. Lincoln had taken a different approach.... Well, I think you can see the comparison from where we English sit. But Mr. Adams, it is not my intention or my place to lecture you on this matter. I ask that you please not consider my comments a redress. Rather,

164

consider them but an attempt to explain view of the difficult position in which we both find ourselves."

"Having said that, let me to state the position of Her Majesty's government," Russell continued. England diligently tried to maintain a position of strict neutrality. Our government did this until it reached a point where, in our opinion, this strict neutrality was no longer being honored. The events at sea culminating in the death of English subjects and a perceived lack of interest by the United States in guaranteeing our neutrality have led Her Majesty to declare the 1861 Act of Neutrality now null and void. In taking this action, England does not join forces with the Confederate States government. Our nation does not seek conflict with either side. *However*, henceforth we will take every step to protect our interests, our shipping on the seas of the world and British subjects wherever they may be. Let there be no misunderstanding of this policy."

"As to the issue of recognition of the Confederate government which petitions us, Her Majesty will decide this issue based on the interests of Great Britain, the apparent ability of said government to establish itself as a new nation, and the virtues of the request. If it should develop that recognition is given to the Southern government, this does not in any way constitute an English declaration of war or other hostilities with the United States. I have a prepared statement to this effect for you, and I present it to you at this time." He moved around the desk and handed a large envelope that contained the Royal Seal affixed in wax. Lord Russell continued, " Mr. Adams, if this war has truly become a crusade to free the slaves of your country as President Lincoln says it has, then I submit to you that England could be a great ally to your country in bringing this about. If on the other hand, the issue is not the elimination of slavery, but a desire to maintain an political establishment without change, this will become apparent to the world. I urge you to talk with your government and relay to them our position and stress the fact that we do not want war or hostilities of any sort with the United States."

Charles Adams sat motionless for a moment as if mentally

recording what had been said. He looked at the envelope in his hands and then said to Russell, " Lord Russell, is the recognition of the Rebel government an imminent action, or is there some time and room for negotiation?

Russell responded, "Recognition is not a fact at this time. That is all I can tell you. Her Majesty will decide in the very near future what will be done in this regard."

Adams was standing now, looking extremely serious and troubled as he spoke to the Foreign Minister, "Sir, I am deeply distressed at what has developed here. I will of course relay this information to my government immediately, and I will do so in person. I hope for the best, but I fear the worse. I can not bear the thought of our two great peoples fighting each other for a third time. Please continue to work for a resolution to this matter with your government's leadership. I pledge to you to do the same." Russell assured Adams that he too would work to avoid confrontation. With that, the two men shook hands and Minister Adams left the Foreign Minister's office.

A PLAN FOR WAR

A week passed since Lord Palmerston had talked with the American Minister. Understanding full well the need to be prepared if the United States reacted by declaring war, the Special War Committee had assembled and was now all seated. The Chairman of the Committee, Lord Granville, had introduced the Secretary of War who began.

"Gentlemen, as you know we have been looking at the situation in North America for some time with an eye toward our military actions should they become necessary. At this time, Lord Herbert shall give you and overview and then General Sir Williams and Admiral Milne will fill in the details and answer such questions as you may have."

Taking a pointer in hand, but not using it just yet, Lord Herbert began,. "We feel that the most likely situation we will face is that the Americans, North Americans that is, will declare war on us once we have formally recognized the Southern government. If there is a delay this declaration, it will surely come after we make an attempt to cross the Union blockade. When this happens, we will immediately put our plan of action into effect. This will include offensive military operations against United States assets. It is our considered assumption that the Confederate States can be counted upon to join with us at some stage of action either formally or informally. Therefore it is logical to plan for moderate support from the Confederates and seek to coordinate such support at the earliest opportunity."

" We have made the following assumptions in our planning:

1. England will *primarily conduct a naval war* against the United States with only moderate land forces being committed in North America.
2. The Confederate government will *primarily conduct a land war* against the United States with only moderate naval forces being committed by them.
3. Our land forces will initially be committed to Canada. Their primary mission will be to defend Canada, with a secondary mission to enhance Confederate operations as

167

possible and practical. We should make every effort to coordinate with the Confederate land forces for maximum effect.

4. Our naval forces will be used at sea and not in the inland waters of the United States. Our naval mission will be to defeat the U.S. Navy at every opportunity, to break the blockade of Southern ports open them for trade, and escort to the degree possible, all English merchant shipping to and from Southern ports.

5. The limited Confederate naval forces consisting of mostly cruisers and raiders will seek out and destroy the U.S. Merchant Marine anywhere it can be found on the open seas. Their numbers can be greatly augmented as our shipbuilding facilities are opened to build new naval vessels as required for the Confederate Navy.   Other Confederate naval assets consisting of ironclad and gunboats will be used in inland water ways in support of land operations, and for use against like assets of the Union Navy. We should make every effort to coordinate with the Confederate naval forces for maximum effect.

6. As quickly as naval assets of the United States are reduced, a naval blockade of major Union ports will be put in place by both the Royal and Confederate Navies."

Turning to the large map of the world, Lord Herbert now used his pointer to illustrate as he continued, "Our plan is code named *Royal Oak.*   Allow me to orient you, gentlemen. Confederate ports run from here to here... Major Southern ports are *Charleston...Savannah...Mobile...New Orleans* located up the Mississippi River, here... and *Galveston,* here. All together, some 3,500 miles of coast line. Union forces have substantial naval blockading forces before all these ports except Galveston, Texas, which was just recently opened by the Confederates. Union naval forces number some 200 plus ships on station at any given time, scattered across each port as noted.

We propose to break the Union blockade at each of these ports. We will inflict maximum damage on the naval forces located in each blockading squadron. This will open Southern ports for the export of cotton and other items to England and other ports as available. Initially, we will escort English merchantmen into these major ports for the purpose of off loading much needed war supplies being sold to the Southern government. On the return voyage, these merchant vessels will initially carry large quantities of cotton that are being made available to the Crown. War materials for the Confederates will be first priority to allow them to prosecute the land war. Priority of support will of course be to English merchant shipping.

At the same time the blockade is being opened, troop ships will depart from England carrying the first of some 55,000 troops being deployed to Canada. A strong naval escort squadron will accompany these troop ships on the runs as necessary. Timing is critical here, as the winter storms and ice will soon appear in the North Atlantic making this effort extremely difficult.

The Admiralty will provide the Confederate Raiders with all available information concerning the U.S. merchant fleet locations. We will recommend their continued concentration on the destruction of the whaling fleets, Asian trading fleets, and general commerce shipping. We know that they have had considerable success with very limited assets as of this date. We expect these Raiders could effectively eliminate American shipping from the seas while we concentrate on American warships.

We will then blockade several key points of the American coast. These consist of the coast of Maine, here... off the coast of New York, here... and off the coast of California. We think Confederate cruisers can accomplish the California mission as more vessels are brought on line for their navy.

As for land operations, the 55,000 troops in Canada will be used to threaten an invasion of Maine. This will place great pressure upon the U.S. government to pull troops away from operations against the Confederates. Should the opportunity and timing be right, our Regulars and the Canadians can mount an invasion of Maine. The would move south to destroy port and shipping facilities if the population can not be convinced to join us. It is no secret that the New England portion of the United States is very pro British. They may well seek to become neutral or possibly even to join Canada.

Canada is willing to call out 100,000 militia to defend their borders immediately against attack. Their need right now is munitions and weapons. The first of some 10,000 rifles are being manufactured as we speak and these will be sent to Nova Scotia as soon as is practical. I must say, that on the negative side, Canadian forts as noted …here, here, and here on the map, are in rather poor condition. Royal engineers have already been dispatched to assist in the immediate refurbishing and strengthening of these forts." Lord Herbert again pointed at the map, this time along the great lakes separating Canada and the U.S. and continued, "Canadian and Royal Navy assets are below par with the Americans. The U.S. has the superior forces on the lakes, although their assets are small. Since we plan no across lake operations, we feel have time to deal with this.

Gentlemen, this is an overview of operation *Royal Oak*. As we sit here, initial steps are being made to provide the assets to support this plan. Should minor or major changes be decided, the current efforts will still be of use in support of whatever we direct. At this time, I would ask for any general questions pertaining to the overview of this plan. Specific questions as to exact ships, numbers, dates and such will have to come at our next meeting unless General Williams or Admiral Milne can answer these today." "What are your questions…?"

The President of the Council, Lord Granville spoke first, "May I compliment you and your staff for this planning effort, Lord Herbert." Lord Herbert responded with thanks and awaited the questions he thought would follow.

Lord Palmerston then said, "Although I don't expect it, I pray that the Americans will understand our actions to move away from strict neutrality. I pray they will not see the need to declare war out of hand. As I say, I pray for this, but I have little faith that the Americans will see the error of their ways." Everyone nodded in agreement, as most had already come to the acceptance of the fact that war was almost inevitable.

"Assuming the Americans give us some time, I am concerned about the troop movements to Canada in bad weather. We are now coming into bad weather for the winter. Do you think we can make substantial troop movements before it becomes too difficult?"

Lord Herbert responded, "Only limited movements, Sir. We propose moving 8000 to 10,000 troops as soon as possible *before* any situation develops with the Americans. They can be ready to begin sailing within a fortnight if we use contracted commercial shipping. These troops would have the engineers as part of the initial transfer. They would help prepare for the arrival of the troops in the spring or when U.S. naval forces are dispersed or reduced by the Royal Navy."

Palmerston continued, "Well, the U.S. Navy might not disperse as easy as we might hope. I would expect them to fight very hard when pressed against their coast line. We must not get our army split in two places and not be able to support them, or have them wind up the object of a naval attack in winter weather. I know you have thought of these points, but I felt they need mentioning."

"By all means, Prime Minister," Lord Herbert said, "I certainly agree and assure you we are looking at this. I feel the key here is for the Royal Navy strike fast and violently at the American blockade squadrons. While they are indeed on alert status, they should be less professional than the Royal Navy, since they are all new volunteers and conscripts. They should be a little stale from sitting at anchor on blockade duty and they will likely not be expecting a major attack from the sea. The last point I should make is that we have the option to attack these relatively fixed points with overpowering force before the Americans can reinforce their blockade squadrons. As we eliminate each squadron, the option for them to shift and concentrate forces greatly diminishes. I feel the Royal Navy will be well prepared to strike hard and I personally expect short work of the initial naval actions."

"Perhaps so, Lord Secretary, but I again caution you to plan well and execute as planned. The Americans should never be

171

underestimated. I remind you that we have fought them twice, and it is *they* that have succeeded - twice. Likewise, consider a war is raging in North America that both sides thought would not last 90 days. It goes on with incredible carnage and ferocity on both sides... both side are Americans, both sides give no indication of stopping." The meeting was quiet for a moment as everyone reflected on what the Prime Minister had just said. Then the PM spoke again, "In any event, gentleman, I think we need only to make a good plan and execute it if the time comes. The Confederate Army is doing fairly well without any help whatsoever. I am sure with our help we will both see justice done for our peoples." This had broken the quiet and now several questions were asked.

"When do we expect recognition to be given and announced?...How soon do we think it will take for the Americans to respond to our recognition? ... If the Americans do not declare outright war, are we committed to try to break the blockade immediately? ... Other questions were asked and answered as the meeting went on. After about thirty minutes of discussion, the military officers were given an opportunity to provide some additional details as well as to discuss priorities and needs that required attention. By noon, the meeting was adjourned for specific work and coordination to continue. The plan known as *Royal Oak* for the conduct of the war, if war was declared, was now approved in concept and it would presented to the Queen. The Prime Minister expected a swift approval by Her Majesty.

WASHINGTON

It was a very cool day in Washington. The first of the cool snaps reminded everyone that autumn and then winter would soon be here. Charles Adams hardly felt the cold weather at all as he hurried toward the White House with Secretary of State Seward. He had just arrived in the Capitol City from London, and he was going directly to see and brief the Secretary. They were then scheduled to meet with the President for what Seward had termed, "A matter of the greatest urgency."

The unfinished Capitol building dome was looming over the city and was a striking backdrop as the men entered the White House. Secretary Seward went directly into the oval office, hardly slowing down for the new guards who were outside the President's door. The sergeants on guard duty were placed there by Secretary of War Stanton who had gotten wind of a possible kidnap or assassination plot that was brewing against the President. He felt that there probably was nothing to it, but he decided it was best to take such precautions just for peace of mind. As the door opened and the two men were announced, President Lincoln asked them to come in. Lincoln gave Charles Adams a warm handshake, then asked both men to be seated. Seward wasted little time with amenities or small talk, but got right to the subject.

"Mr. President, Minister Adams has come to us with all possible haste directly from the Foreign Secretary's office in London. He brings news of great concern that I felt you should hear immediately."

"By all means, Mr. Secretary," said Lincoln. "Mr. Adams, less I appear discourteous, may I say welcome to you and thank you for the fine work you have been doing for our country." Adams thanked the President and waited for him to continue. "Now, what is this distressing news you have from the Queen's court?"

Adams knew this would not be easy for Abraham Lincoln to hear and he regretted having to be the one bearing the news. "Mr. President, I do indeed have distressing news. As you know, Great Britain has been extremely angered over the *Mount Blanc Incident.* Prime Minister Palmerston has been in consultation with Queen Victoria and Parliament and the situation has now escalated beyond what an apology and political expressions of regret seem to be able to repair. Sir, this incident, coupled with the *Trent Affair,* and the well publicized recent victory of the Rebels in Maryland, have led the British to decide to withdraw their Neutrality Act of 1861. Coupled with this, they *may* very well decide to give full diplomatic recognition to the Rebel government in Richmond."

Seward spoke up immediately, "By Heaven, that will mean war! We won't sit still for that!"

Lincoln did not acknowledge Seward and never took his eyes off Adams. "Is the withdrawal of the Neutrality Act an accomplished fact ? I mean is it done, or do we have time to make some offer to stop this from happening?"

"It is done, Sir. Lord Russell, the Foreign Secretary told me the day I left that it was already decided. By the time I rode out on the tide from England, the papers were carrying the story and these are surely on their way to us."

"What did you mean by, '*they may well decide*' to grant recognition to the Rebels?," asked Lincoln.

"Well, Sir, when I left England," Adams began, "Parliament was still debating about the Southern recognition matter. The slavery issue was the primary stumbling block. This may or may not stop recognition by Parliament. As things stand, I honestly don't think recognition will pass at this time. However, I can not be sure. I was told by the Foreign Minister that the Rebels had proffered some sort of agreement to end slavery if England would recognize them. I felt I had to depart and deliver to you what I know first hand. What I was told, very clearly, was that British ships would no longer recognize our blockade of Southern ports or our inspections and stops of British shipping at sea. I was told very clearly that if there were any further incidents involving British ships and British subjects, there would be immediate military action by the Royal Navy as well as recognition of the Rebel government. Lord Russell was very

174

clear on this."

Lincoln responded, "What kind of agreement have the Rebels offered on slavery?"

"I don't know, Sir," replied Adams. "Secretary Russell would not elaborate on this point. However, it was clear that if the Rebels would make a firm offer that was workable, recognition was probably going to be offered to them. He said... well...he said if you were serious about ending slavery, then they would work with us to do so, but if the war was only about the Union...well...."

Lincoln responded without moving a muscle or a change of expression. "The war *is* about slavery, but it has *always* been about the Union! The Union cannot be, it must not be divided! I am surprised the English don't see this." He shook his head from side to side and said, "Has this last incident at sea been what drove England to this? It is hard to believe that one ship and two casualties caused by a mistake should drive them to the verge of war. Can't they see what we are going through? It seems insane for them to fight a war over this!"

"Mr. President, the British look at this situation very differently. As you know, that *Trent* incident almost caused them to go to war with us. Now they see this last event not as an isolated action, but rather as the second, and far worse, event in a *string* of such situations that they think will continue. Sir, I was told point blank that our 'lack of, or un-willingness to seriously punish the Captain of our ship, and the fact that this second incident has happened, shows that we are not serious about avoiding confrontations. To some degree, I think the British feel challenged at sea. You know that is something they will never accept."

"Well, the Queen is no fool. She knows we have our hands full with this war. Otherwise she might be a little more flexible," noted President Lincoln. "This withdrawal of the Neutrality Act...do they see this as an act of war on their part... do they think we will declare war or attack them when they do this?"

"It is definitely *not* an act of war to them, Sir. In fact, I was specifically told that we should not consider this as an act of war on the part of England. They feel that since we don't treat them with strict neutrality, *at least in their eyes*, they will not act absolutely neutral. Mr. President, if I may say so, I honestly think that the English government expects there will be another incident. As soon as this happens, they will surely make a naval response at sea, followed by formal recognition of the Rebels. Based on our announced policy that recognition of the Rebels would result in war with us, I think they would expect us to declare war immediately. I also think their response would likely be substantial."

"You mean they will attack us?"

"In my opinion, yes, Sir. Mr. President, I do not think the English are bluffing about this. The British Foreign Secretary and the Prime Minister expressed to me that that they do not want war with us for the third time. However, they are taking steps to prepare for it if it comes."

"What steps, " asked Secretary Seward?

"A lot of troops are moving, ships moving, weapons and munitions plants are reopening and going to work. Military activity was increasing even as I departed London. The other problem is that if England recognizes the Confederates, my sources tell me that France will almost surely follow with recognition. I do not think France will be so quick to fight, but she would surely love to get at the Southern cotton while we, England and the Rebels are all fighting. Napoleon would have somewhat of a free hand in Mexico while all this was going on."

Secretary Seward was sitting forward in his chair as if totally surprised. He was obviously agitated by what he was hearing. "This is what I always thought the British would do! They will take the first opportunity they can find to recognize the Rebels and go to war with us. We have beaten the tar out of them twice and they want revenge! I say if we have to, we will do it again!"

Lincoln looked very troubled, "I don't believe England really wants to fight us, gentlemen. We have made two bad errors at sea. That's where England is most at home. She is a world power and a world leader, particularly at sea. We must think this through and come up with a way to keep England out of the war. I do not want to fight the Rebels on the land and the Royal Navy at sea."

The President was trying to work the pieces of the situation through in his head and formulate a plan from what appeared to be a disaster in the making. "You say the decision to nullify the Neutrality Act is done?"

"Yes Sir, that is what Foreign Secretary Russell told me," said Adams.

"But there is no declaration of war coming with this act...? They just seem to think the hot headed Americans will do something else to start hostilities..? Correct?"

"That is correct, Mr. President."

"And the recognition of the Rebel government is *not* assured, *unless* we do something to set England off?"

"Yes Sir, or unless the Rebels come up with an offer about slavery. Who knows what else the British are willing to accept" replied Adams.

Lincoln continued, "Mr. Adams, what do you hear about the Confederate Commissioners Slidell and Mason? How are they faring in all this? Happy as a spring calf, I would assume?"

"That is correct, Sir. Mason has been to see the Prime Minister only once, but this was recently. It was the first time the PM had received any representative from the Rebels. Mason seemed pleased with his visit when he left. I am told he is working up orders for several new Confederate fast Raiders to have them ready. Such orders are still not honored by the British shipbuilders, or should I say by the British government, but he may be looking for the changes we are talking about."

"Well, we are sitting on a really big keg of gunpowder here, gentlemen," said Lincoln. "The first order of business is to make sure, *absolutely sure*, that we do not get into another naval incident with the British that would set this off. Next, we must work against Southern recognition with all our assets! We can ignore the British nullification of their Neutrality Act. As long as they don't actively help the Rebels or hinder our forces, we can live with this. We will *have* to live with this. They drafted their Neutrality Act, and we simply can not afford to go to war with them over their withdrawal of it! The fly in the honey will be recognition. *If* Britain recognizes the Rebel government," Lincoln paused, "I see no way to avoid a war with them. I can see no alternative to this. We must stand by our word and not allow the British or anyone else to help the Rebels. We must do everything in our power to hinder and stop recognition!"

Seward spoke first. "Mr. President, if our navy loosens its grip on ships flying English colors, we could lessen the threat. This, coupled with a truly stern warning, might give us some space." Lincoln was nodding in agreement. "Then, if we work on the idea to move France into a position to oppose England, we might make Victoria think twice about going to war with us!"

"Good, very good, Mr. Seward. "If we work with France, by maybe guaranteeing to keep our hands off as Napoleon tries to solidify his grip on Mexico, we could make it worth France's time *not* to recognize the Confederates. Couple this with some incentives and a chance to see England limited in North America…it might have a real impact."

Seward continued, "We also should immediately make it plain that *if* we go to war with England, Canada would be open to U.S. attack! That would make them think twice! Matter of fact, that has a lot of appeal in any case!"

"Mr. Seward…remember…one war at a time!" Lincoln was serious as he both made his point and gave his Secretary of State instructions. "We are moving all across the southern United States in this conflict. I remind you, we can not, we must not, get into another war at sea, let alone a land war in Canada! The American people would never stand for the casualties we would suffer."

Seward always thought he was the better man for the Presidency. He was sure he had a better grasp of what could and could not be done. His ideas would, under certain conditions, work if the man leading it was up to the task! "I understand, Sir. I was only saying that *if* a situation presented itself, such as the

Rebels were almost defeated and we were still fighting the British, we might get the Southerners to stop fighting, join us, and help us, together, take Canada! Why, this might end the war and bind the North and South together to fight a common foe, the natural foe we have always had, the English!"

Lincoln knew that Seward had roughly formulated this idea early in his job as Secretary of State, but nothing ever came of it. Lincoln also knew that Seward underestimated the South in thinking they would give up their cause for something as shallow as an *opportunity* to fight England. He was aware that Seward almost hated the British and had, in fact, said it was his mission in life to antagonize and oppose them at every opportunity! Until now, he thought Seward had put that behind him.

"Mr. Secretary," Lincoln said, "the South will not stop fighting us to fight England. I repeat, we must avoid war with England. Your idea to get France to say no to Southern recognition, or to possibly outright oppose it, has great merit. I think this is a plan we need to work on quickly, as it could have great impact on the war and on England's plans. Please start working on this immediately. Make sure I am informed before any action is carried out."

Seward, although somewhat disappointed his plan was not seized upon, agreed to start immediately to develop this idea.

Lincoln was now addressing Charles Adams, "Mr. Adams, I must ask you to return to England with all haste. We need you to do all you can to stop the British from this path they are taking. Use every legal and moral means at your disposal. I will prepare a personal letter for you to deliver to Prime Minister Palmerston. It will offer the hand of friendship while making it perfectly clear where the United States stands on the issue of Rebel recognition. On this last point, there will be no compromise. We can only hope and pray that they will see our point."

"Mr. President, if the British do recognize the Rebel government as a separate government, what are my instructions?" Adams was wanting to know exactly how to proceed if the worse were to happen.

Lincoln did not hesitate. "In this case, you are to obtain what official documents you can pertaining to the English government's recognition, then you are to return to the United States by the most expeditious route. You will automatically consider yourself *recalled* by your government. There is to be no discussion or pronouncement of war *or* peace beyond what will be made clear to them by my letter and your written instructions. I do not want you and your family in London or at sea with war breaking out. Any declaration of war or other hostilities will be made only after you return and we can see what the English government has formally done. This is why any documents you may obtain will be of great help to us in making the hard decisions we will have to make. However, let me say this, Mr. Adams, when you leave London, do so with the attitude that you will not be returning, as we will almost certainly soon be at war with Great Britain."

It was a sobering statement. It seemed only a step away from reality to Minister Adams. While he understood, he was almost depressed at the thought of this terrible war expanding to become a war with England. He wanted to rush out and leave immediately for London to try to help. Soon he was out of the President's office and was alone with Seward.

"Don't give in to the British, Charles," said Seward with a stern face. "Be firm and make them understand that while we don't want war with them, we don't plan to lose a war with them either!"

Adams was feeling a little uncomfortable as this was a little more forceful than the President had told him to be in this matter. He would, however, do what had to be done, in the manner that it had to be done. After more rather pointed instructions from the Secretary of State, he was at last on his way back toward Boston with hardly a moment's rest. There the *USS Kearsarge* had been ordered to await his arrival to take him directly to England. The *Kearsarge* had been chasing the *CSS Alabama* all over the Atlantic and had almost caught her in a French port, but missed her by a day. Now the *Kearsarge* was sidetracked for this special duty. It would not be long until they were in action.

GRANT ARRIVES

Responding to the President's call for him to come to Washington at once, General U.S. Grant arrived in the middle of the afternoon and checked into the Willard Hotel. No one knew who he was when he entered the over crowded hotel. In a sea of blue uniforms and so many generals and colonels, Grant was just another face - that is until he signed the register. At the mention of his name, and not so quietly at that, people scurried around him. His treatment instantly became that of a celebrity. It seemed as though everyone in Washington knew who he was and why he was there.

As everyone spoke to him and called him by name, Grant was surprised and mused to himself, "No wonder there is no such thing as a military secret in this town!"

The evening passed quickly and the next morning Grant and Secretary Stanton were on their way to the White House to see President Lincoln. The two men were ushered immediately in to see the President.

"General Grant! I have looked forward to meeting you for some time. Please...be seated," the President said in a most cordial manner. "It seems we have something in common. We are both from Illinois!"

Grant thanked the President and joined the President's small talk about home, family, and people they knew in common from Illinois. Then President Lincoln leaned forward and began to address the real reason for their meeting. "General Grant, I must say to you that the war is not going well, or least is it not going well as quickly as we need for it to do. We seem to have a setback or two for every big victory we have. Now, time is running against us. What I am about to tell you, I will say in the strictest of confidence. It appears that England is probably going to recognize the Rebel government and in doing so, they will eventually join the war on the side of the Rebels. It also appears that the Confederate Army in Virginia is going to dig in and hold us at bay until the elections come up in November. They are hoping this administration is defeated and the new one under George McClellan wins. The Rebels are convinced, as are a great number of other people, that McClellan would indeed make peace. Do you know McClellan, General?"

"I met him a time or two, Sir, but don't really know him," replied Grant.

"Well, I know him pretty well, and I am among those convinced that if McClellan is elected and things don't change on the battlefield, he very likely *will* end the war by making peace with the Rebels and allowing the Union to be broken," said Lincoln. "It would mean that all you and the army have fought for would be lost. To me, it's one thing to be defeated on the battlefield, but its quite another to have someone give it away."

Grant said, "I fully agree, Sir, but I think this war can still be won, Mr. President."

"How would you propose to do that, General?," asked Lincoln.

"Well, we must go after Lee's Army and destroy it. We attack and not let up. Lee must be almost at the bottom of the barrel for his source of men and material. Particularly in men. We must keep pounding him till he cannot recover. The more he loses, the faster he will lose. Mr. President, from what I have seen, we tend to fight Lee and then, win or lose, we move away to regroup, reform and build up again. We can sustain the losses better than Lee can. We should never let him recover or even catch his breath. Instead, we must stay on him until he gives in."

Lincoln nodded slightly in agreement, smiled slightly and then looked at Stanton. "Mr. Secretary, I think we have found our *fighter*." Stanton, smiled and agreed. Lincoln responded, "General Grant, this is precisely what I have asked the Generals who have commanded the army to do! I will admit to you that I have been very active, in truth too active, in making suggestions and in pushing for us to attack and destroy the Rebels. I do not profess to be a military man, but procrastination on the part of previous commanders and pressure from the people and Congress have forced me to issue a series of *Military Orders*. I am not sure all these were correct. In fact, I know some were not correct. All I have wanted is someone who would take the responsibility and act, letting me use the power of the government to support him in his actions. You, Sir, have just clearly and simply stated what I have been asking someone to do all these months!"

Lincoln leaned forward in his chair as he looked straight into Grant's eyes. "General Grant, let me get right to it...You know why I have asked you to come here today. I would like to offer you command of the Armies of the United States., including command of the Army of the Potomac. It is a formidable task, but one I think you're up to doing. Will you accept this command?"

Commanding General of the Army of the United States! Even to Sam Grant, an officer not easily impressed by titles and ceremony, *this* had a *very special* sound to it! Grant did not have time to savor the honor. He hesitated only for a moment. "Yes, Mr. President, I would be honored to accept this command."

Lincoln sat back and slapped his hand on his knees as he had done so many times as if to say, "Done!" "Excellent, General Grant! Congratulations! And may I also say, thank you! We are at a difficult time in this war and I personally thank you for assuming this important job. Now! General, my orders to you are, do just what you said needed to be done." Lincoln smiled and paused, "...and what may I do to help you do this."

Now Grant smiled and then became serious, "Mr. President, right now I don't know what, if anything is needed, beyond trying to keep the English out of the war. I need to get to the field to see where the Army of the Potomac stands. I need to see how soon we can move on Lee, and then I want to get going. I don't hold much with taking cities; the key is breaking the Rebel's ability to fight. We must destroy his army. I understand Lee is now in Richmond, so we must go to Richmond. If Lee leaves Richmond, I will follow him. If we can capture the city in the process, so much the better. However my object will be the Rebel army."

"Yes, good! Taking the enemy's capital would be excellent

for the people's morale, but you make that call, General. If you can defeat their army *and* take the capitol, the impact of that would be great indeed. Well, we are off to a good start…Sam. You go by Sam, don't you?"

"Yes, Sir," smiled Grant.

"How did you get *Sam* out of Ulysses?," asked Lincoln.

Grant laughed and said, "Well, its a long story, Mr. President. It goes back to when I was at West Point."

Lincoln was grinning now as he said, "Well, perhaps you will explain it to me over dinner this evening? Mrs. Lincoln and I would very much enjoy your company for dinner and the theater. There is a new play at Ford's Theater and I feel your new command is an occasion to celebrate! Will you join us, Sam?"

Grant smiled and nodded, "Thank you, Mr. President. I would be most pleased." It would be General Grant's first truly relaxed evening in months, it would also be his last for a while.

BRANDY STATION

General Grant was off by train for Meade's headquarters at Brandy Station early the next morning. He had enjoyed the previous evening spent with President and Mrs. Lincoln. He had heard much about Abraham Lincoln. After spending time with him, Grant was now assured this was a man of high integrity and deep personal commitment to the country. Grant felt that Lincoln would indeed stand behind him. Now it was up to him to attack and bring the Confederate Army under Robert E. Lee to its knees. He knew it would not be an easy task. Lee seemed to have a sixth sense about war. His reputation among Federal officers was growing, and he caused no small amount of fear in those who knew they had to face him. Grant respected him, but he did not fear Lee in the least.

"He *is* good," thought Grant, "but I am better. Lee can not stand up to what I can throw against him. I have good troops and more of them. If Britain will stay out of the war, I can whip him. All we need is a little time."

The country side in Maryland whizzed by as the train sped down the tracks. It was hard to tell there was a war on by looking out the window. Grant thought about Vicksburg and the country side in Mississippi that was torn, burned and scarred by the war. "The mark of Cain," he thought. He hoped the North would be spared that pain.

The Union Army, now some 72,000 strong was reforming and regrouping from the debacle at Monocacy. Fresh troops were pouring into the Army from towns across the North. It would take a few weeks perhaps a month or two, and the Army of the Potomac would be ready to fight again. Grant's special train was only six miles from the station at Brandy Station when it had to stop to wait while a train in front of him off- loaded new troops. These were among the hundreds of troops being transferred in to fill out the Corps that had been hurt so badly at Monocacy. After a 45 minute wait, his train lurched a few times and slowly began to move toward its destination. These last few miles took almost half an hour. At the station, Grant saw a beehive of activity. Troops and horses going and coming, wagons everywhere, Quartermasters were off-loading train cars from side rails, while other supplies were being loaded on to wagons. Troops were working on the rails and side tracks, and train cars were pushed on to these tracks almost as fast as they were finished.

Grant's staff off-loaded the horses and General Grant was soon on his way to Meade's headquarters. Some troops saluted as he passed, others just looked, most did not know who he was.

"Just another desk General," most thought. "Hard to keep up with them all as they come and go."

Sam Grant finally arrived at George Meade's headquarters at about four o'clock in the afternoon. Meade was standing outside his tent talking to several Brigade officers when Grant rode up. As he dismounted, the officers all came to attention and saluted. He returned their salutes and acknowledged them with a nod and a "Gentlemen". Then walking to Meade, he said, "General Meade, I'm Sam Grant. Let's talk."

Once inside the tent, Grant mentioned to Meade that he had met him casually during the Mexican War. Neither man remembered much about that meeting, although it did give them something more in common. Grant handed Meade a letter from the Secretary of War Stanton. It simply stated that U.S. Grant was now Commander of the Armies of the United States, and Meade was to obey whatever orders Grant gave. Meade knew full well that he was to be relieved because of Monocacy, so this was no surprise to him. "Of course I understand, General Grant, I will move my things out and clear the tent for you before dark tonight. If you would like me to do so, I will give you a run down on the staff before I go and I...."

Grant was shaking his head in the negative as he lighted up a new cigar. "You will stay here, General Meade, as Commander of the Army of the Potomac. I will assume overall command of operations, but you will stay as Army Commander." Meade was stunned and Grant could see it in his face.

Grant continued, "We have had enough of this changing commanders and moving in and out. Let me be blunt, General, you stay until I fire you. If I do, you will be done. No headquarters, no lateral moves, no western transfers. You will be finished in the Army. So you need to consider that there is nothing to slide over to, and there is nothing to fall back on. You are stuck with me." Grant paused and slowly lowered his cigar toward a map of Virginia that was on the table. Then he pointed the butt of the cigar at Richmond. "Together, you and I are going run Bob Lee out of Richmond, and it begins now. Questions?"

Meade felt a rush of confidence as Grant looked at him waiting for an answer, and he smiled, "No questions, General!"

Grant reached out to shake hands. "Good! Then let's get to it. First of all, I go by Sam. Now, I need a good briefing as to where we stand... troop numbers, effectives, artillery, stores, dispositions, and the like. Then I want a full run down on Lee's Army as much as you know. Our plan is simple. We will move on Richmond and bring Lee into a fight, or we will drive him away from Richmond. If he fights, we whip him. If he runs, we burn Richmond and chase him down. George, tonight over dinner I will bring you up to date on the situation from Washington. Just you and I... Plan for a late evening. Now, please see to getting tents for me and my staff officers. Somewhere close to you would be fine. I need to wash up." Grant had taken command.

LONDON

Duncan F. Kenner of Louisiana, arrived in London by way of France. He was worn out from his trip, having made the trip from Cuba to France, then directly to England with virtually no rest or stops. His physical exhaustion was compounded by the fact that he was under great pressure to deliver the dispatches he was carrying to his friend, James Mason. He arrived in London at three a.m. and went straight to Mason's apartment where he awakened the surprised Confederate Commissioner.

The men met in James Mason's parlor well before the sun came up. Kenner began to tell the Mason the details of his mission and Mason's instructions to immediately carry out.

"This can not be!," exclaimed Mason. "You expect me to walk into the Prime Minister's office and tell him that with a wave of the hand we will give up the very institution that has built the economic wealth of the South? NO! A thousand times NO! I can not do it! I will not do it! What has happened to our government...have they all given up?" Mason waving his arms and pacing the floor in disbelief.

"James, calm down and hear me out, " said Kenner. "President Davis and Secretary Benjamin knew you would be upset. That's one reason they asked me to come, so I can explain the government's position as well as to tell you what is going on back home."

"Explain? Explain to me how Jeff Davis could sign on to this? How could he agree to give up something that will destroy the economy of the South? I've known Jeff since we were young men. I've hunted deer and fox with him at his home in Vicksburg. For Heaven's sake, I've...."

Kenner looked up and said, "James! Vicksburg is in Yankee hands. The people there were starved out after weeks of eating mules and rats! The Davis' plantation was looted and probably destroyed! Jackson, Mississippi was burned... most of the state is in shambles! Louisiana is occupied by Federal troops and a Yankee general named Butler has threatened to turn his troops loose on the women of New Orleans! Get a grip on what I am telling you, my friend. Our options are fading with each day! If we don't soon get some outside help in some form, there won't be a Confederacy for you to represent, or to come home to!"

Mason was quiet as he absorbed what Kenner said. "I thought we would be able to come back, to maybe retake what we have lost! Is it truly that bad...have we lost?"

"No, we haven't lost, James. We fight on. It's just that we are so outnumbered and strapped for supplies, that it seems to be...well, more a matter of time." Kenner continued, "the Yankees can absorb the losses they suffer, but we just can't keep losing men, supplies and territory! Don't you see? Recognition and support from England is the key. If we can soon get recognition from England and get their active support, we should be able to make this war into something even Lincoln cannot afford to support. They would have to let us go!"

Mason replied, "Well, don't assume that recognition of the Confederacy is a declaration of war on the Union by the Queen! Palmerston has made it clear to me that England will do its utmost to avoid war with the North. They want our cotton and will not take any more arrogance from the U.S. Navy, but they are not going to attack Washington any time soon!"

"They won't have to declare war, Lincoln has already said he would do it for them," Kenner explained. "He said our recognition meant war with anyone who granted it! That means the British Navy would be fighting with us! Ports would open, cotton would move, funds and supplies would flow again! Our Armies have the will to fight, but they need the weapons, gunpowder and even shoes to help them fight." Kenner waited while Mason absorbed his logic. He continued, " James, the President of our country instructed me to personally come to give you these instructions. I know you will do as he asks. Every hour the Confederacy goes without help is an hour that more of our boys die for lack of the means to fight. Help them, James. Please...."

Mason turned and looked at Kenner. "I don't believe this is the way, Duncan...but I will do what I am instructed to do by my President. Come, you need some breakfast. I have a paper

190

to write and then I must dress. I hope to have an early appointment with the Prime Minister this morning!"

THE CONFEDERATE STATES OF AMERICA

Confederate Commissioner Mason entered the Prime Minister's office to a cordial welcome. "Thank you very much for seeing me on such short notice, Lord Palmerston. "

"Not at all, Mr. Mason. I was told that you had news of the utmost importance. I was glad to make time for you."

Mason had his portfolio in his lap as he spoke. "Sir, I have just received, by way of a high level courier, dispatches from my government and among these was President Davis' wish that I extend his personal greetings to you."

Palmerston nodded and replied, "Thank you very much."

"In addition to the President's personal greetings, he asked that this personal note be hand delivered by me for your eyes only." With this Mason reached inside and removed a large envelope bearing the Great Seal of the Confederacy in the corner, with Lord Palmerston's name written on the front. He handed it to Palmerston. "While of course, I have not read this, I was told that what I am about to tell you is among the items reiterated in this letter from President Davis. I was asked to discuss a matter of great importance with you. Following that, I am to request that you please read the communiqué from President Davis."

"Lord Palmerston," Mason continued, "I contacted my government and informed them of items we discussed in our last meeting. Needless to say, my government was most encouraged and appreciative of your comments and the support that you extended. The difficulty of your position and that of Her Majesty in dealing with the United States and our government is well understood. Your status as a non belligerent, neutral nation is recognized by the Confederate government. While we have always sought to recognize and respect British neutrality, we would like to state that we formally pledge not to interfere with, or cause difficulty to, Her Majesty's interests within the British Empire or at sea." In somewhat diplomatic language, Mason had just said that the Confederacy heard the British anger over present events, and pledged to stay out of her way. In actuality, the last thing the Confederates wanted to do was upset England!

Mason hastened on, "Prime Minister, in our last conversation, you asked that my government make some concession, some pledge, some move toward an alternative to the issue of slavery. You pledged that if we would do so, recognition for the Confederate States would be forthcoming." Palmerston was leaning forward on his desk as he slightly nodded in agreement. "After a great deal of deliberation, my has government as authorized me to say to you that *for* the formal recognition of our government, England's support and assistance on the world's stage as was discussed, and for a cooperative military effort as may be possible…" Mason hesitated as if having difficulty in saying what he knew he must… the Confederate government pledges to Her Majesty to work for the active elimination of slavery within the Southern states within ten years."

Palmerston noticeably, but gently patted his hands on his desk and leaned back as if to say "At Last!"

Mason continued, "Sir, you have this pledge from the Confederate States government. This pledge is also confirmed by the document that I just presented to you from President Davis. I am instructed to say that the ten year period is absolutely necessary to allow us to get through the war and to work out a plan to reestablish our economy when peace is finally established. The only caveat to this pledge would be if the war for some reason continues for an extended period of time. We do not think this will happen, but if it does, our time schedule will slide as well. Sir, you asked for our response and good faith pledge. I think you see the government of the people of the South have given you exactly that." Mason again paused and then said, "May I report to President Davis that England will immediately recognize the Confederate States?" Mason's heart was again racing.

Palmerston rose to his feet and walked around his desk. "Commissioner Mason, I assured you that I would give you my full support, should your President be able to take this course of action." Palmerston extended his hand, "You have my support!

I will request to see Her Majesty immediately to present this matter to her. I am confident that her approval of recognition is but a formality."

Mason was so relieved and excited that he almost wept. Emotionally, he felt relief and victory all rolled into one feeling. The men continued to shake hands for some time. Palmerston oddly felt much the same way. His feelings of relief and victory stemmed from the knowledge that if war came with the United States, as he was sure it would, England would now have an ally with a powerful army in North America. It would be an ally that could help keep pressure off Canada. His sense of victory came in knowing that England had taken a giant step forward in removing slavery from a part of the world where even war did not seem to be able to resolve the issue. Mason thought of Abraham Lincoln and wondered how he would feel knowing it was England that finally dealt slavery a death blow.

As the men again took their seats, Palmerston asked Mason for a moment while he opened and read the letter from Jefferson Davis. After some minutes, he looked up and said. "Fine. It is as you said, Mr. Mason. I will want to shortly prepare a letter to President Davis as well."

The men discussed other issues of a general nature and agreed that before other discussions continued, the Prime Minister's meeting with Queen Victoria was the next order of business. Both men noted subjects that should be the topics of the next meeting following Palmerston's meeting with the Queen. Following this creation of an agenda, Mason again thanked Palmerston and excused himself saying he would await a call from the PM's office.

There was a reason for such assurance on the part of the Prime Minister as to how this would all turn out. Parliament had approved recognition if such concessions were made, and the Queen had likewise concurred this was the action to take in such circumstances. With the letter from Jefferson Davis, it was a closed deal! By taking his time, Palmerston was buying time for the Royal Navy. Each day was one more day needed to move more British regulars to Canada. It was another day for the Royal Navy to reposition its ships for the naval actions that would be needed. It was also another day of peace before a time of war. He knew that he must prepare himself to meet with Charles Adams to tell him of the recognition of the Confederates.

Palmerston knew what this would surely mean, and the thought of war was pervasive in his thoughts. A third war with the United States…a war that could prove by far to be the worse one yet! Well, no time to worry about that now. He needed to get an audience with Her Majesty to tell her of the developments and to confirm his intentions to grant recognition to the Confederate States. The date was December 21, 1864.

PALMERSTON CALLS ADAMS

Prime Minster Palmerston had called for Charles Adams. He and John Russell were waiting in Palmerston's office. The men were both anxious as they waited. It was a momentous occasion that both wished would pass from them. No one in their right mind wanted to tell the representative of a country news that would probably result in war! Still, Palmerston hoped there was a way to salvage peace from all this. Perhaps Lincoln had reconsidered? Surely Lincoln knew the danger of taking on the Confederates and Britain at the same time.

Perhaps Lincoln thought the French would aid him. He probably did not yet know John Russell had just been assured that the French would also recognize the Confederate government as soon as Britain made recognition public. Russell had learned that the Confederate Commissioner in Paris had promised France that the Confederacy would not interfere or get involved with Maximillian's efforts in Mexico. Britain had quietly said the same thing through a third party. They did not want France involved in the war that was coming. By keeping Napoleon III busy helping the French Prince in Mexico, Napoleon should not have time to start something in Europe before England could dispose of the U.S. Navy in the Atlantic. Hopefully, there would also be an end to the land war in North America.

The door opened and Palmerston's secretary announced Charles Adams. The men observed pleasantries in accordance with protocol. Lord Palmerston began, "Minister Adams, I must get right to the issue. I have come from meeting with Her Majesty today, and I must now inform you that Great Britain will immediately recognize the Confederate States as a separate and independent government. This will be announced publicly tomorrow morning."

Adams stared at the Prime Minister, took a deep breath and slightly shook his head as if in disbelief. Palmerston continued, "Her Majesty asked that I once again reiterate that this does not have to mean war between England and the United States. Your war with the Confederates is your business. We have no desire to join it. We have discussed the reasons for this decision. I can only say Her Majesty feels this is in Britain's best interest."

Adams spoke, obviously upset by what he was hearing. "With all due respect, Sir, I can hardly see how recognizing an insurrectionist government is in the best interest of the people of England. May I ask if the Rebels promised to free the slaves they now hold in bondage?"

Palmerston could see this meeting would deteriorate rapidly if he allowed it to do so, yet he was not one to be questioned in his own office. "Our dealings with another government are not open to discussion, Mr. Adams. With all due respect, I can only say that England has decided what is in the best interest of England. Mr. Adams, I have repeatedly said to you and I say it once more, England does not want to fight a war with the United States. I can make it no clearer than that, but in the words of your President Lincoln, '…the issue of war is in your hands'. I urge you to consider well what this will mean. We are not preoccupied as in our previous wars with your country." He let these hard words sink in to Adams.

"Then there is no recourse, no time for discussion, no possibility for England to change its position on this matter? You are saying the United States should accept this as your last word?," asked Adams.

Palmerston settled the issue once and for all. "I am saying to you, Mr. Adams, that recognition of the Confederate States by England is a fact."

Adams calmly replied, "Then Sir, I must inform you that the United States embassy will close and I am to return to Washington immediately."

"I regret that your country feels this to be necessary, Minister Adams. I assume that this action does not mean that hostilities now exist between our two countries, does it?," asked Palmerston.

"No Sir, no hostilities exist *at this time*." Adams was very specific in his answer.

Charles Adams stood first, signaling that the meeting was

over. "Lord Palmerston, I deeply regret this turn of events. I wish we could have found some other resolution to this situation. I must bid you farewell, but I do want to thank you for your personal kindness and that of your government during my time here in London. I have grown very fond of England and its people. Goodbye, Sir."

Palmerston reached to shake hands with Adams who likewise extended his hand. "I wish you well, Charles. You have been an excellent representative of your government. I hope Mr. Lincoln will reconsider what we have discussed. Our two peoples should not be enemies. In any event, God speed to you and your family and a safe journey if you must go."

Adams left the office with a long face. Russell looked at Palmerston and said, "Well, that was short and direct. It was apparent that Adams had orders to return if this happened. I would rather guess war will be declared about as fast as Adams gets to Washington."

Palmerston replied, "Yes, unless a miracle occurs, I would say we have about two weeks or three at the most before we will be at war with the Americans! I don't think Lincoln will back down on his pledge of war, so we need to make the most of the time we have. I want a time set up for the Queen to receive *Minister* Mason of the Confederate States. Following this, we need to meet with him to discuss getting one or more Confederate Naval officers and perhaps an Army officer to serve here as liaison officers with our military. Let's include Lord Herbert, Lord Granville and the Duke of Sommerset in this meeting. No need to have the military in on this as of yet. Let's also prepare a list of questions concerning areas of coordination and cooperation we could put into place if, or should I say when, the U.S. declares war. We also need to work up a plan to pick up the cotton that was offered to the government. We will surely need the money with the upcoming events!

The men discussed other issues for a time. Then Lord Russell left for his office. Both men were glad this part of the developing events was over.

WASHINGTON

The *USS Kearsarge* had taken Charles Adams back to England only days before, and now it again sailed back across the Atlantic with Charles Adams on board. This time there would be no trip back to England. The next time the *Kearsarge* went to sea, it would be to hunt British ships as enemies.

Abraham Lincoln also noted the fast turn of events as the former Minister to England sat before him. This time Secretary of State Seward, Secretary of War Stanton, and Secretary of the Navy Welles were in the Oval office as Adams told of the events that had developed.

"Mr. Adams, word came to us yesterday by wire that ships arriving ahead of you said the English papers had announced recognition of the Confederates. I wanted not to believe it, but last evening we again heard the same story. Now you confirm it is indeed true." Lincoln was leaning forward in his chair.

"Did you clearly explain the Prime Minister that to recognize the Rebels meant war with us?, Lincoln asked?

"Yes Sir, I made it perfectly clear again and again. I asked him if there was any room for negotiation on this. He said it was not negotiable. It was now a fact."

"Typical arrogant English attitude," said Seward, looking even more sour than usual.

"Well, there is little sense in wondering what we can do to change it now. It is a fact now, and one we have to address." Lincoln sat quietly for a few seconds. "Gentlemen, I have thought much on this. I expected it to come down to the meeting in which we now find ourselves. I want to know your opinions and recommendations."

Seward spoke up almost instantly as if he had already thought it through and had his mind made up. "Mr. President, you *must* go to Congress and ask that they declare war on the British immediately! Once again, the English prove that only what suits England is of importance. This time, perhaps, we can make sure they don't ever want to fight us again!"

Edwin Stanton sat up slightly and then said, "Sir, I think the

Secretary of the Navy might have a different opinion than I, since it will likely be our Navy that will quickly meet the Royal Navy if we opt for war. However, I must say I agree with Secretary Seward. I would take it to Congress and let them decide."

Seward responded tersely. "You missed my point, Edwin, I don't want Congress to *decide*, I want them to declare war!"

Secretary Welles looked completely drained. "This will be a tough fight, Mr. President. The navy will have to expand and now look to the seas of the world as well as to the ports of the South. This will be most difficult."

Lincoln was looking at Charles Adams. "Mr. Adams…?"

"Mr. President, I am only a representative for our government. But since you asked, I would *not* ask Congress to declare war…at least not just yet! I have seen the Royal Navy. It is more than formidable! If we just ignore the English recognition, I don't see that we will be any worse off politically. But we will avoid a costly, and possibly disastrous, war with England! I just cannot see how war with the British can be anything but harmful to us under the present circumstances."

Lincoln replied, "You're correct in much that you say, Mr. Adams. I see nothing good in our fighting England. However, even if we ignore their recognition of the Rebels, we will almost immediately come into conflict with English shipping trying to sail past our blockade. When this confrontation takes place, the Royal Navy will likely be just over the horizon waiting. The result would be the same. An even worse case situation would be if the French or Spanish or someone else tries to ignore the blockade since they see the British getting away with it. We would wind up with them as adversaries as well. No, I see no choice but to deny the British access to Rebel ports and deny the Rebels the goods the British would bring to strengthen them. The slap in the face over recognition I would accept, but the support of the Rebels that follows is unacceptable. I see no choice, regrettably, I will ask Congress to declare war on England." Lincoln again felt very tired. After a few seconds, Lincoln said, "Mr. Stanton, please arrange for me to address a joint session of Congress tomorrow as soon a possible. I will also need to see the Congressional leadership immediately. I must tell them what has happened."

As the men left the Oval office to carry out their instructions, President Lincoln felt more than just alone in his office, he felt alone in the world. The United States would surely be at war with England by this time in a day or two at the most. "We are at a turning point now," he thought. "We must not let a strong coalition form against us. We must strike soon. The key is in defeating the Rebels on land. If this is not done quickly, they will be strengthened by England, making it harder still to defeat them. I don't know if our people will stand up to an even longer, drawn out war. We can threaten Canada. That should help pull English assets away from the South, but this will take even more men. That means we will have to increase the draft for the Army *and* Navy. Elections are coming. The threat of a longer war and more men will not help my re-election! George McClellan's promise of an armistice will surely play against my call for larger drafts along with the army's loss in Maryland. *Time!...I must have some time!"* Lincoln was looking out of the window and, almost as if he were calling out to him, he said, "General Grant, you must buy me some time."

RICHMOND

It had been a grand meal, complete with small talk, laughter, and a relaxed atmosphere. The men moved from the dinner table to the parlor for cigars and conversation as the ladies moved to follow Varina Davis for "ladies talk". President Jefferson Davis' guest list included Vice President Alexander Stephens, Secretary of State Judiah Benjamin, Secretary of War James Seddon, Secretary of the Navy Stephen Mallory and Generals Samuel Cooper and Robert E. Lee. Other members of the Confederate Cabinet, or Administrators, as they were actually known, were either out of town or ill, as was the case with Christopher Memminger, the Secretary of the Treasury. The men were in high spirits.

"Gentlemen, I don't know when I have enjoyed a dinner more!" Everyone laughed as Judiah Benjamin noted that the news of the United States declaring war on England, and the news that France had agreed to also quickly recognize the Confederacy made for a marvelous condiment to the evenings meal.

Davis smiled and pulled on his lapels as if to make an announcement. "You know, I am even looking forward to going to the office tomorrow. I will be receiving our new Minister from Great Britain! I think in a day or two we will likely have to have another dinner, Mr. Benjamin. This time to honor Her Majesty's representative and our new ally!"

"By all means, Mr. President!," replied Benjamin.

"General Cooper, perhaps you can persuade General Lee to join us once more!," said Davis.

General Samuel Cooper, as Adjutant General, was the highest ranking officer in the Confederate Army and a close friend of Jefferson Davis. "I will work on him, Mr. President, but General Lee has a habit of not staying in one place too long."

"Much to the dismay of the Yankee Army!," added Secretary of War Seddon. Everyone had a good laugh.

Lee smiled and said, "Thank you, Mr. President, but I must

regrettably decline as I plan to leave for my headquarters day after tomorrow."

President Davis became more serious. "General, let me speak to you about one of the main reasons I wanted us to meet here tonight after dinner. Gentlemen, please..." Davis motioned for the men to be seated. "After I receive the British Minister tomorrow, I think we need to meet immediately and discuss the practicality of conducting some joint operations against our now mutual enemy. If a joint operation is not immediately practical, at least we should coordinate our actions so as to be mutually beneficial to each other's forces. I have given this some thought and I have several ideas I thought I would place on the table for your comments." This was vintage Jefferson Davis. His military background as a colonel of Mississippi volunteers in the Mexican War, as a former U.S. Secretary of War, and even his short stint as a Major General commanding all Mississippi troops until he was elected President, tended to get him in the middle of planning that his Army officers would normally be doing. It had caused some problems in the past, and Davis had learned the hard way not to get too involved. At least this time, he was trying to put his ideas on the table rather than to put them in place.

He continued, "Now that the Federals have declared war on England, I think it safe to assume that the English will make it a top priority to break the blockade at our major ports. Simply stated, they want to purchase our cotton and our get trade. This will also let the Royal Navy strike most expeditiously at the Yankee navy, since this is where they are!

"They will also want our *free* cotton you promised them," quipped Vice President Stephens, still somewhat miffed over the offer that was made along with the agreement to discuss elimination of slavery.

"They will indeed...and they will have to open our ports to get it," remarked Davis as if to both agree and respond to his quip.

"Gentlemen, I have in mind to discuss one of several operations with our English allies. One such option would be a landing of British troops on the Mississippi coast, then a move inland up the Mississippi River to help us retake Vicksburg and Port Hudson. This would again allow us to stop the flow of Northern shipping along the river. It would also threaten both the Union troops in Louisiana and give the Union forces opposing the Army of Tennessee something to think about. The retaking of Vicksburg would give a great boost to the morale of our people."

Before anyone could respond, Davis continued. "I also thought about a second option that would see the British landing in South Carolina and moving to join forces with General Bragg to attack Sherman. There are other possibilities, but I would be interested in your thoughts on these ideas. Looking at General Lee, Davis directed his comments to him. "General Lee, since you are leaving, your comments would be most appreciated before you depart. As an Army commander, what do you think of these options? Do you think they could have a positive effect on your Army?"

Lee thought for a moment. Then, ever the gentleman and soldier understanding the chain of command, he responded. "Mr. President, I think successful implementation of either of these plans would certainly have a positive effect on my Army's efforts, as well as those of the whole country. I do feel these operations would be difficult from the standpoint of getting the British to commit land forces on our soil to fight as an ally in a secondary role. Historically, the British want to be independent in their military actions. It might be difficult for them to see how this could help the British interests, as easily as perhaps another approach. I would add that the operation through Mississippi would likely have a greater morale value than a military value. The lower Mississippi River would still be controlled by the enemy, which denies us any use of the river."

"Again, coming from South Carolina to fight in the interior of our country might be difficult for the British to accept. Their Army would certainly be smaller than that of General Bragg."

Davis was about to add another point to his ideas, when Judiah Benjamin spoke up, "Mr. President, if I may....?

"Of course," replied Davis.

"General Lee, you alluded to the British possibly taking another approach. Do you have something specific in mind?," asked Benjamin.

"Well, Sir, if the Royal Navy strikes the enemy navy as hard as I think they will, it would then be possible to land a considerable force of British regulars in Canada. I would expect this to make great sense to them, since they must be worried about an invasion of Canada by Federal forces. By joining with the Canadians, their regulars would pose a considerable force to be reckoned with. They would threaten the most northern states like Maine and Vermont just by their presence. If they develop a strong defense, this would multiply their force greatly. "

"This is very much like what we have tried to do for much of the war," added Benjamin.

Lee continued, "Yes Sir. As for the effect on our actions, while the addition of several thousand British regulars would be a great asset in our meeting the enemy, I think it would be not easy to bring about. What having thousands of British troops in Canada would do is to pose a threat that could not be ignored by Washington. Either new forces would have to be created to face these troops in Canada or substantial forces would have to be drawn from other theaters of the war to perform this duty. I feel sure the enemy would not leave its northern most states and its capital undefended."

Lee then added, "If a plan could be developed to have the British and Canadian troops cross into the north and begin to move toward Washington, we might be able to attack the enemy before us at the same time. If he were weakened by being forced to face in two directions, we might defeat him and capture his capitol."

General Lee had clearly presented another option with his comments, and President Davis quickly saw the logic and the impact such a plan could have if were well developed and coordinated. The idea that Washington, and not Richmond, could be captured was particularly exciting to him knowing that Richmond was constant in the sights of the Army of the

Potomac.

James Seddon commented that a recommendation of such an idea might find favor by the British, since it allowed them to operate mostly on Canadian soil. Others commented on the pros and cons of such a plan and the discussion continued for some time. It was clear that a plan was indeed being formatted through this discussion. Then a servant entered with a note for President Davis.

Davis read the note and then said, "General Lee, there is an officer outside to see you."

Lee excused himself and stepped outside. It was during this time that Judiah Benjamin took the opportunity to remind everyone that the discussions of the evening should be treated in strict confidence and not shared even with staff members as of yet. Then, noting the lateness of the hour, the President thanked all for coming and was about to bring the evening to a close when General Lee returned to the room. Everyone looked at him to see if there was a problem.

"My apologies, Mr. President, I thank you for a delightful evening, however, I must now get Mrs. Lee home and depart immediately to see to my command. I have just been informed that Grant is moving. He is moving toward Richmond."

The effect was electric. After a wonderful evening discussing how things would surely soon turn in favor of the Confederacy, the news had come that Richmond was again being threatened. It was a sobering reminder that this war was far from over.

President Davis decided to broach the subject of joint military operations and perhaps a plan similar to what Robert E. Lee had mentioned with the new British Minister to the Confederate States. He would do so shortly after receiving the British Minister Bunch, the former British Consul in Charleston before the war started. Time was again becoming a factor.

As mentioned the evening before by President Davis, it was enjoyable to come to the office. Meeting and receiving a Minister from another government was a new and exciting experience! Then again, almost every day was something new for Davis who practically had to develop a foreign policy and establish diplomatic policies as he went. There was no previous President or government history to draw upon. Normally protocol would initially have the Secretary of State receive a new minister, however for this very first minister ever to be received and under the special circumstances, Davis had decided to do it personally. Secretary of State Benjamin was surely his strongest help in such matters. He was intelligent and extremely perceptive to what was actually being said and what was meant in such diplomatic exchanges. President Davis asked him to be present when he received Minister Robert Bunch as the representative of the Queen and the English government.

"Mr. President, I present my credentials to you, and extend to you the kindest wishes of Her Majesty and Prime Minster Palmerston." Minister Bunch was seemingly very pleased to be in Richmond.

"I have looked forward to welcoming you for some time, *Minister* Bunch! I understand you were in Charleston until early 1863 as British Consul there. However its been some months since you were in the South has it not?" asked Davis.

"Yes, Sir, it's been just over a year since I left Charleston. I must say there have been a lot of changes since then, but I am delighted to be back in the South. I very much enjoy the warm hospitality and kindness for which Southern people are so well known." Bunch was being more than just diplomatic. He really was happy to be back in the South where he had spent so much time just before the war. He had come to enjoy and like the Southern people. He was truly happy to return.

President Davis continued, "I wish that time afforded us more of an opportunity to think on such times, but I fear we find our countries in a struggle with a relentless foe. I hope we shall be able to discuss mutual actions and cooperative efforts that will help us to end this terrible struggle soon. I would much prefer to talk about commerce, trade and travel than to talk about armies, navies and supplies!"

"I fully understand, Sir. Your valiant struggle for independence from the United States has been noted for some time with admiration by the British government. We hope that as England now joins in our own fight with the Northern government, you may be aided by our actions." What Bunch had carefully said, without actually saying it was that England had her *own* fight with the North. She was not ready to dive into being a fully cooperative ally just yet. Davis figured it would cost the South yet more to bring England in to full partnership, but he was not ready to pay more just yet.

"Well, Minister Bunch, as the Royal Navy opens the blockade of our ports to give you access to the bountiful supply of cotton we have waiting, this in itself will be a tremendous help to both of our countries. We think that trade with England will quickly flourish and grow *if* the Royal Navy can keep the ports open for this purpose." Davis was playing with Bunch now as he said, *"...if* the Royal Navy can keep the ports open...."

As expected, Robert Bunch quickly moved to hold up the English colors. "The Royal Navy *will* keep the ports open, Sir, I *assure* you of that." He smiled.

"Minister, these difficult times call for me to be direct, so forgive me if I do so on this our first meeting," said Davis.

Benjamin was hoping that Davis' reputation for directness, even when there was not and emergency would not force Confederate policy in a direction it did not need to go. Benjamin was thinking that as Secretary of State, he would at least like to have a go at it on his own!

Bunch made it easy for Davis. "Certainly, Mr. President, I understand. Please ask whatever you wish."

"I would deem it most helpful to our two nations if you could provide a naval liaison with the necessary staff assets to work with our navy department to effect, let us say... a high degree of cooperation in naval matters of mutual interest." Davis and Benjamin were looking to see how this was received.

"I think this is a most productive idea, Mr. President. I presently have one naval officer on my staff that could initially fill this role for us. Captain Sir James Wilmot. He might wish to add additional staff officers as needed, with your agreement of course," Bunch assented.

"Excellent, excellent!" Davis replied. "Along the same lines, a British Army representative would be most welcome at General Lee's headquarters as well. When Colonel Freemantle was with General Lee's Army, this was very helpful. I am sure that, given the current situation, this would provide even greater opportunities for coordination and cooperation."

"Of course, Mr. President."

"I might also add, Minister Bunch, I desire the closest and most cooperative working relations between you and Secretary Benjamin on behalf of our governments. Secretary Benjamin is one of the most qualified and capable men in the Confederate government. I know he will offer you every assistance."

Benjamin acknowledged his President's comments, "By all means, Mr. President."

Davis continued, "Minister Bunch, one other item I must mention. As you undoubtedly know, France has notified our Commissioner in Paris that they will very soon extend recognition to our government. I feel this is in no small part a result of the recognition extended by England. I would be remiss if I did not express the thanks of our people to you for this as we begin."

"Thank you, Mr. President. We are very pleased to see France follow England in recognizing the Confederacy as a nation among other nations." Bunch had returned the compliment, while he carefully restated that England had taken the lead in this just as President Davis noted.

After some other conversation, Davis began to stand, signaling that this first meeting was over. "Minister Bunch, again welcome to you! We are just delighted to have you in Richmond. I will have my secretary contact your office very soon, as I would like to host a dinner in your honor." Davis paused and smiled, "I will look forward to toasting Great Britain and Her Majesty."

Minister Bunch smiled, "I would be honored, Mr. President, and I look forward to toasting *you*, Sir, as well as the Confederacy!"

Jefferson Davis was most pleased as he felt that formal

relations between Great Britain and the Confederate States were now off to a good start.

As Secretary Benjamin and Minister Bunch left the President's office, Bunch said he felt it important to meet immediately with Benjamin to discuss some military operations that *were already planned and about to take place.* Benjamin was slightly surprised at the offer to share military plans, but not surprised that Britain had already made them and was about to carry them out. Benjamin arranged a meeting with selected civilian and military personnel for later in the afternoon in a secure setting. It was to be a most informative afternoon as the plan to attack the Federal blockade at Charleston and half a dozen other Southern ports was laid out, along with a plan to invade the United States! Operation *Royal Oak* was already in motion.

CHARLESTON

It was a night made for Rebel blockade runners. The sky was almost completely overcast with no moon and without the lightning that was often observed from thunderstorms far out to sea on warmer nights. A steady cold Atlantic wind blew toward the South Carolina coastline. For the Union ships on blockade duty, it was even colder off shore than it was in Charleston. It was almost March. The cold winds of winter would soon be gone, but for now it was a wind to cut a man to the bone. Still, the dark night required extra alertness. Most of the time, the men standing watch duty on the *USS New Ironsides* were looking toward Charleston. They watched for Confederate ships that might try to leave the South Carolina coast and run the blockade at night. Now that war with England was a fact, lookouts needed to watch offshore as well as inland. The big 4200 ton New *Ironsides* was the pride of the Atlantic Blockading Squadron, and indeed the squadron's commander, Admiral DuPont, had made it his flag ship. Similar to the English ironclad, *HMS Warrior*, the *New Ironsides* was a truly formidable warship, mounting fourteen 11" guns and two 150 pound Parrot guns. A 4" iron armor belt placed over a 12" thick oak hull made it one of the strongest fighting ships on the sea. If she had a weak point, it was her bow and stern, where there was no armor. Only extra wood and sandbags provided protection here.

"You don't think the skipper meant what he said about a thirty day extension do ya? My Lord, I don't want to stay out here another month without getting some shore leave... I tell you this much if we get stuck again just sitting here, I..." Seaman Jamie Christian stopped in mid sentence and then slowly pulled the upside down pipe from his mouth and pointed out toward the dark Atlantic.... Did you see a light out that way... just off to port? "

The other sailor straightened up from bulkhead where he was leaning and turned to the left side of the ship. Both men were now quiet as they stared seaward into the dark sky.

It was common for sailors, as they moved around the deck during their watch, to spend a minute or two chatting when they came together just under the mizzenmast. It wasn't supposed to be that way, but it helped break up the hours of the long nights on blockade duty. With the Admiral gone, the ship relaxed even a little more. After almost four months on station, the routine had become very monotonous. It was punctuated only by the now occasional blockade runner that tried to leave the port of Charleston. Of the last four ships to try and break out, one was turned back by the guns of the first line of frigates and gunboats closer in to the shore, one was captured after a brief flight, and the other two ships managed to break out. The latter two had come through the blockade a the weakest point on the western side. Chances were now only 50-50 that a 'runner' could break free. With each prize captured, there was one less Rebel ship to try and make a run. The blockade was taking a slow relentless toll on Confederate shipping. In fact, there had been no activity for the last several days. None at all.

"I don't see anything, Jamie," the sailor responded. "You saw a light out this a way? How far out?" He was staring into the blackness searching for a glimmer of light or an outline of some ship.

"Couldn't tell, but sure looked like a light…just for a second." The sailors were quiet for a time as they both looked for any light or movement. Jamie spoke without taking his eyes off the sea, "No matter how many watches I stand, it always seems spooky out here on nights like this. I don't like this sittin' and waitin' when you can't see a blessed thing." He was still peering into the darkness, but to no avail. The other sailor had now turned and was looking at the Charleston coast line.

"You don't think it could be some of them Brits …?" Christian did not answer. "No signal lights or unusual lights along the coast that I can see. Looks normal toward the shore. I've noted that the Rebs put most of the coast lights out when a 'runner' is going to make a run for it. You think they'd know we see the change. It helps us know something is up so we look harder!" Still there was no answer from Seaman Christian.

"Guess it was just some ship way out just passing clear of the coast," Christian said as he kept looking. "If we see anything else, I'll send up a rocket. Keep alert, now."

Out in the Atlantic sailing toward Charleston Harbor, the English naval squadron and several Confederate vessels were bearing down on the U.S. Navy ships sitting quietly at anchor.

"Midshipman Oxmoore is on Captain's report, Mr. Avery," said the English Lieutenant. "My God! He should know better than to open a hatch where the Quartermaster's lamp can show," he said sternly. "See that ALL lamps are out… now!"

"Aye Sir," said the Chief as he moved away smartly to see to the order.

The Lieutenant turned and moved to where the ship's captain was observing the coast with his telescope. "A stupid error, Sir. I shall see to it. Do you think the Americans saw the light," asked the Lieutenant?

"If they did, we will likely see a signal rocket in a moment or two," said the Captain as he scanned intently through his telescope. The lights from the shore helped provide a contrasting background to aid the English officer's observations. "Several of the smaller American ships have lights showing. Very cordial of them to offer us the navigational assistance, I must say." He abruptly stopped scanning. "Ah, there is a frigate… and another one… now a small schooner... The frigate is surely the American ironclad we were told about. A point to port, Mr. Watkins."

"Aye, Sir. A point to port. All guns manned and ready, Sir, " replied Watkins

"Very well." The Captain replied without ever moving from his observations. "Most of their vessels appear anchored parallel to the shoreline… all except this frigate and a smaller ship behind her. Both have their bows seaward. Ready for a fast pursuit, no doubt. We will take the frigate down our larboard side close aboard and fire our first broad side before she knows we have closed with her." Lowering his telescope at last, the Captain continued speaking to his Lieutenant, "First target is an ironclad frigate. I want our fire to concentrate on the

213

stern and bow at the water line…its not armored there. Two guns to fire and cut her masts down. When we clear her stern, we will cross behind her and then resume course to take the next smaller ship in line with our starboard guns. Pass the word quickly, but quietly, Mr. Watkins."

The Lieutenant immediately headed for the chief gunner who awaited his orders. The Captain was hoping that he could tear open the armored ship at the water line and put water into her by the stern or bow. It figured that if she quickly took on a lot water, she would likely roll or sink because of the heavy armor. It had been a great point of discussion by many of the Captains of the fleet. He was convinced it would work. Now he would see for himself if this armor plating that was being introduced might be the ruination of the ship it was meant to protect. Other shots penetrating at the ends of the ship would travel well into it bowels and wreak havoc with the crews and boilers. In any event he would not waste a close aboard, first round volley against armor he probably could not penetrate anyway. He would make the most of this surprise and his gunnery.

The distance was closing fast now. The British sailors were almost motionless as they stood by their guns. Gunners strained to see their approaching targets and each was giving hand signals for final adjustments before firing. On board the *New Ironsides*, the two men on watch had made another round. Each sailor was now nearing the opposite ends of the ship. Seaman Christian stopped at the bow, scanned across the horizon, and then looked up to note a particularly slow meteor streak high up across the dark sky right between two cloud lines.

"A shooting star…sailor's good luck!," he thought.

With another quick visual scan, he shrugged his shoulders deeper into his pea coat and turned away to start back down the starboard side of the ship. He was looking westward for any suspicious movement in the night. As he reached amidships, he turned and moved across the deck to again make his way toward the bow.

Suddenly, like some nightmarish apparition, what looked to

be the largest ship he had ever seen began to appear out of the dark. It was only 200 yards away, moving fast and coming down the port side of his ship with only the sound of the parting water to announce its passing. For a moment Christian stood transfixed in disbelief. Then he turned to run toward the ships bell to sound the alarm. He saw the other watch was already running toward the bell. Christian started yelling as he ran to fire a signal rocket to alert the other ships.

"Ship off the port bow!!" "Ship off the port bow!!"

The alarm bell began to clatter shattering the night. Then in a thunderous roar, the British fired. The Naval Battle of Charleston had begun!

The heavy 7" breech loaders and the 68 pound smoothbore guns of *HMS Defence* fired less than one second apart. At such close range the fire from the big ironclad frigate was devastating. The stern portion of the American ship was shattered into splinters with every shot as the large projectiles found their mark. Some exploded on contact, some tore deep into the ship. Every shot hit home. On deck, both American sailors dove for cover to avoid the shrapnel and splinters flying from the stern explosions. The ship shuddered and rocked at the pounding it was taking. Men scrambling to get topside to man their guns were knocked down by the concussion of round after round tearing into the ship. Almost at once the big American ironclad began to list to its port side. It listed slightly at first, then more and more. With even a slight list, the gun crews that got to the deck were unable to bring guns to their bear. The U.S. ironclad, seeking maximum armor protection, had been designed with only small openings in which to move its guns. Loose items began to slide to the port side as water poured into two large holes made by numerous hits at the water line forward. Then British ship fired another tremendous volley. This time, the guns were aiming at the American warship's stern. Once more, large holes in the iron plate and chunks of oak were torn from the ship by the large guns. The *HMS Defence* passed to the left behind *New Ironsides* and after a moment, she again turned back to the right. She was swinging on course to bring its starboard guns to bear on the small 600 ton screw steamer *Stettin*.

All across the American blockade, ships were now firing. Some had targets, others only thought they did. The heavy guns of the British ships and their unanswered volleys sparked fires that had set at least two ships to burning. Rocket after rocket was streaking into the night sky, their bursting light flicking and casting eerie shadows across the ships and the sea. The night sky was suddenly brightly illuminated as one of the burning ships exploded in a ball of fire when its magazine ignited. Was it U.S., British, Confederate? In the darkness, there was no way to tell. For the combatants, the only part of the fight that mattered was the one in front of their guns. It was a melee... a melee being fought in darkness with only flickering light.

HMS Defence now was passing *Stettin*. As the small steamer began firing at the British battleship, the English man-of-war unleashed a full broadside literally shooting the steamer to pieces with this first volley. On a smaller, less protected ship, *Defence's* fire had been even more concentrated and the resulting damage and loss of life was much higher. In eleven minutes, three U.S. Navy ships of the blockade had been reduced to sinking hulks. The story was pretty much the same up and down the line. Only the ironclad monitor *Passaic* been spared heavy damage. It had been pounded hard, but the rounds only dented the armor and banged the crew around. In fact, the ironclad took the best the British could give it, and then it replied by firing direct hits with several rounds from its heavy guns to drive the attacker away. Since the American monitor did not have full steam up, she could only sit in the water firing when she had a target. She took hit after hit while her boilers built up pressure to maneuver. The *Passaic* would be among the six ships to escape from the guns of the British and Confederates.

In less than 45 minutes the battle was over. Of the eleven U.S. ships on blockade duty at Charleston, five were sunk, burned or run aground. Two others suffered moderate damage. Two particularly heavy losses were the *New Ironsides,* which sunk despite a valiant effort by her crew to save her, and the gunboat *Sebago,* which had blown up when its boiler exploded and set off the ship's ammunition. The American loss of life was heavy. Four American ships made their way to open sea, while the ironclad *Passaic* and the squadron supply ship were sailing north along the coast toward Port Royal.

Two British ships had sustained moderate damage and several had minor damage. One of the British ships more heavily damaged was the ironclad sloop, *HMS Enterprise,* which attacked the monitor *Passaic.* The monitor had gotten at least three rounds from its eleven inch guns into its attacker, one of which started a fire near *Enterprise's* boilers, forcing the English ship to break off its attack. The *Passaic* could have had an even greater impact on the battle had it been able to get up steam and navigate to seek out targets. Being slow and difficult to maneuver, it was forced to retire to avoid ramming and sinking.

The two Confederate ships that were part of the British squadron had suffered only slight damage. The *CSS Georgia* had attacked and set afire the steamer *Flag,* which ran aground to avoid sinking. The newly acquired *CSS Rappahannock* had helped damage the *USS Augusta.*

The Battle of Charleston had been a British and Confederate victory. The port of Charleston was now open. It remained to be seen if the U.S. Navy wanted to try and close it again. In any event, Britain had broken the blockade and was, for the third time, at war with the United States. Now the United States would no longer have the shadow of a navy to fight. It would have to face the most powerful navy in the world in open sea warfare. The Confederate cause had a new life!

EVENTS SPIRAL

Almost like clock work, the blockading squadrons of the U.S. Navy were decimated by the heavy ships of the Royal Navy. The morning after the Charleston attack, blockading squadrons off the mouth of the

Mississippi River and at Mobile were simultaneously attacked by British steam driven ironclads. At Mobile, *HMS Warrior* took a particularly heavy toll as it sunk three U.S. steam powered warships without any of her sister warship's assistance. *Warrior's* armor plate, her size, and her heavy guns made quick work of her foes while she remained almost impervious. The *Warrior's* sister ship, *HMS Black Prince* had similar success against the Federal squadron at the New Orleans approaches. The most serious damage to the British attackers was caused, not by the American navy, but rather from a defect in the new Armstrong breech loading guns, one of which blew up on the frigate *HMS Resistance* with considerable loss of life.

Within days, the American blockade was falling apart. It was simply overwhelmed by the powerful Royal Navy. The Confederate government was stunned at how fast the British had broken the blockade. It appeared that the only ones not surprised at the results were the British. The Gulf Coast from Texas to Florida was soon opened to British merchant shipping. The merchant vessels wasted no time in getting into the Southern ports. Charleston was quickly open, and within 48 hours following *The Battle of Charleston*, cotton was being loaded on British ships. Charleston was delirious with excitement and joy. British sailors, military and civilian, were treated as heroes. It took a great effort on the part of the officers of the British merchant crews to keep their crews together and working.

Off the coast of Long Island, the U.S. Navy was not so easy to attack. The U.S. warships ships that met the British there were not just sitting on blockade duty. They had been warned that the Royal Navy was gunning for them. They were ready when the British arrived. The battle off New York ended in a draw with the British withdrawing and the Americans rather glad they did. As the British withdrew toward Nova Scotia, other elements moved to Bermuda to re-coal and rearm. It was apparent that a serious blow had been dealt to the U.S. Navy's *Anaconda Plan*. While the American Navy knew the blockade was broken, it was sure it could gather its forces and again seal off the South. For now, the damage had been done, but to the U.S. Navy, this was only the first round with the British.

As the Royal Navy was reeking havoc off the coast of the U.S. and C.S., Confederate raiders were growing ever more bold in their attacks against American merchantmen. Their operations were greatly aided by the now easy access to friendly British ports for supplies and repairs without fear of American Navy interference. The *CSS Alabama*, *CSS Georgia* and the *CSS Florida* were sinking U.S. merchant ships at an increasing rate. The *CSS Shenandoah* joined these raiders by helping to clear the Indian and Pacific oceans of ships flying the American flag.

In England, Confederate Naval Commander James Bulloch, the once not so secret Confederate agent trying to quietly purchase ships for the Confederate Navy, was openly shopping and negotiating for ship contracts as if on a European shopping tour! The *CSS Stonewall and CSS North Carolina* were quickly configured to join *Alabama* and *Florida* in roaming the seas for the Confederate States Navy. The *CSS Mississippi* and *Albert Sidney Johnston* as well as several other new cruiser class raiders were quickly put into construction. The *CSS Vicksburg, Manassas, Charleston*, *Monocacy* and *Oak Hill* were all part of a new class of Confederate Corvette that would soon make the CS Navy strong enough to clear Union shipping from the sea lanes.

INVASION

Abraham Lincoln was working late again. It was now dark and the lamps burned brightly in his office. More and more often in the last few months, this late night work was becoming the norm for him. He had just finished his sixth or seventh meeting of the day. He wasn't sure how many meetings there had been and how many people he had seen. Mary Todd Lincoln had come by to see about him and Tad stopped by to see *Papa* as he went off to bed. Anyone around Lincoln could notice him almost aging before their eyes. The stress and pressure of the war was draining him as surely as it was the nation, slowly at first, but now it was noticeable.

This evening he was working on several of his re-election speeches. His last meeting of the evening had been with leaders of the Republican Party who were working on the re-election strategies. They had urged him to bring some good news to the public, something encouraging. The papers had begun to seriously question the Republican direction. The war seemed endless. About the time something good happened, something bad seemed to over shadow it. George B. McClellan, whom Lincoln had been fired twice as commander of the Army of the Potomac, was running as the Democratic nominee against Lincoln. Each time the Confederates or the British sank a U.S. ship or made a gain, McClellan was quick to point out the fallacy of the Lincoln administration's approach to running the war. At first it looked as though McClellan would probably carry only his home state of New Jersey in the upcoming election. This was changing weekly.

Great Britain's entry into the war brought a great depression upon the rank and file citizen of the North. After all, it was they who were bearing the burden of the losses. Now they had to seriously consider the threats of British attack to their very homes. The thought of 90,000 Canadian militia and 18,000 British regulars just across the border was unsettling to the northern states, to say the least. The Governors of Maine and Vermont had come to Washington to demand that Federal troops be sent to their borders with Canada. New York, which had more troops in Federal service than any other state, informed the Federal government that it *would be* recalling some of its troops back for home defense. When Lincoln said this could not be done until there was *a real threat* of invasion, tempers flared and threats were thrown out across the floor of Congress. One senator from Nebraska casually remarked to a colleague that perhaps the South did indeed have a point about States Rights, since it appeared the Northern states had none! A call of *Copperhead!,* and then *Traitor!* rang out, quickly followed by a flying fists and cane fight between two elderly statesmen. It was quickly over and just as quickly it was pointed out by other Senators that such comments and reactions had no place in the U.S. Senate. In truth, to do so risked arrest since Lincoln had suspended the *Writ of Habeus Corpus,* therefore no reason need even be given for such a federal arrest. It was evident that the fear of a British/Canadian invasion, real or not, was creating very real problems for the Union government!

Lincoln was in the midst of a Cabinet meeting, his second in as many days. The situation in Virginia was not producing the results that were needed. While the Rebel capitol at Richmond was seriously threatened, it was still holding firm against Grants efforts. At sea, the situation with the British Navy was bad and growing worse. The blockade had almost fallen apart and it appeared it was intact only in those places where the British had not seriously tried to break it. The Cabinet members were discussing the problems and options and suggestions had been flying all around the table, ranging from gathering naval forces to attack the British naval base at Bermuda, to turning loose U.S. raiders similar to what the Confederates were using to cripple the U.S. merchant fleet. Just before lunch, the President's secretary came in, handed him a note and spoke quietly with him for minute or two. Lincoln seemed troubled by this and then left the room for a few minutes before returning. As he sat down, the table was quiet for a minute before Navy Secretary Wells spoke.

"Mr. President, we have been talking about what action we

might take that would give us the greatest impact on the situation as well as on the upcoming election. We think the idea of raiders being loosed to prey on British shipping and an immediate coordinated attack against the Canadian naval base at Nova Scotia would have a very…positive…effect." It was apparent that the President was not really hearing what Guideon Wells was saying. Wells stopped and waited for the President to say something.

Lincoln spoke in low tones, "I fear we have more pressing problems now, gentlemen. I have just been informed that British regulars have crossed into Maine and have seized the state capitol of Portland."

The men were stunned! Maine *invaded*? Portland *captured*? The meeting quickly became a series of conversations, questions and angry comments about the British and the Confederates. "How?… When?… Casualties?… Where are they now?…" Questions again abounded.

Lincoln quieted everyone and said, "I am told that there was only minor resistance and little bloodshed, so at least we can be thankful of that. British troops crossed into Maine during the night and were in Portland with cavalry before anyone could do anything. They appear to be moving southward, but their intentions are not clear at this time. "

"Maine has always been pro British!," said Seward. "You would think they would fight or call out the militia," he added.

"What militia?" said Stanton. "Maine has most of their able-bodied men in the Army of the Potomac! There probably was not much in the way of troops or arms to oppose British regulars!"

"Do you think they could be coming to Washington?" asked Treasury Secretary Salmon Chase timidly.

"Good grief! No!" said Seward. "Not even a large force of British and Canadian troops could come through Maine all the way down to Washington! We have the largest Army in North America. British forces would never be so stupid as to get strung out from their support base and then run headlong into the Army of the Potomac!"

"You're forgetting the Army of Northern Virginia," said Lincoln. "Robert E. Lee won't sit by and miss an opportunity to strike. If Grant moves north to stop the British, Lee would probably attack Washington. It would be too good of a target to pass up." Lincoln was rubbing his jaw and thinking the situation through as he talked. "In fact, this might be part of a coordinated plan between the British and the Rebels. If we aren't very careful, this could just cost us the war!"

"Oh my God!" said Gideon Welles.

Seward then said, "When word of this gets to the New England states, they will be all over us to send their troops home."

Lincoln replied, "They *already* know. I was informed on the same note that Senators from the New England states, New York and Pennsylvania have asked to meet with me *immediately*. It appears that the Fox has scattered the chickens and we have only a short time to gather them up before they are lost."

Stanton spoke up, "Mr. President, I suggest that General Grant withdraw the Army back to near Washington, then move troops to meet this threat. He could leave a strong force to protect Washington. At the same time, we should call for General Sherman to withdraw from Chattanooga and move toward Richmond. Perhaps we can still bag Richmond and Lee. Sherman could do it for us instead of Grant."

"What about Bragg's Army of Tennessee?," asked Lincoln.

"Well, he may have to be left unchecked for a while. I don't like it, but I don't think he will follow Sherman north. If Bragg stays in Tennessee and Georgia, we can come back to him after we have met and checked the immediate threat." Stanton waited to see what the President would say.

"There is merit in what you say, Edwin, but I think we need some military advice on this," said Lincoln. "One thing is for sure, we *must* send troops to meet the British. The British and Canadians may not plan to advance much beyond Portland, but we must be sure. They have invaded our soil and we just cannot let them advance unchecked. I have to meet with the Senators now, and they surely won't want to hear anything less! I assume we agree on this much, correct?"

Everyone nodded or said yes in agreement. "All right, I will ask their states to call out what militia they can. Mr. Stanton, we will need militia and other troops from non-threatened states, the western states, or from wherever you can get them. They need to start assembling to meet this threat." Lincoln raised his finger to make a point. "But don't strip Grant. I do not want him weakened in the midst of this until I can talk with him. We will need an officer to take command until we can confer with General Grant. Look to see who you have available to send immediately." Stanton was making notes and nodding as he said he would get right to it.

Lincoln then addressed the cabinet, "Gentlemen, we must react quickly and correctly in this. The initiative is slipping away from us. We can very easily lose this war for the Union. I need your full attention and best efforts here. Let us go now to see what we can find out in each of our areas. We will meet back at six o'clock tonight. I will have supper for us here as we meet and work. Any questions?"

With this, the men adjourned and quickly went to work to gather the assets to help formulate a new plan.

RICHMOND

General Ulysses S. Grant moved toward Richmond. His sudden lunge at the capital of the Confederacy surprised everyone, even Robert E. Lee who was seldom surprised by any general who had come against him. Lee had quietly summed Grant up early.

He said, "This man will come at us again and again. Losses will not stop him, we must defeat him soundly." General Lee did not really know just how well he had described his adversary.

To stop Grant, Lee had decided to meet him away from Richmond. If for some reason he could not stop Grant, the city's outer defenses could hold Grant. If necessary Richmond could be evacuated. Lee also purposed in his own mind that if Richmond was taken and burned, the Army of Northern Virginia would give no quarter to Northern towns and cites. His army would follow the Union policy to destroy and burn what it could, whenever it had the opportunity. In particular, Lee would fix his eyes on Washington. Deep down inside he hoped, he prayed, it would not come to this. The Lee home at Arlington had long since been lost, but he never brought up the subject with Mrs. Lee, who was in ill health. The Lee's front yard and home grounds had been turned into a Union cemetery by the Union Quartermaster General Montgomery Meigs. Before the war, Meigs had served with Lee, but when his son was killed in Missouri by Confederates, Meigs transferred his grief to a personal hate for Lee whom he specifically blamed for the war. Lee too had suffered much, but he never complained or talked of his loss. However, he had now made up his mind that if his capital of Richmond was *burned*, he would make the North feel the war with an equal fire. This war had rapidly become a war for more than just the soldiers in the field.

By the time General Lee returned to his headquarters, he had two recent messages telling him that Grant was indeed moving across the Rappahannock toward Richmond. Estimates were as many as 100,000 troops or more were moving. According to the reports, the Army of the Potomac was moving clumsily, but steadily. Lee quickly determined that if he could meet Grant away from Richmond, perhaps the capital would avoid the risk of siege. Lee pondered why the Federals were moving *clumsily, but steadily*. He deduced that *time* was an element here. The Federal forces needed a victory and they needed it soon. England had opened the Southern ports and influx of shoes, weapons and supplies was making the Confederate forces stronger each week. Lee correctly figured that Grant would come for the throat of the Confederacy. Grant would make a massive strike at Richmond and the Army of Northern Virginia in an effort to destroy it. Robert E. Lee now knew what he had to do. He called for James Longstreet, Richard Ewell, and A.P. Hill. J.E.B. Stuart was on his way to Lee's Headquarters and would be arriving shortly. There might be a chance to end the war in all this!

The three Generals upon which Robert E. Lee depended so much had arrived and were in the briefing tent awaiting their commander. Hot coffee had been served around and the generals were conferring and exchanging news.

"What is General Lee doing? It's not like him to be late to a staff meeting," said Ewell.

"When I came in, I noted the General was meeting with a couple of officers and what looked like a British officer in his tent, " said A.P. Hill.

"A British officer?," asked Longstreet. Hill nodded affirmatively.

"Maybe old Fremantle is back...?" Said Longstreet referring to Lieutenant Colonel Arthur Fremantle of the British Coldstream Guards who had been an observer just a few months before with Longstreet command. Longstreet raise his eyebrows, lifted his nose up and broke into a stiff English accent, " Bit of all right if he is... I say, Old top! Pip Pip!" Ewell and Hill laughed freely at Longstreet's imitation. "Actually, I hope it is Freemantle, and I hope he has brought his Guards with him! To use his words, he was a jolly good show!" said Longstreet. The other generals laughed again.

"Well, for my part I am just pleased the Brits provided us with the shoes and ammunition we have been getting the last few weeks," said Hill.

"Amen to that!" added Ewell.

"Maybe there is a…" Hill never finished his statement as General Lee entered the tent. He was accompanied by a British Colonel who followed him in, then stood almost at attention in the general officers presence.

Lee spoke immediately, "Gentleman, may I present Colonel Lawrence Jeffreyes of the British Army." The officers shook hands and greeted Jeffreyes, who seemed very pleased to be present. Lee motioned for all to be seated, but he remained standing.

Lee actually slightly smiled as he addressed his generals. "For once, gentleman, there appears to be good news with very little bad news to accompany it! Colonel Jeffreyes was escorted here from Richmond by two officers from the staff there. Colonel Jeffreyes has been assigned to my staff as liaison officer and shall we say... *coordinator* for our Army and the British command in North America. Not only does the colonel's arrival speak to improved communication and much needed coordination between our forces, but he brings news of immeasurably positive actions now in progress by Her Majesty's forces in Canada." Lee put his spectacles on and began reading the dispatches that had just been delivered to him only moments before by the couriers that had accompanied Colonel Jeffreye." Yesterday, 11,000 British regulars accompanied by 25,000 Canadian militia crossed into the state of Maine and captured Portland, the state capital."

"By God that's just what we have needed!" Longstreet slapped his leg with his gloves in sheer delight as the other two generals grinned and showed their happiness with the news.

Lee continued, "I am told by Colonel Jeffreyes that the plan is for British troops to continue just past Portland to near the Maine and Vermont border where they will stop and fortify positions against a Federal attack. No doubt you can see where this leading. If you will look on the map here with me." The men stood and leaned forward over the map table as Lee rolled out a map and placed it over the situation map already on table. He pointed to an area just south of Portland, Maine. "As British forces settle in across here to defend their gains, the Federals will surely react. They have only militia and some troops around Washington to use unless…"

Ewell added, "…unless they pull troops from somewhere else."

Lee looked over the top of his glasses. "And I do not think they can assemble a militia force of sufficient size or quality to attack and dislodge entrenched British regulars. They will have to have seasoned, experienced troops, and a lot of them."

"Grant!, said Ewell.

"Precisely!," replied Lee.

Longstreet spoke up, "If we can see this, you know Grant must see this and Grant won't be fooled into weakening his Army by moving half of it to Vermont."

"Correct, but just like at Monocacy, Mr. Lincoln may just do it for us," said Lee. "As Grant balks, Lincoln will surely push him to move a lot of troops northward. I expect there will be no choice here as the state politicians will raise a furor to get some or most of their troops home to protect their homes! What we must do is hold steady and let Grant be forced to withdraw some of his troops. Then we may have opportunities develop for us to attack him. If not, our ability to hold against him will surely be increased. Time will work against him because the Federal elections are just over a week away."

The officers could now see what was needed to really have a chance to end the war. They must hold firm.

The defense of Richmond took on an entirely different importance now. They could help defeat Lincoln by standing firm.

WASHINGTON

The furor and near hysteria across many parts of the North had shifted the direction of voters on an almost daily basis. The United States had been invaded! Who was to blame? Lincoln? Congress? The Peace Party supporters who made the U.S. appear less than committed to continuing war effort? The Army generals? There was plenty of blame to go around and as in all elections, the men at the top were the primary targets. The election was quickly becoming a referendum on the war itself.

As the votes were being counted, Abraham Lincoln sat alone at his desk reflecting upon his time in office and waiting for the first returns. Mary Todd was keeping the children quiet and away from their father until events would unfold to see what was happening with the vote. Lincoln was convinced that he had very little chance to win. Northern papers, such as the *New York World,* no longer supported the war and claimed the country was steadily going bankrupt due to the conflict. Horace Greely was calling for a new ticket to replace Lincoln. The recent turn of events caused most of the Republican party to agree with him. Lincoln thought it amazing that he had even been able retain the nomination for re-election now that England was in the war. He thought it was likely due to the fear that things would get even worse, if a new Republican were to run against a sitting Republican President. Worse of all, the Democrats had been calling for cessation of hostilities at the earliest practical moment.

As President, Abraham Lincoln had known only war. How he wished it had been different. Now a new man would surely be elected. That man would be George B. McClellan, the General that Lincoln had fired...and fired twice! It would be a bitter pill to turn the government over to him. McClellan would soon be President elect and with the change in Presidents, Lincoln knew the war would be surely be lost. McClellan had said he wanted the Union restored. He also said would declare a cease fire as soon as he was President and work to bring the Rebels back into the Union *peacefully*. He claimed he was the one man who could make peace with Great Britain, since he had lived in Europe since being relieved by *Mr.* Lincoln. There was no love lost between Lincoln and McClellan and everyone knew it.   Everyone also knew that if this terrible carnage ever stopped, *no one* would be able to start it again. The people were sick of war! It was also certain that the Rebels would never voluntarily reenter the Union after all that had happened. Lincoln closed his eyes and rubbed his head to try and relieve a splitting headache.

Lincoln tried to think of something else, but to no avail. "Perhaps if Grant could take Richmond and Sherman could take Atlanta, we could get the Rebels to come to terms for a settled peace," he thought.   There had been much talk that if the Emancipation Proclamation were withdrawn, the Rebels might come to the table…but…"No…no, I can not do this," he thought.   "If I were to put colored soldiers back into slavery after all they have done, history would judge me and this nation harshly. I cannot do that! "

"Perhaps if we could make peace with England…*and* if Grant could take Richmond…"   For a moment Lincoln was almost hopeful as he saw a glimmer of a workable plan, but then he considered the chances of being able to make this happen. Peace with England would be difficult to sell to Congress since the Royal Navy had wreaked so much havoc with the blockade and the English government was now being so helpful to the Rebels.   Yet, Grant was the key, "…*if* he could take Richmond… *if…* We need more time," Lincoln thought, "but time is something we have run out of now. Time is against us and is no longer an ally. Grant, you must…"

"Mr. President?"   Lincoln turned to see Secretary Seward standing in the doorway, a somewhat pleasant look on his face. "We have some election returns and I thought you would want to see these."   For a man about to lose his job, Lincoln thought Seward looked somewhat satisfied. "The first of the vote count from the Army is coming in along with first results from New York, Delaware and New Jersey." Lincoln motioned for Seward to come in. He was reading from the papers in his hand as he

230

approached the President's desk. "The Army vote is going for you, Mr. President, and it is doing so by a *substantial* majority!"

Seward looked up and continued, "These first returns show that New Jersey and Delaware are going to McClellan by a large percentage," said Seward. "It looks as if he will carry those states just as we thought." Seward paused, then added, "New York is close…McClellan is doing well there, much better than expected, but it's still an even race right now. I just thought the news about the Army vote would be good news."

Lincoln knew his failure to release New York troops back to the Governor when the British began building up their force in Canada was hurting him badly. His exchange with the Governor had been bitter, and it was surely showing up in the election.

"We *must* have New York," Lincoln said quietly.

"Yes Sir, I know," replied the Secretary of State. "Perhaps the vote will swing a little more as the rural vote comes in, to offset the city." Seward was simply trying to make a bad situation sound better. He knew that because of the population, whatever direction New York City went, so would go the state.

"Any other results?," asked Lincoln.

"Maryland is pretty well split," added Postmaster General Montgomery Blair as he came in the door with Gideon Welles.

"We were in the neighborhood…," said Blair.

Lincoln smiled slightly and motioned for the men to have a seat. "How close is Maryland?," he asked.

"Actually, a little in our favor so far. I must admit that I was a little worried about Maryland, but it looks like we have a good chance to take it!" said Stanton.

"Well, it was not great news, but at least it was still a horse race," thought Lincoln. "Sounds like we are even in some and losing the rest so far, except for the Army vote. To be honest about it, the Army vote means more to me than the vote of most states. These men understand what it's about. They put their lives on the line daily. Yet they vote to continue this conflict when they could just as easily vote to stop it. That means a lot to me."

"If we can carry the western states… Ohio, Iowa and

Minnesota…coupled with the Army's vote. By Jove, we might just make it!" , said Welles.

Lincoln knew they were being optimistic. Ohio and Minnesota were probably going to vote for McClellan. He had to do more than *hold his own*, if he were to win this contest. It was going to be a long night, and it would be sometime tomorrow before the telegraphs brought a more definitive word on how the election was going. For now, at least, it was not turning into a landslide for George McClellan.

After conversation about the election results and how things might go, Lincoln excused himself. He said he was rather tired and thought he would try to get some sleep for the busy day they had to face tomorrow. He sat by his bed before retiring and read a passage or two of scripture from the Bible as he had done so many times before. He then lay down and was asleep in minutes.

Abraham Lincoln awoke in a semi-dark room. The curtains were pulled and the usual ritual of one of his children waking him had not occurred. He sat up and felt somewhat better. Yet he was still tired as he immediately began to pick up the problems of the day where he had left them the night before. He moved to the door and heard Tad running down the hallway.

"Mama, Papa's up and I didn't do it! It was John!," yelled Tad Lincoln.

"Tad!," replied John, just home from law school to be with his father for the election.

Lincoln smiled as he rubbed his face.

"No matter, boys. Your father has slept long enough," said Mary Todd Lincoln. She had kept everyone away in hopes to let her husband get some much needed sleep.

Lincoln's mind was already on the election results. He was eager to finally be getting the results as well as to be getting the election over. He had a heavy foreboding that he had lost the election. He quickly dressed and walked toward the Oval Office. He saw William Seward, the Postmaster General, Montgomery Blair and Gideon Wells waiting outside his office door.

Lincoln tried to sound pleasant. "Good morning, gentlemen. Please come in. I am sure we have much to talk about."

Lincoln went straight to his chair and motioned to the men to be seated as he still stood. He could tell by the lack of smiles that the news was not good. "Montgomery, I surmise from the look on your face that we have not faired well over this past night."

Montgomery Blair was Abraham Lincoln's closest confidant, friend and among his greatest supporter. "No, Mr. President, the reports are not good. I fear we are losing the election."

"How bad is it?," asked Lincoln.

"Its not good, Mr. President. Right now, New Jersey, Delaware, Kentucky, Maine, Massachusetts, New Hampshire, Connecticut, Indiana and Maryland are all going for McClellan. New York moved into McClellan's camp during the night. Missouri is still split. Rhode Island is very close, but looks like it may well wind up in McClellan's column. We are winning in West Virginia, Ohio, Illinois, Minnesota, Wisconsin and Pennsylvania and these look to be certain to wind up on our side. I think we can assume California and Oregon will be ours, but we won't know for a while. I could go on, but when it adds up, it already appears that we can't make it." There was silence in the room. "I'm sorry, Mr. President, but … it looks like McClellan will take the election by sometime this afternoon or tonight."

No one added anything to this for a few moments as Lincoln sat rubbing his chin and just looking at Blair. Finally, Lincoln replied, "Well, I must say, I have seen this coming. I did not want to accept it, but I did see it coming. The entrance of England into the war, and all that that brought with it, I think made the difference. Our losses at sea and in Maine, our defeat at Monocacy, and our general lack of success as of late, all pointed to the people getting discouraged, and particularly getting discouraged with me. Can't say that I blame them."

"I am truly sorry, Mr. President," said Seward. "I think we could have brought the Rebels down if we had just had more a little more time. I agree with you that England cost us the time we needed. If they had not joined the Rebels, we could have ended this thing in a few more months. I really believe that."

"Perhaps you are right, Edwin, but no matter now." Abraham Lincoln had been depressed for only minute that showed. There would be plenty of time for that later, time to reflect on what might have been if the North could have won and if he could have worked to rebuild a South back in the Union. For now there was little time to lose. Perhaps he could pull victory out of defeat if he worked at it even harder.

"What we must do is to look to winning this war in the few months we have left. I am convinced that however well-meaning General McClellan may be, he cannot possibly win this war, so we must do so before he takes office Gentlemen, I'll ask you to excuse me now. I would like to speak with Mrs. Lincoln and my family. Perhaps we can meet a little later."

The men got up and each one shook hands with Lincoln expressing regrets as if there had been a death in the family. After they left, Lincoln looked out the window for a time. He was quietly gathering his strength, the strength that he had gathered so many times before.

"I must be strong, " he thought. "I need to be strong for Mary, for the children, for the people...the people. We must show the people and the world that our nation can continue even in the midst of a civil war and an election. Democracy and our country go on even as the government leadership changes in a war. Yes, this is our strength! We will make a kindly transition to the new leader! I must now send *President elect* McClellan a note of congratulations." He looked out at Washington for another short time, then turned to talk with Mary. McClellan could wait a little longer.

RICHMOND

Jefferson Davis stood alone, quietly looking out of his office window. In his hand were two telegrams. One that had informed him that Abraham Lincoln was all but beaten in this the first American election during a time of war, and the other saying that France had recognized the Confederacy. Davis felt a tremendous rush of emotions. Strangely, he almost overcome with a mixture of elation of the Confederacy's victory and recognition as well as a deep sadness for the loss and the cost of this victory to the South. He had great apprehension of the task that lay ahead, and he was personally exhausted. He knew the word would soon be out that Lincoln and the Republicans had lost and that France had recognized the Confederacy. Church bells would ring out and there would be celebrating across the South. Jefferson Davis also knew that the war was still not over, and the Confederacy could lose even in this late hour, Lincoln or no Lincoln, France or no France.

There was a knock at the door. "Come in," said Davis. Entering the office were Judiah Benjamin, Stephen Mallory and George Trenhom, the newly appointed Administrator of the Treasury. They were all smiling and jubilant as they made their way to Davis to shake his hand, pat him on the back, and share in the joy of the news.

"Recognition by France *and* the defeat of the Republicans and Lincoln. Truly the happiest day for the Confederacy since England joined us!," said Benjamin.

"It is marvelous!," said Mallory, "...just marvelous! Congratulations, Mr. President! You have prevailed!"

Davis was smiling but he was surprised at the comment from Mallory. "My friends, the *South* has prevailed...our glorious *Army and Navy* have prevailed... our *people* have prevailed. I am truly humbled at the victory that is so near. God has truly smiled on us this day!"

The men became somewhat quiet and nodded in the affirmative as they almost prayerfully voiced their agreement with their President.

After a few seconds of almost tearful happiness, Davis spoke up. "Well! Let not my seriousness of the moment overcome the joy of the hour! Truly there is much to be thankful for, but there is also much yet to do!" Davis was now smiling. "First of all, we are all aware that this war is not yet won! It is no secret that ultimate victory is surely more in our favor with this good news, but we must seize the moment. I would propose we have a meeting of the Administrators this evening to discuss a formal proposal of a *Cease Fire* with the Federal government. Judiah, I think you and I need to speak with the British Minister as soon as possible today. We should see what England's position will be now that Mr. Lincoln is about to become a private citizen again. England has been very fair in their dealings with us. I do not want to make a move that will be detrimental to them if at all possible. Likewise, we should at least talk with the French representative, although I am not sure if Mr. Lincoln will be so quick to declare war on France as he on with England, since little was to be gained from it. Would you see to this for me?," asked Davis.

"Of course, Mr. President," replied Benjamin, "I will arrange a meeting as soon as possible."

"Let us plan to have a meeting of the Cabinet this evening after dinner...say at 7 p.m.? I will have more information then, and I will have a draft document for us to discuss in which I ask for an immediate Cease Fire!" Davis said.

"Cease Fire...That has a wonderful sound to it!," said Trenholm. "It certainly does!," said Mallory.

The men began to smile broadly again and were very happy as they filed out. Judiah Benjamin waited and was talking with Davis about the meeting with British Minister Bunch, when the church bells of Richmond began to ring.

"The news is out!," said Benjamin.

"Yes," said Davis smiling broadly. "I hope they ring the bells loudly enough to be heard in Washington!"

LEE'S HEADQUARTERS

General Lee had just come back from looking over the defenses around Richmond and was in his tent reading a dispatch from Richmond. James Longstreet and A.P. Hill entered the briefing tent where they found Richard Ewell sitting at the map table writing notes and preparing messages to be delivered when they were done.

" Hello there, Dick!," said Hill as they entered the tent. They men were obviously in good sprits.

"Howdy boys," said Dick Ewell looking up from his notes. "Ya'll must have come on the same wagon!, he added in a joking manner."

"No, we just joined up down the road before the Yankee artillery starting coming in," replied Longstreet. "I swear, they don't seem to have any limit on the artillery they can throw into a fight!"

The tent fly swung open and Lee's Adjutant, newly promoted Lieutenant Colonel Walter Taylor stepped in, smiled and said, "Gentleman, General Lee will be with you momentarily."

As he started to leave, General Hill spoke up, "Colonel Taylor, how is the General doing…? Physically, I mean. I know he has had some difficult days here of late."

Taylor replied, "Yes Sir, the General has been right well the last few days. It seemed as though the ringing of bells in Richmond and the subsequent news of the Federal election have actually made him feel better."

"Sure as the dickens made the rest of us feel pretty good too!," said Longstreet. Everyone laughed and as they did so, Taylor stepped back to hold open the tent for Robert E. Lee to enter. The three generals all stood as the commander of the Army of Northern Virginia entered with J.E.B. Stuart and Colonel Lawrence Jeffreye.

"Well, it sounds as though you all are in very good spirits, I must say!" Lee was smiling as the spoke. Hill said the recent news of Lincoln's defeat and the British invasion of Maine was *almost* as good as a nice glass of Tennessee whiskey. Again everyone laughed. Lee motioned for the men to be seated.

"General Stuart has just arrived in time to honor us with his presence. It seems that he always manages to be away from my headquarters when I have a meeting scheduled," quipped Lee as he played with his young cavalry officer of whom he thought so highly.

"Not at all, Sir. You know I love to attend your meetings…almost as much as I do attending the Yankee's meetings in their headquarters!," Stuart grinned broadly.

General Lee closed his eyes and slightly bowed to the cavalier. "General Stuart, I yield to your choice of meetings!" Everyone again laughed and Ewell gently slapped Stuart on the back.

"My friends, it is well that we find time now to laugh. There have been so many days when we had little to laugh about. God in his infinite wisdom and mercy has seen fit to bless us in this struggle. I am pleased to tell you that He continues to do so." Lee held up several pages in his hand. "I have just received this dispatch from President Davis. In conjunction with the British government, our government has now decided to offer the enemy an option for immediate Cease Fire." The officers were surprised, but delighted with this news. Lee continued, "This offer is made as a result of the election of General McClellan to be the new President, and the fact that the British have taken the capitol of Maine, while the Royal Navy has destroyed much of the Federal Navy. We, in turn, have had good success against the enemy and, except for a shortage of manpower, our supplies and material are improving almost daily. There is every hope that General Grant and the Federal government will see that the time to end this conflict is now." Lee paused, "Gentlemen, if this offer is accepted,… it could mean the end to war."

The assembled generals sat quietly for a moment as if they could hardly believe what they had heard their commander just say. Longstreet slowly put his stub of a cigar in his mouth, leaned back in his chair and then smiled. "I have hardly given any thought of this thing ending, but now that I do…it surely has a nice ring to it!"

Dick Ewell likewise seemed almost unable to give serious thought to the idea of maybe the fighting coming to a halt. "General, you don't think the Yankees might think *we* have lost the stomach for the fight do you? If we ask for a Cease Fire…they might think we have lost the will to continue…"

"No, I don't think the enemy will come to that conclusion. This offer is very specific about that, and outside of this document, the situation speaks for itself. Grant is stalled to our front. He could attack in force, but if he does he will almost surely loose a large portion of his army. This offer of a Cease Fire is very plain to say that if this offer is turned down and Grant loses here, the next offer of peace will likely be dictated on the steps of the U.S. Capitol building by Confederate and British forces."

Lee began to read from the Cease Fire proposal in his hand, "…This offer of an immediate and unconditional cease fire for all parties to include the United States, Confederate States and England, is being made with the belief that the United States can no longer win this war with the Confederate States and the British Empire. This cessation of hostilities is made in good faith with the desire to immediately bring an end to the devastation being experienced by all parties. The only conditions required are for all parties to stop fighting and to remain in place without being reinforced until a peace can be negotiated with all parties."

Lee read ahead to himself and then continued, "…It must be understood that a failure to agree to this Cease Fire will result in a renewed and intensified conflict. The nature of this war will change from a defensive effort on the part of Confederate government to one of offensive war against the United States…" Lee removed his spectacles and looked at his generals.

"You see that this document is very clear in stating that the purpose of this offer is to stop the carnage on *both* sides, but the choice is in the hands of the enemy. Gentlemen, I must make a confession to you. Even before I received this dispatch from the

President, I had already reached the decision that if Richmond was overrun and burned, I would make every effort to visit the same fate upon the enemy and his cities. It took me a long time to come to this, but I am convinced we must force the enemy to stop this war. We might not take his capital, or even make an effort to do so, but his countryside is covered with large cities that could be made to feel the anguish of war as our country has been forced to do these past several years. We are at a crucial point here. I pray the enemy will see this. If they do not," Lee was growing more serious and stern than his officers had ever seen him. "...God will need be their source of refuge and comfort, for I will bring war to their very hearth."

No one spoke for a moment. They had never heard General Lee threaten to make war on the Northern population as the Union Army had done to the South.

A.P. Hill broke the silence, "Sir, I would be honored to deliver this message to the enemy commander."

Lee was again calmed. "Thank you General, but I have already asked Colonel Taylor to deliver this to General Grant as soon as it is light and he can do so safely. As he does so, we shall be planning our actions either to respond to a Yes or a No from the enemy." Lee smiled, "I need all of you gentlemen here with me."

Stuart spoke up, "Sir, I would be likewise be honored if you would permit my command to provide a cavalry escort for Colonel Taylor."

"I was going to ask for that, General Stuart. Please have your escort dress well and present the very best possible appearance to General Grant's headquarters. It is important they look their best."

"Of course, Sir," replied Stuart.

Lee continued, "Gentleman, I do indeed hope our offer is accepted, but I will not be shocked if it is not. Mr. Lincoln has shown himself to be a man of single-minded purpose. General Grant has demonstrated that he will readily accept heavy losses to attain his goal. I remind you that Mr. Lincoln is President until March. Grant will surely be in command of the enemy armies until that time, if not beyond. They remain a dangerous combination and may now become even more so as they desperately try to force a victory at any cost. This is our first task…to prepare for a desperate effort by the enemy to our front."

Lee continued, "Secondly, if they do not attack, they may choose to leave part of their force in place while moving a large part of their forces north to counter the British forces now in Maine. The forces left behind would seek to hold pressure on Richmond by keeping us in place in a defensive posture. If the first option takes place, we will try to inflict as many casualties as possible upon their army when they attack. If the second option is their choice, I propose to hold the troops to our front while our main force moves around to attack them from the flank or rear."

Each general found something to like about any of these scenarios. Longstreet and Ewell favored the defense and hoped that if the fighting resumed in earnest, the Federals would attack their works which were improving daily. Hill favored the move to attack if the enemy was weakened. Stuart, as always, wanted to ride around the enemy and attack him from the rear or a weak flank. It appeared the Union forces would likely be at a disadvantage in either case. Of course, none of this assumed the Federals could break Confederate defenses and spill into Richmond, overpowering a large part of Lee's army in the process. If this were to happen, it would be a different matter altogether. Still, plans would have to be made to have the government ready to move on a very short notice should the city begin to fall. Several routes out of the city to Petersburg and other locations were planned using rail and road as the case dictated.

As the discussion and planning continued, Stuart stepped out to send instructions to his men to prepare for the escort, then he talked briefly with Colonel Taylor to put everything in place for the morning ride to the enemy headquarters. The other generals each sent word that they would be staying at General Lee's headquarters well into the night.

Morning arrived to find the Confederate headquarters already awake. The smell of breakfast and hot coffee permeated the air. The supplies that now flowed to the Confederate Army were evident even with things as simple as the coffee, blankets, and plentiful food that had become available. General Lee was warming his hands around a cup of coffee and greeting the sunrise, when Colonel Taylor came to him for final instructions. Taylor looked as if he were going to a parade as he saluted General Lee. He was dressed in a neat gray uniform, shined boots, polished sword, leather dispatch case and a smart new kepi he had saved for *special occasions.* Fresh haircut and a trimmed beard and mustache made him look every bit the professional staff officer he was.

"General, I believe I am ready, Sir. My escort is here and I have inspected them and they look fine. With your approval, Sir, I will be on my way," said Taylor.

"Colonel Taylor, this morning you represent the Confederate government and our army. I have the utmost confidence in you. Insure you give this dispatch case only to General Grant, or, if he is not there, to his adjutant or the acting commander. My compliments to General Grant and tell him that I respectfully request a response in 72 hours to this dispatch. After that, I will assume a negative response. Do you understand?"

Colonel Taylor carefully repeated exactly what he had been told. Lee nodded yes and then said, "God go with you, Walter. I shall pray for your safe return."

The young colonel mounted his horse, saluted and then moved to join his escort at the exit point. The escorts were each clean, well dressed and well mounted. With a large white flag being carried by the rider next to him, Taylor and the other four men rode two by two toward the Confederate lines, where they halted and gave the enemy pickets time to see and understand what they doing. Then, at a trot the riders proceeded through their lines and toward Federal lines. The troops in blue were stirring. Some stayed down behind their emplacements, others stood up and watched the approaching riders. They knew the white flag meant there would be no fighting for a time.

The small road the riders were traveling was well blocked and fortified at the point where it entered the Union lines. When Taylor stopped in front of the barricade, he was met by a young Captain who stood making no move at first. Taylor's horse turned slightly and Taylor saluted. "Sir, I am Colonel Taylor of General Robert E. Lee's staff. I have been ordered to personally deliver a dispatch from General Lee to General Grant. Will you provide an escort for us, Sir?"

The young officer in blue came to attention and smartly saluted. "Colonel, you must wait here while I inform my colonel of your arrival."

"He already knows of his arrival," said the Union colonel as he walked up. "Colonel, please state your business." Saluting once more, Colonel Taylor restated his mission.

The Union officer saluted and then said, "Come with me. I will take you to deliver your message. Your men will stay here. Tell your men dismount. Captain Franks!"

The Union captain responded loudly, "Sir?"

"Get these soldiers some coffee and a biscuit or so. This officer and I will be back directly. These men are to remain here, understand? I want these men treated with respect"

The Union colonel finally took his gaze off Colonel Taylor and turned to the young Captain. "They are under a flag of truce. Clear?"

"Yes Sir, I will see to it." The captain sent two soldiers off to come up with coffee, bacon and biscuits for the Confederate *visitors* now in their lines. The two colonels and the Confederate sergeant with the white flag rode off down the road toward Grant's Headquarters as everyone gawked at the strange scene.

General Grant was meeting with several officers to discuss plans when a major stepped into the tent and said, "General Grant, excuse the intrusion, Sir, but I think you better see this!" Grant stepped out of the tent, his coat open, no hat, coffee in hand and his ever-present cigar in his mouth. He was followed by the officers to which he had been talking. Immediately, Grant saw the white flag carried by the approaching riders and quickly noted one of the men was a Confederate officer. He made no move or change of expression, instead he took a long, slow drink of coffee.

The men stopped just short of riding up to Grant. The Union rider told Colonel Taylor to remain in place, he dismounted and approached Grant. He saluted, and told Grant the story of the Confederates riding up to the forward lines and the Confederate colonel's request. Grant told him bring the Confederate officer forward at which time the Union colonel motioned for Taylor to dismount and come up. Taylor dismounted and quickly walked to Grant.

Saluting smartly and remaining at attention, he said, "Sir, I am Colonel Taylor of General Robert E. Lee's staff. Please forgive me, but you are General Grant are you not, Sir?" Grant gave him a soft salute and then said, "I'm Grant."

"Sir, General Lee's compliments. I am instructed to provide you with this dispatch and following your reading of it, I am to give you a verbal message, Sir." Colonel Taylor remained at attention.

Grant relaxed, turned and headed for his tent all the time talking to Taylor, "Stand easy Colonel, lets go into my tent. Would you care for a cup of coffee as you wait while I read this?, asked Grant.

"No, thank you, Sir, " replied Taylor.

Sam Grant motioned for Taylor to sit down, but Taylor remained standing. "For Pete's sake, Colonel. Sit down… I am going to be a few minutes here and there is no sense in your standing all the while!" Colonel Taylor sat down maintaining an erect posture and ready to stand and resume attention on a moment's notice.

"West Point"? Grant said as he opened the dispatch case without looking up.

"Sir?," replied Taylor.

"West Point...Did you attend West Point?," asked Grant.

"VMI, Sir," Class of '57.

"Yes, of course… VMI…" Grant began to read the paper. When he had finished it some minutes later, he read it again.

Then without comment or expression, he looked up at Taylor. "What message did you have for me now, Colonel?"

Taylor stated the message as to the time limits and the conclusion of there being no response.

General Grant removed the cigar from his mouth and then said, "My compliments to General Lee. Tell him that I must forward this dispatch to Washington and await a reply. I will try to provide an answer within the time frame stated, but if not, he should not assume anything by an absence of a reply. Tell him as one soldier to another, surely he understands the difficulty of getting one's government to respond in a timely matter. You assure General Lee that I *will* do him the courtesy of a reply one way or the other just a soon as possible. Anything else?"

Taylor answered, "No Sir, I think that covers my instructions,".

Grant nodded to the Union colonel. "Very well, the officer that brought you here will escort you back to the lines. Grant stood up as did Colonel Taylor. "Good luck to you, Colonel Taylor."

"Thank you, Sir." Colonel Taylor saluted smartly and then walked back to his horse and the Union colonel who would escort him back to the front lines. His mission was complete. Now it was all up to General Grant and to Abraham Lincoln.

WASHINGTON

Abraham Lincoln was on his way out of his office when he saw Edwin Stanton coming down the hallway. Stanton was red faced and he was out of breath. "Mr. President, these papers just arrived from General Grant. Sir, you need to see them!" Stanton was puffing.

"Well, come into the office, Mr. Secretary. Lets see what this all about.," said Lincoln turning to reenter his office followed closely by Stanton,

"A messenger just brought this straight in. He came by train from General Grant and then rode at a gallop to get this here. It's a message from the Rebels! General Grant got it this morning!" Stanton was going on and on, but Lincoln had already shut him out. He saw the message was signed by Jefferson Davis himself and had come by way of Robert E. Lee. He began reading and felt his face flush as he read...

"...This offer of an immediate and unconditional cease fire for all parties... is being made with the belief that the United States can no longer win this war... The only conditions required are for all parties to stop fighting ...failure to agree to this Cease Fire will result in a renewed and intensified conflict. *The nature of this war will change from a defensive effort on the part of Confederate government to one of offensive war against the United States...*" This last article burned as he read it. He did not like the threat that the Rebels were making, but Lincoln also knew this was now a much more real option than it had been in 1862 and early 1863. With the British as allies, cities of the North were much more susceptible to invasion than ever before. He knew the offensive war being waged in the South now could well come to the North. An end to the fighting - it was what Lincoln had wanted so much, but it was not the way he wanted it. He knew to accept it would be the end of the war, for the conflict would surely never start up again if the killing and destruction was ever stopped. He also knew it would mean an end to the Union as he knew it. The Rebels would have won. No! He could not accept that! But... he was about to give up the control of the government to McClellan and he knew that McClellan would accept it!

"Mr. President?" Lincoln realized that Stanton was talking to him. "Mr. President, are you all right? Is it bad news? Stanton had seen Lincoln almost drift away as he read the message.

"It's a letter from Jefferson Davis. He is offering a Cease Fire…an end to the fighting.," Lincoln seemed to almost act puzzled as he talked to Stanton.

"A Cease Fire?…" Stanton looked puzzled, "You mean… he wants to quit?"

"No, he wants *us* to quit. He wants to *just end the fighting* now." Lincoln was looking at the document. "And he says if we don't accept this offer, the Confederates and British will take an *offensive posture*. In other words they will begin to attack us in our territory. I take that to mean they would burn and destroy as much as they get their hands on."

Stanton looked totally surprised. "My Lord!" He sat pondering what President Lincoln had said. Then he began to become stern. "Of course you won't accept this. We can fight them. We will mobilize an army and a navy like the world has never seen. We will…"

Lincoln interrupted him. "Edwin, in less than 90 days *we* won't be in office…McClellan will! If I don't accept this offer and I hand over the government to McClellan, who I feel will not prosecute the war as it must be prosecuted, we can not only lose the war and the Union, but we could be devastated in the process! I was already concerned with the French recognition of the Rebels and the possibility of their actively coming into the war." Now, add to that the pressure for me to recall the all of Vermont and most of the New York regiments to follow the all Maine troops we have already sent home, and …well… I must consider all options."

Lincoln called for his secretary. "Ask the Cabinet officers to come at once. I need to meet with them about a matter of urgency. One hour!" He again turned to Stanton. "If we are to fight, we will need to *finish it* in 60 days. If we can not do so, we may be forced to accept this Cease Fire proposal. I am at a point where I might hand McClellan half a Union, or on the other hand, I could give him a Union in the midst of war and in very real danger of being put to the torch." Lincoln looked again at the proposal as if he were trying to see something else he could use to help him in his decision. "Hard times, Mr. Stanton. Hard times."

Lincoln felt as though his office had become a prison cell. He was spending as much as 18 hours a day in his work now and was taking more and more meals in his office. When Mrs. Lincoln tried to scold him about his rest and eating habits, he had replied that the boys fighting the Rebels would also like to have time away to rest. As long as they did not rest, he could not feel the liberty to rest too much either. Mary Todd Lincoln was not impressed.

It was now some hours later following the Cabinet meeting to discuss the Rebel offer of a Cease Fire, and Lincoln was standing at the window of the oval office. He was watching the workmen going and coming as work continued on the new Capitol Dome. The construction was, to Lincoln, a symbol of the permanence of the Republic. It was a symbol of the people. The building went on in spite of the weather, the war, and even nation's changing of a President. Lincoln longed to return to a simple, quiet life, away from casualty lists and hard decisions that cost men their lives. How easy it would be. Just stop. Just stop fighting and let the Rebels go their own way. But this had always been an option. It was what Jefferson Davis and the secession states had always wanted. Peace could have come at any moment the Northern states said they just did not want to fight anymore. Now, after three years of the most brutal war ever experienced in the hemisphere, a cease fire was still the only option that would stop the slaughter. How easy it would be. Lincoln turned to his desk and as he sat down he took pen and paper and began to write.

"Dear General Grant,
It was only a short time ago that you and I discussed the

need to quickly bring this war to a close. Now, as you know, events have made this need imperative for the nation. You have read the message from Jefferson Davis. He says simply we must stop fighting or face the possibility of our nation being put to the sword. The weight of the decision rests on me alone. I do not ask you to share it, but I do need your counsel to help me decide our course."

"If we agree to the cease fire, the war will end. If we continue to fight and do not win before the new administration assumes its duties, I do not believe it will continue the fight and the war will end with the Union broken. However, if we continue to fight and we can capture the enemy capital and its government, we might win the war with the Rebels, leaving us to then deal with the British and if need be, the French."

"General Grant, I must ask you. Can you now take Richmond? This appears to me to be the only real option for a victory for the Union. If it can be done, it must be done. If it can not, I will not shed more blood and risk harm to our cities and towns when the outcome will be no different. If you have another plan and I need to come to you, I will do so. If you need to come to me, please do so.

Know that I have the utmost confidence in you and our Army. I will support you in whatever decision you recommend and then I will decide what I alone must decide. Together we must do what is best for our country and our people. I wait to hear from you.

A. Lincoln

Lincoln read over his letter, sealed it and placed in the pouch that had been provided. He called his secretary and handed the pouch over with instructions for an armed military courier to take it immediately to General Grant and await a reply. Lincoln's mind was already made up, but he would wait to see what Sam Grant said.

GRANTS HEADQUARTERS

Sam Grant was reading the Washington newspaper and noting how almost all the details reported about the war were wrong, misleading or outright lies.

"Sherman was right," thought Grant, "newspapermen are not much better than spies. Why don't they report something good and something correctly for a change?," he muttered.

The tent fly moved back and a major said, "Beg pardon, General. Courier's arrived from Washington with dispatches for you."

"Send him in," said Grant.

Immediately a cavalry captain appeared at the tent entrance. He was covered with dust and dirt from a hard ride. Grant motioned for him to come in.

As the young officer saluted he said, "Dispatch, Sir. From the President. I was told to deliver directly to you and await a reply."

"Very well. You go get some coffee and something to eat. I'll call for you when I am ready to reply. Major!"

"Sir!" the major replied as he immediately entered the tent .

"See to the Captain's needs and keep him at hand, I will want him shortly. And see that he has a fresh mount. You alone?," said Grant looking at the courier.

"No Sir, there are two armed escorts."

"See to them as well, Major." Grant was now opening the dispatch case as the two officers left him alone.

"Dear General Grant,

It was only a short time ago ... I must ask you. Can you now take Richmond? ... If it can be done, it must be done. ... I will support you in whatever decision you make ...We must do hat is best for our country and our people.

A. Lincoln

Grant sat back and took a deep breath. It had all come down to this. Take Richmond and we *might* win. Stay stalled at

Richmond or do anything else and we lose. It was just that simple. Grant needed a drink of whisky. He settled for a cup of coffee from off his small pot bellied stove.

Grant started to call for General Meade, but thought better of it. There would be time for that. He spent the next few minutes considering what would happen if he did not try to assault Richmond. George McClellan would soon be President! Grant quickly decided even *he* could be a better President than that pompous toy soldier McClellan!   Lincoln was right, if Richmond was not taken, McClellan would lose the war in his first month in office. Before he would let that happen, Grant purposed that he would settle for a cease fire *now* and save the lives of many a good man. So what to do… should we have an all out dogfight or just quit…? This would be the hardest call of the war.

Sam Grant knew that the Army of the Potomac was getting stronger each day.   Its numbers were growing as new replacement units arrived, and even considering its great loss at Monocacy, the Army was recovering well.   Morale, however, was only fair. British attacks in Maine had many New England and northern border troops wanting to go home to protect their own homestead and states which they thought might be threatened. Maine troops had already been released as had half of the New York troops. Vermont troops in particular were getting troublesome.   Other states balked at making up the manpower shortage that was being created.

Confederate defenses at Richmond were strong.   Lee and Longstreet were both known to be masters of the defense.   The Army of the Potomac had seen that first hand in Maryland.   The Rebels were growing stronger each day as well.   Grant also knew there would be little help available to support him. Bill Sherman was struggling hard south of Chattanooga as he tried to move toward Atlanta.   Rumors were that British regulars had landed at Charleston and on the Gulf Coast to reinforce Atlanta and South Carolina. They were expected to be in Atlanta before Sherman could clear Resaca.   Sherman would have no one to spare for the Army of the Potomac.

Grant would have to go it alone if he attacked Richmond. There was no real weak spot in the city's defense that stood out. The attack would likely be a meat grinder in which sheer numbers of men and artillery would be the factor to break the defense. If he massed artillery, made a feint at another location in the defenses and then stormed the works at a different spot with a large concentration, it might just work. But it would be a blood bath no matter how it came out. He thought of Fredericksburg. Grant also remembered well his assaults at Vicksburg in his attempts to take that city. He lost 5,000 troops trying to storm the Confederate works. Finally, a six week siege broke that city, but that wouldn't work here. Unlike Vicksburg which was cut off, Richmond was receiving British supplies through Petersburg. Had he the time, he would attack Petersburg first and cut off the support to Richmond, but there was just no time. It was Richmond now or nothing. Take Richmond...or lose the war for the Union. Sam Grant chewed on his cigar and paced the planks in his tent.

An hour passed and then two. Grant had gone out of the tent and walked around as if he were trying find his answer among the camp smells and smoke from the many fires that filled his nostrils. His officers could see he was laboring over something and they stayed well clear of their commander. They had seen this before and it always meant that something big was up. Finally, Grant returned to his tent. He poured another cup of coffee and without ever taking a drink, he sat the cup back on the black pot bellied stove and went to his field desk. He picked some clean paper and took his pen in hand to write to the President of the United States.

Dear Mr. President,

I have taken a very serious look at the situation that you have presented in regards to our either accepting the Rebel's offer of a cease fire, or immediately attacking Richmond to capture the city. While military decisions are usually clear in their options for success or risks for failure, I must admit these seem much more complex.

I desire to see our Army spared another costly battle, but I know this could possibly be the last battle. In fighting it, the rebellion could very likely be crushed once and for all. I am also certain that if we lose this battle, our losses will surely be as great or greater than any suffered so far. If this happens, we will likely lose the war. The result in this case would be the same as if we had accepted the Rebel Cease Fire only terrible losses will accompany the final result.

To accept the Cease Fire now would certainly end the years of painful losses our nation has suffered, but in its acceptance, we must understand that the Union will be broken and the sacrifice already made by thousands of men will have been wasted. How the nation would respond to this is something you would know better than I.

Mr. President, I do not desire to spill another drop of our Army's blood, but I can not recommend that having come this far, we surrender the cause for which we all have fought so hard so long as there is a fair chance for victory.

You alone must make the decision and I understand all too well the burden you must now feel, so let me be straightforward in my recommendation in hopes that will assist you. I recommend that we formally refuse the Cease Fire, and immediately attack Richmond in one great effort to capture the city and, hopefully, the Rebel leadership. Understanding that our losses will be very, very high, I still believe we have a high chance of success to break into Richmond. If we lose, we will lose fighting. However, I do not plan to lose!

To this end, I will begin preparations immediately to make such an attack at the earliest possible moment after you so order it. If you decide not to make an attack, I will do as you order and will hold the Army until I am told what action I am to take .

Mr. President, I have the utmost respect for you and your commitment to the best course for the Union. I know you will make the right choice.

U.S. Grant

The General read his letter several times, then folded it and placed on top of an envelope. He then called for his aide whom he asked to find General Meade as soon as possible. In minutes, George Meade was entering the tent.

"Coffee, George?," said Grant.

"No thanks, had enough for a while. Makes me jumpy! What's up Sam?," Meade asked. "Did the President answer that offer from the Rebels?"

"Not exactly, replied Grant. He sent it back for me to make a recommendation. This is my reply," said Grant as he handed the letter to Meade.

"Meade opened the letter read it carefully. After a minute or so, he looked up and took a deep breath and blew it out slowly saying, "Do you think he will go with your recommendation?"

"Have no idea," said Grant.

Meade read the letter again. "Looks like a bad hand. If we fight, we might lose. If we agree to stop now, we lose for sure. We pretty much lose no matter what approach we take, if we don't *take* Richmond." He looked straight at Grant, "You know McClellan will cash us in when he takes office. I know him, he won't fight Lee *and* the British."

"George, what odds do you give us for taking Richmond?"

Meade thought for a minute. " Honestly? ... I would say its a little *less* than even money to break their lines...maybe a little better than that to take the city if we can get in. We will take heavy losses at the break, assuming we do break the line, when we pour the reserves in. I figure we will have another tough fight on our hands from the troops in the city and perhaps the townspeople. I would say it will be real messy."

Grant pointed at the map on his table. "If we break through...say...here. I think we could be downtown before anyone could organize to stop us. I don't think the townspeople will fight. I think they will try to run or hide. They aren't soldiers, and while some may stand, I don't think most will. Its breaking through their lines that troubles me. Our losses could be the worst of the war, George. The other worry is Jeff Davis and the Rebel leadership. If we start to break the line, they

254

might get away before we could bag them. Taking Richmond and not catching Davis could mean we just paid a high price for a piece of city property and nothing comes of it. Davis could set up shop in Charleston or Columbia or go back to Montgomery! Imagine terrible losses here after Monocacy, and then the British marching on Washington with Lee squeezing us from the other side. I don't know... I just don't know. Its risky."

Grant continued, "There's one more thing, George. Jeff Davis as much said that if we choose to fight on, he will turn the Reb army loose to burn and plunder the North wherever they can. This probably includes the British as well. If they get loose, we could wind up with Washington, Portland, or who knows where being put to the torch by the Rebels or the British."

General Meade pondered the options for a minute and then asked, "Do you really think the Rebs will give up if Richmond and Jeff Davis are captured?"

"That my friend, is the *big* question!"

Meade observed, "So far the loss of every Reb city from New Orleans to Vicksburg to Memphis has seemingly had little real effect on their morale until they feel the pinch from the loss of a port, commerce or rail lines. The shock of losing their capital and their elected government *might* force them to reconsider, but..." Meade continued, "You know there won't be any more options for us after this. We win it here at Richmond,or Little Mac will surely give the store away saying he doesn't have enough troops, enough artillery or enough something!" Meade reflected again and then said, "I wonder if McClellan knows about this offer of the Rebs? I'll bet Lincoln hasn't told him yet."

"You can bet he hasn't! If George McClellan knew about this, he would already be calling a newspaper conference! Old Jeff Davis is missing a sure mark if he hasn't passed the word about this offer along to McClellan," said Grant. "Still, we have the problem before us and I have to respond to the President now."

"So, what do you think, George?" Grant clinched his cigar stub hard in his teeth and sat back, folding his arms. "Do we cut our losses, or bet the farm?"

Meade thought for a minute and rubbed his chin. "Take the Cease Fire, Sam."

Grant made no show of surprise or disappointment. "What's your reasoning?," he said.

"We are most likely to lose no matter which way we go. Even if we take Richmond and Jeff Davis, Lee has only to keep fighting and hold on till McClellan takes over in March and they will likely win. If there is one thing I have learned about Lee and his army, its that they won't give in. We will have whip them on the battlefield, and I don't think we have the time to do it now. Add to this, should France come into the war on the side of the Rebels...well...the odds are way against us, Sam. It's a real bad hand. It doesn't have to be played out."

Grant shifted his cigar from one side of his mouth to the other. "What about all the men who died to get us this far...Shiloh, Vicksburg, Fredericksburg, Monocacy? Seems hard to just stop after all they paid."

"We all paid part of that price, Sam. Losing a few more thousand men won't make it any easier to stop. I recommend that we cut our losses and cut the Rebels loose before they turn on our country. God knows we tried. No one can say we didn't try! "

Grant still sat and pondered the options. "OK...thanks for your honest thoughts, George. I'll let you know what I decide to tell the President."

Meade knew the conversation was over. He stood up and told Grant to call him if he could help and with that, Meade started out of the tent. Almost out, he stopped and stepped back in. "Sam, I just want you to know that whatever you decide, I'll back you to the hilt."

"I know you will, George. Thanks." Grant smiled and nodded.

After General Meade had been gone for a few minutes, U.S. Grant picked up his pen and began to again write on the envelope. *President A. Lincoln...*

Only 21 hours had passed from when Lincoln had written his letter to U.S. Grant. Now he was reading Grant's response.

Dear Mr. President,

... this could possibly be the last battle ... if we lose this battle our losses will surely be ... greater than any suffered so far and ... we will lose the war. The result in this case would be the same as if we had accepted the Rebel Cease Fire only terrible losses will accompany the final result.

To accept the Cease Fire... the sacrifice already made by thousands of men will have been wasted.

You alone must make the decision... I recommend ... refuse the Cease Fire, ... attack Richmond ...capture the city and ... Rebel leadership. ... our losses will be very, very high...but we have a good chance of success.

Mr. President... you will make the right choice.

U.S. Grant

It was not what Lincoln wanted to hear. He had fully expected Grant to recommend acceptance of the Rebel Cease Fire. He reread the letter. *Terrible losses...thousands of men wasted...losses will be very, very high... we have a high chance of success.*

Lincoln sat and stared at the wall and ran the options over and over in his mind. "The Union ... dissolved? No! Another 10,000 to 15,000 men lost with little chance of success...No! I just can't do that again!" He paced the floor. Three years of war...it was about to be lost...it might be won. Don't stop now! Press the issue! Is there enough time? The losses...! The Union...! Will taking Richmond make enough difference to end the war?" Abraham Lincoln had a another pounding headache.

An hour passed...another hour... Lincoln sat down and began to write to Grant for the last time.

General Grant,

I shall look forward to sitting down with you when this is all over and talking with you at length of the times in which we found ourselves this day. For now, we must make a decision and act.

I agree that we should not fight such a war as this and give it up at the end for less than what we started the contest to accomplish. So I say to you, if, in your military opinion, Richmond has a good chance of being taken, then take it immediately. This is my first desire. However, if upon careful consideration, you feel you can not take the city or nothing can be gained in your doing so, then notify me immediately and then tell General Lee you want an immediate Cease Fire. I will support you in either option.

If a Cease Fire is to be our lot, I desire this administration to be the one to accept and negotiate the terms of such an agreement. I am enclosing a letter of terms that must be agreed upon should you make the choice in favor of a Cease Fire. I have noted those items that are absolutely non-negotiable. These items deal with prisoner exchange and return for both white and colored troops, territory and property exchange and return, and details concerning a Commission to arrive at a suitable Peace Treaty between us. These terms are not negotiable, and you must make the Confederates understand this. Open this letter only if you decide you must accept the Cease Fire, otherwise return it to me at a future date..

General Grant, you are on the ground facing the enemy, I am not. I am giving you the option to choose what is best course of action on the battlefield. Your choice will be my decision and I will stand by it and by you.

If you decide to attack Richmond, send me a telegram with just one word: UNION. If you decide to order a Cease Fire, send me the word: PAX. I will know what you have decided. After this, please keep me constantly posted and updated as to developments since this is a most sensitive time for us as you know.

I stand here to support you. God Bless you and our Army.
A. Lincoln

GRANT'S HEADQUARTERS

The tent fly opened again and General John Newton entered to join General Grant and Meade along with the other Corps Commanders of the Army of the Potomac. The large tent was full. The guards posted outside the tent would not let anyone else approach the area and security was now tight.

"Gentlemen, I called for you this morning to tell bring you up to date on developments that happened almost as fast as our communications could support them. To summarize, the Rebel government has asked us to accept a Cease Fire." Audible surprise and muttering rose immediately. Grant continued, "This Cease Fire would amount to a virtual end of the war if it went into effect. If no peace accord was reached by this administration, the new administration would complete the peace process."

Some of the generals grumbled at the thought of McClellan taking over, while others expressed no comment on the idea of George McClellan as President to replace Abraham Lincoln.

"President Lincoln and I have discussed the options in some detail. Our choices are simply these: accept the Cease Fire. The war will end with the Rebels having accomplished their goal of secession from the Union. The Union would be re-defined. The other choice is for us to assault Richmond in strength and do it now! If we are successful and can capture the city and the Rebel government to include Jefferson Davis, we might end the war almost at once!" The officers shifted around at these ideas. It was plain to see they liked the idea of capturing the Confederate President.

"Now here are the other things you need to understand. Our chances of breaking the Richmond defenses and taking the city are at *best* fifty-fifty. Capturing the Rebel government is probably *less* than fifty-fifty. Our losses in such an attack will surely be some of the heaviest of the war. To be honest, these losses may be for nothing, since it still may not win the war. There is no guarantee. You also need to know that the Rebels have said that if we *do not* accept their Cease Fire proposal,

259

they and the British may well put Northern cities to the torch, not unlike we have done across the South.

"Lastly, it is late in the day in this war, and you men have served well and faithfully. I want to be honest with you and tell you that the President has left it up to me to decide to accept the Cease Fire or to attack Richmond. I wanted you to know that. The final decision and approval is the President's, but it is my initial call to recommend. We should all remember this day that we owe the President a vote of thanks to allow the Army to make the call on the field of battle.

"I will not ask for opinions as I do not want to cloud the issues, or put any of you in a difficult situation concerning this matter. I just wanted you to understand what was going on here.

"I have made the decision and am ready to inform the President to get his final approval. *We will attack Richmond.* We will give it a maximum effort and seek to break the defenses at a weak point!"

Several of the general officers glanced at one another and took deep breaths as if to say. "Here we go again!" Others leaned forward. No one sounded surprised or disappointed at Grant's decision.

"I have asked General Meade to let me explain this operation to you. He will then take over and provide details of the operation to you Corps commanders." Grant pulled a bed sheet off of a large easel that had been covering a map of Richmond and the surrounding area.

"This is how I see this attack developing…" Grant began to show how the 1st Corps would assemble.   "… create a diversion   here…III   Corps   would   attack   in force…artillery…reserves…" The overall plan began to develop. "The keys to this plan are a massive artillery barrage prior to the assault, engineer assistance in breaching the defenses, and a strong assault by the infantry. I think we can break this line if we hit it hard enough, then we can pour into Richmond. V Corps will follow III Corps into the break of the defensive line and have as their primary mission the taking of the Rebel capitol and any of the government officials that can be captured. General Sykes, I want you to also to take the Tredegar Iron works. Be careful they don't blow it up in your face. Now note this, we are to *capture* the city, *not burn* it. Artillery is to concentrate on the defenses, not the city. Do we all understand?" Everyone nodded. "Questions?"

Several questions were asked and then finally General Grant summed up his part of the briefing. "Gentlemen, the President left the decision to attack or not to attack up to me. I know we can take Richmond. It has been a goal since this war began, and now its in our grasp. If we take it we may end the war for the Union. If we fail, we will likely lose the war. Its just that simple. Hold nothing back." He looked at each general officer. They were looking at him. He saw the resolve, and he knew they could do it. He knew they *would* do it!

"General Meade? I'll leave details to you. I have dispatches to send." Grant turned to Meade who stood and came forward to the map. As he did so all the assembled officers stood at attention. Grant mentioned something to Meade then started out of the tent.

Once Grant was gone, Meade said, "Take your seats. Well, we have our work cut out for us. Lets get down to details." He began again dissecting and explaining the plan.

Grant walked back the few yards to his tent. Now that he had explained the plan to the Corps commanders, and had seen their faces, he felt even more positive about the chances for success. He was thinking about the need to get the artillery massed without causing too much alarm to the Rebels. The artillery would be the key to rupturing the line. Ammunition stocks would have to be increased dramatically. No matter, Meade would take care of that. Approaching his tent, he saw General Meade's Provost Marshal Brigadier General Marsena Patrick walking fast toward him. Grant slowed and stopped for him.

Patrick saluted as he came up to Grant. "General Grant, this message just came in. Since General Meade is briefing right now, I thought you ought to see it straight away!"

Grant opened the two pieces of paper and read the somewhat

hastily written lines. As he read he stopped chewing on his cigar and read carefully what the note said. "Where did you get this?," Grant asked.

"General Buford sent it straight in by rider, Sir. He had some scouts out all the way down to the Appomattox River, way southwest of Richmond. They reported this movement and said it was substantial."

"The message doesn't say if its infantry or cavalry. Any word on what kind of troops these were?, asked Grant.

"No Sir, I can send word back to see what we can find out," said Patrick who was asking if this was what he should do.

"Yes, man, do it now! I need to know what type of troops? Cavalry? Infantry? Artillery? How fast they were moving? I want to know the minute this information comes back! Go!" Grant ordered. Patrick saluted and was gone.

"Buford should know better than this," Grant thought. He read the note again, "...enemy troops moving south *in force* from Richmond *by rail*. Appear to be headed for Petersburg..."

"Something is up," thought Grant. He turned around and motioned for an orderly who was near his tent.

Running up to the General, the young corporal reported, "Yes Sir!"

"Get over to that tent and interrupt the briefing going on there. Ask General Meade to take a break and to come see me immediately."

The orderly took off toward the toward the briefing tent. Within minutes, General Meade was at Grant's side.

"Yes Sir, what's up?," asked Meade.

"Looks like some Rebs are moving out of Richmond, George. John Buford sent this message ..can't tell who signed it... looks like ...Colonel Dev...Devoe?" Grant was trying to make out the signature. Meade looked at it.

"Devin, Tom Devin. He has 2d Brigade of Buford's cavalry. Good man," said Meade.

"Well, this note is not complete! Here, read it." Meade read the wrinkled note.

Grant, obviously somewhat agitated, spoke again, "It just

says troops moving by rail…don't know if it's infantry withdrawing or cavalry moving, or what! I need more details. Your Provost Marshal gave me this note on his way to give it to you. I sent him off to check see if we can get more information from John Buford."

Meade looked at the note again and then looked up. "Sam, we could possibly break into Richmond easily and find no one at home! They may be running to Petersburg to avoid a fight!"

Grant said, "Or we could hurt ourselves on Richmond defenses only to finally capture a shell of a city with the government already gone! Or…the Rebs could be up to something we don't see right now. I don't like it, George."

"What do you want me to do, Sam?"

"Nothing right now. Plan the attack and keep this to yourself. I'll call the operation off if I have to, but we plan to go ahead for now. Meanwhile, we will try to see if Buford can provide us with more details."

Meade agreed and was quickly on his way to his assembled Corps commanders. Grant entered his tent. He wanted a glass of whisky,. Again, he would settle for some old, lukewarm coffee. He sat down and wrote a telegraph message to the President of the United States. It simply said, "UNION", and was signed U.S. Grant.

LEE'S HEADQUARTERS

"Did Stuart get off all on time, Sir?," Longstreet asked.

Robert E. Lee smiled and replied, "Yes, he was actually a little ahead of schedule. I think the railroad engineer was eager to get to Petersburg and out of Richmond." Lee pointed at the map on his table, " He should be coming upon this junction …here…just south of us, even now. It's only ten miles or so from here." Lee moved his finger along the rail line going west. "He will then divert west as far as the tracks go, which looks to be about twelve miles. Still it should get him clear of the city and the enemy lines. The rest of his unit will move tonight and follow the guides he left along the way. General Stuart should be moving into position sometime tomorrow and cross the James late tomorrow evening or at dawn the next day."

"That ought to surprise old Grant!," said Longstreet as he stood, arms folded, looking at the map. "I just hope Stuart doesn't get too tangled up or run into a large Federal cavalry unit out there. If Grant and Meade figure there is a strong force out west loose on their flank and possibly their rear, I doubt if they would make a move on us here. "

"Well, that's the idea, Pete, but I will say this, General Grant is not one who seems to worry about what he can't see over the hill. That can get him in trouble, but it also means he won't be fooled by a lot of movement and shifting. He seems to find a target and go right straight for it." Lee was looking at the map and rubbing his chin. "I wish I could get infantry west of him. That would surely make him take notice."

Longstreet thought to himself, "Surely he isn't thinking of sending part of our force off to engage Grant's and Meade's flank! We would be heavily outnumbered if Grant attacked…we could loose Richmond….we can't…"

"Not enough time," said Lee without ever looking up. "No matter. General Stuart will do the job."

Longstreet breathed a sigh of relief upon hearing his commander say this and then said, "I hear that Meade almost has a mutiny on his hands. New York and Massachusetts units want to go home to face the Brits coming down from Canada."

Longstreet smiled a little. "Seems like States Rights suddenly got a little more personal to those old boys!"

Lee responded, "Their morale may be down, but I expect those units will stand steady. What I think will happen is that more units will be called to active service to face the threat from Canada. This means the enemy army will get larger and larger. Should he be able to concentrate such a force against us or the British… well…it could be most difficult…"

"I wonder if the Northern people would stand behind such a move? Don't you think that's one reason Lincoln was not re-elected…they have had enough of this war? The last few Yankee papers I saw before their election seem to blame him for England being in the war. I think they just want it to end."

"I certainly hope your right, Pete. I know I feel *it is close…* I think we can end it. We must not let the enemy win anymore victories until the new administration takes over. If possible, we need to add pressure to keep his army off balance." Lee again was studying the map before him. "That's what I hope we will accomplish here tomorrow."

General JEB Stuart was looking at a map just like the one Robert E. Lee and James Longstreet were studying. It was laid out before Stuart as his train bounced and rolled along westbound. His officers listened to him as he talked above the noise of the train.

"Once we reach the end of the tracks here at *Coalton*, we will off load, form up and continue west bound turning north. I want scouts out well in advance of us. We must insure that the rendezvous point is clear. When the other brigades meet us here, near *Moseley Junction*, I want to know what is in front and on the side of us. I think we can cross the James here at… *Maiden's Adventure.*" Stuart laughed and said, "…sounds like my kind of place!" His officers laughed loudly knowing there was a lot of truth to that remark from their young commander.

"If this is not satisfactory, our scouts will have to see what crossing is available. I want to cross the river, then swing back toward Richmond and the Federal lines. If the way is clear enough, I want to do more than threaten their flanks. I want to show up between them and Washington!" Stuart smiled and looked at his officers. They were smiling back and nodding. This is what Stuart's cavalry did best, ride around the flanks and rear of the enemy, staying just out of reach and creating havoc with supply lines and railroads.

"We will destroy their supply line and tear up their rail lines. We burn whatever we can't use or tear up!" Stuart was rubbing his left shoulder. The severe wound he suffered in his shoulder at Monocacy was aching. The two trains carrying the first brigades of Stuart's troops and mounts were slowing. They were not far from track's end. Soon they would be mounted and on their way

GRANT'S HEADQUARTERS

Grant was sitting in front of his tent with Generals Meade and Pleasonton when General Patrick again approached with a message in his hand. "More information, General!," Patrick said. "Its from Buford, Sir. I think its what you were looking for." He handed the message to Grant as his commander had instructed.

Grant read the message and then re-read it. "The Rebs are moving *cavalry and infantry* out of Richmond by rail. They are headed south toward Petersburg. Looks to be a Division or more. No flags...no standards...."

The assembled officers listened then Meade asked, "Why would the Rebels move troops out of Richmond when they must know we are likely to attack? And why move *cavalry by rail* to Petersburg?"

Pleasonton spoke, "Davis! They would move Jefferson Davis and the Confederate leadership by rail, and they would send a strong cavalry force to protect them! I'll wager they have figured we are going to attack and they are moving Jefferson Davis out of our path!"

"By God, I think you are right," said Meade. He looked at Grant who was listening, but had said nothing. "What do you think, General? It makes perfect sense."

Grant slowly put his cigar in his mouth and began to slowly chew on it. "Maybe," he said. "May-be" As the three other officers talked and worked out details of how Jefferson Davis would be escaping, Grant went into his tent and got his map. Returning to the circle of folding chairs, he lay the map on the ground before them and leaned forward in his chair studying the map's towns, rail lines, roads, and bridges. What Al Pleasonton was saying made perfect sense. If it were Lincoln, Grant knew he would be moving his President to a safer place as well. A Division or more... a bit large for an escort, but maybe not. Why by rail?...to move the President, his Cabinet , families, perhaps records, and key personnel... that was logical.

After a few minutes, Grant leaned back and thought for a

minute as he chewed slowly. Then, he spoke, "There may be no more to this than what General Pleasonton says. In fact, I think he is probably right, but we have to be careful here. The Rebs have a habit of doing what we don't expect and showing up where we didn't expect them." The men nodded agreement. "General Patrick, please get word quickly to General Buford to continue to apprise me of *any* additional movements in this area. I want to know immediately...that's day or night...if there is more activity."

Grant was well known for worrying little about what he could not see around him. He had considered what this movement meant, considered the force and the possibilities and moved on. There was a battle to fight and it would come in less than 48 hours now. He would worry about a stray Rebel cavalry division when, and if, it arrived on the scene."

THE ATTACK

General Stuart was sitting on his horse on the side of the road when Col. James Drake of the 1st Virginia rode up to report. "The last of the brigades are catching up and crossing the river now, General. I have some of my boys posted to make sure everyone gets across and closes up. They know the area like the back of their hand and they will confirm when everyone is across. "

Stuart nodded and said, "Fine, James. Rejoin your command. I'll move out when everyone is across and closed."

Some forty minutes later the message came. Everyone was across the river. They were now on the same side of the river as the Army of the Potomac. While the infantry was no threat to Stuart's cavalry, he knew that somewhere out there John Buford was also mounted and working to avoid the very surprise that Stuart proposed to spring. He would swing wide and head north before turning east to come behind Meade. He hoped his luck held as it always had. JEB Stuart wanted to make the Yankees howl for attacking Richmond. He knew the importance of this mission as well. Anything to slow up Grant and Meade bought time for the Confederacy. If he could make them chase him, it would take time, and the more time he used, the closer to George McClellan's taking office and the war likely ending. They would ride hard to get into position as quickly as possible.

The assembled Union Corps commanders listened as General Meade talked with them. The men of the Army of the Potomac had worked hard and fast to get prepared for this attack. Artillery had been repositioned and much of it concentrated for the barrage that was to be unleashed only sixteen hours from now. The men knew the desperation of this attack. It was all or nothing. Victory, or almost certain defeat for the Union. The Corps commanders were apprehensive, but eager to go. Everyone wanted to get it started and get it over one way or the other.

Following George Meade's comments and last items of coordination, Sam Grant spoke to them. "Gentlemen, there is not much more to add to this. We have come far together. Everyone here has been with the command through some hard times. Tomorrow we will unleash the largest concentration of artillery we can bring to bear. Probably the largest this war has seen. Even before it ends, you men will move out to force a breach in the enemy defensive line that will let us enter Richmond. We *must break* this line. We *must force* it open. We must take Richmond. You know your assignments. If we find the Rebel government in the city, we must take them captive. Do not, I repeat, do not hurt them! Insure that your men know that this is imperative! Dead leaders become martyrs. Understood?" Everyone nodded.

"Tell your officers, tell your men, tomorrow we fight what may be the final battle for the Union. Let's make it count. God bless you all! God bless the Union!"

After the briefing, Grant returned to his tent as Meade and his officers went about checking and reviewing last minute changes and dispositions. Artillery commanders complained that they needed more ammunition. They were told more was on the way coming from the rear echelon and was to be delivered right to the guns by rail tonight. The troops did what troops always did before a battle. They wrote final letters in case they did not come back. They pinned their names to their uniforms so if killed, they could at least be identified. Others cleaned their rifles and did everything they could to be ready when the word came. A great many, prayed.

Some miles north and west of this concentration of Federal troops before Richmond, General Stuart was riding eastward along the south bank of the South Anna River. He had stayed south of the river on purpose and was feeling his way rather slowly as he moved toward the lines of the Federal forces. As the evening approached, Stuart slowed. He had made good time. He moved off the road to confer with Wade Hampton and Fitz Lee.

On a hill side over-looking the Confederate column, a Corporal from the 8th Illinois Cavalry stood back inside the tree line holding his horse and watching the valley below. He saw three Confederates move out of the column and stop along side the road to talk. "Probably officers," he thought. He watched the advancing column and figured it had to be four or more brigades at least. He decided he had seen enough and needed to get moving to report what he had seen. "Colonel Gamble and General Buford will love this," he thought. He moved parallel to the valley, careful to stay in the tree line, then moved over the ridge and started down the other side. It would be dark soon and he needed to get off this hill side and into the valley ahead so he could make better time. He had to get back to his lines and make his report. Just 100 yards behind him, two Confederate flankers were moving along the same path in the tree line that he had been taking. As they scouted the tree line, they did not see him move across the ridge ahead of them.

At the same time Stuart moved along the *South Anna River*, a Federal train loaded with munitions slowly made its way down from Fredericksburg, carrying artillery ammunition and supplies for the Army of the Potomac. It had been the emergency requisition from General Meade he needed to resupply his guns both during and after the massive artillery bombardment planned in support of the attack on Richmond.

Three hours later it was very dark. Stuart stopped the column to get a report from his advanced scouts that they were only some five miles from the *South Anna Bridge.* From here on out, he had to be very careful not to be observed. He planned to move forward toward the bridge and work his way back toward Yellow Tavern. The Federal supply trains and wagons assembled here would be pretty easy targets for a hit and run attack. If the surprise was good enough, he might even send some troops down the tracks to see what could be hit there. He was already thinking the fires from his attack would be visible from Richmond. General Lee and Grant alike would see where JEB Stuart had been!

Stuart's scouts lead the column closer and closer to the bridge and the rail line. Finally it was in sight. As Stuart approached the bridge he saw riders approaching rapidly. They were part of Fitz Lee's Brigade.

A Sergeant of the group reported to Stuart. "Sir, Colonel Owens' compliments! He begs to report we have captured a Yankee ammunition train, Sir! It's plum full of artillery powder and cannon balls! We have it up the tracks about two miles from the bridge. Seems the train driver slowed his train up for fear we had burned the bridge down! They had a couple of men walking out in front of the train when we came upon the train. He was pretty surprised when we climbed aboard. The engineer is scared to death we are going to blow the train up with him on it! They didn't have too many guards on this train either. Most of them surrendered when they seen how many men we had. One of the prisoners said there is a big supply camp down the tracks about three or four miles. The Colonel wants to know what you want him to do with the train, Sir?"

"Good report, Sergeant!" said Stuart. You ride back to Colonel Owens and give him my compliments and tell him I said he has outdone himself this time! I want him to move the train on to the bridge up ahead and stop it there. He is to clear everyone from the train and then prepare it to blow up! I want Colonel Owens to blow the ammunition cars take the bridge with it! Tell him to blow the train about thirty minutes after he hears us attack the supply station down tracks, then ride west to join us at the river crossing. You got all that, now?" The Sergeant acknowledged his message, then the riders turned and were gone into the darkness.

Stuart turned to Wade Hampton and Fitz Lee, "Boys, they not only will see the fires we leave tonight, they will hear us in Richmond on this trip! I think we will even wake up Grant and Meade in a little while!" It was turning into a typical JEB Stuart cavalry raid. He decided to move forward, turn south along the rail lines and destroy the first big supply base he came to. At the same time, he would set blow up the train to cap it off. His troops moved out.

At General Grant's Headquarters not many people were sleeping. The anticipation of a big attack caused many men to toss and turn or to get up and walk about. Sam Grant was laying on his bunk fully dressed except for his boots, coat and hat.

There was a light at the tent's entrance.

It was General Meade with a lantern. "Sorry to bother you, Sam."

"That's all right, George. Come in," said Grant as he stirred from a light sleep.

"I thought you should see this. More information from Buford. Looks like we have problems brewing!" George Meade handed Grant the note and placed his lantern on the table so Grant could read by its light.

Grant read the message, *"Confederate cavalry sighted near Ground Squirrel Bridge south side of South Anna River. Estimate 4 to 5 brigades of cavalry. No wagons or artillery. Moving east. Am moving to engage them. Buford"*

Grant was quickly awake. "That's what the cavalry was doing on the train this morning. It was moving out to swing around on our flank. That's JEB Stuart I'd bet."

Meade asked, "General, you still want to go with the attack this morning?"

Grant sat for a moment. "What time is it?," he said.

"Its just before midnight," replied Meade. "If there are more troops out there than just a few brigades of cavalry, we could wind up engaged to the front and the rear!"

"You recommend calling the attack off?," asked Grant as he swirled some coffee around in a cup sitting on the tent stove.

Meade thought for just a moment and replied, "No. Not just yet. But we have to watch our rear. If that develops into a fight, well, we might not can handle both. This battle will be tough enough without having to support a fight in our rear area!"

"Well, let's see what John Buford can do. Leave the attack on for now. We have a few hours yet. Coffee?" asked Grant.

Meade nodded in agreement as to the attack and the coffee. Both men were uncomfortable with this news.

JEB Stuart did not go far down the tracks when he heard the train slowly moving on the bridge he had passed. The sound grew fainter as they moved south. It wasn't long until another officer returned with word that the supply base they were looking for was just ahead. The moon was coming up now. It was getting easier to see, as well as to be seen. Stuart called for his brigade commanders and soon was talking to them about their attack. Stuart decided to ride through the supply base in a night raid. It was something that was difficult to coordinate and was dangerous, but it was something Stuart's troops had done many times. They were good at it. They knew how to raid a camp while avoiding shooting each other and how to not double back to avoid confusion among his own troops. Powerful, swift and deadly; this was the Stuart cavalry raid. He knew this one would be topped off with the blowing up of the train back up the tracks he actually looked forward to hearing it go off and seeing the explosion light up the sky to mark where he had been. He toyed with the idea of bringing the train right into the camp and then blowing it up. But this way, he reasoned, would make the Yankees think the force was even larger than it really was!

Stuart's men deployed to attack the sleeping supply and railroad camp known as *Cross Tie Camp*. A shot rang out! The Confederates had been seen by a Union picket. The attack was on. Within what seemed like only seconds, shots were fired in all directions. Then there was a fire…followed a small explosion. More shots, horses panicking, men shouting, sabers flashed in the scattered light. Now there were more fires. More small arms rattling from all quarters. Men ran to try and get away from tents on fire. Suddenly, there was a huge ball of fire and a tremendous explosion as one of the tents loaded with powder and rifle ammunition exploded. Half a dozen horses and riders were knocked over from the force of the blast. Most of them were up quickly, remounted and riding hard.

Six miles south of *Cross Tie Camp*, John Buford's cavalry reined to a halt to listen to the rumble from the explosion and to look at the dim glow showing well up the tracks from where they were.

"Stuart!," growled Buford. "Let's ride!" He spurred his horse and he was off with his command riding hard behind him.

The attack had been on for less than ten minutes when it was over. The glow in the sky that John Buford saw was the fire from the tents, wagons and the tree line where wagons of munitions had stood. Only a large clear spot, a slight hole, and a few toppled trees remained where the two ammunition wagons had exploded. Other wagons loaded with rifle ammunition were popping and burning furiously as were the insides of several box cars sitting on side tracks. Horses ran all through the area, and many were down from the explosions. Federal dead and wounded were scattered about, with a few Confederates among them. The heavy handguns, shotguns and sawed off rifles of the Confederate cavalry had taken a heavy toll of the dismounted men. As the mounted cavalrymen poured into the camp, the barefooted and outgunned supply troops ran into the woods for safety. Some stood to fight and were either killed or wounded. Those taken prisoner were forced to strip off their clothing and told to run for their lives into the woods.

The night raiders set fire to everything that would burn. The sky glowed brighter and brighter. Stuart's aide yelled over the noise to his commander, "About five minutes till the train goes, General!"

Stuart stood in his stirrups and started yelling, "Lets go! Let's go! Time to ride!"

His troops passed the word quickly and the men were mounting their horses and forming to move out. With a wave and shriek of what had become known as the Rebel Yell, the men rode off into the dark.

Many of the men were yelling "On to Fredericksburg! On to Fredericksburg!"

They hoped the Federals who heard this would pass the word along to add confusion to the raid. If they were lucky, the Yankees would be looking for them up the track toward Fredericksburg. It was a cheap way to buy some time as they rode off to the west and back the way they had come. As they rode off, the guides that had been sent ahead to clear the way, led the column through the dark and helped them move faster than would be normal at night.

Stuart was aware of the time as he moved. He waited for the train to explode, but nothing was heard or seen. At least thirty more minutes passed, still nothing. They kept riding hard.

Stuart began to worry that something had gone wrong.

Then he thought, "No need to worry, Tom Owens knows his business. Unless Yankee troops showed up, Owens will burn the train."

Back at *Cross Tie Camp*, General John Buford was coming into the scene of destruction the Confederates left. He tried to find the officer in charge as men rushed around trying to throw sand and water from the near by creek on the fires still burning.

"Who's in charge here?," yelled Buford.

"I am!" came a equally terse reply. A man in a bloody undershirt, officer's trousers, boots and a revolver in his hand was just off to the side of the mounted column. He moved toward the rider shimmering in the light of the fires who was asking the question.

"Lieutenant Colonel Charles Adam! And who are you, Sir?" he called to the rider.

Buford and Colonel Devin both dismounted to talk with the disheveled officer. "I'm General Buford. What in blazes happened here, Colonel?"

"Blazes is right, General! Confederate cavalry! Regulars, I'd say. Rode right through my pickets and into the camp! It looked like several hundred of them to me. Gunfire, explosions…they fired the whole place up. Set off the ammunition wagons... biggest explosion I ever heard! It took out a bunch of my men…knocked me into a stack of cross ties and busted my head," he said as he wiped the big cut on his head with a piece of cloth he had picked up. "They swept through the camp like a twister and took off!"

"Which way did they go and how long ago?," asked Buford.

"I'm not sure … some of the men were saying they were headed up track toward Fredericksburg. I tried to telegraph a warning, but the lines are down. We have contact with General Meade's headquarters, or at least we will have shortly when we get the telegraph tent back together, but nothing to the north."

Colonel Devin looked at Buford and said, "Fredericksburg? We have troops all over the place there. Why would they being going to Fred…"

Suddenly a shock wave hit the camp that sounded like a cannon had just gone off right where the men were standing. Buford stumbled back over a wagon wheel and almost fell down. For an instant he thought it was incoming artillery fire. Horses normally accustomed to gunfire and cannons bolted and spun around. Trees shook and everyone reeled from the concussion as the sky to the north lighted up like daylight.

"What in Heaven's name was that?," yelled Devin as he tried to calm and steady his horse.

Colonel Adam, who had dropped to one knee at the explosion, now stood up looking at the bright light in the northern sky. "Well, I would guess that would be the ammunition train from Fredericksburg!," he said wiping his forehead again. Buford looked at him in surprise at his matter of fact comment. The Colonel continued, "General, I'd say the Rebs are headed up track, and will probably tear it up as they go!"

Buford mounted his horse. "Colonel, looks like you have quite a few men down. Do you need some medical assistance?"

"I'd appreciate that, Sir," the Colonel replied.

"Dev, see that Doc leaves some help here for the camp! We will pick them up later!" Colonel Devin nodded and turned to make it happen.

Buford continued, "Colonel Adam, after you get your men taken care of , you need to see to your own wound. You got a pretty good crack on the head there. After that, send a message to General Meade for me. Tell him what's happened here. Tell him I am proceeding north after what appears to be JEB Stuart. I'm going to chase him down wherever he goes. Got that?"

"Yes Sir, I'll send it right along as soon as we get the telegraph back up. Shouldn't take long. You take care, General. Get a shot in for us." Adam gave Buford a soft salute as the riders moved out smartly again in pursuit of JEB Stuart.

Down the track, General Grant and George Meade were in front of Grant's tent looking north at the glowing sky in the distance. Dozens of officers and men had been awakened by the thunderous boom and were outside also looking toward the northern sky.

"The telegraph lines are down to the north, but it could only have been the ammunition train they were running down to us tonight," said Meade. "We needed that ammunition badly," he added quietly.

Grant was looking at the sky as he spoke, "After the artillery barrage before the attack, what will your ammunition stocks be down to?"

"Something like 40%. We had planned to put everything we could into that effort so we could help the infantry break the line…We needed that ammunition train to bring us back up to a suitable reserve." Meade offered no advice or comments other than this. He knew Grant understood the problem.

Grant stood for a time watching the glow in the sky. "George, we have to postpone the attack tomorrow." Meade said nothing but just listened to his commander talk. "If that was the ammunition train we needed, and I don't see what else it could have been…," he nodded toward the glowing sky, "…then we will be too short on ammunition to sustain this attack. If we had to have more artillery fire during the fight, we might even not be able to provide the support our troops need." Grant stood quietly for a moment and then said, "On top of that, somewhere out there a Confederate Cavalry Corps is on the loose. If they disrupt our supply lines any more, we could wind up down here in even worse shape." Grant was remembering Oxford and Holly Springs, Mississippi when Nathan Bedford Forrest tore his supply lines up and stopped one of the earlier campaigns against Vicksburg.

George Meade looked at Grant and said, "Do you want to reschedule it or postpone it indefinitely?"

"We will wait a time," Grant said. "See if you can confirm that was the ammo train. Maybe see what we can do in a while." Grant was strangely accepting of the situation as he walked off toward his tent. Meade watched him for a time, then turned to go give the order to stand down from the attack.

In his tent, General Grant sat down at his desk and thought about the letter he must now write. After while he took the pen and began…

Dear Mr. President…

I regret to inform you that I have this evening called off the planned attack against Richmond. I had replied to you that we would make a maximum effort to take the city, and indeed this attack was scheduled for tomorrow morning. However, events have taken place that now make the likelihood of success very poor for our Army.

Our ammunition train that was so vital to us to continue the fight has just this night been destroyed while enroute to us. This action was most likely caused by a Rebel Cavalry Corps which we know to be loose in the area of our supply lines between Richmond and Washington. Our own cavalry force, under General John Buford, is trying to catch up with these Rebels, but at this time, he has not done so. We also have some reason to believe that the Rebel government may have fled Richmond by rail headed south. After considering these factors, I think the odds of success in our planned attack are now so low as to be unacceptable. The chance for us to lose the whole Army is greater than the chance for success. If the war continues with the British and possibly the French, we must not lose the Army before Richmond.

Therefore, I have exercised the authority you gave me and I have postponed the attack for an indefinite period. There is a possibility that we could still attack Richmond as planned, but, Mr. President, I must tell you it looks unlikely.

It is now my recommendation that you should give active consideration to acceptance of the Rebel Cease Fire to bring the fighting to a close. If you authorize me to do so, I will make this contact and accept the terms as presented to you in the Rebel's Cease Fire message. Following mutual acceptance of this document, I would request permission to withdraw the Army from Virginia if this is acceptable to you.

Mr. President, I wish I could have done better for you and the nation, but I now think time is working against us. I await your orders.

General Grant read the letter a couple of times, put it in an envelope and sealed it. He placed the envelope on the table and looked at it. Then he made out a telegram to be sent when the lines were again up. *PAX...MESSAGE TO FOLLOW...*So that was it. An end to the war on a piece of paper. Grant thought about the campaigns, the victories, the defeats, the never-ending sadness of it all. He felt he had personally lost the war. He needed a drink of whiskey. There would be no coffee tonight. He opened his trunk and got a bottle and glass. Tomorrow he would send a message to Robert E. Lee asking for a reconsideration to the Cease Fire message. For now, he would have one drink and try to rest. At least the men would be spared tomorrow morning. Many a man would get a second lease on life as the great assault of Richmond became only a plan to be read about in the history books.

WASHINGTON

Only a few hours later, President Lincoln sat at his desk reading the message from U.S. Grant. Strangely, he felt almost relieved that the attack was called off. No more mass casualties. No more graves by the thousands. Lincoln was glad for this, but his sadness for what this meant was crushing. Grant had just told him that the Army could not win the war. After three years of bloody war, the South was to go its own way, the Union would lose its bid to remain whole, and slavery would stand for a few more years.

There were many questions to answer. What would happen with the British troops in Maine? What would happen to the border states of Missouri and Kentucky that both the U.S. and CS claimed and both recognized? What about the Oklahoma and Arizona Territories that were also disputed by the two sides? These were not easy problems. Lincoln put them from his mind. These were not problems with which he would have to deal. His time as President was almost over. He hoped McClellan might do a better job of making peace than he had done making war. Lincoln pondered his place in history. He had become President and the war started. He would leave office as the war ended. He freed the slaves in the United States. But he had also presided over the first defeat in U.S. history, and the U.S. was smaller by far now. He wondered what kind of legacy it would be.

Lincoln began to write to General Grant a confirmation telegram...*PAX*...

GRANT AND LEE

It had been over 14 hours since Grant sent his message to Abraham Lincoln.   Finally his reply came giving him the permission to contact the Confederates as he had recommended. He opened the sealed letter that President Lincoln had told him to open only if the Cease Fire was to be accepted.

Dear General,

If you are reading this, then I have sent you a message saying we will accept the Cease Fire proposed by the Confederates. I am grateful that you and our Army will be spared the need to again enter the crucible of war. I think we have fought the good fight, even though final victory to save the Union appears to have eluded us.   We can take heart that slavery has been attacked and defeated once and for all in our nation. It surely has been weakened everywhere else. We must now look to a peace with our neighbors in the South as we settle the conflict with the British.

To this end, you are authorized to contact the military representative of the Confederate government and if still agreeable, enter into a Cease Fire with them to become effective at the earliest possible hour. The conditions as presented are acceptable with the following notations.

1. *This Cease Fire will be followed as soon as possible by negotiations leading to a permanent peace treaty between all warring parties.*
2. *All prisoners of war and political prisoners will be exchanged as soon as possible. This includes all colored soldiers who are prisoners of war by reason of fighting in the uniform and for the United States.*
3. *Where desirable on the part of the party involved and with the agreement of the other side, military forces may be withdrawn immediately from the field.*

General Grant, you have served your nation well in war. I am thankful of all you have done. I ask you now to serve your nation once more as we begin this process of peace.   Contact

me as soon as you have accomplished this task so we may plan our next steps.
    A. Lincoln

General Grant contacted General Lee asking that a meeting be arranged for the purposes of discussing the Cease Fire offer, if it were still offered. Lee responded with a willingness to meet Grant. The meeting was set for 10:00 a.m. at a site on the Mechanicsville Road where it crossed the Chickahominy River. Since the site was in front of the Confederate lines, Grant set up a tent for the occasion. The field was clear with only a barn some half a mile away to the east. Grant ordered a new tent be used and for the men to look sharp in their appearance to the Confederates. He had also told his staff that from now on the former enemy was to be referred to as *Confederate*, rather than *Rebel*. It was a first step, and would take some getting use to, even for Grant.

Grant arrived,crossed the Chickahominy and was in place some fifteen minutes before ten o'clock. Some ten or so officers were assembled to include George Meade, John Newton, and E.O.C. Ord. Grant's Chief of Staff, General John Rawlins, and Grant's military secretary, Lieutenant Colonel Ely Parker, were also present.

Grant was in a dress uniform that had hastily been borrowed for the occasion, for he had brought no such uniform with him to the field. Grant had hardly thought such an occasion would develop. His staff had quickly assembled a suitable uniform for their commander, lest he be thought to insult General Lee by dressing shabbily. His shoulder boards had been sewn on to show the rank of Lieutenant General, and his boots were shined. Grant's general officer's belt and sword were also polished for the meeting. U.S. Grant looked every bit the part of the Commanding General of the U.S. Army. It was a far cry from how he usually looked in the field.

Some five minutes before the hour, a party of gray uniforms could be seen coming up the road from the direction of Richmond. It was Robert E. Lee and his party of three officers.

Lee was accompanied by General James Longstreet, Colonel W.H. Taylor, who had delivered the original message to Grant, and Colonel Charles Marshall, Lee's military secretary. Two flag bearers carried a white flag and a Confederate national flag, which was also mostly white, with only the Confederate battle flag in the upper left corner. The four officers and the flag bearers were dressed in clean neat gray uniforms, and looked as if they were dressed for an evening parade.

When Lee rode up, all the Union officers except Grant came to attention and at the initiation of Meade, they saluted. Only when Lee had taken some steps toward Grant did he salute. General Lee and his officers returned their salutes to acknowledge the courtesy.

Sam Grant stepped forward and extended his hand, "General Lee."

Removing his right hand glove Lee responded, "General Grant." The two men shook hands warmly and each man felt the significance of the moment. Lee introduced his officers beginning with James Longstreet. Grant did the same with those who were standing nearby.

Following the introductions, Grant said, "Come, let us talk."

Lee nodded, smiled slightly and walked along side Grant toward the tent erected for the occasion. A fair sized camp table was in the middle of the tent and two chairs were on either side facing one another. An equal number of other chairs were along the sides of the tent, well away from the two in the center. As they walked in, neither General said anything in the way of small talk. Obviously, it was a tense and uncomfortable situation for the Federals and a somewhat uneasy situation for the Confederates, given the place where they were meeting.

After being seated, Grant again open the conversation. "General Lee, I don't know if you remember or not, but we met once during the war in Mexico. It was at a staff meeting, just outside Mexico City...one of the many as I recall." Grant smiled slightly.

"I must confess that I do not remember the occasion, General." Lee was looking at Grant as if trying to recall his face. "But then that was some time ago and much has happened since then."

"Indeed it has, indeed it has. General Lee, I regret that we have to meet under such conditions", Grant responded. "I wish the politicians could have resolved these issues that have caused us both so much pain for the past few years. I would have very much appreciated getting to know you as a friend rather than having to face you as an enemy these past years."

Lee smiled slightly and said, "I, too, would have appreciated that, General. I have great respect for you and your Army, Sir. I hope that after today we may set about on that path of friendship for us, as well as for our countries." With this Lee had brought the meeting to the reason for the talks.

"I shall look forward to that," said Grant. "Now, Sir, to the business at hand. You recently sent my government a proposal for a general Cease Fire which would then remain in place, leading to negotiations for a Peace Treaty between …our two countries." Grant had carefully worded this statement to say "..our two countries…" and it was not lost on Lee. For the first time he had heard the Confederacy referred to as an equal country by an official of the U.S. government! Lee now knew that the peace was very close at hand!

"That is correct, Sir," responded Lee, "and I am authorized to say to you that this proposal still stands as presented." Lee started to add, "if you accept this proposal without delay," but instead was trying to sound agreeable and open to an equal exchange. "If you are prepared to agree with us to a General Cease Fire at this time, the fighting can end here today…right now. Fighting elsewhere can stop as quickly as news of this document's signing can be given to them. "

Now, Sam Grant had to be very careful with how he presented these next issues. "General Lee, my government has instructed me to agree to this proposal, provided several conditions can be assured and guaranteed."

Lee responded, "Sir, I can not add or take away anything of significance to what my government has proposed in this offer. This is a Cease Fire only. It will lead to an end to the shooting.

This is not, nor can it become a negotiation of conditions for peace between our countries. I have no such authority. I assume that these conditions are conditions of substance, otherwise they would not be placed on the table. Having recognized them as substantive, I can most surely not negotiate with you for their resolution. I am sure you see my position here."

Lee had set the stage for a clear cut Yes or No on the Cease Fire. He also knew the Federals needed a Cease Fire, otherwise this conversation would not be taking place. Grant was worried since he knew the issue of the colored soldiers would be a sticking point.

"Perhaps we can at least look at these points, General Lee? I think if we carefully weigh and understand what is being requested, it may be workable for us here today. Agreed?" Grant queried.

By all means, General, Lee replied. I merely wished to point out that the eloquence of your presentation will in no way have a bearing on what I can agree to accept. Like you, I am constricted by specific orders." Lee nodded for Grant to continue.

Grant opened a folder handed to him by his secretary , Colonel Parker. "The conditions that are required for our agreement are as follows: First, the Cease Fire will be followed as soon as possible by negotiations leading to a permanent peace treaty between all warring parties." Grant looked up and said, "we have both agreed to this, and I know everyone desires it to take place.

"Secondly, where desirable, on the part of the party involved, military forces may be withdrawn immediately from the field with permission of the other side." Grant again looked at Lee. "This simply allows either side to withdraw their forces from the soil of the other party, provided everyone agrees. In our case, I think your people would appreciate our withdrawal back to Union territory as soon as possible", said Grant.

"Lastly, all prisoners of war and political prisoners will be exchanged as soon as possible. This includes all colored soldiers who are prisoners of war by reason of fighting in the uniform of and for the United States." Grant put the paper down and knew this last requirement would be the point of contention. He quickly added, "Here we simply ask that our soldiers be returned to Union control." He waited for Lee to respond.

Lee did not change expression, nor did he hesitate to understand what had been said. "I think it is understood and agreeable that all Union soldiers who are prisoners would be exchanged without difficulty." He stopped for a moment and then continued. "This would not include slaves who were, by our laws, were illegally set free by military force, then, being required by you or by their own volition, became soldiers in the Union Army. These people are still slaves and are not recognized as Union soldiers."

Grant sat quietly and glared at Lee. Then he asked, "Surely General, you can not separate the slave from the freeman and the Northern black man from the Southern black man?"

Lee responded, "And surely, General Grant, you could not expect that after a war fought by us for over three years, we could simply agree that every black man in a blue uniform was free to go to the North? As I said when we began this part of the discussion, I do not have the authority to negotiate such an agreement. These issues will have be part of a Peace Treaty with agreement to be reached by other men at another time. Today, I can only sign a Cease Fire on behalf of the Confederate Army as was presented to you. I am prepared to do this upon your agreement and acceptance of this proposal." Lee waited a moment and then said, "General Grant, let us sign this agreement and stop the fighting here today." Lee had made it crystal clear. He would not negotiate or be backed into an agreement beyond what he had come to do.

Grant sat back in his chair. He wanted to argue these points, but he knew that Lee would not do so. "I don't think I can do that, General. As much as I too want to end this fighting, I will not abandon my soldiers, white or black, to remain in Southern prisons or as slaves. I just cannot agree to that."

Lee was deeply troubled that Grant thought Northern black soldiers would be held captive. "I would not expect you to agree to that, General Grant. *I would not agree to that either.* What I am saying is that *no* Union soldier, *black or white*, who has come from a state now in the Union would be forced to remain in the South. Only those slaves who were slaves when you came into our homeland and forcibly freed them are affected here. I would say that in cases where there is a *doubt* as to the status of the individual, the man would be allowed to go North." Lee hesitated before carefully wording his next response. "Perhaps... if we can sign this agreement today, the exchange of prisoners could be expedited...? I know we certainly would like to get our soldiers home just a quickly as possible."

Grant leaned forward again. He understood what Lee was saying. The quicker the troops were exchanged, the less time there would be for slave owners to try to find escaped slaves who were serving in the Federal army and who were now prisoners of war. "What assurance do I have that this is what will take place and that it will be honored once we leave here? Forgive me, General Lee, I mean no personal offense to you, but what I am asking is how do I know...how does *my* government know...that this is how *your* government will see this issue?"

Lee was quick to answer, "I can only offer you my word, General Grant. As I have just been given command of the Armies of the Confederate States, I am not without influence in our government. This is not a boastful statement, but a fact that comes from the nature of my office, like that of your office. If it means anything to you, I will give you my personal word that this issue will be honored by my President just as I have presented it to you. I can see no conditions that would change this, but - I remind you that this is a Cease Fire we are agreeing to here today. There is still a peace to be won by our governments after we lower our swords and shake hands. I pray we can at least do our part here today."

"General Lee, your word means a great deal. You are known for the honor of your word. In the short time that I have talked with you, I feel I understand why." Grant sat for a moment and looked at his long time adversary. "Upon the strength of your word, I will agree to this Cease Fire with the conditions as noted. If for some reason it is not honored by others not at this table, we can again pick up the sword. For now let us look to better times." Grant reached across the table and extended his hand to Lee. Lee looked pleased, but he did not smile broadly. He instead took Grant's hand warmly and nodded affirmatively. "We have taken a good first step here today."

General Lee looked at his secretary and nodded for him to bring the documents forward. "Colonel Marshall, please make an additional note to these documents listing the issues expressed by General Grant and agreed to by me. Make a special note that we have agreed to *expedite* the exchange of *all* prisoners." Colonel Marshall collected the two documents went to another table to make the notations. In a matter of minutes, the documents had their notations affixed and were returned for signing.

One copy was presented to Colonel Parker who reviewed it and placed it before General Grant. Colonel Marshall brought the second document to General Lee to sign. When both signatures were made, the two Colonels exchanged documents and, again, the Generals signed their names. The Cease Fire was now in place. The War Between the States was, for all intents and purposes, over.

Lee and Grant chatted for a minute or two about minor details and then the conversation changed to mutual acquaintances. In a few minutes, Lee stood. "General Grant, I apologize that I can not continue our conversation, but I must take my leave now. I have much to do to put this agreement in place."

"As do I, Sir," said Grant. Lee turned, put on his left glove, and waited for Grant. Then the two men walked out of the tent together. Grant then added, "Perhaps we will meet again soon under better circumstances, and we can talk of happier times."

"I trust that will be the case, General," said Lee. Stopping before he walked to Traveler, Lee extended his hand to Grant. "I will pray that all will go well for our two nations from this time forward. If I may be of assistance to you in any way in the coming days, please contact me, General." Lee then put on his other glove, turned and mounted Traveler. Once he was sitting perfectly erect in the saddle, Robert E. Lee saluted and said, "General Grant."

Grant smiled and returned the salute, "General Lee." With this Lee turned and he and his party headed down the road toward Richmond. Sam Grant watched Lee for a time.

George Meade walked up and stood by him. "How do you think it went, General?"

"Well, George, we stopped the killing today, so I guess you could say it was a success. I think that's about all one can say about a Cease Fire. At least the killing has stopped." Grant then turned to Meade. "George, please excuse me…I think I need a little while alone. I have to write the President a letter. Please pass the word of the agreement along to the command. Colonel Parker has the details of the agreement." "Perhaps we can have dinner together tonight. I think I would like that." Grant seem detached.

Meade saw the far away look in Grant's eye. "Sure, Sam. That would be nice. I'll drop by later." Grant walked slowly back to his tent.

Robert E. Lee was riding toward Richmond his head held high. As he looked at the city's skyline, he felt an immense relief knowing the city would be spared any further ravages of war. His men were crowding out to the road looking for a sign from their beloved leader. Was it over? Was the fighting at last stopped or would there be a Federal attack?

As Lee passed through defensive positions and hundreds of soldiers pressed forward, Lee finally smiled broadly, removed his hat and raised it high as a salute to his men. "We have a Cease Fire!"

The cheers and yells that erupted were thunderous. They spread like a cannon fire. Hats went up as did most everything else the men could get hold of. Men danced around holding each other. Tears flowed freely. Many men knelt to pray, unashamed for the new lease on life they felt they had just been given. James Longstreet was waving his hat and cheering with the men as the party rode on toward the city.

Word of the scheduled meeting had spread well before Lee had gone to see Grant. The whole city and the soldiers knew only to well what the meeting was all about. When the first cheers went up and men began to celebrate, everyone knew the fighting was over for the Army of Northern Virginia. Lee made his way to his headquarters and went to his tent. It was difficult to contain the joy the officers and men felt and indeed no one, least of all Robert E. Lee, wanted to try to do so. He told James Longstreet that he would be going to see the President at the capitol shortly. He wished to have Longstreet accompany him, but first he needed to stop for a few minutes at his tent.

As Lee entered his tent, he told Colonel Marshall to see that he was not disturbed. Once inside, Lee neatly placed his hat and gloves on the table along with his sword, unbuttoned his coat and he sat down on the side his bed. With his hands on his knees, sitting erect, he simply sat there for a few minutes. He reflected on the events of the day. General Lee felt the tears come that he had held back for so long. He quietly wept. He wept for God's goodness that spared so many lives this day. He wept for men who were gone but who had bought them this day. Lee turned and knelt at his bed and as he wept, he prayed, "...*He maketh wars to cease unto the ends of the earth; He breaketh the bow, and cutteth the spear in sunder; he burneth the chariot in the fire. Be still and know that I am God: I will be exalted among the heathen, I will be exalted in the earth. The Lord of hosts is with us...*

The day passed as days do. It had been an unusual day... A day of peace.

The two officers sat together looking across the river at the distant smoke from hundreds of campfires. Their faded uniforms showed the wear of long campaigns and hard times. Their faces reflected years of war as recorded by eyes which had seen too much, too quickly. A brilliant orange glow from the fading evening sky seemed to confirm that this was more than just the end to another day.

Slowly the younger officer said, "I just can't believe it's over..."

"Me either," quietly answered the colonel, feeling old far beyond his 24 years. "I thought it would never end. So many hard fights...so many good men...and now, it's finally over. I never thought I'd live to see it end. Now that I have, I don't feel much like cheering. I just want to...." His words trailed off as he put his good hand to his eyes.

"I know...me too," said the other young colonel, feeling embarrassment for his friend. He scratched hard in the dirt with the small stick that young men always seem to pick up.

Looking up he said, "Rob, you know, it will be really hard to try to forget all that has happened and to be friends again...with them". He stared at the distant smoke.

Robert leaned back against the tree He, too, stared at the smoke hanging low over the trees. "I know, but we must. Besides, Chris, most of them are just like us when you get right down to it. They did what they thought was right... just like we did."

Christopher flared back, noticeably agitated, "Like us? No! They weren't like us at all! We fought for our country, but they...!"

Robert raised his hand and closed his eyes as if to calm his friend's rising voice and to the settle the waving stick now pointing menacingly toward the river in front of Richmond. "Easy…easy.. It's over.. Thanks be to a merciful Lord, it's over."

Calmness returned to Christopher as he went back to his scratching in the dirt. The light was dimming rapidly. He looked up again.

"Rob...you know, we almost lost this war?" He paused. "Did you ever think about what would have happened if we had lost?"

The older colonel paused for a long time, looking at the smoke now fading from sight and slowly shook his head, "I don't want to ever think about that...."

Deo Vindice
The End

AUTHOR'S NOTES

This story is based on a great deal of fact. Perhaps these notes might be of interest to you to know what was behind the people, places and events in DEO VINDICE.

In an 1862 naval encounter that became known as the *Trent Affair*, a Union warship stopped the British mail ship, *Trent*. The Union captain forcibly removed two Confederate Commissioners who were bound for England and France by way of Cuba. The men were James Mason and John Slidell. They had been sent by the Confederate government to try to plead the Confederate cause and to work for Confederate recognition. As passengers on an English vessel, the men and their families were under the protection of the English flag. A formal apology was demanded by the British along with the immediate release of the two Commissioners. The British were so infuriated by this event that they seriously considered the option of war with the United States if their demands were not met. To back up these demands, 18,000 British troops were moved to Canada and munitions plants were opened in preparation for war. Queen Victoria was, indeed, furious as was the English Parliament. Some of Lincoln's cabinet were unmoved by these threats, while others realized what a war with England *and* the Confederates would mean. Lincoln was quoted as saying, "One war at a time...." He had the two Confederates released with a watered down apology that basically just acknowledged the incident. We can only consider what might have happened if a *second event* involving the death of British subjects had occurred following the *Trent Affair*.

The British war plan in the book referred to as *Royal Oak* (a fictitious name) was based on the real British plan for war with the United States as created during the *Trent Affair*. During this crisis, the British Prime Minister, Lord Palmerston called a special war committee into session to develop this plan. The resulting plan included actions that would: Strengthen Canada with British Regular troops, arm the Canadian militia (they were poorly armed) and bring them up to a strength of about 100,000 men. It planned for an attack from Canada against the state of Maine. If Maine did not outright secede from the U.S. to join the British as some thought it would, then Portland, Maine would be captured and occupied. The plan also called for the British Royal Navy to blockade the coasts of Maine and New York, while attacking and opening the blockade of Confederate ports. This would provide access to Confederate cotton for British commercial shipping. The threat by the United States to declare war on England, or anyone else who gave recognition to the *Rebels*, was a fact very plainly stated by Lincoln's administration. If war came, Britain planned to recognize the Confederacy knowing that France, and probably Spain, would follow the English lead. This move would place the United States in the position of having to face declaring war on France and Spain if it declared war on England, all the while fighting the powerful Confederate land armies in the field. The problems with logistics, weather, and timing mentioned in the story were actual subjects considered and discussed as the real British plan developed.

The Southern plan of giving the cotton away and freeing the slaves to obtain British recognition is based in part on factual material. The South held back its cotton and is known to have destroyed about two million bales in an attempt to create a critical shortfall in England and Europe. Eventually, hundreds of thousands of manufacturing jobs were affected in England. The Confederate government hoped that this action would *force* the British to break the blockade to get its cotton. A market glut in 1859 and newly developed markets in Egypt, Africa and Brazil eventually offset this loss and caused the Confederate plan to fail. Had cotton been offered for *free,* and *offered at the right time*, it might have had a much greater impact.

It is known that the idea of freeing the slaves as a condition for English recognition was discussed and actively pursued by the Confederate government in early 1865 as an agreeable condition for English recognition. However, by 1865, this plan was too late to have any impact, as it was obvious to the British that the South was going to lose the war.

The characters of the story are, for the most part, actual characters of the time. Some are well known such as Lincoln, Grant, Meade, Davis, Lee and Longstreet. Many of the other characters are also real persons, but may not be so well known. Robert Bunch, the first English Minister to the Confederate States, was actually the British Consul at the British Consulate in Charleston before the war. He remained in Charleston until 1863. Having him become the first British Minister to the Confederacy seemed a nice touch.

Vicksburg did surrender on July 4th, but General Pemberton did not get better terms from General Grant as a result. Confederate General Bowen did die of dysentery two weeks after Vicksburg fell.

President Lincoln really did tell country bumpkin stories, and Secretary of State Seward really did dislike hearing them.

The Irish Colonel Patrick Kelly, who was killed on the bridge at Monocacy; and the two Mississippi Colonels Griffin and Luse, who were casualties at Frederick, were real officers of real units.

General George Custer was not killed at Gettysburg, nor was JEB Stuart wounded there. Custer died at the Little Big Horn and Stuart died at Yellow Tavern.

General Grant did drink heavily, but never during a battle. It did not affect his generalship in any event.

Lieutenant Colonel Ely Parker, military secretary to General Grant; and Colonel James Marshall, military secretary to General Lee, actually held these positions for these two generals.

Colonel Walter Taylor was a Virginia Military Institute (VMI) graduate, Class of '57.

The OCTORARA and MOUNT BLANC were real ships. Their Captains were not.

The British ships that attacked Charleston were real ships of the Royal Navy at the time, as were the U.S. ships they attacked. The various armaments described for the English ships were real. The new breech loading cannon that blew up on the *HMS*

Resistance was one of many such faulty guns that eventually were all recalled from fleet use.

The Confederate Corvettes *CSS Vicksburg, Manassas, Charleston, Monocacy* and *Oak Hill* never existed.

The *USS Kearsarge* actually did more than just chase the *CSS Alabama*. She caught and sunk *Alabama* off the coast of France. *Kearsarge* had no such luck in this version!

The Army of the Potomac Reserve Corps was commanded by General French and the Reserve really was at Frederick.

It did rain very heavily at Gettysburg on July 4, and the roads did become quagmires.

Lincoln really did expect to lose the election in 1864, but he won, defeating General George McClellan handily. Lincoln did fire General McClellan from Commander of the Army...twice.

General Robert E. Lee did pray and read his Bible daily.

ACKNOWLEDGEMENTS

The Map of Gettysburg is modified from a map in *Robert E. Lee, Man and Soldier*, Thomas N. Page, Charles Scribner's and Sons, New York, 1911.

The map of Monocacy - Frederick is modified from a map drawn by Charles F. Von Lindenburg, accompanying the report of MG Lewis Wallace, U.S. Army, 1864.

The scripture quoted by General Lee is from the NIV Psalms 46:9-11.

My thanks to Ms. Una P. Keagle for her patience and kindness in the grammatical editing of this manuscript.

My thanks to my wife, Arlene, for her support during all those many, many evenings when I was off in front of my computer or wrapped up in a book fighting yet another war.

About the Author

R.W.P. Patterson is a native of Columbus, Mississippi. He is a graduate of Louisiana Tech University, and a retired Lieutenant Colonel from the U.S. Army. He served in the Infantry, Signal Corps and Aviation branches. Assignments have taken him to Germany, Korea, Central America and two tours of duty in Vietnam as a CH-47 helicopter pilot.

COL Patterson currently resides in Springfield, Missouri, where he is Vice President of Finance and Administration for Central Bible College. He is a frequent lecturer on the subject of the War Between the States for the college's history classes. He is also Vice President of the Board of Directors for Southern Military Institute. Patterson is Chief of Staff of the Missouri Division, Sons of Confederate Veterans, and Chaplain of the Missouri Society, Military Order of the Stars and Bars. He and his wife Arlene have two married sons.

Author of over 20 magazine articles and two computer based books on the War Between the States, *Deo Vindice* is his first novel.

Printed in the United States
129692LV00001B/6/A